I0760815

AMBUSH

SECTOR 64 BOOK ONE

DEAN M. COLE

CANDTOR PRESS, LLC

Ambush: A Military SciFi Thriller (Sector 64 Book One)

Published by CANDTOR Press, LLC

Dean@DeanMCole.com

ISBN: 978-1-952158-01-8

Also by Dean M. Cole

Get *Solitude: Dimension Space Book One* Today!

(Read the *Solitude* sneak peak at the end of this book.)

The Martian meets *Gravity* when Earth's last man, Army Captain Vaughn Singleton, discovers that the last woman is stranded alone aboard the International Space Station. Commander Angela Brown could reverse the event that swept humanity from Earth's surface ... if only she could get there. If you like action-packed, page-turning novels, you'll love the electrifying action in this award-winning, apocalyptic thriller.

Blurbs

What the critics are saying about the Sector 64 series.

Huffington Post - IndieReader.com - Top Ten Science Fiction

Kirkus Reviews

"Cole tackles the first-contact scenario with bombastic flair. [He] delivers the high-resolution imagery of a Hollywood blockbuster ... A technologically riveting dream for sci-fi action fans."

LiquidFrost - Amazon Top 500 Reviewer

"This series moves into the Space Opera world, officially ... Retribution moves (even) faster than Ambush ... Hits the ground with destruction; ends with destruction, with destruction in-between. So yes, it is a heartwarming tale full of rainbows and kittens."

AudiobookReviewer.com

"SECTOR 64 was a highly imaginative action-packed apocalyptic assault on your mind."

IndieReader.com

"SECTOR 64 is an engaging book from the very first page to the final words of the Epilogue."

Audiobook-Heaven.com

"His descriptions of aerial battle and military procedure are accurately detailed and his knowledge of the aircraft themselves fascinated me ... Sector 64 is a great read."

Another Great Series by Dean

The Complete *Sector 64* Series
1947 - *First Contact a Sector 64 Prequel Novella*
Today - *Ambush - Book One of the Sector 64 Duology*
Tomorrow - *Retribution - Book Two of the Sector 64 Duology*

(Read the sneak peak of *Ambush* at the end of this book.)

PART I

"We stand now at the turning point between two eras. Behind us is a past to which we can never return ..."

— Arthur C. Clarke

CHAPTER 1

Two fighter jets sliced through the night air. A crescent Moon, thin as an orange peel, cast a dim glow across the Nevada desert five thousand feet below the F-22s. Even under the waning crescent, the bright desert reminded Jake of a spaghetti western's night scene. As if filmed during the day with a dark filter to simulate night, the excess visual detail seemed out of temporal place.

"Papa Two-One, this is Lima Two-Four, over."

Air Force Captain Jake Giard scanned his fighter's computer-generated engine indications and then keyed his radio's transmit trigger. "Lima Two-Four, this is Papa Two-One. Go ahead."

The radio crackled to life again as his wingman replied. "Roger, Two-One. Come up internal."

Jake nodded and switched his radio selector to the ship-to-ship laser communication terminal. The autonomous system formed a virtual fiber optic link that allowed data to stream between the two fighters. A secure internal communication link piggybacked on the data stream. Unlike a radio signal, the laser beam couldn't be intercepted. So, fighter crews often used it like a cellphone for air-to-air communication.

"Hey, Vic. What's up?"

Over Nellis Air Force Base's remote desert training area, they flew a tight, echelon left formation. From his position just behind Vic's left wing, Jake studied the moonlit silhouette of his wingman's stealthy single-seat fighter.

"Uh ... thanks for doing this. I know you didn't have to take a flight this late."

Jake smiled under his oxygen mask. "It's not like I had anything better to do at three o'clock on a Sunday morning." The truth was, he had plenty he could be doing. However, the junior pilot was having trouble completing his unit indoctrination training. Having already failed one checkride, Victor was struggling with the high workload of the unit's close air support scenarios. Jake had volunteered to take him out for additional iterations. However, in preparation for a combat deployment, the squadron's fighter wings were in high gear, training around the clock. So, Victor's additional period had been relegated to oh-dark-thirty in the middle of the weekend.

"Yeah right," Vic said. "I'm sure you'd rather be on a night training flight than partying a Las Vegas Saturday night away with Sandy."

"Wow, you're right," Jake joked. He broke his fighter into a left bank and rolled away from Vic's jet. "I'm outta here."

"Hey ... I was just kidding," Vic said.

Having dropped below Victor's line of sight, Jake rolled his fighter level and passed under his wingman's aircraft. Emerging on Victor's right, Jake pulled alongside. In the Moon's soft light, he could see the back of his helmet as Vic searched the sky to his left.

"Over here," Jake said with a chuckle. When the young man's head snapped right, Jake barrel-rolled his fighter over Vic, the maneuver's wide arc carrying him clear of his wingman. It ended with Jake parked off of his wingman's left wing, back where he had started. "This sure as hell beats working for a living. Doesn't it?"

Vic laughed. "When my alarm went off at two AM, it kind of felt like work." Then his tone took on a serious note. "Did you see that report on the news tonight?"

"That report? Can you be a little more specific?"

"Sorry. They found more Russian surface-to-air missiles in Afghanistan."

Frustrated his attempt at levity had failed to distract the young officer from his unending worries, Jake looked across to his wingman and shook his head. *I know where this is headed.*

Fresh out of flight training, Lieutenant Victor Croft had never been in combat. Last week, the man's jittery nerves had kicked into hyperdrive when their squadron received orders to deploy to Afghanistan's Bagram Airfield at the end of the month. Renewed Taliban activity, coupled with enhanced weapons supplied by Iran, had NATO forces reeling.

"I'm sure they'll have it worked out by the time we get in-country," Jake said. He felt guilty playing down the threat. In the last year, the Taliban had employed Russian S-300 anti-aircraft missiles with devastating results.

"Maybe," Vic said dubiously. "I haven't slept since the meeting."

Jake remembered the white pallor he'd seen on Vic's face following their deployment brief. Wide, frightened eyes stared from the young pilot's light-skinned, ginger face. Drained of blood, Victor's skin glowed through his closely cropped red hair.

"Be calm, grasshopper," Jake said. He hoped the poor imitation of a Japanese sensei would allay Vic's continuing apprehension. "You'll be fine, your training will take over once you're in combat, trust me."

"Trust *you*?" Vic asked. The humor in the lieutenant's voice was good.

Victor thickened his soft hillbilly accent in the way that endeared him with comrades—and also won him favor with the Las Vegas ladies frequenting Nellis Air Force Base's officers' club. "Why, because you're from the government, and you're here to help me?"

Exaggerating his own Texan accent, Jake said, "Oh yeah, I forgot, you Appalachians don't cotton to us governmental types."

Victor laughed. "Yep, us hillbillies have a special place in our hearts for outsiders. Now, squeal like a pig, boy."

Jake's laughter broke as a tremendous shock wave, coupled with a blinding flash, rocked his fighter. Overtaking them from behind, a bright ring of lights had rocketed between the two aircraft.

"Shit! What the hell was that?" Jake said. Recovering from the shock, he adjusted the controls, reining in his battered fighter.

"I don't know. It must be doing Mach four or better—" Victor faltered as the object broke right. "What the hell?"

Bolting right, it made a ninety-degree turn, changing direction in an instant. One moment it was rocketing away from them, the next it blazed eastward at the same tremendous rate without curving.

"Holy shit, nothing can take those Gs," Vic said, thunderstruck.

"Oh my God," Jake whispered. Blinking, he tried to clear his eyes. *That's not possible.*

As if it had no mass or weight, the strange object made several more instantaneous course changes. Varying from slight angles, to complete course reversals, the maneuvers kept it near their two-ship formation.

Its zigzagging path circled the fighters twice. Then it stopped for a few moments. Matching their velocity and vector, it parked a mile off Lieutenant Croft's right wing. A moment later, it snapped to within one hundred meters of Victor's side of the formation, closing the mile-wide gap in less than a second.

"Whoa," Vic said with a shaky voice. His fighter jinked away from the object.

"Easy, buddy," Jake said. Jerking his F-22 left, he narrowly avoided colliding with his wingman. "I'm still right here."

"Sorry," Vic said.

"I've got nothing on radar." Jake paused, taking a deep breath to reel in his emotions. "When it was in front of us, I couldn't see it on infrared either."

"Hey, I see something," Vic said, panting. "There's a shadow."

Jake narrowed his eyes. "You're right! I see it against the background."

"Yeah, that's how I spotted it."

Gliding above the distant horizon, the ring of lights had dark voids protruding above and below. A brief eclipse of the background stars provided the only visual evidence.

"So, it's not some kind of ..." Jake paused, searching for words. "Energy source. It must have mass, it's gotta be a ship of some sort." Studying it, he paused, then shook his head. "But I've never seen anything move like that."

"If this is one of ours, it's way beyond anything my physics professor knew about," Victor said.

Looking across his wingman's fighter gave Jake a chance to estimate the ship's size. Judging by the shadow, it was as tall as it was wide. Like a pregnant frisbee, it was broadest across its middle, where the ring of lights still rotated. Horizontally, it was roughly as long as the F-22, making it just over sixty feet wide.

"What the hell is it?" Vic asked.

"No idea," Jake said. He couldn't see the skin, but the silhouette's bottom was round, and it looked like the top came to a point. "This is incredible ..." As Jake spoke, the ship started closing the gap. "Hey, be careful, it's getting closer!"

"Roger," Vic said.

Jake's heart raced as he focused on the ship's middle. "Those lights ..." He faltered, unable to conjure an adequate description.

"I know," Vic said. He sounded as mystified as Jake felt.

A horizontal, pulsing ring of multicolored light seemed to rotate in the air around the object's midsection. As the ship neared Victor's fighter, Jake got a clearer view of its structure. As if radiating from the ship's center, the glowing rays only extended a foot or two from the ship's skin, but he couldn't see any fixtures generating the energy. "I don't see the source of the lights. They look like ... raw energy." Watching the strange ship flying in formation with his wingman was both surreal and somehow familiar.

"I wish he'd pull up front again. My gun camera can't slew that far to the side," Vic said.

Recognition smacked Jake. "Hey, it looks like they want an escort."

"You're right," Vic said, then shouted, "Jake! Do you have your iPhone?"

"Yeah!"

Concentrating on flying his fighter while keeping an eye on the strange ship, he dug blindly through the bag he'd tucked into the small map pouch next to his right leg. *There it is.* Yanking out the phone, he turned it on—a clear violation of Air Force regulations. *I think they'll forgive this one.*

"Got it! I'll take a couple of quick shots, then drop back and see if I can capture it with my gun camera."

"Sounds good, just get it on something."

Staring at the phone's glowing, white boot-up apple, he shook the phone and growled, "Come on!"

Outside, the ship slid closer. When it parked a few feet off Vic's right wing, his fighter lurched.

Jake dropped the phone. "What happened?"

"I don't know. It feels like my right wing is trying to stall—" Victor's voice cut out as the buffeting rocked his fighter left and right. Broken by turbulence-induced grunts, Victor's voice came over the radio. "The stick is ... beating up ... the inside of my thighs."

He banked left to give Victor space. "Get away from the ship."

"I don't know ... if I can hold on," Victor said. His voice strained as he fought to control the fighter.

Jake threw his transponder into the emergency position, alerting air traffic control. Ears ringing, his pulse raced in response to the adrenaline dumping into his system. "Get the hell out of there!"

A crescendo of static rose in Jake's helmet.

Chopped and modulated by the communication laser's failing efforts to maintain connection, Lieutenant Croft's panic-stricken voice broke through the cacophony, "... systems ... going down ... damn warning light ... flashing ... day, Mayday, May—"

Jake switched back to their assigned radio frequency and keyed the mic. "Lima Two-Four ..."

Static.

"Victor, come in ..."

Louder static.

The faint glow from Victor's engines faded, then extinguished. His fighter started losing altitude.

Jake's mounting alarm ratcheted another notch. Slamming both throttles to idle, placing his fighter in a rapid descent, Jake tried to keep up with his plunging wingman.

The external position lights on both fighters began dimming. The static increased to an ear-splitting level, and then it died. Jake's cockpit darkened as all its electronics faded to black. All electrical energy seemed to drain from both F-22s.

Switching radios to emergency, he toggled the mic. "Mayday, Mayday, Mayday, this is Air Force Two-One-Five!"

No side-tone.

Shit, the radio isn't transmitting!

He switched back to the air-to-air frequency. "Lima Two-Four, this is Papa Two-One. Come in, Vic!"

Still no side-tone: he couldn't even hear his own voice. A quick check showed his helmet was still plugged into its socket.

Then, to Jake's horror, both fighters started drifting toward one another. "Oh shit," he whispered. He pulled against the stick, but the unresponsive electronic flight controls refused to budge.

Drifting toward Lieutenant Croft's fighter, Jake's ship started an uncommanded slow roll to the right. He yanked and jerked the stick left. Nothing. Without electricity, they couldn't respond. Jake reached for his ejection handles and froze. Already rolling through ninety degrees, his cockpit was aimed at his wingman's fighter. If he punched out now, he'd shoot into the top of Victor's airplane.

He watched helplessly as his ship rolled inverted. His F-22's dim shadow fell across Vic's fighter. For a surreal moment, the two stared face-to-face across the narrowing gap as both struggled with their unresponsive flight controls.

An unnatural glow caught Jake's attention. The mysterious ship's multicolored ring of rotating light brightened and then flared as it rocketed away—the only evidence of its departure direction lay in the fading image burned across his retina.

"What the hell?"

Instrument lights flared back to life, and his F-22 snap-rolled left as, power restored, the electronic flight controls responded to Jake's desperate tugging. As he rolled away, he saw the ship's blazing departure throw Victor's aircraft into a flat spin.

"Shit!" Jake screamed. He flipped his Raptor over, trying to keep his wingman in sight, but the night quickly swallowed the still blacked-out fighter.

He checked the radio. It was back online. "Come in, Victor!"

No reply.

"You're running out of time! Eject! Get the hell out of there, Lieutenant!" he ordered. As if trying to will the event into existence, Jake visualized his small-framed friend yanking on the jettison handle.

Switching back to the emergency radio, he transmitted, "Mayday, Mayday, Mayday, this is Air Force Two-One-Five!"

"Air Force Two-One-Five, this is Nellis Radio. Please state the nature of your emergency," replied the air traffic controller, her voice maddeningly calm.

Before he could reply, night turned day in a brilliant explosion as Victor and his F-22 slammed into the desert floor.

"No!" Jake screamed.

Tires barked as his fighter touched down. Jake extended the air brake. The fighter decelerated. Heavy-hearted and in an anguished mental fog, he struggled through the after-landing checks.

"Air Force Two-One-Five, proceed to the end of Runway Two-One-Right, right on taxiway Alpha, left onto the ramp. A security police detail is waiting to pick you up."

Security police? They're not normally involved in crash investigations.

"Uh ... roger, Nellis Tower, Runway Two-One-Right, right on Alpha, to the ramp," Jake repeated. His tone was flat, dutiful. Finishing his landing rollout, he saw the promised security detail's flashing lights ahead on the right.

He finished the after-landing checks. *What happened to you, buddy? Why didn't you eject?*

Hoping to spot his downed wingman, he had remained on scene. Jake had made multiple low passes, searching the small, speed-blurred patch of desert his landing lights illuminated. All the while, he'd monitored the frequency of Victor's portable emergency radio. In spite of numerous calls from Jake, it remained silent.

The post-crash fire had raged for thirty minutes, only faltering after it consumed the cache of jet fuel and combustible metals. When the rescue helicopter arrived, its crew performed an extensive search. After an additional thirty minutes, they reported: "No sign of ejection."

Out of fuel and hope, Captain Giard finally obeyed air traffic control's incessant orders and returned to base.

Now that he'd landed, Jake slowed his F-22. Reaching the end of the runway, he turned right onto taxiway Alpha as instructed by air traffic control. Ahead, the swarm of security police vehicles generated a myriad of flashing lights. The strobing red, blue, and amber colors reflecting off every surface of his cockpit were an unwelcome reminder of the ship's strange lights.

Turning left onto the south end of the ramp, he nosed the fighter into the U-shaped formation of vehicles. Locking the parking brake, he finished the after-landing checks.

Ground support personnel, casting nervous looks at the assembled security police vehicles, hooked up the ground power unit. With the GPU connected and powering the aircraft, he received a thumbs-up from an airman who looked ready to bolt. Jake acknowledged the clearance and killed the fighter's engines. To his surprise, the airman did bolt.

As Jake's canopy rose, a security police squad, weapons drawn, stormed the plane. Jake was looking down the muzzles of eight M16 automatic rifles.

"What the hell is this?" he shouted over the whine of the ground power unit's turbine exhaust.

"Out of the plane, sir!" screamed a large sergeant. The non-commissioned officer was pointing his Beretta nine-millimeter pistol at Jake's head.

Overwhelmed by the night's events, Jake stared incredulously at the armed squad. Shaking his head in resigned capitulation, he unbuckled his safety harness and unplugged his helmet. Climbing from the cockpit, he started backing down the boarding ladder. Halfway to the ground, he was ripped from the metal steps and thrown face-down onto the ramp. He could feel several muzzles pressed into his back.

"What the fuck!" Jake yelled. His breath lifted a small dust cloud from the tarmac, its asphalt surface warm against his face.

"Don't fucking move, Captain."

He continued to struggle. "I haven't done anything. This is bullshit!"

The cold, steel muzzle of a large caliber pistol pressed against the back of his neck.

Jake stopped struggling.

The sergeant, now calm and inches from his ear, said, "Captain, I have my orders, and they don't come from any higher, and they don't get any more serious than this. I assure you, this is not *bullshit*."

The muzzle lifted from his neck.

"Now, are we done here?"

Panting, Jake nodded.

In less than five seconds, the sergeant cuffed him and dragged him to his feet. "Thank you, sir." Grabbing Jake's left elbow, he led him to a security police cruiser. The sergeant opened the door, stuffed him in the back, and slammed it.

Jake stared out in confused disbelief. "What the hell did we stumble into, Vic?"

CHAPTER 2

Exhausted eyes stared back from the interrogation room's one-way mirror.

"Damn it, Captain, what were you doing in that area?" The voice echoed off the tiled floors and walls. With only a four-legged rectangular table and two metal chairs occupying its center, the room offered little sound absorption.

Turning from his reflection, Jake locked eyes with the major. For what felt like the hundredth time, he said, "Sir, as I've been telling you for the last twelve hours, Range Control assigned us that training area."

For the hundredth time, the major stared back, unblinking and unbelieving.

Knuckles rasped against the room's single door.

With a disgusted sigh, the major shook his head and turned toward it. "Come!"

The door creaked open. A nervous Air Force airman stuck his head into the room.

Major Tinsdale glared at him. "Damn it! I left clear instructions that I was not to be disturbed."

"Sorry, sir. You have a call from a General Tannehill. I tried to tell him you were busy—"

"No, no, no, I'll take it," the major said, standing, all annoyance evaporating. "Just sit there, Captain, I'll be back." Grabbing his notepad, he strode angrily from the room.

The airman nodded at Captain Giard and followed the major out.

Hearing the door lock, Jake turned back to his image in the mirror. A steady dripping sound emanated from a floor drain at the room's center. The ticking second hand of an old government issue wall clock, hanging over the door, added its maddening rhythm to the staccato dripping noise.

Studying his weary face in the one-way interrogation room mirror, Jake tried to make sense of the situation. It was obvious they knew the two of them had encountered the ship. However, every time he tried to bring it up, the major redirected him. Tinsdale kept returning to the subject of airspace and timelines. *It's as if he thinks we conspired to be there at that particular time.*

Given nothing to eat and only enough fluids to keep him awake, Jake didn't think they'd let him free anytime soon, if ever.

Jake heard the major shouting unintelligible commands as he came down the hall.

The door flew open, and in a storm, Major Tinsdale erupted into the interrogation room. Throwing a stack of papers on the desk in front of Jake, Tinsdale paused, took a deep breath, and sat across from him, head hanging down.

To Jake's surprise, the major looked up with a contrite expression.

"Captain, I owe you an apology."

Stunned, Jake sat back, trying to understand the rapid reversal. Was this some kind of interrogation technique? Was the major propping Jake up, just so he could knock him back down?

Reading the distrust, the major raised his hands, palms facing Jake. "It's ok, Captain. I give you my word, this is not a trick."

"Then what the hell is going on?" he asked. Belatedly, he added, "Sir."

"Apparently, you have friends in high places."

His confusion doubled. "What?"

The major shook his head. "You'll be briefed later." He pointed to the stack of papers. "But, before you can leave, you have to sign these."

Lying in bed, gazing at the ceiling, Captain Jake Giard ran fingers through his short, dark hair. His entire body ached with a bone-deep exhaustion. He hadn't slept in the eighteen hours since the disastrous encounter.

Jake knew sleep wouldn't be the restful reprieve from reality he needed. Only a dark prison waited—a place where he would relive the freakish encounter and the loss of his young friend ad nauseam.

Shifting, he propped another pillow under his head and looked outside. The city's uncountable sodium-vapor street lights set his bedroom walls awash with an orange glow. The drawn curtains of his window revealed a beautiful panorama. Viewed from his East Las Vegas apartment on the side of Sunrise Mountain, the city lights painted across the valley below twinkled like a sea of chipped orange glass beads. From Jake's remote vantage point, the buildings and lights of the Vegas Strip constituted a small portion of the scintillating mural painted across his bedroom window.

The cool, crisp springtime breeze ruffled the curtains, creating a welcome distraction. Jake felt his body relaxing as a coyote's howl drifted down from the desert mountainside. A lonely sound, it matched the darkness of his mood.

His body jerked with a waking spasm as a jet engine's distant roar drowned out the coyote's wail, claiming dominance over the night air. Muffled by distance, the airplane's din rolled like thunder off the surrounding mountains.

"Great," he muttered.

Frustrated and exhausted, Jake slid out of bed and stepped across the cool tiles. Pushing the billowing curtain out of the way, he walked to the center of the wide window, intending to close it. Movement in his peripheral vision drew his attention. Two miles to the north, on

Nellis Air Force Base Runway Three-Left, two hundred feet from where he'd been accosted by the base's security police, Jake could just make out the twin, fiery-blue jet plumes of an F-22 Raptor on a takeoff roll.

The solo fighter was a poignant reminder.

"Damn it! What happened to you, Vic?"

He slammed the glass pane shut. Snapping the curtains closed, he turned and walked back to the bed. Collapsing backward onto its soft surface, Jake stared through the ceiling.

What the hell was that thing?

"I can't even tell anybody about your death," he said to the empty room. He shook his head sardonically. *Great! The UFO contactee is talking to his dead friend.* "Wonderful."

The day spent in the interrogation room had left Jake confused and questioning his decision to reveal the appearance of the strange ship. Not that Major Tinsdale had allowed any elaboration on the subject.

He was under strict orders not to mention the event to anyone. He knew it was standard protocol not to discuss aspects of a mishap during an investigation, but these orders encompassed everything: personnel, equipment, aircraft, and timelines—before and after the accident.

Ordered to act as if the flight had been canceled, he was not to discuss the night's events, nor mention Lieutenant Croft's status. *Since when did a man's death become a status?*

Not that he'd had the opportunity to talk with anyone. Under virtual house arrest, Jake had been instructed not to leave his home. Relieved from duty, he was to spend the remainder of the day and subsequent night resting. Major Tinsdale told him to expect additional instructions the following morning. However, he wasn't sure how that information would arrive. Perfectly functional the previous day, neither his iPhone nor his home phone worked now. Even his Internet was down. Also, a nondescript government issue sedan sat parked out front, its occupant hidden in shadow.

The mortgage-like stack of documents he'd signed promised

forfeiture of his left nut and first-born should he ever discuss any aspect of the night's events.

A metallic chime yanked Jake from his thoughts. It was the doorbell. He checked his watch: 10 p.m.

Rocked by a sudden epiphany, he sat bolt upright on the mattress. "Sandy!"

He jumped out of bed and scrambled to the closet, searching blindly for his robe. *Can't believe I forgot.*

The doorbell rang again.

"I'm coming!" he yelled. Sliding to a stop on the tiled foyer, he opened the door.

His girlfriend, Captain Sandra Fitzpatrick, pointed an admonishing finger. "You'd better not be starting without me—" Seeing his face, she stopped. "Oh my God, baby. What happened?"

Looking into her deep blue eyes, he felt the day's tumultuous stress drain from his body. "I love you."

Eyes softening and stepping through the door, she enveloped him in her sensuous arms. "That's not an answer, but I'll accept it for now."

"Thank you." He nodded toward her embrace. "By the way, that's my job."

Ever the competitor, she raised a skeptical eyebrow. "I'm allowed to comfort you."

Jake gave her a meaningful look. After a moment she capitulated, allowing him to wrap her up in his strong arms. Fiercely independent since their first meeting in Air Force flight school, Sandy was loath to let anyone do anything for her. As an Air Force fighter pilot, it was a character trait that had served her well. It was only during their private moments that she lowered the ever-present shield and exposed her soft feminine side to Jake.

Melting into him, she snuggled her cheek into his chest. Her limpid blue eyes stared deeply into his. "I've missed you."

"I missed you too, baby," he reassured her.

She leaned back in his arms. "So, what happened to you this morning? You didn't call or text me after your flight."

"My phone went on the fritz," he said, only half-lying.

"Your home phone too? Both of your phones are going straight to voicemail. I didn't know your home number had voicemail."

"It does now." *Apparently.*

"How was your flight?"

Unwilling to lie outright, he changed the subject, guiding her toward the bedroom. "I thought you were coming here so I could help you relax."

The previous night—only a few hours before his and Vic's fateful flight—Sandy had complained that the next day's schedule included a grueling twelve-hour battery of tests on a new F-22 avionics configuration.

Sweeping her up, he carried her the remaining distance to the bedroom.

Sandy wrapped her arms around his neck.

Jake smiled. In a French accent, he whispered, "Mon amour, your velocity-induced accelerated stall has firewalled my adiabatic lapse rate."

"Oh, I love it when you whisper dirty pilot talk to me."

Laying her gently on the bed, Jake grasped the top of her flight suit's full body-length central zipper. Drawing it down, he slowly exposed her heaving breasts, then her dimpled abs, and finally the top of her lace panties. With a devilish grin, he said, "There's my favorite landing strip."

"It better be your only landing strip, Captain," Sandy said. She playfully reached between his legs. Looking into his eyes with a mischievous smile, she said, "I have the ball, the hook is down."

"Ease up on the navy crap, or *the hook* might retract."

"Yeah right," she said, laughing. Still holding his member, she pulled him into bed.

WOMP, WOMP, WOMP.

The sound drilled into Jake's brain. Again he reached for the fighter's instrument panel, pressing and then punching the cancel button in a futile effort to reset the incessant alert blaring from the flashing master-caution panel.

WOMP, WOMP, WOMP.

Frustration mounted as the fighter's computer still wouldn't accept his inputs.

My friend is dead, and now my fighter is dying too.

WOMP, WOMP, WOMP.

Even the alert sounds wrong ... Oh shit!

Dragging himself from the nightmare, his arm rose from the sheets and fell on the alarm clock.

The noise continued.

With a start, Jake realized it was his home phone that was ringing. He'd left the handset in the living room. "Guess it's working now."

Sandy stirred, mumbled something unintelligible, and went back to sleep.

After a quick kiss to the top of her head, he leapt from the bed. Sprinting through the living room and sliding to a stop in front of the phone, he checked the number.

No name displayed, but he recognized the area code: 202. From his many calls to the area's Air Force offices, he knew it very well. Washington, D.C. *This should be it.*

After a hesitation, he answered. "Hello."

"Is this Captain Jake Giard?" asked a feminine voice.

"Uh ... yes. Who's calling?"

"This is the Pentagon's office of Air Force Tactical Operations, Planning, and Development. Please hold for Captain Allison."

Before he could protest, inane elevator music told him she'd already placed him on hold. He was usually happy to hear from his old combat wingman. However, this morning he worried the line would be tied up when the real call came. *Hurry up, Richard.*

While waiting, Jake thought about the last time he'd seen his and Sandy's old flight school buddy, Richard Allison. He'd been in a hospital bed, only five hours after a near brush with death.

In spite of his impatience, he found himself wondering how

Richard was handling ground duty. If only that bullet hadn't found its way into his engine.

~

— Twelve Months Earlier —

"Target is fifteen kilometers at two-seven-niner degrees. Estimate entry into Maverick missile range in thirty seconds," Jake said to his wingman.

"Roger, Gunslinger One-Three. Gunslinger Two-Six has visual on the target, now at heading: two-seven-eight, range: eleven kilometers. Target acquisition complete, missile armed," said Captain Richard Allison.

As Richard called out his target data, Jake, from his position off of the right wing of Richard's ground attack-configured fighter jet, was completing the same process for his target.

"I have lock-on, launching now," Richard said.

The Maverick missile roared as it left the FA-16, rapidly accelerating toward an ill-fated anti-aircraft missile launcher.

A shudder passed through Jake's fighter as his missile also ripped into the night sky. "Second missile is on the way."

The Mavericks bore down on the two anti-aircraft weapons. A brilliant flash illuminated the desert as the missiles struck their targets, detonating the warheads and rocket fuel on both launchers. The fireballs incinerated everything within two hundred meters.

"That should do the trick," Richard said.

"Roger, Gunslinger Two-Six. Let's do a quick BDA and head home."

"Roger, keep in tight," Richard replied as he turned inbound.

Beginning his post-attack Battle Damage Assessment, Jake scanned the infrared display. After a few seconds, he smiled. "Scratch two more SA sixes."

"That's two less surface-to-air missile launchers to dodge. I wish the Pakistanis would stop this crap from crossing the—" Captain Allison's radio transmission cut out mid-sentence as a stream of tracers sliced through the darkness directly in front of the two aircraft.

"Break left!" Jake screamed.

With the bright orange tracers slicing between the two fighters, Jake banked his fighter hard right, narrowly avoiding the wall of lead.

"Crap! That was close," Jake said. "Must have been a Zeus." It was the common nickname for Russia's deadly four-barreled ZSU-23-4 anti-aircraft gun. *Good thing he missed. That rate of fire with high-explosive shells...* The thought sent an involuntary shudder down Jake's spine.

"I'm hit, I'm hit!" Richard screamed over the radio.

"Oh shit!" Jake said. He toggled his radio. "Gunslinger Two-Six, how bad are you hit? Is it flyable, over?"

No reply.

"Gunslinger Two-Six, Richard, what is your situa—" A bright explosion flashed from the direction Richard had turned. To his relief, Jake saw the silhouette of a parachute canopy briefly outlined by the light of the exploding fighter jet.

Rolling his aircraft to bring weapons on the ZSU, Jake jumped into the job of protecting his wingman.

Another burst of fire shredded the night. Like flaming orange basketballs, a new volley of explosive twenty-three-millimeter shells rose from the desert floor, blindly seeking out his aircraft. Apparently, the weapon's operator knew not to turn on his radar. That mistake would attract Jake's HARM radar-seeking missile. Still, his initial success against Richard's aircraft had made the enemy gunner overconfident. His odds of repeating the original feat were nil. Firing again into the screaming darkness merely supplied Jake with a bright orange dotted line pointing to the source of his friend's demise.

His last Maverick missile locked onto the anti-aircraft gun's infrared silhouette. Lifting the guard, Jake fingered the missile launch trigger. "Bye, bye." With a pull, he launched the missile. It rapidly accelerated toward, and then destroyed the ZSU in a brilliant explosion, briefly bringing daylight to another small patch of desert.

"Good shooting, Gunslinger One-Three," Jake heard over the emergency frequency.

He breathed a sigh of relief at the sound of his downed wingman's voice. "Keep your transmissions to a minimum, Two-Six. After all my hard work, I don't want a load of artillery raining down on you. What's your condition?"

"I'll live, but this is Indian country, so hurry with the cavalry already," Richard said. Apprehension seeped through his humorous façade.

Jake heard an electronic click as the inane hold music ended. "How the hell are you, buddy?" Richard asked.

Leaning against the bar top separating the apartment's kitchen from its dining room, Jake looked at the ceiling. He took a deep breath and slowly let it out. "I've been better. Sorry I haven't called, things have been ... crazy here. How's the leg?"

"It's better. As a matter of fact, I just returned to flight status."

"Listen, Richard, I've got—"

Not pausing to let Jake finish, Richard kept speaking. "In the meantime, I've been assigned to a special unit in the Pentagon. Actually, that's why I'm calling."

"I'm sorry, Richard, I have something going on here. As much as I'd love to catch up—"

"I understand," he interrupted again. "I've been watching your situation develop. We need to talk."

"Richard ... wait, what do you mean? What do you know?" Jake asked, confused.

"I'd rather not discuss it over the—"

Jake's frustration boiled over. "Damn it, Richard, nobody wants to discuss this thing. Every time I try to bring up details, they cut me off. I haven't been able to tell anyone what really happened!" Lowering his voice, he looked toward the bedroom. "I haven't even told Sandy."

Richard ignored Jake's rant. "You're meeting me in D.C. tonight."

What the hell? How can Richard be involved in this? After an extended pause, Jake said, "Okay."

"I'll tell you more tonight. You're booked on a noon flight out of McCarran. An e-ticket is waiting for you at the United counter."

"Okay, Richard," Jake said. His mind reeled. "I'll ... see you tonight."

"Good, tell the lovely and talented Captain Fitzpatrick hello for me. And, tell her she's still the second-best fighter pilot I know."

"You bet," Jake said. He grinned in spite of the confusion. "It's quite chivalrous of you to place yourself third."

"In your dreams, buddy," Richard said through a laugh.

CHAPTER 3

Sandy woke to the sound of Jake's voice in the living room. Heard from across the apartment and spoken in subdued tones, the words were indecipherable. Near the end, his voice rose, and she even heard laughter. The conversation had ended before she deduced that Richard, their flight school classmate, had been on the other end of the line.

Jake was so distracted when he returned to the room, he didn't notice she was awake.

Sandy studied his face. Gone were last night's uncharacteristic stress lines and baggy eyes. Either a night's rest or news from Richard had washed it away. However, she saw something new in his face, an underlying look of confusion.

He climbed back under the covers.

"Who was that?" she asked.

Jake twitched as her voice broke through his apparent trance. "Richard," he answered after a brief pause. His tone was distracted. Lying on his back, he stared at the ceiling.

His change in demeanor concerned her. "Is everything all right? How's his leg?"

"He's ... fine. His leg is better." Jake raised his eyebrows. "Actually, he's back on flight status."

"That's great!" Sandy said. Her head on his left shoulder, she rested her left arm across his chest. "What's wrong?"

Jake fell into an uncomfortable silence. After a while, he planted a kiss on her forehead. "I need another hour of sleep."

Still lying on her right side, she lifted her head and touched his cheek with her left hand. "Okay, baby."

The questions running through Sandy's mind must've paraded across her face. Jake smiled, a resolved expression chasing away his distracted look. "I'm sorry I've been so mysterious. Let's get some more sleep, then I'll tell you all about it."

Sandy stared into his eyes. After a moment, she pinched his nose. "You better, mister." She kissed his cheek and rolled onto her back. "Now, get some sleep."

He smiled. "Yes, ma'am." After setting an alarm on his phone, he placed it on the nightstand. Laying his head back on the pillow, Jake closed his eyes.

After a few moments, rhythmic breathing told Sandy he'd fallen back to sleep. He'd always been able to do that. Jake fell asleep with ease, a fact that often annoyed her. Sandy regularly took an hour or more to find it.

Being careful not to wake him, she rolled back on her right side to study his face. Even asleep, the underlying confusion she'd glimpsed earlier still furrowed his brow. Looking at him, she remembered the first time they'd met.

She'd thought Jake was an asshole. He and his best friend Richard were cocky to the point of annoyance. While Richard had, in fact, proven to be an arrogant, impatient asshole, she'd grown to love them both.

While Jake and Richard had attended the Air Force Academy together, Sandy, a Stanford grad, had recently completed officer candidate school. All three were freshly commissioned second lieutenants, the Air Force's entry-level officer rank.

The first time she saw them was at Air Force flight school indoctrination. The two were loud and obnoxious, so involved in their antics, they scarcely noticed or acknowledged their fellow classmates.

While Jake's short, dark hair and angular features attracted her attention, she quickly tired of their antics.

Later that evening, she saw them again, this time in the officers' club. Seeing Sandy in civilian clothes and not having recognized her, they had assumed she was an officers' club waitress.

While Richard was slightly taller than Jake, his abrasive, impatient demeanor left Sandy unimpressed. He immediately began flirting, bragging about being in flight school and how he was "certain to go straight into fighters".

Sandy had played along, to a point.

After a moment of boasting, Richard asked her to be a good "bar wench" and get them a couple of beers.

She went to the bar. On Jake and Richard's tab, Sandy bought herself the most expensive drink listed. Placing it and their two beers on a round, cork-lined plastic tray, she walked back to their table. Sandy handed Jake his beer and set hers on the table. As they stared in confusion at the expensive umbrella-clad cocktail, she allowed the unbalanced tray, and the single beer it held, to fall into Richard's lap.

Richard scrambled and cussed.

In mock horror, Sandy placed a hand over her mouth. "Oops, I guess my center of gravity calculation was off, but what's a lowly *bar wench* know about calculating weight, arm, and moment anyway?"

Hearing her appropriate use of arcane aviation vernacular, both men stared, mouths agape. While Richard's face only showed surprise and a particular level of distrust, Jake's flashed with recognition. He grinned and said, "Sandra Fitzpatrick."

Sandy decided she might like this one.

After the initial friction, they had spent the rest of the night drinking, laughing, and swapping life stories.

Inseparable throughout flight training, they maintained their friendship in spite of the fierce competition created when the trio shot to the top of their class. Week by week they exchanged places, each occupying the number one position for varying lengths of time.

In the end, Sandy was the Distinguished Honor Graduate. Jake and Richard had finished second and third, respectively—a fact Sandy believed still offended Richard's self-important inner asshole.

All three went directly into fighters. It was during their F-16 fighter transition training that her and Jake's relationship had grown beyond the bounds of mere friendship.

The hurt in Sandy's eyes tore at Jake's heart.

"Why didn't you tell me about this last night?" she said.

After catching another hour of sleep, he'd thrown an overnight bag on the bed and jumped into the shower. When she asked what he was packing for, he'd struggled with what to say. Finally, with no other outlet for his pain, misery, and confusion, he had told Sandy the whole story.

Instead of the expected look of disbelief, her face was a mixture of hurt, confusion, and sympathy.

"Why didn't you tell me?" she repeated. "You shouldn't be going through this alone. I'm no wallflower, Captain Giard. I'd like to think I'm more than a girlfriend." She stepped up to him. Placing her left hand on his arm, Sandy caressed the back of his neck with her right. Her deep blue eyes gazed into his. "I'm supposed to be the shoulder you can lean on."

"Sorry, baby," Jake said. He crowned his eyebrows in his best puppy dog face. "I just wanted to keep my left nut ... and our first-born," he said, jokingly referring to the confidentiality agreement he'd signed. He over emphasized the last part, hoping to make her laugh.

To his relief, a coy expression replaced the hurt look. "Don't start making assumptions, Captain Giard—on either account. I believe I own said property, regardless of the bachelor machinations manifest in your interior design, or lack thereof," she said casting a meaningful look at the apartment's sparse decorations and scattered sporting equipment. "And, as to part two of your assertion, you'll need to append a hyphen to my name long before I'll allow said property to facilitate such outcomes."

Jake stared into her eyes for a moment. Knowing Sandy was giving him a pass, he fell another day deeper in love with her. Squeezing the hand she'd placed on his arm he stepped to the overnight bag. "Captain Fitzpatrick, I believe you missed your calling: you most certainly should have been a lawyer."

"Pshaw," she scoffed. "I'm the best fighter pilot you know." Laying out his formal, dark blue uniform, she adjusted the rows of combat ribbons crowding the area between his aviator wings and the jacket's top left breast pocket. Finishing, she stood and faced him with a knowing look. "Nice diversion, by the way."

Jake nodded, a sheepish grin on his face. Kicking off his shoes and hopping on one foot, he none too gracefully changed pants. "Guess I didn't want you to think I'd lost it," he said catching his balance and looking into her beautiful eyes.

Smiling, she playfully slugged him on the shoulder. "Next time you run into an alien ship you better let me know, mister."

He hugged her. "Yes, ma'am, but I didn't say it was alien. It could be some top-secret technology. For all I know, it could've been an Air Force ship. Hopefully, Richard has some answers for me."

"If he doesn't, you're going to have to elevate this, Jake."

Surprised to hear her echoing the thought hovering in the back of his mind since waking, he gave her a questioning look.

She shrugged her shoulders. "They can't ask you to cover up an Air Force pilot's death. I don't care what they had you sign. It's not a lawful order. It'll be your duty, hell, it'll be my duty as well, to report this to the Judge Advocate General."

Jake nodded. "I've been thinking the same thing. I'll be damned if I'm going to let them bury this, but I trust Richard. So, I'll give them two days to make it right. If they haven't done anything about it by the time I get back, I'll go to the JAG myself."

She nodded. "If it comes to that, I'll go with you."

Jake placed a finger under Sandy's chin. Tilting her face up, he kissed her.

She leaned back, looking at him with her left eyebrow cocked. "You'll be back in two days, right?"

"Two days," Jake promised. "There's not much under the sun that could keep me away even that long."

Running fingers through his short brown hair, Sandy looked at him, her penetrating blue eyes peering into his soul. After a long stare, she pushed him away. "Come on, Captain, you have a plane to catch."

She picked up his packed overnight bag and moved it to the front door.

Jake finished dressing. Inspecting his uniform in the mirror, he locked eyes with Sandy's reflection. "I love you, lady."

"I love you more," she said with a smile.

They headed toward the front door. Sandy bent over to pick up the overnight bag.

Admiring her form, Jake grinned. He loved the way the flight suit conformed to her perfect contours. "You keep doing that, and we'll never get out of here."

"Well then, by all means," Sandy said. She bent again, casting a devilish grin over her shoulder.

Jake laughed. She always knew how to make him smile. He spanked her playfully and took the bag. "That's my job."

"Yessir!" Giving a playful salute, she opened the door for him. "Age before beauty."

Chuckling, he stepped outside. Seeing the unmarked dark government sedan still in the parking lot, ominous with its black windows and matching plain black rims, Jake stopped laughing. Shaking his head, he gestured toward the Crown Vic as he walked to the back of his red Corvette. "I'm really over all this cloak-and-dagger bullshit."

Sandy cast a wary glance at the car. "They'll probably follow us to the airport," she said.

"Probably," Jake agreed. Popping the rear hatch, he threw in the overnight bag.

Opening the driver's door, Sandy grabbed the key fob from him. "I'll drop you off."

He stopped, mouth agape in mock exasperation. "First you try to carry my bag, then you open the door for me, and now you want to drive. You're killing my chivalry, you know."

"Told you I'll never be a wallflower, baby. You better keep up," Sandy said as she slid into the Vette's seat and started the engine.

Jake shook his head in feigned exasperation. Walking to the passenger side, he watched the sedan's occupant watching him.

Pulling the Corvette to the terminal's curb, Sandy looked at Jake with a smile. "Tell our old flight school buddy hello for me. He's still the third-best fighter pilot I know."

"You two!" Jake laughed and shook his head.

"Be careful, Jake. I love you."

"I will. You be careful too. I'll call you when I get settled in D.C. If anything comes up, call me."

"Yessir," Sandy said with a smile and another salute.

Walking around to her side of the car, he grabbed the bags from behind the seat. Pausing next to her, he ran a hand across the car's gleaming surface, then patted the top of the driver's door. "Take care of my baby while I'm gone," he said with a wink.

"I will, and I'll take good care of your car too," she said with a smile.

"See you in a couple of days, beautiful." After a passionate kiss, he turned and walked toward the doorway. Crossing the curb, he saw the government sedan pull into the drop-off zone a few car lengths behind the Vette.

Jake pointed to the unwelcome visitor. "You were right."

Sandy studied the Corvette's rear-view mirror. Spotting the dark Crown Vic, she grinned. In typical Sandy fashion, she raised her arm through the car's open roof and extended her middle finger, giving their unwelcome visitor the bird.

"Have I told you lately how much I love you?" he said, laughing.

The one-finger salute shifted toward Jake and then morphed into a beauty pageant hand wave. Sandy winked at him. "Hurry home, Captain Giard."

~

Northbound on Interstate 15, Sandy headed back into town. Apparently only interested in the comings and goings of Jake, the government tail had not followed her beyond the airport.

She passed the iconic black pyramid of the Luxor Hotel and Casino. Behind it, heat waves shimmered above the main east-west runway of McCarran Airport. In the bright blue sky over the dark, triangular building, a single-engine Cessna 150 lumbered into the atmosphere. Having just departed, the airplane probably had a student pilot behind the controls.

That reminded Sandy of her father. She'd been a daddy's girl from day one. He always professed to want a son. However, she'd been such a tomboy—more interested in frogs and mud pies than Barbies and unicorns—her parents had never tried to have a second child, boy or girl.

Growing up as an only child, Sandy was fiercely independent. In military flight school, she'd learned that greater than sixty percent of all Air Force pilot trainees were either an only child or first-born. Less than a fifth were their family's youngest sibling. But Sandy credited her love of aviation to her father more than her birth status.

Up until the supporting airport closed in 2002, her dad had owned a small civilian flight school outside Monterey, California. Carmel Valley Vintage Airport, southeast of the city, had been her childhood stomping ground. She'd been raised as much by her father's small cadre of flight instructors and aircraft mechanics as she had by her parents. While her mother's office-based secretarial job left no one home to watch Sandy, her father's self-directed schedule—coupled with the fact he owned the business—made his hangar a wonder-filled day care. There, parallel rows of spark plugs became white stallions towing a silver coach in the form of a pitted, cone-shaped chrome spinner from an ancient propeller. There, after a hot day of flight training, sweat-stained instructors dutifully sat at her too small table, drinking tea and eating imaginary crumpets. And, also there, standing on her daddy's toes, she learned to waltz as Neil Diamond's *Mr. Bojangles* blared from an old car speaker that hung from a rusty nail.

As Sandy exited the highway and turned down a palm tree-lined Las Vegas street, more memories flowed past her mind's eye like an Instagram photostrip. She always remembered those days with the oddly faded colors of a Polaroid picture. Forever frozen in a mental snapshot, Sandy waved excitedly as her father cruised overhead in his Cessna. Its seventies-tastic paint scheme, white with a horizontal, two-tone brown stripe running down the side of the fuselage, contrasted starkly against the Polaroid-color-shifted blue sky.

Growing up, she'd spent many summers, holidays, and after-school hours in her father's hangar. He and a small collection of polyester-clad and mustachioed instructors trained a never-ending string of mullet-sporting students clad in acid-washed jeans. As the years marched past, the eighties and its hair bands were ushered out by Kurt Cobain-loving, grunge-clad, Gen-X pilot-wannabes. However, her father and his small cadre of instructors as well as the airplanes never changed their colors ... or their style, for that matter.

With names like Tom, Chuck, Bob, and Jim, they had taught her everything she knew about civil aviation. Dad hadn't even left much for the Air Force to teach her. She still remembered laughing like the schoolgirl she was when her father, trying to teach her how to do a strafing run on an unsuspecting herd, inadvertently chased old man Creech's cows through a wood fence.

She loved her mom dearly, but as with most mother-daughter relationships, they had often butted heads, especially in her teenage years.

Pressing a button on her phone brought her father's wise, loving, and wrinkled face to its screen. After only one ring, his cheerful voice filled the car's speakers.

"Pumpkin!"

"Daddy!"

~

Stepping through the exit into the evening's humid air, Jake felt his uniform starting to cling to his body. For Washington, D.C., it was unusually warm and muggy. He checked his watch: a quarter past seven left forty-five minutes until his meeting with Richard. In spite of the ever-present hustle and bustle, the terminal's passenger pickup area had a dark, lonely feel. The visible portion of the sky was rapidly approaching total nightfall. Harsh bronze light cascaded from noisy overhead fixtures, amplifying the uninviting atmosphere.

Behind Jake, the automatic doors kept opening and closing. A drunk curled up next to the exit tripped its sensor every time he raised a brown bag-covered bottle nestled in his wizened hands.

Jake flinched as a harsh voice erupted from his right. "Jesus, Olaf! I told you, you can't sit there," an airport police officer said with apparent impatience. Walking toward the vagrant, he pointed at the brown bag. "And what the hell is in that? If it ain't Perrier, we're going to have a problem."

Jake turned from the drunk's Eastern European-accented slurring response, returning his gaze to the cars lining the passenger pickup zone. He noticed a man watching him from another dark Ford Crown Victoria, the same color, make, and model as the one that had followed them to the Las Vegas airport. When Jake's gaze lingered, the driver looked away too quickly.

"Son of a bitch," he swore under his breath. Walking to the head of the taxi line, he opened the waiting cab's rear door. The taxi driver was climbing out, but Jake held up his small suitcase. "Get in, this is my only bag."

Guilt-ridden, angry, and frustrated, Jake felt his blood pressure rising and his face reddening. Last year, he'd watched his best friend get blown out of the sky. Now Victor was dead. The survivor's guilt was bad enough, but the military's obvious mistrust, evident in the ever-present tail, poured salt, pepper, and acid into a festering wound.

In the side-view mirror, he watched the stranger cast off his guise as a bored ride waiting for an arrival. Discarding the paper he'd feigned reading, the observer started his car as the cab driver dropped into his seat.

"Fuck this shit! I'm tired of these bastards."

Ignoring Jake's rant, the cabby asked, "Where'd ya wanna go, pal?"

"O'Hara's Bar and Grill," Jake growled.

"You got it, bud. That's about ten minutes past the Pentagon on the Three-Ninety-Five."

"OK," he said. Looking over his left shoulder, Jake glared at the sedan. Having been to Washington several times, both as a kid and as a military officer, he had a good feel for the lay of the land. Jake looked at the cab driver's eyes reflected in the rear-view mirror. "Go north, first. Then head east, across the river."

"That ain't the right direction," the cabby said.

"Just do it."

"It's your nickel, pal."

As the cab pulled out, Jake watched the sedan in the side-view mirror. Just prior to disappearing behind a corner, he saw it edge away from the curb.

"Once you cross the river, find a place to double back. Then we'll head to O'Hara's. There's a twenty-dollar tip in it for you if you can lose that Crown Vic," Jake said, hiking a thumb at the tail.

Spotting the sedan and looking nonplussed, the cabby studied Jake in the rear-view mirror. "Look, pal, I don't want no trouble here."

Jake pulled a money clip out of his front pocket. Peeling off two twenties, he leaned forward. "Well, mister ... uh," Jake paused, searching the framed driver's permit hanging on the cab's dash. "Mister Skolowski." He laid one of the twenties across the man's shoulder. "Here's twenty now." He held up the other so the driver would see it in the rear-view mirror. "And here's the twenty I'll give when you lose that asshole."

Skolowski grabbed the bill from his shoulder and pocketed it. "Now you're talkin' my language, pal."

"I thought so," Jake muttered. While the driver merged with interstate traffic, Jake checked their rear. He spotted the black Crown Vic about a hundred yards back, hovering behind a yellow 350Z, positioned so the driver could observe the cab yet still blend with the other commuters careening down the interstate.

"So, why's dis guy following you?"

"Guess he wants to take a poll," Jake said sardonically.

Shaking his head, the cabby moved into the left lane.

Jake spotted the Potomac River bridge ahead. Off to the left, through gaps in the trees lining the highway, he glimpsed D.C.'s night cityscape. Parks and monuments formed the only breaks in the ocean of lights.

As the cab crossed the bridge, Jake glimpsed the sedan indiscreetly following too closely.

Jake was thrown forward in his seat as the cabby braked hard. Their pursuer caught off guard, the gap between the two cars rapidly decreased. Skolowski cut across four lanes at a forty-five-degree angle, barely making the exit on the far side of the river.

Impressed by the cabby's dedication to the cause, Jake looked back, grinning. Too late to make the exit, the dark sedan careened across the highway. The off-ramp dropped below the level of the interstate, cutting off Jake's line of sight.

Just as he was sure they'd lost it, the dark sedan shot into view. Leaping the curb, it careened down the side of the embankment.

"Jesus!" Skolowski exclaimed. He stomped on the accelerator. "What in the *hell* does dis guy want wit you?"

"Even if I could tell you, which I can't, you'd never believe me."

Directly behind them, the Crown Vic struck the bottom of the embankment, sending up a spray of grass and mud. It bounced over the curb and onto the off-ramp, only two feet behind the cab's rear bumper.

"Son of a bitch!" screamed the cabby, swerving hard right and shooting down a side road. "Dis is your lucky day, pal. I grew up in dis neighborhood."

Jake viewed the *neighborhood* wondering where his supposed luck would find him. Abandoned cars, sans wheels and windows, lined both sides of the road. A lone street light illuminated the path ahead. Jake caught a brief glimpse of three teenagers kicking a fourth on the ground.

Several consecutive quick turns put some distance between them and their pursuer. Rounding another corner at high speed, the cabby turned off the car's headlights.

Jake tensed. Their speed didn't reduce with the visibility.

Without warning, the cabby spun the wheel hard right, firing the cab into a dark, very narrow alley, one Jake would have laid odds couldn't accommodate a subcompact, much less a four-door sedan.

Still, Skolowski refused to slow.

"Had lots of practice losing the cops in dis neighborhood."

Jake gazed through the rear window, watching for the Crown Vic. The wall across from the alley's opening glowed with the lights of the approaching chase car. Long shadows rapidly shortened as the unseen car closed. In a flash of white headlights and red tail lights, the car sped past, the glow's quick fade signaling their success.

"Let's get the hell out of here," Jake said, handing the cabby the other twenty.

Skolowski made a turn out of the alley. One turn later, lights on, they were back underway. For a moment, they traveled along the river. The interstate came into view. Skolowski said, "O'Hara's it is."

Jake checked his watch: eight o'clock. He handed the cabby two more twenties. "Here you go, Skolowski, keep the change. I appreciate your help."

"No problem, pal."

Jake stepped out and closed the door. The cab pulled away. He walked up to the tavern's rustic wood door. Pulling it open, he stepped into the dark interior. Searching for Richard, he spotted a raised hand in the back. Returning the wave, Jake scanned the tavern for more stalkers. An old couple was seated at the brass-trimmed oak bar. They were watching the overhead television. Otherwise the place was empty.

As Jake approached, Richard stood, extending a hand. "You look like you're expecting someone to jump you."

Jake relaxed a bit, smiling at his old wingman. "Today, they'll have to take a number."

Richard gave him an appraising look. After a moment, he nodded. "It's good to see you." Without addressing Jake's comment, he sat and gestured to the opposite chair. "Sit down, buddy."

As Jake sat, Richard grabbed the pitcher and filled a half-thawed frosty mug sitting on a damp, pressed-paper coaster. Jake picked up the mug and tilted it toward Richard. "It's good to see you, too." After studying the beer for a moment, he set it down. "Listen, Richard, sorry if I'm being too short or direct, but what the hell is going on?"

Richard gave him another appraising look. When Jake opened his mouth to say more, Richard held up a hand. "First, I need to hear your version of what happened yesterday morning."

Confused, Jake leaned back in his chair. "My version? Who else's could there be?"

Richard looked at him for a long moment. "I can't say much." He paused again, then nodded. "This is sensitive shit. I went out on a limb for you yesterday morning."

Remembering the interrogator's words, Jake leaned forward. "You're my friend in high places?"

Richard nodded. "But, before I climb farther out on that limb, I have to know how it all happened: the timing, the location, everything."

After a moment, Jake nodded. Leaning back, he took a draw from his mug. In hushed tones, he related the story. He started with the encounter over Nellis and its effect on Victor's aircraft and ended with the arrest and subsequent interrogation.

When Jake finished, Richard nodded and sat back.

"You don't seem surprised by any of this."

Richard shrugged. "I'm not."

"And?" Jake looked at him with raised eyebrows. "What do you have for me?"

"I can't really tell you anything tonight."

"Damn it, Richard, this is bullshit."

"I think someone already told you this isn't *bullshit.*"

Jake froze, mouth hanging open. He hadn't mentioned the security police sergeant's words.

"Listen, Jake. What you told me matches what we already thought."

Jake raised an eyebrow. "Who's we?"

Richard only shook his head.

"What about Lieutenant Croft?" Jake said. "A good man is dead, and everyone is acting like it didn't happen."

"I promise you, no one has forgotten Victor. Your story checks out. So, by noon tomorrow, things'll be much clearer."

"But—"

As if swearing an oath, Richard raised his right hand. "We didn't bring you all the way here just for steak and beer. Tomorrow, friend, tomorrow."

"We?"

"Let's just say, you've stumbled into something bigger than you can imagine. Until you've been fully vetted, you'll be watched and followed."

"Well, that explains that," he said with a chuckle. Grabbing the pitcher of beer, Jake filled their mugs.

"Huh?"

After setting down the empty jug, Jake tipped his mug in a toast. "Guess it's safe to say you'll be hearing from a pissed-off agent."

Jake told him about the exciting taxi trip.

Richard laughed. "I can't believe it cost you forty dollars."

"It didn't cost me a thing. I'll be giving you the expense report."

"Yeah, good luck collecting on that one."

"So, what else can you tell me?" Jake asked.

"Like I said, tomorrow."

Jake stared back at him. After a few moments, he lifted both hands. "Okay, I surrender."

CHAPTER 4

Captain Jake Giard woke with a start and a feeling of joy. Blinking the sleep from his eyes and looking around the room, he squinted against the glare of a lone sliver of light knifing through the dark air. As he studied the dust motes drifting through the street light's phosphorescent casting, Jake felt the elation fade with the dream that birthed it.

Remembering where he was, he slid to the edge of the bed adjacent to the window. No longer blinded by the street light's laser-like beam, he looked around the dark, musty room. Slowly, it drifted into focus. To Jake's right, an ancient digital clock radio sat atop a bedside table. With an audible click, its dimly lit black metal tabs with white numerals flipped over to reveal 06:00.

With a grunt, Jake sat up. Reaching over, he turned on a small lamp standing next to the clock. He flinched as its harsh rays burned into his sleep-addled brain. As Jake tried to rub the pain from his eyes, the events of the previous night washed across his thoughts, the latter parts a bit fuzzy—they'd shared more than one pitcher of beer.

Light banished the last of the dream. The fog of sleep evaporated, taking the elation with it. While he couldn't remember the details of the dream, he vaguely recalled speaking with Victor. It was a nice notion. However, now sitting in the beam of harsh street light falling through the parted curtains, he needed to deal with reality: his wingman was still dead.

"Fuck," Jake croaked through his parched throat.

Flinging the covers back, he stepped from the bed and walked to the window. Sliding the curtains open, Jake studied the few predawn stars that managed to burn through the city's light pollution. "What happened to you, Vic?"

~

"Please sign in here, sir, and have a—"

Walking quickly, Richard swept into the office. "That won't be necessary. He won't need to sign in. As a matter of fact, he isn't here at all." Gesturing to Jake, he added, "Come with me, Captain Giard."

"Who won't need to sign in, sir? I don't see anyone," said the young Army private through a conspiratorial smile.

"Thank you, Betty. Please forward my calls to voicemail." He hiked a thumb at Jake. "The invisible man and I will be out for the rest of the morning."

"Yes, sir," she replied.

Playfully grabbing Jake by the back of the neck, he pushed him toward the door and back into the Pentagon's labyrinth of hallways. Walking down the long, sterile corridor, he looked at Jake with an exaggerated grimace. "You look like shit. How's your head this morning?"

Jake grinned. "My head's not too bad, but when I woke up, my liver was on the pillow next to me, crying." Actually, in the two hours since waking, the combined effect of coffee and aspirin, coupled with a surprisingly peaceful cab ride had left Jake feeling much better, physically. "But enough about me. What's the plan?"

"Patience, grasshopper."

Rounding a corner, they stepped into a dead end hallway. At the far end stood a very serious-looking guard next to a table and an elevator door. Jake didn't see a call button. However, a keypad and some kind of lens sat above its expected location.

As they approached, the guard nodded to each of them in turn. "Good morning, Captain Allison, Captain Giard."

Jake blinked his surprise at the guard's foreknowledge of his name, his gaze snapping from the apparent camera lens back to the sergeant.

"Good morning, Doug," Richard said as his fingers danced across the keypad. Bending slightly, he looked into the lens. Jake heard a beep and saw a green light illuminate on the keypad's small screen.

"Good morning, Captain Allison," a computer-rendered male voice said.

"Good morning, Hal," Richard said, looking at Jake with a crooked grin. Gesturing, he said, "Step over here and look into the lens."

He complied. As soon as Jake looked into the glass eye, a red glow filled his vision, followed by the same beep and computer-generated voice. "Good morning, Captain Giard."

Jake looked at Richard. "How does it know me?"

"Don't ask, I could tell you, but I would have to kill you," Richard said with mock seriousness.

Jake spun on him. "Goddamn it, Richard! Enough with the fucking jokes, already. Someone really did get killed over this shit."

Richard's head snapped back as if Jake had slapped him. To his credit, the sergeant didn't flinch.

Richard raised both hands. "I'm sorry, Jake. That was thoughtless of me." The elevator doors opened, and Richard motioned for Jake to enter. "Bear with me a little bit longer."

After a moment, Jake shook his head and walked into the elevator. Still fuming, he studied its interior walls. All four surfaces were brushed stainless steel with no discernible fixtures or buttons. The doors slid closed and, to his surprise, the elevator went down from the ground floor.

Richard merely smiled with that maddening, humorous indifference.

The elevator continued downward. Jake felt the pressure building on his ears. Pinching his nose, he performed the Valsalva maneuver.

His ears popped and the pain subsided. "How the hell did that computer know me?" he asked again.

Richard pinched his nose in an apparent effort to clear his ears too. In a nasal tone, he said, "For the last twenty years, the military covertly scanned all recruits' retinas."

"How?"

"A camera built into the ophthalmoscope the doctors use for their initial entry exam snaps a shot of each retina. It's added to the recruit's file and to the master database."

The elevator slowed and stopped. The doors opened, revealing a modern hallway, its design far removed from the comparatively ancient architecture of the Pentagon—now an unknown distance above them. Another pair of serious-looking guards flanked a double door at the end of the hallway.

The walls and doors were highly polished black onyx, trimmed with brushed stainless steel.

Jake recognized the type of flooring. "There must be a lot of computers on this level."

Richard looked surprised. "What makes you think that?"

He pointed at the floor's grid of panels. "That's a raised floor. The underlying crawl space is used to distribute chilled air and run cables between server racks."

"Astute observation."

They approached the doors. "So, what is this place?"

"I could tell you." Richard pointed at the larger of the two guards. "But then he'd have to—" Seeing Jake's warning glare, he stopped mid-sentence. "Sorry."

In a deep, humorless monotone, the mountainous guard said, "Captain Allison, Captain Giard, IDs, please."

Taking their cards, he passed each under a laser scanner. It beeped twice. Nodding, he returned them. "Please proceed, sirs."

Turning, Richard reached out, placing his palm against a panel next to the doors. A red glow emanated from the pad. It beeped like the one upstairs. "Good morning, Captain Allison," the computer said.

The double doors parted. Noise from the busy room beyond flooded the quiet corridor.

Richard walked through, and Jake followed. Inside, the architecture was identical to the entry hall, but on a much larger scale. While the corridor was empty, this area was teeming with activity. Personnel, both civilian and military, scurried about.

It looked like NASA's Mission Control. Large monitors adorned the far wall while rows of computer consoles filled the large chamber's center.

Jake scanned the room, surprised to see so many foreign uniforms. Strange accents and languages were interspersed in the bustling room's din. Whatever it was, it had to be a multilateral, multinational effort.

He turned to Richard. "Again, what the hell is this place?"

Smiling, Richard pointed to the back wall.

Turning, Jake saw a beautiful scene on one of the large monitors. The image feed came from a camera orbiting high above the planet. The video quality was amazing, like looking through a window into space. Earth's curving horizon filled half the image. Irregular, halting movement drew Jake's attention. One of the stars in the image's right side appeared to be moving. Then it blossomed to fill half the screen. To his shock and bewilderment, no one in the control room reacted to the development.

Looking around the room, mouth agape, his pulse quickened. Confused and angry, he turned back to the monitor, and glared at the ship that had killed his wingman. It darted out of frame, its extreme acceleration leaving only a hint of its departure direction.

Jake was dismayed that those who had obviously seen the spaceship continued with their tasks. He turned to Richard, only to see that same infuriating smile on his face. Jake blew up. "What's so goddamned funny?" Then he realized Richard wasn't grinning at him, he was looking over Jake's shoulder.

A familiar voice spoke up from behind him. "It's about time you got here, Captain."

Jake turned and came face-to-face with his suddenly not so dead wingman.

Standing in the bustling underground control room, Jake stood with his mouth agape. Head spinning he stared at Lieutenant Victor Croft. A mix of emotions and confusion flooded his thoughts. "What the hell?"

"Well, it's good to see you too, Captain," Vic said, laughing.

Victor's chortling broke through Jake's shock. He grabbed the young man in a bear-hug, nearly crushing his reanimated wingman. "Holy shit, Vic! You ... you got out after all. Thank God!" Jake shook his head. "I thought ... hell, I *knew* you were dead," he said, finally setting him back down. "Why didn't you—?"

"Let's move this to the conference room," Richard interrupted, placing a hand on Jake's elbow and nodding toward the control room's occupants.

Jake turned in the room's abrupt silence. While the appearance of a strange ship hadn't fazed the assembled personnel, the reunion had brought all activity to a standstill as everyone watched.

Confused and unsure of what to say in spite of all the questions running through his mind, Jake looked from the onlookers to Richard, to Victor, and then back to the large monitor. Overwhelmed, he allowed Richard to guide him to a door on the side of the control room.

After climbing a flight of stairs, they passed through another door into a conference room. A long table surrounded by chairs occupied its center. A glass wall separated it from the control room.

Jake walked to the clear wall. Watching the activity below, he again felt overwhelmed. His mind raced with a multitude of questions.

Moving to stand on both sides of him, Victor and Richard joined Jake at the window.

Richard said, "It's a lot to take in."

"You think?" Jake shook his head and turned from the window. He grabbed a chair and fell into it. With his back to the conference table, he looked from Richard to the strange control room and finally to

Victor. He struggled to comprehend the developments of the last five minutes. "What the hell is going on here?"

"Lieutenant Croft," Richard said, pointing to the head of the table. "Please debrief the good Captain."

Vic walked toward the end of the table nearest the door. "I still don't know the whole story, but I can tell you my part of it."

Richard nodded. "That's fine, Lieutenant."

Jake stared at him. "I'm all ears."

"Ok," Vic said. Sitting down, he turned to Jake. "As you know, when that ship showed up, everything went to Hell. When it got too close, I lost control of my fighter."

"Yeah, me too," Jake said, nodding.

Victor also nodded. "I figured that, when your fighter rolled on top of mine, but when it left, mine didn't recover like yours did. Somehow, its departure threw me into an inverted flat spin. No matter what I tried, I couldn't recover it."

"So, you were able to eject after all."

"Nope," Victor said, with an indecipherable grin.

— Fifty Hours Earlier —

"Oh my God!" Victor screamed over the radio. With a white-knuckled death grip on the controls, he fought to rein in the violently shaking fighter. He keyed the radio transmit button again. "The stick is ... beating up ... the inside of my thighs."

Through the building roar of turbulence buffeting the airframe, he heard Jake over the radio. "Get away from the ship."

"I don't know ... if I can hold on," Victor said, his voice straining as he was thrown against the harness.

Multiple caution and warning lights illuminated, filling the cockpit with their red and amber brilliance. Blaring from his helmet speakers, squealing horns and mounting static drilled into his head. In a cascading collapse, system after system crashed. Still struggling to control his bucking fighter, Vic looked from the flashing warning lights to the strange ship. "Get the fuck away from me!"

Panic's icy fingers gripped his heart. He squeezed the radio transmit trigger. "My systems are going down. Every damn warning light is flashing!" he shouted into the building static. He couldn't tell if the radio transmitted.

"Mayday, Mayday, May—" he screamed. His helmet audio cut off mid-word as all electrical systems crashed. The cockpit lights faded to black, and the screaming static evaporated.

The fighter's electrically actuated flight controls locked up. Victor struggled with the stick, but his aircraft remained unresponsive. He looked across to the strange ship. "Move!"

A shadow crossed his cockpit. Looking up, he froze. Upside down and on a collision course, Captain Giard's fighter loomed overhead, blocking out the Moon.

"Come on!" Victor screamed. Looking across the narrowing gulf, yanking futilely against the flight controls. He tried to slide lower into the fighter's ejection seat.

Light flooded his cockpit, banishing the fighter's shadow. Dragging his eyes from the impending doom and surreal image of Jake looking down on him, he watched the strange ship's ethereal ring of lights grow blindingly bright, then it flashed away from his jet.

A tremendous shock wave threw Victor against his restraints. "Shit!" Somehow the ship's departure knocked his fighter into a flat spin. Knowing Jake was only a few feet away, he cringed.

Alternating waves of light swept through the cockpit as his spinning fighter emerged from under the shadow of Jake's airplane. Looking up, he saw Captain Giard's F-22 rolling away. Victor's momentary elation was quashed as his fighter tumbled inverted.

"Mayday, Mayday, Mayday!" his quivering voice squeaked into the dead radio. "Damn it!" he screamed, pounding the lifeless instrument panel.

Following his emergency restart procedures, he flipped switch after switch to no avail.

Knowing he was running out of options and time, he looked up from his upside-down fighter to see the Nevada desert floor way too close. In panic's icy grip, he frantically clawed at the ejection handles. An eternal second later, his fingers wrapped around them. He yanked with all his might.

Nothing! They didn't budge.

"Fuck!" He tugged and yanked several more times.

Still nothing!

Inverted, knowing death was imminent, Victor tilted his head back to watch the desert race up and devour him. He blinked, not believing his eyes. The strange ship had returned. It was outside, falling in formation with his fighter. "What the hell?"

Looking past the ship, he realized they weren't falling. They were still descending but at a much slower rate. "Shit," he whispered.

Vic's heart skipped a beat as a loud explosion ripped him from his awed trance. As if belatedly reacting to his ejection handle pulls, the canopy's jettison bolts exploded. Victor squeezed his eyes shut and ducked his head, bracing for the anticipated rush of wind, but it never came. Opening his eyes, he watched the separated canopy float away as if it were in the zero gravity of space.

In spite of the slow-motion fall, Victor could feel the desert growing closer. "Time to get the hell out!" He actuated the seat belt release, intent on a manual bailout. As soon as the harness unlatched, he felt an odd tugging sensation in his abdomen. Before he could react, Victor was yanked clear of the fighter. "Oh shit!" He flailed, belatedly grasping for a handhold. All senses screamed free fall, but there was no wind, and the desert still wasn't rushing up.

The tugging sensation increased, pulling him across the narrow gap. In an adrenaline-induced temporal disconnect, he perceived the half-second crossing in slow motion. Bridging the gap, he watched the ship's incredible pulsing, multicolored ring of lights pass less than two feet overhead. Reaching out, Victor's hand grazed the ethereal beams. For a fraction of a second, it felt like the center of the ship contained the mass of a black hole. Caught in its tremendous gravitational field, his hand slammed down like a metal rod to a magnet, but the instant it passed out of the light, the force evaporated. However, the gentle tugging sensation in his gut persisted.

Passing beyond the ring of lights, Vic flew under the strange ship. Like a hole in the sky, it loomed over and ahead of him, obscuring half the world. Its barely perceptible black mirror skin appeared to absorb almost all light that fell on its surface. Heart racing, he threw his hands up to absorb the imminent impact.

Just as Victor was about to hit, he heard tearing paper, and the skin in his path vaporized. He floated into the ship, and the skin resealed, plunging his weightless body into a silent, mind-swallowing void.

Hyperventilating, he floated in darkness. His panicked mind raced as he tried to comprehend what was happening. Wide-eyed, Vic snapped his head left and right in a desperate search for visual clues.

Nothing.

Something touched the sole of his boot. Victor screamed. After a moment of panicked flailing, he realized it was the floor. Gravity was returning. A few seconds later, he crouched on a textured metallic surface. Still in complete darkness, Vic reached overhead. Finding no obstructions, he slowly stood.

"What a pantywaist," his mother chided through a mirthless laugh.

"Not now, Mother," Victor whispered. Looking down, he shook his head. Now that her pestering persona had set up camp in his thoughts, she'd not soon stop. In the deafening silence, his heart pounded like an express locomotive. "Pull it together," he whispered. Closing his eyes, Victor held his breath in a desperate attempt to rein in his terror. After a few seconds and with no further comments from his overbearing maternal mental hitch-hiker, he exhaled. Feeling calmer, he extended his arms sideways and ahead, probing for a wall. After a moment, he realized he could see his hands as dark silhouettes against a dimly glowing background.

Facing away from the wall he'd passed through, Victor edged forward until his hands brushed against a surface. As he swept them left and right, the ivory glow intensified, revealing he'd passed into a small, oval-shaped room. A gray floor formed the only flat surface.

"What the hell is th—?" The wall vaporized under his fingertips as a tearing paper sound echoed through the small space. Victor jumped and stumbled backward, not stopping until slamming his back into the outer skin.

Blinking and panting, he stared at the new opening. A six-foot section of the wall had dematerialized, creating a doorway leading deeper into the ship's interior. Beyond, impenetrable darkness swallowed the light from Victor's small room.

Standing, he studied the door and dark void beyond. As his eyes adjusted, he began to perceive soft light in the next chamber. It was much larger than his small oval-shaped room.

Inching forward, sure any moment a fanged alien would pop out and snatch his life, Victor worked his way to the opening where he froze, unsure how to proceed.

The disembodied voice of his widowed mother chastised, "Come on, pussy, grow some balls!"

The woman's nagging and berating began in earnest during Victor's eleventh year, following his father's untimely death. Every time she found her only child unworthy of the title 'man of the family', she showered him with insults, belittling Vic in front of friends and family alike.

In his head, her unending denigration continued. "You pansy, if they wanted you dead, you'd be a crispy bug stain on the desert floor."

Goaded into action, he crouched and poked his head through the opening for a quick scan. Inside, he discovered a large, circular room that appeared to span the entire width of the ship.

As his eyes adjusted to the darkness, his heart skipped a beat. Three figures stood in the center of the large space. Victor was on their left. They weren't looking in his direction. Although, in the darkness, he couldn't be sure.

Thinking of Neil Armstrong's famous words, he extended a trembling leg into the ship's main cabin. *One small step, my ass.*

Not comfortable with the thought of sneaking up behind unknown aliens, and unwilling to shout 'Here I am!' he turned left, planning to follow the curving exterior wall until the aliens acknowledged his presence. *Or eat me.*

Before Victor finished his third step along the curved surface, the entire wall—a full one-third of the ship's horizontal circumference—vanished. The view outside shocked him into momentary paralysis. Recognizable from any altitude, the brilliant lights of Las Vegas receded over a shrinking, curved horizon. Looking down between his boots, Vic saw the black void of the Grand Canyon slide into view. Finding himself precariously balanced on a ledge miles above the surface, broke his paralysis. Launching backward toward the middle of the ship, Victor landed gracelessly on his ass. He crab-walked a few feet farther before dawning realization froze him.

If the wall had vaporized, he'd have been sucked out. Vic didn't know their exact altitude, but he knew they were already well above an airliner's cruising level. Judging by Earth's curvature, they were gaining more altitude every second. Considering the contained pressure differential, he knew there must be something physical present. Either the wall had turned clear or a force field was in place.

Loath to let any gaff go unnoticed, his mother chimed in. "Sure, just sit there, pussy. I'm sure the big, scary aliens are duly impressed."

Victor shook his head. He could practically hear the spittle flying from her pursed lips. Subvocalizing, he said, "Shut up, mother." Gathering himself and steadying his nerves, Lieutenant Croft stood and crept back to the wall. Looking down, he could see they had climbed above the atmosphere, reaching orbital velocity and altitude in the few moments it took him to clear the small room. Looking back to its opening, Victor recognized it as an airlock.

The acceleration must have been incredible, but he'd never felt the ship move. Somehow, this vessel's interior was disconnected from inertia. Thinking of how they'd pulled him into the ship, Vic realized the ship must also control gravity.

Looking over his right shoulder, he saw the three beings still hadn't acknowledged his presence. As far as Victor could tell, they hadn't even reacted to his graceless dismount of the imagined planetary-scale precipice. A walking thesaurus in the vernacular of her son's unending failures, his mother would've described that little foible as maladroit.

Shaking off the thought, he studied the figures. From his closer vantage point, he realized they were standing behind a console. Oriented toward the center of the wide clear wall, it was about four feet tall and topped with an angled, curving glass. Like holograms in a science fiction flick, enigmatic three-dimensional multicolored figures floated over its surface.

In height and width, the three beings appeared to have the same proportions as a human. Each had two arms and two legs. However, Vic couldn't discern anything beyond that in the ship's dark interior.

The holograms seemed to respond to their manipulations, although it was impossible to tell what they were doing from this distance. He saw the center figure's shadowed head look beyond the control panel as if studying something outside.

Falling back to his original plan, Vic crept along the invisible wall —keeping a respectful distance from the miles-high ledge.

He divided his attention between the aliens on his right and the incredible panorama to his left. Below, cities formed beautiful pools of scintillating lights. As the ship continued eastward, their prevalence increased until there was more city than dark countryside. Then it abruptly ended. White light gave way to the zigzagging black boundary of a dark ocean. "Holy shit," Vic whispered. They were already passing over the Atlantic Ocean.

The ship started a slow rotation. Originally oriented backward, its clear wall had been facing west. Still traveling east, the vessel turned through north. As it slowly rotated to face the oncoming eastern horizon, a carmine sun peeked from behind Earth's curved surface. A thin, red beam sliced from right to left across the cabin's dark interior. Rising through the layers of the atmosphere, the orb changed from red to orange and then to yellow. As the vessel continued its clockwise eastern rotation, the sun painted a sweeping mural of shifting colors across the room's left wall.

Having reached the front center, Victor took a deep breath and turned to face the beings. Silhouetted against the eastern horizon's glow, he stood between their apparent control console and the clear wall, feeling naked, exposed. However, the ship hadn't finished its rotation. His hosts remained dark voids in the room's brightening interior. Behind him, the sun continued along its horizontal arc, its brightening rays slowly banishing the ship's internal shadows. Marching inexorably across the ship's interior, the sun's light finally fell across the trio.

Victor froze, unable to comprehend what he saw.

"This doesn't make sense." Confusion morphed into anger. He screamed, "What the hell is going on here?"

Unresponsive, the three perfectly normal human beings simply stared back.

"What are you doing? You nearly kill me and my wingman, you crash my fighter, and scare the *shit* out of me. What the *fuck*?"

Silent and expressionless, they continued to stare at Victor.

He looked around. "Where'd this ship come from, anyway?"

Infuriatingly, they just stared back, mild humor the only detectable emotion.

Finally, the center one answered in a heavily accented language. Victor didn't understand the words. They sounded like Afrikaans, but all wrong.

"What?" he asked.

The apparent leader held up his right index finger in a hold-on gesture. His other hand moved back to the strange-looking panel.

A rotating, three-dimensional green hologram of a human brain emerged from its surface. Rising above the control panel, it hovered between them. Victor looked from the hologram to the man with a questioning look. To his surprise, the holographic brain mimicked his head's movements. Thinking it might be a coincidence, Vic turned his head left and right. The green brain did the same.

A vertical stack of holographic cubes streamed through the air to the left of the brain. Each block had a different color and a unique symbol. No longer worried the ship's occupants might be toothy aliens with a taste for human flesh, Victor stepped in for a closer look. He thought the symbols on the boxes might be part of some arcane computer language.

The center man apparently found what he was looking for. He

made a gesture, and the cascading cubes rolled to a quick stop. Reaching into the hologram, he tapped a virtual box. To Victor's surprise, the cube moved as if it had mass. As it slid out of the column, a new cube, identical in color and symbol to the one now in the leader's hand, coalesced out of thin air, filling the vacated slot. Raising it to eye level, the man looked at Victor through the semi-transparent purple cube and grinned. The holographic brain swelled to the size of a beach ball. Winking at Victor, the man tossed the cube into it.

Forming concentric rings, small waves radiated from the point of impact, like water disturbed by a falling rock. An oil can popping sound rang out as the cube breached the surface.

Dizzying vertigo buckled Victor's knees. He fell backward. Something resembling a lounge chair rose from the floor and caught him. He sat unmoving, disoriented by a strange tingling sensation. It felt like something was tickling his brain. As the impression passed, he shook his head.

Victor looked up at the three men staring down on him. Before he could ask them what had happened, the leader spoke again.

"Before I could say anything, he spoke again." Victor said. The enigmatic smirk returned. "And I understood him perfectly."

Confused, Jake closed his gaping mouth. "What do you mean? Was he speaking English?"

"No, he was still speaking in that strange language."

"And you could understand him?"

"Yep."

Maddeningly, Vic didn't elaborate. He just sat there grinning.

Jake grew impatient. "What? What did he say?"

After a theatric pause, Lieutenant Croft continued. "He said, 'Welcome home, brother.'"

CHAPTER 5

"This is where it gets interesting," a new voice said from the doorway.

Jake turned to see a wiry, middle-aged Air Force brigadier general enter the room.

All three men scrambled to their feet and snapped to attention in response to the sudden appearance of a very senior Air Force officer.

The officer chuckled. "At ease, gentlemen."

Relaxing from rigid attention, Jake turned and read the general's name tag: TANNEHILL. It was the uttered name that had ended his interrogation. Looking at Richard, Jake cocked an eyebrow. "And the plot thickens."

Walking to the head of the long table, General Tannehill motioned for them to take a seat. He grinned at Jake. "You don't know the half of it, son."

The three men sat down. Jake leaned back in his chair. "Well, sir, I haven't felt this naive since Betty Sue Alford kissed me during third-grade recess."

The general smiled. "I'm not sure I can be as enlightening as Betty Sue, but I'll try to clear up a few things for you." Sliding out the end chair, the general sat. Leaning forward and resting his elbows on the table, General Tannehill pointed at Jake. "Let me start off by saying I'm very impressed by how you've handled yourself. All the way through the incredible events of the last two days, you've acquitted yourself nicely." Tannehill gave him a knowing look and winked. "Even considering last night's taxi flight to freedom."

Jake's face flushed. Richard and Victor both laughed.

The senior officer leaned into his chair and held his hands up in a penitent gesture. "I hope you'll accept my apology for all the subterfuge."

A million questions ran through Jake's mind. "Sir—"

General Tannehill extended an index finger. "Before you ask, allow me to give you a brief history lesson. Hopefully, that'll clear up most of your questions."

Surrendering, Jake leaned back in his chair. "Sir, you have my complete and undivided attention."

"Well, as you may have guessed, we're not alone. It turns out the Milky Way galaxy is teeming with life." He pointed through the ceiling. "There are thousands of sentient species out there." General Tannehill paused, allowing Jake a few seconds to absorb the news.

Jake's mind reeled with the new revelation. He looked around the room, expecting to see one of its occupants grinning. They weren't. The general's assumption that Jake had guessed they weren't alone was wrong. He'd been prepared to accept that the Air Force or some other governmental agency had acquired radical new technology. The presence of humans aboard the strange ship only reinforced the notion.

Jake turned incredulously to the general. "Thousands, sir? No disrespect, but you're pulling my leg, right?" He pointed at Victor. "Lieutenant Croft said the ship's occupants were human."

With an understanding smile, General Tannehill held up a hand. "Bear with me, Captain."

"But sir, if there are thousands ..." He paused, searching for words. "They'd be hard to miss. Surely we would've seen them long before this."

The general's smile expanded. "We did. May I continue?"

Shocked, hands raised in surrender, Jake sat back. "Sorry, sir, please do."

Tannehill smiled sympathetically. "It's okay, Captain. I've been in that seat myself." Leaning forward, he activated a computer embedded in the table.

The room darkened and a storm of lights swirled overhead. Looking up, Jake froze in open-mouthed amazement. After a few seconds, the pinpoints of light coalesced into a vibrant hologram that filled the space between the long table and the ceiling. "It's beautiful," he whispered.

Nearly filling the room, a stunning twenty-foot-wide, three-dimensional rendering of the spiral-armed Milky Way galaxy rotated majestically over their heads.

General Tannehill continued as if a hovering hologram were an everyday occurrence. "The predominant species is an ancient race called the Argonians. Steeped in tradition and spread throughout hundreds of star systems, they founded a transgalactic government thousands of years ago."

"While it was started by the Argonians, it is an inclusive, representative government, providing peace and stability equally to all, regardless of species or stature."

He toggled the computer's touch screen. A truly alien bust filled the display. Chirping melodiously, a feathery, birdlike creature's obvious sentient eyes peered through a colorful plume.

"Argonian?"

Tannehill shook his head.

Fading, the avian was replaced by a furry, squeaking, mouse-like being. Beaming with intelligence, its eyes twitched nervously back and forth under a gold flight helmet. Then an alien with a grouper's fish face spoke in a deep tone, the meaning of its gurgling words a mystery. An accelerating myriad of visages paraded through the hologram, morphing through various species: reptilian, amphibian, and several more avian and mammalian analogues. Jake was unable to class some—including one that looked like a talking rock with a matching gravelly voice.

The last one faded, and the hologram vaporized.

Jake's gaze dropped to the general. "Their eyes." He paused, searching for the right words. "Regardless of color or shape, they all burned with ... intelligence."

"Astute observation, Captain," General Tannehill said with an appreciative nod.

"So, which one was Argonian?" Jake asked.

"None." Apparently disinclined to expound, the general continued his presentation. His fingers danced over the embedded keyboard, and a new hologram coalesced overhead. He pointed at the rotating icon. "The Seal of the United Galactic Federation, the Argonian-founded institution that has successfully governed the galaxy for thousands of years."

Several unidentifiable symbols adorned its surface. However, Jake was surprised to see familiar images of interlinked rings, birds, and green leaves prominently displayed on the revolving hallmark.

The hologram changed back to the rotating galactic plane and the general continued. "It's a *big* galaxy—unimaginably big. Even with all of their assets and technology, the Argonians still haven't charted every sector. So, a couple of thousand years ago, they deployed a self-propagating network of sensors."

Jake watched a grid of luminous green points spread across the twenty-foot-wide galaxy. Numbering in the tens of thousands, the rendered devices gave the entire galaxy a green hue.

"They're designed to look for a myriad of signals associated with burgeoning technological societies."

Jake nodded, enthralled.

"In nineteen forty-five, we got their attention," the general said, with a meaningful look.

After a moment, Jake put it together. "We detonated our first nuclear weapon."

"Yep," Richard chimed in. "Apparently, unnatural fission reactions rate pretty high on their list."

The general nodded. "When the Argonians detected the electromagnetic pulse, they deployed two scout ships to our sector of the galaxy. Upon arrival, they identified Earth, a previously unknown and uncharted planet, as the source. When they began observations, they made a stunning discovery, one requiring an immediate report to the Galactic Federation," the general paused, a grin spreading across his face.

Jake was on the edge of his seat. "What was it?"

The rotating Milky Way morphed into a human head and shoulders. A man in his mid-twenties stared at Jake. Aside from the odd cut of his uniform, he looked like a normal person.

Jake looked from the holographic man to General Tannehill. "I'm confused, sir."

The general pointed. "There's your Argonian."

Jake leaned back. "What?"

"To the surprise of the scouts and the Argonian leadership, Earth had been populated by Argonians—or as we refer to ourselves, humans."

"Holy shit ..." Jake whispered. Embarrassed, he looked at the general. "Sorry, sir."

The general chuckled. "I think I said the same thing."

With dawning realization, Jake turned to Vic. "That's what he meant by *brother*."

In reply, Vic said something, but Jake didn't understand him.

"What?" Jake asked.

Victor said a few more words, and Jake realized it wasn't English. Actually, it was a language he'd never heard.

Jake turned to General Tannehill as the man finished entering a command into the computer. A two-foot-wide holographic brain popped into existence over that end of the conference table. To its right a vertical queue of four-inch-wide cubes matching Victor's description streamed past. As each box in the descending column reached the table top, it vaporized. At the same time, a new cube coalesced at the top of the line. Every box was a different color, and each had a unique symbol.

The general studied the boxes. When a translucent purple one came into view, he reached in and grabbed the four-inch cube between thumb and forefinger. As if it were solid, the box left the streaming line of icons. Again, just as Victor had described, a new box appeared in the emptied space.

Holding the cube at eye level, Tannehill studied its symbol.

To Jake, the figure looked like a curved-leg numeral seven with a horizontal equal sign bisecting its center.

Looking at Jake through the translucent icon, the general grinned deviously.

"Wait—" Jake started. Before he could finish the protest, the general tossed the icon into the disembodied mind.

An audible metallic pop rang from the point of impact. Concentric rings radiated across the holographic brain's surface.

A sudden wave of nausea struck Jake as dizzying vertigo made him feel like the room was spinning. Jake grabbed the table with both hands. A strange tingling sensation flooded his head. As it passed, he blinked several times. "That felt weird." Jake froze in shocked amazement. He'd spoken in the same strange tongue as Vic.

"Can you understand me now?" Vic asked in the same language.

"Oh my God, that's amazing," he said through an unnerved laugh. Jake switched back to English. "I can completely differentiate the two languages," he grinned widely, "as if I've spoken them for my entire life."

Looking at General Tannehill, Jake pointed to the holographic brain and the scrolling icons. "Is that just for learning languages? Can it teach other subjects?"

The general smiled. "There's way more than that. Want to learn kung fu or at least the Argonian equivalent?"

Richard leaned over the table, pointing at the hologram. "It's like *The Matrix* without a big hole in the back of your head."

Head spinning from all the revelations, Jake felt both mentally exhausted and simultaneously exhilarated. The significance of what this meant for himself, his family, and his friends—hell, the entire world—was incredible.

His grin never faltering, General Tannehill seemed to enjoy the flood of emotions and questions streaming across Jake's face. He imagined the general probably had the same reaction upon receiving his first briefing.

Giddy with the possibilities, Jake nodded. "Please continue, sir. How are we and the Argonians the same race?"

"We don't know for sure. They've told us that some of their early colony ships disappeared, never to be heard from again. As I said earlier, it's a damn big galaxy. They theorize one may have been stranded here tens of thousands of years ago. Although we have no idea what became of their technology or scientific knowledge. Apparently, they were close enough genetically to the Neanderthals to coexist."

"According to recent genetic discoveries, they did more than *coexist*," Richard added.

"Amazing," Jake whispered.

"Anyway, returning to the nineteen forties," the general said. "After reporting their discovery, the scouts were ordered to proceed. Unfortunately, before they could make contact, there was a mishap. One of the scout ships encountered a severe thunderstorm over New Mexico and crashed." The general smiled and raised his eyebrows. "An incident most refer to as Roswell."

Jake sat bolt upright. "Roswell was real?"

"Yes," the general said. "It was a freak accident. Guess it just goes to show, even though they've advanced significantly, they're still fallible humans."

"But why would they be in Roswell?"

"That was before the Air Force split from the Army. Roswell Army Air Field was home to the Five-Oh-Ninth Bomber Group. It was an elite air wing and at the time the only nuclear-armed military unit in the world."

"Also, it was only a hundred and ten miles from Trinity, the test site where we detonated our first nukes," Richard said.

"Go figure," Jake said. "No wonder that was their first stop."

Tannehill continued. "The story has been altered and bastardized. However, many of the fundamental parts are true. The ship and its impact debris were collected. After several moves and several years, it ended up in an Area Fifty-One hangar."

"Is it still there?"

"No, it was eventually returned to the Argonians."

"But wait, Roswell happened in nineteen forty-seven," Jake said. "I thought you said we got their attention in forty-five."

"You're right, Captain. The Argonians' drive technology allows them to travel significantly faster than light, and their zero-width wormholes allow instant galactic-wide communications. However, the signals their passive sensors listen for are limited to the speed of light."

A storm of dissociated points of light swirled overhead. After a moment, they coalesced into the Milky Way galaxy. Bent over the keyboard, the general tapped out another command. Standing, he pointed into the twenty-foot-wide hologram as the tide of green dots spread through the image again. "Even with more than a million equally spaced sensors, they are still a thousand light years apart."

"A thousand light years?" Jake said in a dubious tone. Standing to his full six feet, his head was immersed in the hologram. As the slowly rotating galactic plane slid past, he eyed the spacing of the sensor grid with open skepticism. "I'm sorry, sir, but that doesn't look like it could be anywhere close to a thousand light years."

Walking toward the far side of the room, General Tannehill smiled and pulled a laser pointer from a shirt pocket. Activating it, he placed a red dot on the wall behind Jake. "Move to the outer edge, Captain."

With a final skeptical look at the grid floating through his vision, Jake ducked out of the hologram. He stepped to its far side and stood opposite the general. Through the translucent brilliance of the rendering, he could just make out the man's face.

Without turning it on, Tannehill lifted the laser to eye level and aimed it at Jake's face. "Okay, Captain, I just fired my laser light at you."

There still wasn't any light coming from the device. Jake saw the general's point immediately. "You're saying that it would take a long time for the light to travel across the galaxy."

General Tannehill nodded and turned on the laser pointer. "A *very* long time. In the real galaxy, that light would take one hundred thousand years to travel from me to you." With his opposite hand, he ran a finger through a region of the hologram that looked like flowing sand. "Every pixel of this glowing dust is actually a star separated from its closest neighbor by light years of empty space."

Nodding, Jake stared in stunned comprehension. None of it was new information. However, the general's practical demonstration slammed home the galaxy's scale in a way raw numbers never had. "So, it could have taken up to five hundred years for them to detect us."

The general grinned. "Yep, it was pure happenstance that a sensor was less than two light years from our solar system."

As they moved back to their chairs, Jake gave the general a contrite expression. "Sorry for the skepticism, sir."

Tannehill waved it off. "You're not the first person I've given that little demonstration." Sitting down, he studied the table's embedded computer screen. "Where were we?"

"I think you were about to tell me what happened to the remaining Argonian scout ship?"

"That's right," the general said, leaning back in his chair. "It made first contact with the US military."

"With the military? Why not the government, sir?"

The general shrugged. "It's been their policy for thousands of years. They say it reduces the possibility of a hostile reception."

Jake considered it and nodded. "Guess it's better to talk to the armed husband at the front door before trying to sell his wife an encyclopedia set."

"Pretty much," General Tannehill agreed.

"So, what were they trying to sell to the wife?"

"As I mentioned, our galaxy has tens of thousands of worlds inhabited by thousands of species. The Argonians were the first star travelers. So, over the millennia, they've helped hundreds of species, at varying levels of technological development, make the transition to star-faring status. Through trial and error, they established a regimented process of first contact and integration. This process allows newly discovered societies to be smoothly integrated into the galactic community while minimizing the short-term cultural and economic impact."

"In spite of our being the same race, they decided to follow the same procedure for our induction into the galactic government and economy. The entire process is slated to take seventy-five Earth years. For us, that clock started around 1950. The technological advances scheduled for the next decade will make the last sixty years seem trivial by comparison."

Obviously well versed in the details of the briefing, the general continued with a practiced ease. "The coming years will see the introduction of game-changing technologies. The biggest effects will be in the medical, communications, and energy sectors. Additionally, there will be more and more hints of the existence of extraterrestrial life."

"All of this is designed so that, by the time the world becomes aware of the existence of aliens, we will have advanced enough to reduce the cultural shock," the general concluded.

"Why such a long process?" Jake asked. "Humanity is resilient. Surely they don't think we'll fall into anarchy the first time CNN televises a UFO landing in Central Park."

The general nodded in understanding. "They have to consider all of the potential ramifications of early disclosure. Initially, their first contact efforts garnered everything from smooth transitions to global civil wars. Over the subsequent millennia, they fine-tuned the process. Several factors determine the length of the transition. If our world economy had been globally aligned and if energy trading weren't such an integral part of it, we would've had a shorter transition. Energy is the biggest sector of our global economy. Just imagine what would happen to the world markets if free energy was dropped on our doorstep tomorrow."

Jake nodded in understanding. "The millions of jobs and billions of dollars tied into all the steps between oil exploration, drilling, production, and distribution of petroleum products would be lost overnight."

"Exactly, and that's just one part—albeit a very big part—of the world economy. While seventy-five years sounds exceedingly long to us, when you consider it from their position and timescale, it's a blink of the eye."

"So, what happened back in the forties when they told the US leadership about the galactic government and the seventy-five-year process?" Jake asked.

"Initially, there was a lot of reluctance and skepticism. Our military commanders were especially concerned with the requirement to include all of Earth's significant governments, especially the Soviets. The Argonians explained that the galactic economy was a hybrid of capitalism and socialism based on free trade. They also told them the process of bringing us into the fold would require a gradual transition of all Earth governments to a compatible economy."

"In other words, they were proposing changes that weren't going to be popular anywhere," Jake said.

"Pretty much," General Tannehill agreed. "In January of nineteen forty-eight, the heads of state for all of Earth's significant countries were brought together and briefed by the commander of the remaining scout ship. The seventy-five year timeline and the reasons for it were laid out."

"As I'm sure you can imagine, there were serious objections from the Communist nations. The scout commander pointed out that governments that chose to exclude themselves from the process would also be excluding themselves from the opportunities and technologies that would be realized during the undertaking. The Communist delegations declined the invitation, insisting their superior governments and economies would achieve these goals on their own. They refused to be any part of it. Over the following decades, as the Cold War continued and the West prospered in the face of the failure of Communism, the abstaining governments slowly came around."

Jake nodded. "So, over the last couple of decades, we've witnessed the transition," he said. Raising a hand, he counted off the steps with his fingers. "First the fall of the Soviet Union, followed by the gradual transition of the Chinese economy, and then by the formation of the

European Union and the United States' gradual increase in social programs—regardless of which party was in power."

"Yep, you're connecting the dots. Today all of Earth's significant countries are in the loop. We're well on the road to Galactic Government integration," concluded the general.

"Thank you, sir. That definitely answers a lot of my questions," Jake said, looking at both of his friends, then focused on Lieutenant Croft. "It's damned good to see you alive and well, Lieutenant."

Victor squirmed under the attention. "You're telling me," he finally managed as he stared down at the desk.

That reminded Jake of another bothersome issue. He turned back to General Tannehill. "Actually, sir, there is one more thing. I don't understand why the ship caused problems with our fighters. If it could interfere with our aircraft, why didn't they keep their distance?"

Richard nodded. "I got this, sir," he said. "The Argonians use a gravity drive and inertial dampening system. It generates a field that simultaneously moves all matter within its effective range. The field's envelope extends several meters outside of the ship. Since all of the molecules within it move together, any object or person within the field won't feel G-forces or acceleration. For instance, the reason you feel G-forces as your Corvette accelerates from zero to sixty in three point five seconds is due to Newton's Law of Inertia. The molecules in your chest want to stay in place while the molecules in your back are being pushed forward by the power of the engine. Now imagine you could pull all of those molecules simultaneously: there would be no compression due to inertia. You would literally feel no G-forces at all."

Sitting back, Jake envisioned the ship plowing through the atmosphere, trying to visualize its effect on the surrounding air. "That explains the buffeting Vic's F-22 experienced as the ship closed in. Since the effect extends beyond the ship's external skin, there must be a pocket of air dragged along by the ship's drive. When it got too close to Vic's wing, it lost lift, causing it to stall out."

"Makes for one hell of a rough ride," Lieutenant Croft said.

"Yeah, but that brings me back to my original question. Knowing this, why would the Argonian pilot allow his ship to get close enough to cause problems?"

"I'll take this one, Captain," General Tannehill said. He nodded to Jake and Vic with a contrite expression. "Quite frankly, gentlemen, we screwed up, and by *we* I mean *I*." He tapped another string of commands into the keyboard. Leaning back in his seat, the general continued. "There was a meeting scheduled with the Argonians that morning. We have F-22s assigned as escorts. They are shielded against the gravity drive's effect."

A hologram of an F-22 flying in formation with an Argonian ship materialized over the table. Rendered as a magenta fog, a bubble of energy completely encapsulated the Argonian ship just as Jake had envisioned. As it neared the holographic F-22, pulsing concentric arcs radiated from two points on the side of the fighter. They appeared to blow back the gravity drive's effect, creating a concave dimple in the Argonian ship's bubble.

Tannehill continued. "Unfortunately, due to a simple scheduling error—an error I failed to catch—the assigned F-22s were late for the meet-up. The same error allowed you and Vic to be vectored into the area designated for the rendezvous. When the Argonian commander detected your fighters, he mistook you as his escort to the meeting location."

Richard chimed in. "The shielding is also necessary for your electronics. The gravity field affects your electrical lines and equipment much like a spinning, hugely powerful magnet. The gravitonic flux lines cut across unshielded lines in a way that drains all electricity."

Jake nodded to Richard and turned to Tannehill. "Thank you for your frankness, General. So, where do we sign up?"

"Excuse me?"

Jake spread his arms wide, palms up. "It seems to me you could have forgone all of this, sworn us to secrecy, shipped us off to Iceland, and written the whole thing off. So, sir, I'm thinking you have something better planned for us."

"Captain Allison told me you were a smart fella."

"Actually, I told him you were a pretty fart smeller," Richard quipped.

Following hours of weighty discussion, Richard's joke brought a welcome levity.

As the laughter settled, General Tannehill continued. "Captain Allison's assertion notwithstanding, I do believe we have a place for the two of you in our program. If you'd be so inclined."

CHAPTER 6

"Commodore Salyth, charge the weapon, and prepare to drop the ship out of parallel-space," growled Lord Thrakst.

"As you command, Lord," the younger officer replied. Rising from an inadequate half-bow, Thrakst's second in command forwarded the orders to the appropriate stations.

Pretending to ignore the slight, Thrakst impatiently stared into the main display. Ahead, their light curved into a sphere by the parallel-space drive's faster-than-light velocity, the compressed star field shone with the brilliance of a million suns. Without the ship's shielding and light filters, the hard radiation streaming from the sphere would incinerate flesh and char the naked bones to dust in seconds. Outside of that ball of light, all was black. As they burned their way into Argonian space at superluminal speed, they traveled too fast for the light of the stars abreast and astern of their position to reach them. Illuminated by the light ahead, only the other ships of his fleet broke the impenetrable inky void.

Agitated, Thrakst dug a razor-sharp talon into the damp rough rock armrest of his black-stone throne. The design and atmosphere of the hollowed-out iron asteroids that formed the ship mimicked the damp interior of their home world cave dwellings. The environmental control system maintained the humidity level at one hundred percent. However, even the constant sound of dripping water that echoed through the spaceship's interior brought Thrakst no comfort.

A low, rumbling growl rattled deep in the chest of the ancient warrior posted on his right. The wizened old Zoxyth was Raja Phascyre, Lord Thrakst's most trusted advisor and oldest friend.

The Lord's razor-sharp scaled lips parted in a toothy grin. His pointed, black tongue danced across silver fangs. In a hissing voice backed by a deep rumble that originated from the same depths as his confidant's growl, Thrakst spoke in words only the Raja could hear. "What is it, Phascyre?"

The Raja's scarred arm rose. In menacing agitation, the old warrior's razor-sharp, sickle-shaped dewclaw talon repeatedly slid in and out of his forearm. Extending a grizzled finger at Commodore Salyth, Phascyre turned to face Thrakst. "That one thinks his time draws near."

Thrakst regarded the remaining eye of his old friend's mutilated face. It burned with anger. Having sworn a life oath to protect the Lord, Phascyre looked ready to attack the young Commodore. Even the polished rock he'd bolted into the socket of his gouged-out right eye appeared to scowl. In spite of his age, the Raja was second only to Thrakst in size and physical stature. Turning to scowl at the commodore, Raja Phascyre's eye slits narrowed. "My Lord, let me take the hatchling down a notch."

Thrakst's grin widened. "Do not worry, old friend. I can handle this one." He paused with a deep, low laugh. "Actually, he reminds me of myself."

"Yes, exactly," Phascyre said. He turned his sole eye on Thrakst. A toothy smile parted the old warrior's scaled lips. "So, let us not forget how you rose to this station."

Thrakst wrapped the thumb and three talons of his right hand around the Raja's upper left arm and pulled him down to a knee. He gripped the old warrior so tightly, the dagger tips of Thrakst's steel-reinforced talons pricked green blood. "I never forget, old friend."

Phascyre bowed his head deeply. "Forgive me, my Lord."

Releasing his arm, Thrakst gave the warrior a respectful nod and gestured toward Salyth. "The day I stop heeding your words will be the day that hatchling deserves this seat." He tapped steel-tipped talons on the throne's damp rock surface, depositing small drops of Phascyre's green blood.

Paying no heed to the fresh wounds, the Raja nodded and stood.

Leaning back into his black throne, the huge and menacing Zoxyth Lord scanned the bridge of the dark warship, *Tidor Drof*. It was dark times in the Zoxyth Empire. The recent radical reversal of fortunes had the High Council questioning Thrakst's decision to press the battle beyond Zoxyth space.

In the early days, their war to purge the Argonian infestation had succeeded beyond all expectations. After their original successes, the Zoxyth High Council had pressed their Lord of War to sue for peace, not to take the battle beyond the Forebearer's ancestral borders. Thrakst had even considered it. Then the Argonians had done the unthinkable.

Looking through the Forebearer's left eyeport, Thrakst studied the dreadnought flying on his left flank. As with the *Tidor Drof*, it was a giant conglomeration of hollowed iron asteroids held together by steel superstructures. Like all ships in his fleet, the bridge at the front of the ship was a massive bust of a Forebearer's head chiseled from a dedicated asteroid. The combination of natural and unnatural structures and the power their mass signified were designed to strike fear into all who ventured within its sphere of influence, a sphere Lord Thrakst intended to extend today.

Gesturing for Phascyre to look at the bridge of the adjacent dreadnought, Thrakst pointed at the sculpted Argonian skull clenched in the Forebearer's stone fangs. "This weapon will bring the bastards to their knees."

The ancient Raja bowed respectfully. "You will have your vengeance, my Lord."

"Oh, they will pay. I will avenge ..." Lost in the memory, Thrakst gnashed his silvery teeth and dug the steel-tipped middle talon of his right hand into the armrest again. Black and rough, its damp rock surface reminded him of his grotto back on Zoxia. He'd loved coming home to her, her scent, the sound of her and their son's cooing. He longed for her touch. The image dissolved, chased away by fire and a woman's death screech.

Clawing at the stone floor with his lower, steel-tipped talons, Thrakst stood. The massive, scaled muscles of his legs flexed and rippled. Standing to his full eight-foot height, he stepped to the center of the bridge. His imposing bulk filled the area between his black throne and the forward bank of consoles.

Stepping forward, Phascyre stood to the Lord's right rear.

Thrakst nodded at him and then faced forward. His black tongue ran across dripping fangs.

"Ready to deploy," reported Commodore Salyth, this time his bow non-existent.

Lord Thrakst's long, sinuous arm struck so quickly that the movement was almost imperceptible.

Commodore Salyth fell to a knee, clutching his bleeding face.

"Do not forget your place, Commodore, or next time I may *forget* to retract my arm talon," said Lord Thrakst.

Lowering his hands, Salyth bowed deeply and backed away from the towering Zoxyth leader. "Forgive me, Lord, it was not my intent to disrespect." In a final display of servility, the ambitious officer's swept-back, horn-shaped ears lay flat against the hunter green scales of his angular skull.

Thrakst gave him a curt nod. "Transmit this to the entire ship."

"Yes, my Lord," Salyth said. After a respectful bow, he forwarded the order to the officer standing at the communications console.

The Lord was pleased to see his protégé shake off the pain. Not waiting for confirmation, Thrakst turned and walked back to his rock throne.

Standing in front of his high perch, he addressed the fleet. "A hundred thousand years ago, when the Argonian infestation first ventured out of their solar system, they found us holding the galactic keys. They attacked us then as they do today. Following our near genocide during the War of Argonian Aggression, the Forebearers were forced into an unholy alliance. The aggressors doled out crumbs of power. Strung along by the Argonians, we were told that our representation in their galactic government made us *equal* partners in the Galactic *community*," Thrakst said, spitting out the words *equal* and *community* with unbridled disgust, hatred, and contempt.

"Now that we fight for our independence, they again seek to genocide us!"

A cacophony of angry growls and indignant screeches echoed through the cavernous ship.

Nodding his massive head, Lord Thrakst continued his tirade. "Making the ultimate sacrifice, many great warriors have since joined the Forebearers. In spite of heavy losses, it is only through their brave efforts that the Argonians have yet to re-enter Zoxyth space. As during that first war, their advanced technology turned our early successes into a chain of defeats."

Angry rumblings passed through the ship.

For millennia, the Zoxyth Empire had struggled to understand Argonian technology. Complicating the issue, their genetic security protocols had blocked Zoxyth efforts to reverse-engineer captured ships. If you don't have Argonian genetics, the systems resist all attempts at discovery, self-destructing if probed too deeply. Their ship's semi-sentient intelligence could also differentiate between living and dead tissue, as well as free will versus coerced cooperation, thus thwarting efforts to gain access using cadavers and prisoners.

Thrakst continued his rant. "The Argonians arrogantly assume their technology renders the outcome of this war a forgone conclusion. This weapon will turn the tide! The gods of war will see our dreadnoughts rain death upon all opposing our rightful ascension to the galactic seat of power. The Argonians will beg for our mercy!" proclaimed Lord Thrakst. The steel-reinforced talons in his clawed feet scratched at the floor while he thrusts a clenched fist into the rock ceiling, sending out a spray of shattered stones. "With this weapon, we will chase the Argonian infestation from the very galaxy!"

In answer, his warriors raised their arms as their roars joined his.

Thrakst pointed at his second in command. "Commodore Salyth, after this test, your dreadnought fleet will be the first to attack an Argonian star system."

Grinning through green blood, Commodore Salyth bowed sharply. "Thank you, my Lord. It will be the highest honor to visit the Forebearer's vengeance upon the Argonians."

With a nod, Lord Thrakst sat in his cathedra. "Very well, Commodore, your command ship will be renamed as the *Forebearer's Revenge*. I know you'll earn their gratitude."

"Thank you, Lord," Salyth said, returning to his station.

Thrakst sat. "Now it is time to introduce the Argonians to their fate. Drop only this ship out of parallel-space."

As planned, the dreadnought dropped back into regular space amongst a large formation of mismatched, decrepit spaceships. Like an angry nest of flies, the refugee ships scattered. Exactly as Thrakst had hoped, some turned to attack while others fled for the perceived safety of distance.

After waiting for the fleeing ships to gain adequate space to test the weapon's full range, Thrakst pointed to Commander Salyth. "Fire!"

CHAPTER 7

Admiral Ashtara Tekamah studied the myriad stars that filled the infinite space beyond his stateroom. Usually, the tranquil view from his private quarters provided the fleet admiral a reprieve from the daily stress and clutter of command. Today, it only served as a reminder of all that was wrong with the universe. Frustrated and irritated, the leader of the Galactic Defense Force turned away from the panorama. Behind him, the clear variable-phase polymetallic wall opaqued, taking on a dark-stained wood finish.

The Argonia-born Commander of the United Galactic Federation's defense forces accessed his electro-organic network. Feeding data directly into his visual cortex, the self-assembling nanites of the EON superimposed icons over his view of the real world. Demanding his attention, one of the symbols hovering in his peripheral vision oscillated between amber and red. It was a report he'd already read. Due to the urgency of the message the admiral hadn't removed the flag.

Sitting down, Tekamah tapped the icon with his virtual hand. Scanning the intelligence officer's report for the third time, he considered its implications.

"Damn it!"

A swipe of his virtual hand wiped the report from Tekamah's synthetic vision. Two annoying red and amber flashes later, he double-tapped its icon and removed the flag. Still finding no solace, he shut down the EON's synthetic vision, leaving him an unobstructed view of his office.

From behind his antique ornate bronze desk, Admiral Tekamah studied the collection of ancient battle implements that hung on the wall to his right. His gaze shifted to the central two revolvers hanging in opposition. One was from an age lost in Argonian antiquity. Barely a hundred years old, the other was much newer. While only a narrow gap separated their muzzles, a hundred thousand years and half a galaxy hung between their inceptions.

Independently developed by two isolated branches of the Argonian race, the weapons symbolized the base nature of the species, a nature Tekamah had believed was long in their past. However, the news contained in the report had his blood boiling. In spite of a lifetime immersed in an empathetic society, he would love to have Thrakst in the iron sights of both pistols.

A hundred millennia ago, when the Argonians first ventured outside of the home system, they ran headlong into the burgeoning Zoxyth Empire.

Having subjugated every sentient species they encountered, the Zoxyth had already established a serious superiority complex. When they came across the Argonians, the first technologically advanced species they'd encountered, the Zoxyth attacked.

The aggressive reptiles had expanded their empire beyond the boundary of their solar system as quickly as their nascent spacefaring technology afforded it. However, the Argonian race didn't spread outside of its home system until the virtual immortality afforded by their medical and technological advancements created the need for additional resources and real estate. Consequently, humanity's ancestors more than held their own against the antagonistic Zoxyth, soundly defeating them in that first engagement.

However, believing there was plenty of real estate for both, the Argonians disengaged. To avoid future confrontation, they shifted their exploration and colonization efforts away from the Zoxyth Empire's territory.

Spurned by their first defeat, and unwilling to accept the growth of another empire on their border, the Zoxyth took the battle to the Argonian home world. When an armada of their asteroid ships dropped out of parallel space above Argonia, the planet's inhabitants unleashed a counter-attack that killed every reptilian combatant. To ensure Zoxyth rulers got the message loud and clear, the Argonian defense forces went on an offensive sweep and vaporized every Zoxyth ship between Argonia and the self-declared Neutral Zone.

It turned out that the only thing the Zoxyth respected was force. An uneasy peace settled between the two species. Over the subsequent millennia, the Argonians encountered a multitude of other space-faring species without repeating the calamitous events of that first contact. They allied with several alien races and eventually set up a galactic free trade zone.

By the time of the forming of the first galactic government, the Zoxyth had joined the zone. They even assigned a representative to the newly formed galactic senate.

From the early days of the United Galactic Federation, the Zoxyth were a constant thorn in Argonia's side. However, in spite of their antagonistic posturing, the Zox remained a productive contributing member of the galactic community during the intervening millennia.

In recent decades, a wave of religious fundamentalism had swept through the Zoxyth sector. Ancestor worshipping fanatics elevated the Zoxyth that had originally attacked Argonia to sacrosanct deities. The worshipper's maniacal leader, Lord Thrakst, citing the documented destruction of one of the Forebearer's massive egg carrier colony ships, claimed they had narrowly avoided genocide in what he called the War of Argonian Aggression. According to Thrakst, the Argonians had forced peace terms and drawn the Forebearer's into an unholy alliance through lies and deceit.

Two years ago, fanatical followers of Lord Thrakst seized control of the Zoxyth Empire and declared their independence from the United Galactic Federation. Subsequently, state-sponsored attacks and seizures fell on ships traveling through Zoxyth space. What started out as harassment actions soon escalated to outright rebellion.

A GDF cruiser disappeared when it went into Zoxyth space to investigate an Argonian outpost that had fallen silent. Then the pair of Galactic Defense Force scout ships sent to find the cruiser disappeared as well. In a recon-in-force action, the *Galactic Forge* battlecruiser and space-carrier *Deliverance* dropped out of parallel-space a light-second from the last reported coordinates of the missing cruisers. Within seconds, over a hundred of the massive Zoxyth asteroid dreadnoughts materialized around the two warships. They were surrounded. The ensuing battle left thousands dead on both sides.

Against Tekamah's recommendation, the leadership of the Galactic Federation recalled all GDF outposts and vacated all United Galactic Federation facilities within Zoxyth space. Essentially, they allowed the Zox to secede from the UGF without negotiations or accountability for their unwarranted attacks.

Admiral Ashtara Tekamah told the council the Zox would see the move as weakness. Unfortunately, they proved him correct all too soon. Within days of the recall order, swarms of asteroidal dreadnoughts began attacking settlements outside Zoxyth space. Somehow the Zox had secretly amassed an enormous fleet.

That was two years ago. While the Zoxyth initially had major victories, the last few months had seen the tide of war shift inexorably in favor of the Galactic Defense Force. Once the council fully appreciated the scope of the Zoxyth threat, they had thrown the full force of the Argonian Galactic Defense Force into the battle. Tekamah, his hands untied, had swept the Zox infestation from every system outside of Zoxyth space.

Since the last engagement, two months previous, an uneasy ceasefire had settled across the region. As both sides regarded each other across stagnant battle lines, refugees had begun repopulating the liberated planets.

While the United Galactic Federation contained thousands of species, there had been little blending of populations. With a few notable exceptions near the galactic core, the denizens of most colonized worlds consisted of one species. The radically differing atmospheric and gravitational standards rendered cross-species cohabitation a near impossibility. The subsequent genetic polarization carried across many aspects of the galactic community. To simplify environmental systems and to prevent proliferation of weapon technologies, the Argonians maintained sole control of the Galactic Defense Force. While they often worked hand-in-hand with other races, only Argonians staffed the fleet's warships. Superficially, it sounded xenophobic and had been called as much by the Zoxyth. However, over the millennia, the GDF had earned a reputation as a force for good. Whether providing disaster relief or coming to the rescue of an embattled ally, the Argonians of the Galactic Defense Force were goodwill ambassadors and the glue that held the United Galactic Federation together.

Following the cessation of hostilities, great convoys of returning refugees now streamed back into the border worlds. The mission of the GDF had shifted from offensive to defensive as they provided protection to the various species re-entering the zone.

Now there was a problem.

Admiral Tekamah closed his eyes for a moment. Sitting back in his chair, he reactivated his EON and accessed the disturbing report again. It was from a unit assigned to escort duty.

Prior to linking up with that military escort, and still well outside the border region, a fleet of Argonian refugees preparing to return to their liberated colony world had come under attack. The distress call cut off midstream, but not before reporting a sole Zoxyth dreadnought.

The escort squadron had leapt into parallel-space in a mad rush to come to their defense. What they found at the last reported position of the refugee fleet sent a chill down Tekamah's spine.

In the hour it took the squadron to close the four-light-year gap, the dreadnought blasted and burned all the ships of the Argonian convoy and made its escape. In spite of the fleet's extensive destruction, there should have been some survivors or bodies, or something other than what they'd found ... or not found, in this case.

Every ship remnant and cinder they'd searched was devoid of any Argonians, alive or dead.

CHAPTER 8

The late spring sun beat down on the Nevada tarmac like a never-ending nuclear detonation. In spite of the lengthening late-afternoon shadows, the high desert sky retained the deep blue hue of a midsummer day. The surrounding mountains would look at home on the Moon. Their rocky peaks scratched roughly at the lighter edges of the azure, overarching atmospheric ocean. Forming an unbroken halo, they guarded Area Fifty-One's secret Groom Lake Air Force Base from prying eyes.

Chasing their elongated ambling shadows, two Air Force officers walked in front of a long row of hangars. In the base's ghost town silence, their footsteps echoed off the metal sides of the large buildings. As they progressed east, toward an expansive aircraft ramp, each hangar appeared to be older than the previous.

"I always thought when I became a super-secret special agent I wouldn't have to sweat anymore," Jake said to Vic.

"Yeah," Vic said. Casting a resigned glance at the blazing sun, he fanned the zipper-lined lapel of his flight suit. "It's like stepping into an oven."

They had just finished their first week at the officially non-existent military base. The security briefings and safety classes had been exhausting and mind-numbing. The secretive and compartmentalized policies of the facility prohibited discussion of their assignments or job duties with their instructors, a fact driven home by ubiquitous signage and incessant aural security reminders blasted from an overhead public address system. As far as Jake knew, the instructors had no idea of the not so alien aliens or any of the myriad unknowable projects currently operating at the base.

Wiping a fresh bead of sweat from his brow, Jake scanned the expansive concrete plain. From here, it appeared they were walking through an abandoned airfield. He knew most activities took place in a vast underground web. Their briefings had been in a small part of that network. One of the orientations had alluded to an intricate maze of tunnels, connecting various facilities. This trek to the flight line was their first foray beyond the administrative area.

"Those were vague instructions," Victor said, breaking Jake's thoughts.

"I know. Considering how anal they are here, being told to walk to the end of the hangars and wait seems, I don't know, loose, I guess."

"I know, I keep waiting to see security police running at us, guns drawn," Vic said. His hand pointed at Jake's head, pistol-style.

Jake winced as the gesture reminded him of the events that followed their disastrous UFO encounter.

"Oops, sorry." Vic lowered his arm and grinned. "I had it rough, too, you know."

"Yeah right. You get gently floated from your fighter. I get yanked down and tossed unceremoniously face first onto the tarmac. You're taken to a nice, plush facility, and fed tea and crumpets. I'm taken to an interrogation room and berated for twelve hours, and I'm the one left feeling guilty," he said through a sardonic grin.

Vic looked dejected. "Sorry."

"Dude, I'm just messing with you." Jake punched him in the arm. "Time to put on your big-girl panties, Lieutenant."

Rubbing his shoulder, Vic smiled self-consciously.

Stopping next to the last hangar, they looked around, unsure of what to do next. When they had received their instruction, Vic had asked, "Wait for what?" The instructor merely shrugged his shoulders. They'd encountered the gesture so many times the two officers called it the Area Fifty-One salute.

"These hangars look like they've been here since the—" Vic stopped as a black Hummer zipped from behind the building.

"Well, I'll be a son of a ..." Jake said through a startled chuckle.

The vehicle slid to a stop in front of them. "Are you ladies just gonna stand there all slack-jawed?" Captain Richard Allison asked.

"I was wondering when your lame ass would show up," Jake said.

"Go to Hell," Richard said through a grin.

Wiping more sweat from his brow, Jake glanced at the sun hovering over the western mountains. "I think we're already there."

Richard gestured to the sweat stains adorning his own flight suit. "I hear you, brother."

"It's good to see you," Vic said as he and Jake climbed into the Hummer. "We've seen nothing but admin types all week."

"Well, it's time for that to change. I'm here to show you the meat and potatoes of the operation." While speaking, he pulled onto the flight line and headed toward the runway complex.

Jake studied the maze of tarmac, taxiways, and concrete runways. "I know more about the layout of this place from what I saw on Google Earth than I learned from all the briefings we suffered through." He pointed ahead. "For instance, from what I saw in their imagery, I know those are some of the longest runways in the world, a few extending well into Groom Lake's dry bed to the north."

As Richard pulled onto a ramp linked to one of the main runways, Victor pointed at a jet-blast shield in front of a low, flat hill. "There's a familiar structure."

"Yep," Jake agreed. "There's been at least one at every Air Force Base I've been to." Positioned behind an area designated as a jet ground-run area, the blast shield worked like giant louvers. The curved overlapping slats diverted a jet's exhaust away from the ground.

"Not like this one," Richard said, turning south toward the structure.

Jake studied the metal panels. Airport planners usually positioned them in front of buildings or roads. However, this shield was cut into the side of rising terrain.

As they approached, the shield began to lift and fold horizontally, revealing a large hangar hidden in the mound.

"That's not a natural hill," Jake said. "It looks like the hangar was built and then covered in earth."

"Bet you didn't see that on Google Earth," Richard said through a smile. As he pulled the Hummer through the opening, the blast shield-clad hangar doors lowered.

Within, Jake discovered it lacked a few of the necessary fixtures to qualify it as a hangar. No hoists, offices, or ancillary equipment adorned its well-lit interior. They were in a huge metal box, big as a hangar, just not equipped as such.

Just as Jake and Vic opened their mouths to comment, a deep clunking noise sprang from the box's metallic walls. A tremor shook the Hummer.

After a few moments, Jake sensed vertical motion. "We're descending?"

Richard nodded. "The upper levels we're passing through are used for projects too sensitive to use the above-ground hangars. The lower we go, the more sensitive the project."

"Guess we're heading to the bottom," Jake said.

"As far as I know, but as far as the crews in the floors above us know, they are the lowest and most secret project here." Pointing to the wall ahead, Richard continued. "Each level has its own blast and soundproof door separating it from the lift. In addition to their normal functions, they prevent prying eyes from seeing or hearing more than they should."

"Need-to-know and all that," Vic said.

"Compartmentalization," Jake said. "Gotta love it. Sometimes I wonder if any one person knows everything that happens here."

Richard nodded. "With all the military branches, plus the CIA, NSA, and who knows how many other 'A's ..." He shrugged, letting the Area Fifty-One salute finish his sentence.

"As you already know, your I.D. badge contains a tiny radio frequency or RF chip that allows access to your authorized facilities. The lift works the same way. Approach and it opens. Enter and it takes you to your assigned level."

As Richard finished, the lift came to a gentle stop.

Another clunk echoed through the box as the door ahead lifted open.

In the topless Hummer, Richard grabbed the upper frame of the windshield and pulled himself out of his seat. Sitting on the driver's seat back, he spread his arms wide over the windshield with an exaggerated flourish. "Gentlemen, I present Earth's most advanced fleet."

CHAPTER 9

Hurtling past damp, rough, black stone, Lord Thrakst stomped down the hallway. Bursting onto the bridge, he glowered at the busy officers as they monitored Commodore Salyth's fleet preparations for the coming light-jump. Growling, Thrakst pointed at the communications officer. "Remind the young Commodore to have his ships disable their drive suppressors," his deep voice thundered, more felt than heard.

"Yes, Lord," replied the officer, forwarding the order. "Commodore Salyth confirms drive-level set to five and drive suppressors off, my Lord."

"Excellent, I wouldn't want him to get there too early. And, if they're too quiet, the Argonians might miss the party."

Through the bridge's view-wall, he watched Commodore Salyth's attack party move into formation for the Light-Jump to Sector Sixty-Four. Like his command ship, the dreadnoughts were a combination of natural and artificial structures. Engineered asteroids cobbled together by massive superstructures, their menacing appearance brought terror to all those unfortunate enough to cross them.

Except for the sculpted bridge section, the asteroids maintained their natural, rough, cratered rocky exterior while the zoxa-formed interior was engineered to provide a Zoxyth atmosphere and climate. The zoxa-forming also fashioned bays for systems, weapons, and personnel. The ship's rocky jutting angles formed jagged silhouettes interspersed with smooth, glistening metal of the connecting superstructures.

Thrakst scanned the nearest ship, Commodore Salyth's newly renamed command ship, the *Forebearer's Revenge*. Glowing green portals interrupted the patchwork of rock and alloy. Shadows moved across ports, as warriors within hastened about, performing their assigned pre-jump tasks.

At the allotted time, Salyth's ships appeared to wink out of existence as his fleet slipped into parallel-space.

Thrakst's talons anxiously scratched at the floor. Drool dripped from his gleaming gnarled teeth as he salivated at the thought of feasting upon his soon to be defeated enemies. "Happy hunting, Commodore."

CHAPTER 10

Studying the object of her concern, Sandy ran a hand across her flat stomach. From its perch on a bed of perfectly folded toilet paper, the pregnancy test stick sat like a religious offering waiting for an Indiana Jones wannabe to scoop it up. After another glance at her washboard abs, she dissolved into a fit of laughter. The comic book mental image of her round, pregnant body rolling down the cavern, chasing the idol-snatcher from her own temple of doom, was more than Sandy's hormonally charged emotions could contain.

Just as quickly as it started, the laughter morphed into silent tears. "Shit!" Sitting on the closed toilet, she continued through her full library of choice curse words. Muffled by the hands cradling her face, her diatribe sounded like Charlie Brown's schoolteacher in the midst of a Tourette syndrome-fueled meltdown.

Her profanity reserves tapped, she sat in silence. Placing tear-soaked hands in her lap, Sandy stared at the ceiling. She took a deep, calming breath. Letting it out in a long exhalation, she looked at her phone on the vanity top. Picking it up, Sandy turned it on. Jake's goofy grin stared back from the phone's screen. She nodded her head toward the pee stick. "What are you going to think about this little tidbit of news, mister?"

After a moment, she pressed the send button. Without ringing, the call went direct to voicemail. "Hi, this is Jake. I'm either flying or doing something really important. So, you know what to do." After the phone beeped, Sandy said, "Hey, babe, it's me. Give me a call when you get in. I miss you, Mister Mysterious."

Ending the call, she stared into his eyes. "What are you guys up to?"

In the two weeks since he'd returned from D.C., Jake had been very tight-lipped about what happened. His whole attitude had changed overnight. He'd left dejected and confused and returned happy and confident.

The return of Victor was incredible news. Outside of the major that had interrogated him, Sandy was the only person Jake told about the loss of his wingman. So, she was the only one wondering what had happened to Vic that night. All Jake would say was that they'd stumbled into a highly classified program. A wall of secrecy had slammed down over the whole situation.

Also, the two disappeared each day. When she tried to call either of their phones, it went straight to voicemail.

Sandy looked at her watch. It was six o'clock in the evening. *Where the hell are you, Jake?*

CHAPTER 11

From the Hummer's front passenger seat in the giant elevator, Jake watched the slow rise of the secret hangar's folding steel blast doors. As the horizontal field of view expanded vertically, two recognizable sets of landing gear came into sight.

"Are those the shielded F-22s?"

Richard nodded.

The door continued to rise, revealing the sleek, stealthy black fighters resting on the gear. The hangar beyond bustled with activity as personnel of various specialties scurried about. While Jake wasn't surprised by the two F-22 Raptors parked diagonally along the left wall, he was shocked to see the UFO he and Vic had encountered parked beyond the fighters, in the hangar's back left corner.

"What the hell?" he said, turning to look at Vic and Richard.

Vic's shocked face mirrored Jake's thoughts.

Grinning, Richard said, "No, it's not the one you two encountered. However, minus weapon systems, it's the same."

Dropping back into the driver's seat, Richard edged the Hummer into the hangar. Easing past the Raptors, he headed straight for the alien ship.

Peeling his eyes from the spaceship to look at the F-22s, Jake noticed a couple of unfamiliar antennas. Four oval depressions with short metal rods protruding from their centers adorned each fighter. Two left and two right, they looked like side-facing oblong aerodynamic satellite dishes.

Jake pointed at the devices. "Do those shield the fighters from the ship's gravity drive?"

Richard nodded. "They project a negative waveform that cancels out the gravity wave."

Jake considered the concept. "Like noise-canceling headphones dampen sound waves?"

"Exactly," he said. "Within the area where the two fields interface, the two sine waves, one hundred eighty degrees out of phase, nullify each other."

Nodding, Jake turned back to the strange ship as Richard pulled to a stop in front of it.

Stepping from the vehicle in reverent silence, they moved to stand side-by-side facing the ship. Its dark metallic curved surface was perfectly smooth. The skin had no angles or edges. It looked as if it had flowed into its present shape.

"It's like looking at a dark mirror made from black mercury," Vic said.

"Yeah," Jake said. "I can see the Hummer's reflection, but barely." Bending at the waist, he squinted at the image. "The headlights look black. It's like the skin is absorbing the light."

"The way it absorbs the brighter light more than the dimmer makes it look like a photo negative," Vic said.

Richard nodded again. "The skin actively absorbs incoming energy, making it virtually undetectable in all but the visible spectrum."

"So, that's why I couldn't see it on my infrared scope," Jake said.

"And, why our threat radar never went off," Victor said. "But it looks cool."

"Yes it does. I've worked with it for six months now, and I'm still fascinated every time I see it," Richard said.

Jake stood, silently taking it in. The ship was much taller than the fighters, and a little wider than they were long. Disc-shaped, it looked tall enough for at least two internal levels. The flattened conical top flowed seamlessly into the ship's vertical side about five feet above a central horizontal bulge. The semicircular protuberance was about three feet wide.

Richard stepped up to a pedestal mounted to the floor between them and the ship. After entering a couple of commands into the computer mounted on its top, he returned to their side.

Jake felt, more than heard, a deep hum emanate from the ship as a horizontal multicolored pulsing ring of energy emerged from and began to rotate above the ship's equatorial bulge.

"That's the lights we saw," Vic said in an awed tone.

"The ship generates a rotating energy field the Argonians manipulate to maneuver the ship. The only energy we've been able to detect with our sensors is in the visible light spectrum: in other words, just what we're looking at."

"Visible light only, no other radiation?" Jake asked.

"Well, none we can detect."

"Are you sure we're safe this close to it?" Victor asked with a nervous step back.

"Yes, the Argonians promise it's completely safe."

Jake nodded, entranced by the ethereal lights floating only two feet overhead. "How does it work?"

"Basically, that central bulge contains a spinning magnetic ring with an oscillating quantum field. The column Victor saw in the ship's center is a powerful superconducting coil. The strength of the coil's field, coupled with the ring's incredibly high RPM, creates a powerful and tunable anti-gravity force."

"How does a ring spinning in one plane create a bubble that surrounds a three-dimensional ship?" Jake asked.

"Varying the quantum oscillation transmutes the ring's polarity, changing the angle it cuts through the coil's horizontal field. RPM variations modulate its vertical component."

"Okay ... that was all Greek to me," Victor said.

Jake tried to visualize how a ring rotating on a horizontal plane could have an effect in the vertical plane. In a flash of insight he said, "So, oscillating the quantum field adds a vertical component to the horizontally spinning ring's field."

Nodding, Richard added, "It creates a second, virtual ring that is omni-axial and omni-rotational."

"Huh?" Victor asked with a bewildered look.

Jake looked at him and turned back to Richard with mock exasperation. "Lieutenants!"

"Can't take 'em anywhere."

"Hey, I was a psych major, not physics like you two."

"Just kidding, buddy," Jake said. "To put it in layman's terms, if you had a pair of goggles that could see the force Richard is describing, you would see a cocoon of rings spinning around this ship."

"They'd be spinning and tumbling in every direction," Richard added.

Nodding, starting to catch on, he asked, "Where does the light come from?"

"I was going to ask that too, but the forces you're describing sound familiar. I read an article about a theory that works something like this," Jake said, pointing at the ring of light. "If I'm right, those are called gravitophotons."

"I thought you might pick up on that," Richard said, shaking his head with an impressed grin.

"Gravit-a-what-ons?"

"Gravitophotons," Jake said. "The article I read was about some new work a group of theoretical physicists are doing with an old theory."

"Old?"

"Yep, as in nineteen fifties and sixties. It's called Heim Quantum Theory."

"You mean somebody on Earth figured this stuff out fifty years ago?" Vic asked. "Why haven't I heard about it?"

"The theory was created by an obscure, self-taught German physicist named Burkhard Heim. This guy was a true genius. In an effort to get around the limitations of chemical rockets, he came up with a modified quantum theory. His equations could predict both the position and energy state of a quantum particle, a feat no one can duplicate, even today."

"It's something quantum physics tells us can't be done," Richard added.

"He claimed it successfully bridged the gap between quantum physics and Einstein's general relativity."

"Okay, so again, why doesn't the whole world know this guy's name?"

"Most physicists of the day dismissed him. His work, all in German, was very arcane. However, some of the Germans working on America's rocket program knew of him and greatly respected his work. It is rumored that Wernher von Braun even approached him in the early nineteen sixties asking if they should shelve their work on chemical rockets."

"Wait, how does a unifying theory nullify the need for chemical rockets?"

"His theory postulated that if you spin a large, extremely powerful magnet through a hugely powerful electric field you will generate gravity waves." Turning to Richard with a meaningful look he added, "He also postulated those waves would manifest a new, previously unknown particle: Gravitophotons."

Pointing both hands toward the ring of lights, Richard said, "Ta-da."

"If the ship is 'cocooned' in these rings, why don't we see lights all over the ship?"

Jake started to open his mouth. Reconsidering, he turned to Richard. "That's a good question."

"They're only generated where the virtual rings cross the physical ring."

Jake nodded. "The oscillating quantum field causes the color variances while its spin imparts the rotational aspect."

"Exactly," Richard said, obviously excited by the subject. "The antigravity field has another beneficial effect."

"What's that?"

"It decouples ninety-nine point nine percent the mass of everything within the field's influence from the space surrounding it, enabling the instantaneous course changes you saw, without crushing its occupants."

Jake shook his head. "How could it do that?"

"It decouples the ship from the Higgs Field."

"The God Particle?" Victor asked.

The final piece fell into place for Jake. "So, the anti-gravity wave creates a quantum bubble that shields everything in it from the Higgs Field."

"Almost all of it. They had to leave that tiny fraction of a percent. Otherwise, it would turn photonic and move at the speed of light until the universe ended. Anyway, because it disconnects the vast majority of your mass from the outside world, it's the perfect inertial dampener."

Victor shook his head. "Huh? Photonic?"

Jake turned to him. "The photonic thing ties to Einstein's theory of relativity. Basically, it says that anything with zero-mass, like a photon, will always travel at the speed of light." He gestured toward the vessel. "To the outside world, everything in the bubble, including the ship itself, has no apparent mass. You could accelerate it from zero to a hundred miles an hour in an instant." Jake flicked his finger. "As easily as thumping a party balloon, but inside you wouldn't even slosh your coffee."

Vic nodded, accepting Jake's description with mute amazement.

Another epiphany hit Jake. "So, they must generate a separate artificial gravity field so they can stand on the floor. Otherwise, the interior would be a bubble of weightlessness."

"Yep."

Tearing his eyes away from the lights, Jake studied the ship's bowl-shaped bottom. It flowed up into the horizontal central bulge about eight feet above the ground. In three places, its skin stretched down to support the ship. He pointed at the legs. "I don't remember seeing these on the one we encountered."

"They're retractable," Richard responded.

"That metal looks permanently stretched to me."

"Hang on," Richard said, stepping back to the computer terminal in front of the ship. After he had punched a few keys, the deep hum emanating from the ship changed frequency.

"What's that hum—" Vic started to ask but stopped as the ship began levitating a couple of feet above the floor.

Aside from the subsonic drone, the ship sat in total silence.

"That is awesome!" Vic said.

"It's weird to see something rise off the ground so quietly," Jake said.

In a half-second, the protrusions silently retracted, leaving smooth skin as the ship continued to hover.

"Okay, okay, quit showing off," Jake said to Richard after a few moments. "I'm dying to see the inside of this thing."

"All right," Richard said, feigning dejection.

Jake held up both hands and laughed. "I'm impressed."

"Me too," Vic added.

Richard smiled. "You're too easy." He typed more commands into the interface. "And for my next trick ..." The legs noiselessly re-extended, and the humming ceased as the ship gently touched down. Overhead, the ethereal gravitophoton-generated lights evaporated.

Richard finished up at the keyboard and rejoined them. "Close your mouths, boys."

"Well, I was just thinking that was probably the smoothest landing I've ever seen you make. As I recall, the mechanics back in Afghanistan were always amazed your aircraft could still taxi after one of your typical landings."

"Screw you," Richard said through a grin.

Pointing at the ship, Jake asked, "What happened to the one that crashed in Roswell?"

"As far as I know, it was returned to them. The Argonians gave us this ship in the eighties as part of the integration program. We're allowed to learn from it and reverse-engineer what we can. However, we're not allowed to take it apart."

"Can we get to the mechanism that generates the ring of lights without taking it apart?" Jake asked.

"Nope."

"In other words, no access to the drive technology, at least not yet," Vic said.

"Exactly, they want to keep us in our little corner of the galaxy, for now," Richard said, and then clapped his hands. "So, are you two ready for more?"

"I thought you'd never ask," Jake said.

"Lieutenant Croft, do you remember where the exit was?"

"When they dropped me off, I think the door was right about … here," Vic said, stepping between two of the legs. As he did, an opening suddenly appeared in front of him.

Jake heard a whisper of static like a charged sock pulled from a clinging towel.

"See what I was talking about?" Vic said.

"Yep," Jake said. He stepped up for a closer inspection. From overhead, the opening stretched from a foot below the bulge and continued in front of them, ending where the flat bottom of the ship's belly formed a threshold.

They stepped into the airlock, and the door resealed with the same static sound. A moment later, just as Vic had described, an opening appeared in the opposite wall.

"This way, ladies," Richard said, stepping through.

Jake followed. Stepping into the large room beyond, he paused. "What the hell?"

The room was too wide. They had entered at ground level where the circumference of the belly section was significantly smaller than the main body. "This room looks like it's as wide as the whole ship."

Vic nodded. "You're right, I didn't notice that the other night."

"The airlock doubles as an elevator," Richard said.

"Yeah, but that means it moved eight feet in less than a second. I didn't feel anything," Jake said.

Richard smiled. "It's amazing what a gravity drive can do for you."

"Cool," Vic said, nodding his head.

Walking deeper into the ship, Richard continued. "This is an Arg scout and general utility ship. Like the one you saw the other night, it's identical to the one that crashed near Roswell. They have several configurations, but this is the most common."

Jake studied the interior. "I see what you meant about the walls, Vic." They glowed softly. The ceiling, about ten feet above the floor, left space for another room above, although, Jake didn't see a way to get to it. Aside from the central, meter-wide column running from floor to ceiling, he saw no other items or structures in the cabin.

"Where's the control panel I saw," Vic asked.

"Like the chair that supported you when the edification encoder kicked in—"

"*Edification* encoder?" Vic interrupted. "Is that *really* what they call it?"

"Loosely translated, yes," Richard said with an understanding nod. Then he said the Argonian word.

Utilizing the Argonian language knowledge imparted by the encoder's *edification,* Jake thought it was the best translation, although it seemed a bit condescending.

"You get the feeling they're a little full of themselves," Jake said.

"Guess that's a hazard of ruling the galaxy," Richard replied with a shrug.

That brought up a question Jake had been meaning to ask. "I know they started the Galactic government, but I thought General Tannehill said it's free and inclusive, treating all equally."

"It is, but they are, by far the most widespread and populous species. They hold more than half of the government seats."

"Guess that'll be good for us too, in the long run," Vic said.

"Especially we military types," Richard added.

"Why's that?" Jake asked.

"Like General Tannehill said, they do share power, but the Argonians kept the military to themselves. Apparently, mixing crews with biologies requiring radically different gravitational and atmospheric environments is a bit more complicated than portrayed in the Star Wars universe."

"I imagine they don't fully trust other species with their advanced tech and weapons systems," Vic said.

Jake nodded. "That must rub some species wrong."

"I'm sure you're right, and it's probably another manifestation of that conceit," Richard said.

Vic grimaced and ran fingers through his short, red hair. "Sounds like we have more briefings to attend. You know so much about them. Jake and I haven't even scratched the surface."

"What do you think we're doing here?"

Jake's eyebrows rose. "What do you mean?"

"You've finished your base orientation." He pointed at the ship's floor. "Tonight you begin your induction into the Galactic Integration Program."

Jake and Vic exchanged excited looks.

Richard laughed. "You look like a couple of schoolgirls." After a moment, he gestured ahead with his right hand. "Mind if I continue the tour?"

"Please do," Jake said with a huge grin.

Richard started walking across the wide room. "Back to your question about the control panel. When needed, equipment grows from the floor. If you are actively maneuvering the vessel, the control panel stays in place. Once you're cruising, the interior changes its configuration." He gestured toward an area that Jake took to be the back half of the vessel. "It converts this into a living area and the Argonian version of a kitchen."

Turning forward, Richard stepped to an area halfway between the wall and the center column. Moving to join him, Jake froze mid-step, startled by sudden movement in his lower peripheral vision. Like a reversed and radically accelerated time-lapse video of a melting ice sculpture, a structure grew from the floor.

"Holy shit," Jake whispered as it finished forming. He stepped closer. Matching Vic's description, a curving glass control panel topped it. Everything seemed straightforward. Oddly recognizable symbols denoted controls and systems status. He smiled in amazement. "I can read the Argonian writing." Turning his attention to its metallic sides, he asked, "How does it *grow* from the floor?"

"The Argonians are masters of nanotechnology. You're literally standing on an ocean of molecule-sized robots."

Jake and Vic cast nervous glances at the floor, shifting from foot to foot, looking under their feet.

"Don't worry, they play nice," Richard said. Then with a sardonic grin he chuckled ominously. "Y'all are going to love the EVA suits."

"EVA suits?" Vic asked nervously.

Apparently tiring of Vic's constant trepidation, Richard gave Jake an exasperated look. He turned to face Vic. "We'll come back to that later, Lieutenant." Turning toward the console, he continued. "Anyway, there are several types of nanobots. They're able to do everything from forming structures to making complex electrical circuits. Each nanobot has as much computing power as a PC. The billions of them networked together form the ship's artificial intelligence or AI."

"So, this AI can recognize your intentions and provide what you need?" Jake said.

"For the most part. It also responds to Argonian voice commands. We think the Argonians have another way of communicating with it, but haven't been able to figure that one out yet."

Richard ran his hand across the control panel and the ship activated. A large section of wall ahead seemed to vanish.

Apparently detecting no change, the workers walking past the thirty-foot-wide window didn't respond. Jake guessed the effect was like a one-way mirror. If the wall were indeed clear, the emission of the ship's internal light and energy would negate the efficacy of the ship's energy-absorbing skin.

Jake hadn't heard or felt anything, but through the view outside he could see they had lifted a meter or two. He was about to mention it when the ship started moving toward the blast doors.

Richard touched another section of the panel. "Groom Lake Tower, this is Turtle One, over."

Jake chuckled. "You call it the *Turtle?*"

Richard nodded.

"That's fitting."

Richard looked over his shoulder. "Kinda says it all, doesn't it?"

A voice sprang from the panel's surface. "Turtle One, this is Groom Lake Tower. You are cleared as filed, please report in position and ready for departure."

"Groom Lake Tower, Turtle One, Wilco," Richard said.

Jake's heart raced in anticipation. "Are we doing what I think?"

Vic made a show of displaying a fake yawn. "Been there, done that." Although, excited eyes betrayed his true feelings.

Richard turned, offering Jake the controls. "Here you go, buddy. This'll be the easiest nickel flight you've ever had."

Jake, adrenaline pumping, approached the control panel. "Considering this is the first spaceship I've ever flown, you better hope it's an easy transition."

Pointing to a graspable, hand-shaped depression embedded in the panel, Richard stepped aside. "Just place your hand in there. It responds to forces in all three axis. Slight upward causes a slow rise. Left pressure moves us left, and so on. Twist it for yaw and roll it for ... well, you get the idea."

Jake nodded his understanding.

"Remember to relax. This ship's Stability Augmentation System perfectly adjusts for all external disturbances like wind or turbulence. It's even better than our fighter's SAS. Basically, it's a point-and-go system. Easier to maneuver than a car, it can be operated by anyone, much less a steely-eyed combat fighter pilot such as yourself." He bowed with mock reverence.

Hiking a thumb at Richard, Jake looked at Vic. "I told you he was an excellent judge of pilot skills."

Ignoring Jake, Victor turned a concerned face to Richard. "Without training, what stops someone from screwing up so bad they can't recover?"

"The ship's AI is smarter than any of our supercomputers. It won't allow the ship to collide with anything. It constantly surveys its surroundings, calculating velocities and trajectories for itself and near ships. Using all the data, the computer buffers or blocks inputs that would put the ship in danger."

Studying the control panel, Jake nodded. "So, it takes over the controls if it thinks you're screwing up."

"Yep, but it can do a lot more than that. With a verbal command, this ship can fly itself out of this hangar, perform the departure, and complete the flight plan. It monitors our conversation and understands our intentions just as well as a normal human would."

"Holy shit," Vic whispered. He looked around. "Is it self-aware?"

Jake wondered the same thing. "How do they know it won't wake up on the wrong side of the hangar one morning, and decide it wants to go *Terminator*?"

"I guess the Argonians saw the movies too," Richard said after laughing at Jake's reference. "Because they programmed special algorithms that prevent it from becoming self-aware. The last thing they want is a computer this powerful and linked to the ship's controls to start thinking independently."

As Richard finished, Jake surreptitiously tried to run the ship into the hangar wall, keeping the speed down in case Richard had overstated the ship's abilities. Anticipating an impact or a maneuver to avoid it, Jake gripped the control panel. Just when he thought the ship was going to hit the hangar wall, it came to an instant stop.

Richard shook his head. "You just had to test it, didn't you?"

Lieutenant Croft looked up surprised. "Wow, I didn't feel it stop."

"Me neither. Guess I should've expected that," Jake said, laughing and relaxing the death grip he had on the panel.

"Remember, the ship's gravity drive moves all molecules—"

"Within the drive's sphere of influence," Jake and Vic finished in unison.

"Okay, okay, I just wanted to make sure y'all were paying attention."

"Knowing it on an intellectual level is one thing, but experiencing the disconnect between sight and seat-of-the-pants is amazing," Jake said.

"I know. Pretty cool, huh?" Richard said, nodding. "The effect is a perfect inertial damper." He raised his hands overhead like he was on a roller coaster. "Standing right here, you can take Gs that normally would kill you."

"Look, Ma. No hands," Vic said.

Jake turned the ship away from the hangar wall and continued toward the lift. As they approached, the doors opened, revealing the large elevator already in position.

He turned to Richard with a questioning look.

"Take her in," Richard said.

"When is it going to be my turn?" Victor asked with mock impatience.

"Age before ... well, as a soulless ginger you ain't all that easy on the eyes, so I guess we'll just say, rank has its privileges," Jake said as he guided the ship into the lift.

Vic flipped him off.

Once they passed into the elevator, a holographic display of the ship and surrounding lift formed over the control panel. They watched the miniature version of the blast door slide closed behind them.

"Cool," Vic said, forgetting Jake's jibe.

Jake nodded and pointed into the image. "Is this where you saw the holographic brain?"

"Yep."

"I was wondering how we'd see what was behind us," Jake said. He looked at the opaque rear wall. "It's not like we have a rear-view mirror."

As they ascended the shaft, the display updated their vertical position in real time: *-150, -140, -130.* However, he still felt no movement.

Looking out, Vic walked to the clear wall. "What's the plan? Are we just taking it up for a quick trip around the traffic pattern?"

"Patience," Richard said. "You'll see soon enough."

Suddenly, the lift darkened. Inside the *Turtle,* the hologram and the soft glow of the ship's interior walls provided the only illumination. Jake looked down. The altitude display read *000.*

Outside, the exterior door started to lift. Filling the entire width of the giant door's opening, a blue-black sliver of night grew vertically from the floor.

Like diamonds scattered across a black velvet-lined drawer sliding from a black cabinet, the rising door revealed a background of scintillating stars. Ending in sharp contrast against the black silhouette of the surrounding mountains, the stars seemed to hover within easy reach.

Staring at the night sky, Jake ran his free hand along the side of the control panel. *Which one of those did you come from, girl?* He turned to Richard. "Can she travel faster than light?"

"The gravity drive, as they call it, has been disabled. Like I said, they want to keep us in our corner of the galaxy, at least until we complete our integration."

"How fast is it with the Light-Drive disabled?" Vic asked.

Richard chuckled, shaking his head. "Where's the fun for me if I spill all the beans upfront? All in good time, Lieutenant."

Jake moved the ship into the open and noticed a hint of flashing colors reflecting off the tarmac.

Richard nodded toward the light. "There's a stealth mode that damps down the drive's gravitophoton emissions." Reaching around Jake, he toggled the command. Outside the multicolored reflections faded. Richard pointed toward the mountains to the east. "We don't want the UFO groupies over at the Little A'Le'Inn to spot us."

Jake raised an eyebrow. "Why not suppress the light all the time?"

"It reduces the *Turtle's* maneuverability, but usually you don't need both stealth and maneuverability at the same time."

Jake nodded. "Makes sense. If you need maneuverability, it's probably because someone already knows you're there, someone you're trying to keep up with, or get away from."

"Exactly." Richard activated the comm panel. "Groom Tower, Turtle One is in position and ready for departure."

"Roger, Turtle One, you are cleared for takeoff. Contact Space Control passing flight level niner-niner-niner."

"Roger, Groom Tower, Turtle One cleared for departure. Thanks, guys."

Pulse racing, Jake stared at Richard. "*Passing* flight level niner-niner-niner?"

"You betcha!"

"That's ninety-nine thousand, nine hundred feet."

"Yep, everything above a hundred thousand feet is Space Control's domain."

Huge grins spread across Jake and Vic's faces.

Jake turned to Victor with a hand held up for a high-five. "Holy shit, we're going into space!"

"Hell yeah!" Vic shouted, smacking his hand.

With a crooked grin, Richard shook his head. "Amateurs."

Jake scoffed. "Yeah right, asshole." Elbowing Victor while pointing to Richard, he said, "Sandy and I went to flight school with this guy. I'll bet a dollar to a doughnut that the first time he went up, his silly ass was standing right there, giggling like a schoolgirl."

"I don't know what you're talking about," Richard said, feigning innocence. Bringing them back on subject, he changed to a serious tone. "Back to the mission, boys. We're cleared for takeoff."

Their smiles evaporated and they both nodded.

"Jake, I want you to take us off, vertically for the first five seconds —like an elevator—then pull the nose straight up."

Looking back at the rear wall, twenty-five feet behind them, Jake imagined falling backward when he turned the nose up.

Seeing this, Richard said, "Let me have the controls for a moment."

Jake stepped right. "You have the controls, Captain."

With Vic on the left, Richard moved to stand between them. Placing his hand into the controller, he said, "Roger, I have the controls."

Without warning, he flipped the ship upside down.

"Shit," Jake screamed. He and Vic clutched at the edges of the control panel. He hadn't felt any movement, but the visual disorientation of seeing the horizon flip so quickly was overwhelming.

Richard started laughing. "Don't worry, I had the same reaction."

With a discomfited chuckle, Jake eased his death grip on the control panel. Looking up at the runway, ten feet overhead, he said,

"Standing outside looking in, we'd look like bats hanging in here by our feet."

Looking irritated, Vic said, "Any chance we can get a heads-up next time?"

"Nope," Richard said, stepping back, gesturing to Jake. "You can have the controls, Captain."

Stepping back into position, he said, "I have the controls." Gripping the control pad, he slowly turned the ship upright.

"Chicken," Richard chided.

Jake turned, facing him eye-to-eye. Without looking away, he snapped his hand to the right. The ship executed a perfect snap roll through three hundred sixty degrees, stopping instantly once level. To his delight, a moment of disoriented concern flashed across Richard's face.

"Gotcha," Jake said.

"Damn it!" Vic yelled. "Cut that crap out."

Regaining his composure, Richard continued. "Now that we've gotten that bit of training out of the way, are you ready for takeoff?"

Jake and Vic looked at each other. A mixture of anxiety, excitement, and apprehension was evident in Vic's face. Jake felt some of the same emotions crossing his.

"Let's do it," he said, facing forward.

"Make it so number one," Richard said, in a poor imitation of a British accent.

Jake gripped the control pad and pulled up. The world outside blurred.

CHAPTER 12

From the captain chair of his command ship, *Helm Warden,* Admiral Ashtara Tekamah surveyed his fleet through the vessel's broad view-wall. Utilizing the display's pan and zoom features, he studied each silhouette. Light-absorbing skin rendered the armada's huge battlecruisers and carriers as black voids drifting across the crisp star-field. In the expansive bridge, a floating holographic version of the fleet surrounded his elevated perch. The green holograms lent the dark silhouettes a third dimension. The ancient fleet was the culmination of technologies accumulated over the uncountable millennia since Argonians first ventured into the great vacuum.

The admiral shifted his gaze to the brilliant bulge of the galactic core. Without the obscuring dust, its billions of stars were clearly visible from the fleet's current inclination and proximity. On nearby habitable planets, the core was often visible during the day. Seeing the center third of the spiral armed galaxy brought out Tekamah's inner anthropologist. Unlike the earthbound Argonians, inhabitants of planets in this sector would never refer to the bright blue stripe dominating their sky with a moniker as inane as Milky Way.

The backstory to the name of his command ship, *Helm Warden,* still fascinated Tekamah, even though he'd been alive long enough to have witnessed a not insignificant percentage of its multimillennial history. It was more mission statement than title. Since ancient times, Argonians had called the galaxy the Helm, an archaic mariner term for wheel. Warden, meaning defender, gave the name its full meaning: Galactic Defender.

Staring into the brilliant core with a sardonic grin, Tekamah cocked an eyebrow. *And, the Helm truly needs defending.*

He pushed the negative thought away. If only for a moment, he wanted to revel in rumination.

Long ago, medical advancements coupled with a full understanding of DNA banished death by disease and old age. The ever-expanding population birthed by their virtual immortality had fueled the Argonians' drive to explore and populate the galaxy. It was during those early efforts that Argonians must have first populated Earth.

Esoteric and tradition-based, the Argonian culture developed and matured over the subsequent millennia. While the earthbound branch had somehow lost their technological roots, generation after generation of Argonians developed technologies and machines, each better and more advanced than its predecessor, each bringing societal and economic changes. Eventually, their cultural and technological achievements plateaued. Further advances had required the Argonians to grow beyond their mortal bodies.

To take advantage of the expanded mentality afforded by the virtual world and the rich textures and unpredictability of the real world, as well as to buffer themselves against unplanned terminations arising from accidents or warfare, most Argonians experienced a parallel existence. Simultaneously, they lived within the digital realm and the organic.

In order to maintain continuity of thought and self with their computer-based version on Argonia, each vessel or community maintained a real-time data link utilizing a zero-width, one-dimensional communications wormhole. Exceeding the speed of synaptic-based thought, the transgalactic data transfer rates seamlessly connected the organic brain to the computer-based just as the corpus callosum connected the two hemispheres of the brain, rendering the parallel existence as one. Unless you sought the boundaries, you couldn't sense where one ended and the other began.

Originally, Argonians had uploaded themselves as copies, maintaining their sense of self within the organic body. Over the intervening centuries and millennia, the thoughts, memories, and life experiences stemming from their computer-based reality far surpassed their corporeal existence. Now most Argonians considered the organic half of their existence as an extension of their essence, not the home of it.

Leaning back in his chair on the *Helm Warden's* bridge, Ashtara took a moment to enjoy his surroundings. Throughout the ship, naturally antiqued metal decorated every surface. Over the millennia, the metallic alloy had taken on a dark bronze tint. While not as big as the ship's largest halls, the bridge had a respectable ten-meter ceiling. Tall, pointed arches marked the three corridors entering the bridge. Shifting his gaze to the ceiling, he surveyed the cube-shaped room's upper four corners. Large, metallic sculptures of predatory birds pointed toward the bridge's center. The artist rendered each frozen in full dive, wings pinned back, talons outstretched, and carnivorous beaks thrust into the onrushing wind.

Across a multitude of species and cultures, galactic history revealed a persistent theme. Once a society reached a plateau of wealth and technology, it switched to developing cultural richness, entering the Age of Legacy. In that epoch, projects of every type and scope aspired to eclipse mere function, endeavoring to maximize cultural wealth.

The Galactic Defense Force's space fleet was a pure manifestation of this legacy, every ship a massive floating cathedral to prosperity, art, technology, and life. Each as ornately decorated as they were functional, the vessels were replete with cavernous halls. Their ceilings towered fifty meters overhead. Elaborate passageways decorated with towering, twenty-five-meter bronze arches connected the ship's various sections. Interspersed throughout, elegant and ancient botanical gardens gave the ships a regal air.

Cultural studies were Admiral Tekamah's passion. The similarities between races separated by millennia and light years fascinated him. His studies of the closely guarded secret of the earthbound Argonians—the lost colony—revealed amazing parallels between their development and Argonia's ancient history.

Earth's society, evolving in complete isolation, employed many of the same traditions and governmental organizations as the Argonians. Even the military organizations had separately evolved a synchronicity of traditions and command structures.

Earth's history was replete with Age of Legacy examples: the early Egyptians' pyramids, the Roman Empire's Colosseum, followed by the rise of the Roman Catholic Church and its Vatican.

Earth was now in the Disposable Age: a time when a society repeatedly finds yesterday's *new* technologies and materials rendered obsolete by the relentless march of discovery. Out of necessity and the expectation that whatever they build today will be worthless tomorrow, little, beyond minimal artistic appeal and bare essential engineering, is invested in projects.

Having exhausted all the time the current situation afforded for an old man's reminiscing, Admiral Tekamah shook off the thoughts and stood. He ran fingers through his wavy, permanently salt-and-pepper hair. With an apparent age in his mid-forties, the admiral had a dignified air. While Argonian medical technology allowed him to maintain any apparent age, he felt this one best represented his inner self.

Turning his gaze from the view-wall, he studied the bridge. The command level's elevated floor was a transparent, permanently stable force field that placed the observer in the center of a room-filling, three-dimensional holographic display.

Computer-generated representations of the vessels and planetary bodies in the *Helm Warden's* vicinity filled the bridge. In every direction the admiral looked, holograms of the fleet's ships flew in formation with the *Helm Warden*. The size of each vessel was exaggerated. The fleet's formation spanned several light seconds of space. If rendered at true scale, the massive ships would be little more than tiny specs.

Slowly passing through one of the birds of prey in the bridge's upper corner, a hologram of the planet they were departing was drifting out of view, its curving surface receding into the ceiling.

The permanent force field floor was augmented with on-demand features. For instance, if you want to sit you simply lean back, and the field adjusted to support you. To leave the elevated pedestal, walk to the edge marked by a softly glowing yellow line and step over. A gravity lift then gently lowered you to the bridge's bottom level.

Finishing his survey, the admiral watched as one of his senior Corps commanders rose to the pedestal bridge.

Standing at attention after landing on the clear floor, the commander saluted. "Admiral Tekamah, I've received an unusual report regarding the Zoxyth."

"Forward it to my EON," ordered the admiral as he dropped into his force field-generated captain's chair.

After a brief pause, the commander said, "You have the file now, sir."

The admiral accessed his EON. After a quick scan, he cocked an eyebrow. "This doesn't make sense."

"My thoughts too, sir."

"They never send dreadnoughts away from the action ... and such a large force."

"Yes, sir. Dividing their military like this is pure folly. This may be our opportunity to bring the war to a close."

Admiral Tekamah went through the various possible scenarios. He couldn't understand why they would send a force of that size into that sector. Far removed from the main shipping routes, the area in that direction offered nothing of strategic importance.

Utilizing his EON he accessed the bridge's hologram. The rendered fleet and planetary body dissolved into a swirling storm of disassociated pixels. After a moment, the vortex of light coalesced into an animation of the Helm galaxy, or the Milky Way as the earthbound Argonians would call it.

"Show the last known position of all Zoxyth military ships."

A tight grouping of red icons popped into existence about a third of the way out from the galactic core. A second grouping appeared less than halfway out from the center. In the relatively empty space between the spiraled bands, the second grouping of ships appeared to be crossing to the adjacent galactic arm.

Subvocalizing through his EON interface, he commanded the display to draw a line from the enemy's main fleet to the reported position of the other ships. Connecting the two groups, a red line crossed an appreciable portion of the galaxy's radius. "Extend the line to the galactic perimeter."

As the red line lengthened, it penetrated the adjacent spiraled arm about midspan.

Tekamah studied the area with growing concern and mounting unease.

"Superimpose sector numbers."

His heart skipped a beat when he saw the line passing through the Sixty series. "No," he whispered. "They can't know." Hell, even his commanders didn't know of their existence. Subvocalizing, he ordered the display to zoom in on sector Sixty-Four. To his horror, the red line cut through the center of a solar system with a very familiar G-type main-sequence star.

"Oh Lords!" exclaimed the admiral, standing as a sinking feeling struck his gut. "Deploy Third Carrier Group and three attack squadrons to sector Sixty-Four immediately!"

"I don't understand, sir. The Zoxyth only attack Argonian systems: there are none in that sector."

Ignoring the commander, he said, "Tell Admiral Thoyd Feyhdyak he'll have his deployment orders once they're underway. Have all other commanders report to the briefing arena in one hour. If they can't be there, their holograms had better be."

"Yes, sir," the commander said.

Wondering how they knew, hoping he was wrong, but knowing he wasn't, Admiral Tekamah monitored the orders cycling through his EON.

Gods, please let Thoyd get there in time.

CHAPTER 13

The outside world blurred the instant Jake applied upward pressure on the flight controller. As if it anticipated his intentions, the ship rocketed up like a homesick heavenly elevator almost before he commanded it. The artificial intelligence's instantaneous interpretation of his rapid input made the AI seem prescient.

The ship lifted so quickly Jake's knees buckled under the visually perceived G-forces. He saw Vic respond the same. While Jake had felt no acceleration, the visual input through the view-wall convinced his mind, tripping the instinctive response.

The scene outside was astounding. Under shocking acceleration, the airfield and then the surrounding mountains rapidly shrank below their line of sight.

Looking up at the brightening stars, Jake applied slight back pressure to the controls. The ship responded by gently pitching up. Continuing to apply accelerative pressure on the flight controller, he ushered the ship upward, nose first.

Like a swimmer coming up from the depths, the ship broke free of the planet's ocean of air. Shining in more colors than he imagined possible, stars morphed from soft, twinkling lights to crisp points.

Jake had never seen pictures, videos, or even cinematic special effects that approached the level of beauty he was witnessing.

"Now neutralize all pressure," Richard said, pointing at the controller.

Jake slowly relaxed his hand. From this altitude, unknown miles above the planet's surface, with only stars filling the view-wall, nothing seemed to change. Applying a slight forward pressure on the controller, the stars slid up as the ship pitched forward.

His heart soared as an incredible sunset rose into view. With the beautiful panorama filling the view-wall, he released the controller, freezing the scene.

Watching the day's second sunset from an apparent altitude of a hundred miles above North America's West Coast, the three officers stared in silent reverence. Peeking over the distant horizon, the sun's beautiful rays streaked across the Pacific Ocean. The golden river of light flowed around towering cumulus clouds. Like fingers in the stream, their long shadows stretched into the east's encroaching darkness.

I can't believe I'm here. Wish you could have seen this, Dad, he thought, sending a prayer to his deceased father. It was he who had nurtured Jake's love of aviation. Ron Giard had taken his son to countless air shows and space shuttle launches. Jake could still see the awe in his father's eyes at the first launch they had attended. Jake had found it infectious and ultimately irresistible.

As the sun dipped below the horizon, the atmosphere flashed with golden brilliance, its thin, life-supporting blanket glowing brighter than the underlying surface.

A few poignant moments later, they turned away from the panorama. Stifling sniffs, they coughed, looking anywhere but at each other.

"Let's not hang at this altitude too long," Richard said, breaking the uncomfortable silence. "Even the light-absorbing skin can't soak up this much sunlight. We might be visible." Richard pointed at something beyond the view-wall's right side. "Why don't you take us over there?"

Following Richard's gaze, Jake grabbed the controller. As he rotated the *Turtle* eastward, a half-lit orb slid into view at the far right end of the ship-spanning panoramic display.

Victor drew a sharp breath.

A huge smile spread across Jake's face. "The Moon?"

Visible along the left side of the view-wall, Earth's night-darkened, curved horizon spanned from floor to ceiling. Much smaller, only occupying a small portion of the vertical field, the first quarter or half-moon hung near the right side of the panorama.

Without answering, Richard stepped next to Jake. He toggled a command into the panel's interface and a glowing, three-dimensional model of their ship coalesced at eye level.

Sticking his thumb and forefinger into the holographic Turtle and spreading them apart, Richard magnified the display. Repeating the movement, spreading his fingers apart as you would on a smartphone, caused the rendered ship to grow in size and detail.

Vic looked duly impressed. "They didn't use it like that last time."

"I'm just demonstrating its capabilities," Richard said as the ship grew to fill the space available.

Not interested in the large virtual model of the *Turtle*, Jake walked to the view-wall. The illuminated right side of the Moon was blindingly bright. Without the dulling effect of the atmosphere, craters and mountains stood in stark relief.

Dragging his eyes from the incredible scene, Jake turned back to his wingmen. He looked through the translucent, computer-rendered ship at Richard and Vic's hologram-illuminated green faces. "The Moon?"

Still ignoring him, Richard slid his open hand into the hologram. This time he pinched his fingers together. As it would on a smartphone, the gesture reversed the magnification process. The faster he made the movement, the farther the display zoomed out. A couple of gestures later, the *Turtle* shrank to a tiny point of light as Earth's curved surface slid into the bottom of the scene.

A particulate haze floated over the planet's arcing surface.

Following curved paths, pixels of light seemed to drift in every direction. Jake pointed. "Satellites?"

Richard nodded.

"There's so many of them," Vic said. Bending over, he lowered his face into the display. Tiny green dots appeared to pass in and out of his head. With childlike, wide-eyed amazement, Victor watched them zip about like a swarm of flies.

Impatient and apparently irritated, Richard elbowed the young lieutenant out of the display. Grinning, he winked at Jake.

"The Moon?" Jake persisted.

Richard's grin morphed into a frown. Spreading his arms apart like he was trying to grab a large beach ball, he reached into the hologram. "Watch this." He brought his hands together. The image quickly zoomed out, Earth shrinking while the comparatively small Moon slid into view.

"And, now for my next trick ..." Richard said. He walked to the miniature Moon. With his face mere inches from the glowing sphere, Richard raised his right hand. After a dramatic pause, he extended his index finger and poked the cratered surface.

Ripples and a loud pop emanated from the point of Richard's touch. Moving like pond water disturbed by a tossed pebble, the surface undulated as concentric rings radiated across the virtual Moon.

After toggling another command into the control panel, Richard leaned back. A chair rose from the floor, smoothly capturing his falling physique. Reclining, he laced fingers behind his head. "That's it."

"What's it?" Vic asked.

"We're on our way," Richard said, pulling a hand from behind his head and pointing through the view-wall.

Jake turned to see Earth's horizon sliding out of sight as the Moon moved to the center of the star-filled panorama.

The ship was starting the two hundred twenty-five thousand-mile journey.

Shocked and trembling with adrenaline, Jake surrendered to the ship's gravity field and plopped down next to Richard. He mouthed a silent 'thank you' when a chair rose to support him.

Speechless, Vic did the same.

"This is amazing," Jake whispered. He patted Richard on the shoulder. "Buddy, I have to admit, I didn't see this coming ... ever." Leaning closer, he asked, "Are we going to land?"

"No, our flight plan doesn't allow for that. Speaking of." Richard leaned forward and toggled the comm panel. "Space Control, this is Turtle One, over."

"Turtle One, this is Space Control. Radar contact, report lunar orbital insertion."

"Roger, Control, talk to you in a few minutes."

"A few minutes?" Jake asked. "There's no way we—" His protest died mid-sentence as he looked outside.

The Moon now filled half the view-wall. In the few minutes they'd been underway, the Moon's apparent size had quadrupled.

Crisper and clearer than any picture, the vision of its cratered surface along with the stark contrast of the ancient lava seas lapping against their ringing mountain ranges left him breathless.

Again he sat in shocked silence.

Their ship closed at such tremendous velocity that the Moon grew visibly while Jake studied the scene.

Unable to tear his eyes from the incredible sight, Jake tapped Richard's arm. "How fast is this thing? The Apollo missions took days. I figured the *Turtle* would be faster ... but this ..." He trailed off, shaking his head.

"We could explore the solar system with this thing," Vic said in an awed tone.

Richard gave him a meaningful glance. "What makes you think we haven't?"

He turned to Jake. "Not so fast you could reasonably travel to the stars without the light-drive capability, but it has opened the solar system to us."

Self-consciously closing his gaping mouth, Jake nodded.

Studying the Moon's nearing surface, he saw craters, within craters, within craters. "This is so cool."

When the Moon expanded to fill the entire view-wall, he saw their speed drop dramatically. Traversing its surface from west to east, the *Turtle* entered a counterclockwise orbit around the Moon.

Richard activated the comm panel. "Space Control, Turtle One entered orbit at zero-six-thirty hours Zulu."

Jake checked his watch. While it was 10:30 PM back home, in Greenwich, England, it was 6:30 AM or half-six, as the Brits called it.

The thought triggered an idea. Shooting to his feet, he turned to Richard. "Hey, can you turn the ship toward Earth?"

"Yeah, but you won't be able to see it much longer. We'll be passing behind the Moon soon."

"Exactly! That's what I want to see."

Smiling, Richard nodded. He grabbed the control pad with one hand and actuated the comm panel with the other. "Control, we're about to pass out of radio range. We'll talk to you on the other side."

"Roger, Turtle One, catch you in forty-five."

Responding to Richard's inputs, the ship began to rotate about its vertical axis. It transitioned from facing east to north and then to the west. As they flew backward, toward the Moon's far side, the desolate surface slid away below them.

Moving closer to the view-wall, standing three abreast, they watched Buzz Aldrin's *splendid desolation* spool out under their feet. Earth's vibrant globe loomed large over the monochromatic, cratered horizon. North America, barely discernible by its city lights, shone from the dark-side. Farther east, across the Atlantic, the sunlit side formed a beautiful crescent, Europe and the islands of Great Britain visible as they greeted the morning sun.

Continuing their mute vigil, they watched as Earth touched the Moon's horizon. In an existential moment, Jake considered how fragile and insignificant their home looked. Raising his outstretched arm, he bracketed Earth with his thumb and forefinger. "All of mankind lives on that little rock," he said, breaking the silence. One eye closed, he watched the pinched world slowly slip behind the Moon.

Then it was gone.

CHAPTER 14

From the bridge of the newly renamed flagship, *Forebearer's Revenge,* Commodore Salyth watched his fleet of dreadnoughts plow through the interstellar void. Looking ahead of the formation, he studied the relativistically compressed multicolored spherical star field.

The fleet's faster-than-light speed squeezed the incoming photons streaming from the stars abeam and forward of the fleet into a fish-eyed cluster of light. Within the glowing ball, concentric rings of color surrounded a blindingly brilliant point. From its ultraviolet center, the visible spectrum of light shifted through the full rainbow of colors, finally fading into a red-shifted outer ring. At the perimeter of the visible light lay a razor-thin, infrared ring. Salyth's heat-sensitive reptilian eyes could just detect it against the absolute cold that was the universe outside that sphere. The rest was a virtual black hole, the light from stars behind them unable to catch up with the fleet's super-luminal velocity.

Parallel-space outside the central ball of stars was so completely devoid of light that it wasn't difficult to imagine it the domain of innumerable and unimaginable evils. It was a place in which Salyth—and Zoxyth in general—felt at home.

He imagined the ancient Forebearers staring back at him from that dark Valhalla.

Salyth glowered into the abyss. *Today, I bring your vengeance to the enemy.*

Pivoting with a grace belying his massive bulk, he turned and stomped back to his cathedra. The enormous stone throne was the same size as the one that dominated the bridge of Lord Thrakst's command ship, *Tidor Drof*. Because of his superior genetics, Salyth was the largest Zoxyth specimen in his fleet. However, as the spacious accommodations of this seat of power demonstrated all too well, he still hadn't attained the domineering mass of Lord Thrakst.

Glancing self-consciously at the large gaps between his leg scales and the cathedra's sides, Salyth stood. After a quick scan of the bridge personnel revealed no appraising stares, Salyth marched to the communications console. Knocking aside the officer standing over it, the commodore activated a fleet-wide call. "All ships, drop out of parallel-space at the designated space-time coordinates and proceed to your pre-assigned attack positions."

Moments after receiving Salyth's order, the fleet dropped back into real-space.

The commodore stomped to the forward view port. Ahead, half a universe worth of stars exploded from the fisheye. As the light streaming from the stars astern joined the photons from ahead, the star field fully encircled the formation of ships.

Glaring through the port, Salyth studied the water-rich world that had blossomed ahead of his fleet. The celestial body hovered where the ball of stars had been a moment earlier. The planet filled the *Forebearer's Retribution's* viewport. Salyth scanned the visible continents. Greeting its final sunrise, their ship's initial target lay clearly visible along the day-night terminator. The light-loving mammals were in for a rude awakening.

Radars of varying bandwidths painted all sixteen of his ships within moments of their arrival. Some originated from the multitude of orbiting machines surrounding the blue planet. Salyth drew his sharp, scaly lips back in a fearsome snarl. *Look at us all you want. It will make no difference. Soon, Lord Thrakst will know he chose wisely.*

Turning, he faced the assembled officers. Silhouetted against the blue, brown, and green sphere, he lifted two clenched fists. "Now the Argonians will truly know the pain and fury of the Forebearers."

CHAPTER 15

Jake's position, inches from the view-wall, afforded a beautiful panorama. Richard had rotated the *Turtle* back to the east. Facing forward, the ship glided ten miles above the Moon's barren surface in graceful silence. More cratered than the familiar nearside, this half didn't have the gravitational umbrella of Earth hovering permanently overhead. Looking down, he watched as pock-marked proof passed intransigently under the *Turtle*.

Lieutenant Croft turned toward Jake with an excited expression. "We might be able to see a lunar lander from this altitude, definitely if we're a little lower." He turned to Richard. "Can we visit one of the Apollo landing sites?"

Richard considered it for a moment, then nodded. "There's one not too far from where we'll emerge from the far-side. I think we have time for a flyby. We'll have to change our flight plan when we contact Control ..." He paused to check his watch. "In thirty-five minutes."

Jake and Victor exchanged glances.

"Too bad we don't have time for a landing," Jake said with a meaningful look.

"Good try, buddy. It wouldn't matter how much time we had. We can never land there. They're designated as historical sites, and we have strict orders not to go there."

After a moment, Jake and Victor nodded.

"Guess they don't want us trudging through Neil Armstrong's historic footprints," Jake said.

"Cheer up, boys. Like I said, we'll still do a low pass. In the meantime, are you ready to see the rest of the ship?"

"Upstairs?" Jake asked.

"Yep."

Scanning the interior, Jake didn't see an obvious way to the upper floor. The room had no stairs or openings. Although, considering how they had passed through walls to enter the ship, he knew the latter wasn't a problem.

Apparently reading the confusion on his face, Richard held up a finger. "Guess it would be easier to show you than to explain." He turned and walked toward the center column of the ship. A green, meter-wide glowing ring appeared on the floor. Reaching the circle, Richard stepped into it. After two seconds, his feet left the floor as an invisible force lifted him toward the ceiling.

An instant before Richard smacked headlong into the solid ceiling, a familiar crackling static sound echoed through the ship. An opening with the same diameter as the lower ring appeared in its smooth surface, and Richard disappeared through it.

"Come on up."

Jake and Victor looked through the view-wall at the scrolling terrain. Reluctantly, they pried themselves away from the incredible scene.

Richard's voice drifted through the overhead opening. "Don't worry, you're not gonna miss anything. We'll be on the far side for a few more minutes. Besides, this side is pretty boring anyway."

"Boring?" Jake said. "That's the last thing I'd call it. Jaded much?"

Ahead of him, Victor hesitated at the ring's perimeter.

"Anytime now, ladies."

Tentatively, Victor extended a probing boot into the circle. Impatient, Jake gave him a shove. "Let's go, Lieutenant." Stumbling into the halo, Victor looked at him with an apparent protest forming on his lips. Before he could speak, Vic's eyes widened, and he looked down. Then he lifted from the floor.

Jake stepped into the glowing ring. At first nothing happened. Then he felt an invisible force encase his lower legs, and he rose from the floor.

"It grabs your legs to keep you lined up with the opening," Richard said.

Overhead, Vic reached the top and slid sideways. Jake saw Richard perched on the edge of the opening. The lift gently deposited Victor on the floor next to him.

As Jake passed through the gap, the propelling force shifted him sideward and set him next to Richard opposite Victor.

Faint static noise came from the hole as the floor solidified. Another glowing green ring marked its prior location.

Slightly smaller in diameter than the lower room, the width of the upper compartment correlated to the narrower upper section of the exterior.

The ship's central column terminated about four feet above the deck. As Richard walked toward it, Jake noticed some familiar controls in the upper surface of the pedestal. While not as complete as the set on the bridge, they apparently facilitated flying the ship from this level.

"Why did they put a set of controls up here?" Jake asked. "You can't see out."

With a practiced dramatic flourish, Richard lifted both arms. Raising his voice, he spoke with the exaggerated inflections of a magician introducing his next illusion. "This room serves many purposes." With an arcing sweep of his right arm, Richard reached down and activated a control.

Jake's heart leapt as the top half of the ship vanished. Involuntarily, he stopped breathing. Appearing to expose the floor, pedestal, and three officers to open space, the entire circumference of the wall and ceiling disappeared.

Once he realized they hadn't plunged into vacuum and weren't dead, he turned and glared at a laughing Richard.

"That never gets old. You can breathe now."

Jake slugged his shoulder. "A little warning next time."

Turning, Jake inspected the full three hundred sixty degrees. The Moon's horizon was equally visible in every direction. It looked like they were standing on a round platform suspended over an ancient, alien desert. Ahead, in the direction of flight, lay the day-night terminator. The line where lengthening shadows gave way to a fourteen-day-long lunar night drew closer every second.

"Let me try something," Victor said as he stepped up to the center column.

Richard nodded.

Placing his hand into the controller, Victor pitched the ship forward, turning the floor perpendicular to the moonscape. Then he stepped around the column and walked to the edge closest to the Moon's cascading surface.

Richard cast a questioning look at Jake.

Jake gave him an Area Fifty-One salute.

With his back turned toward them, Victor raised both arms overhead, fingers extended like a plunging diver. Looking up, he stared in the direction of flight.

Finally realizing what he was doing, the other two moved to stand on either side, and did the same. With the *Turtle's* bulk blocking them from the setting sun, only the faltering light reflecting off the Moon's undulating surface illuminated their laughing faces.

Side-by-side, with arms extended and heads tilted back, they flew across the Moon's cratered surface like three superheroes flying in formation. As the ship slid into shadow, the moment passed. They lowered their arms and wiped away tears of laughter.

"If we're still laughing like that when Space Control calls, they'll figure we've gone off the deep end," Richard said. He actuated the controls and the walls shifted back to opaque. "Want to see the EVA suits?"

"EVA suits?" Vic said. His face brightened with nervous excitement. "Spacesuits?"

Jake looked around. "Where are they? No, wait, let me guess. In the floor?"

Richard held up a finger. "Watch and learn." With his other hand, he actuated another portion of the control panel. Midway between the central pedestal and the rear wall, a semicircle of cabinets grew from the floor.

"How in the hell does that work?" Jake asked.

"It's all about nanotechnology."

Jake pointed at the freshly formed six-foot-tall cabinets. "I know, but even considering that, how do they get this much material from a floor no more than two inches thick?"

"Carbon nanotubes, the same matter in carbon composites. Except, instead of being arranged in sheets, the molecules roll into tubes one carbon atom wide. They're strong enough that if you put together enough of them to equal the thickness of a human hair, that tiny thread could easily lift the weight of a full tractor trailer."

"How do the nanites use the nanotubes? Are they made of it, or do they use it?"

"Both. Their internal structures are made from it, but they live in an ocean of the stuff."

Jake tilted his head. "So, they're like spiders with a virtually endless supply of super-strong silk?"

Richard nodded. "Exactly."

Victor froze. "Spiders?"

Ignoring him, Jake did a quick cabinet count. "Looks like it's equipped for up to ten personnel."

"Yep," he replied, checking his wristwatch. "But since we're coming up on earth-rise, I'll have to show you how they work later. Let's head down."

"Spiders?" Victor asked again.

Richard shook his head and activated the control. The cabinets melted back into the floor. He gestured to the glowing green ring. "Gentlemen."

Vic relented and stepped tentatively into the ring, jumping noticeably when it started down.

"Skittish, that one," Richard said under his breath, nodding toward Lieutenant Croft.

"Yeah, he's smart enough, but a little insecure at times," Jake agreed. He stepped into position and started down. Richard followed.

Back at the control panel, Richard pitched the ship up, returning it to level.

On cue, Earth began to peek above the Moon's night-darkened limb.

A loud klaxon rang through the ship. The wall's soft glow shifted to dark red.

Jake's suddenly flowing adrenaline ratcheted up another notch as the *Turtle* self-actuated its holographic display. One glance at Richard told him this was an unprecedented development.

Five feet beyond the console, the rendered Earth coalesced with its familiar swarm of green satellites. At the same time, a holographic Moon formed between Jake and Richard.

Centered over the console and pulsing with an ominous red hue, a formation of indiscernible objects hung between the Moon and Earth.

"Where the hell did those come from?"

PART II

"In our obsession with antagonisms of the moment, we often forget how much unites all the members of humanity. Perhaps we need some outside, universal threat to make us recognize this common bond. I occasionally think how quickly our differences worldwide would vanish if we were facing an alien threat from outside this world."

— Ronald Reagan

CHAPTER 16

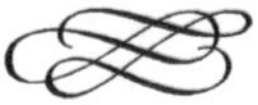

"What the hell *are* they?" Vic asked.

"I don't know!" Richard yelled over the blaring horn.

Stepping to the control panel, Jake squinted at the red dots. Unable to make out details, he placed both hands into the center of the holographic formation with his palms together. Reversing Richard's previous command gesture, he spread his arms. The image magnified and the red points resolved into an organized collection of irregular shapes. Arranged in a four-by-four diamond formation, sixteen rocky bodies cast a red glow across Jake's face. He looked over his shoulder at his two wingmen. "They look like asteroids."

"How could asteroids be in formation?" Victor said.

Jake shook his head. "They couldn't." Using a reversed pinching gesture, he zoomed in on one of the knobbly bodies. In the magnified image's higher resolution, the selected asteroid resolved into a collection of enormous boulders cobbled together by trusses and superstructures. What he'd mistaken for rocky protuberances jutting from the main body were themselves separate asteroids.

Richard looked as confused as Jake felt. "It looks like someone stitched together a bunch of rocks."

"They look like ... ships," Jake said.

Wide-eyed, both wingmen nodded.

"Are they Argonian?" Jake asked, worried he already knew the answer.

Finally finding the correct command, Richard silenced the still bleating klaxon, plunging the ship into screaming silence. He turned to Jake and shook his head. "No."

"Has this happened before?" Victor asked shakily.

"No, not since Roswell, anyway. The Argonians keep a tight lid on planets like ours. No one is allowed to contact us." He paused, running fingers through his hair. "Hell, even our existence is supposed to be a galactic secret."

"Not anymore," Jake said. A deep foreboding burned through him as he regarded the *Turtle's* red walls and the red holographic rendering of the alien fleet.

"The *Turtle's* response has my short hairs up," Richard said, mirroring his thoughts.

"I know," Jake whispered.

Each vessel had a common feature at its front. However, at the current magnification, he couldn't quite make it out. Reaching in with another gesture, Jake expanded the lead ship. Stepping next to him, Richard made a rotating motion, and the ominous vessel turned to face them.

"Huh?" Jake said.

Victor moved to stand on Jake's left.

Breathless, the three officers leaned closer. Not believing what he saw, Jake zoomed in again, and the resulting clarity removed all doubt. "Oh shit!"

All three men took an involuntary backward step.

"Oh my God," Victor whispered.

Manifested evil glared from the hologram.

A chill shot down Jake's spine as any hope for alien benevolence evaporated. And, unlike the Argonians, this was truly alien.

The bow of the ship was an enormous reptilian bust, the sculpted visage of an alien head. Arranged similar to a human's, it had a pair of eyes that burned with the ferocity of a rabid dog. Instead of a nose, two dark slits formed an irregular V-shaped central orifice. Below that, its mouth sported snarling, drawn-back, scaled lips that looked razor-sharp. By themselves, the exposed teeth would have chilled anyone's blood. However, the source of Jake's horror lay trapped in the alien's mouth.

Frozen in the act of consumption, the monster's fangs crunched into an obviously human skull. Clamped in the alien's jaw, the skull hung at an angle. The beast's upper right fang penetrated through the top of its cranium. Cracks radiated out from the puncture. Below, the lower left fang dug into the skull's chin.

Judging by the size of the bust relative to the visible ports and catwalks, it was as big as a sports arena, yet constituted the smallest part of the overall ship.

Richard broke the shocked silence. "Shit!" He rushed to the communications panel. Toggling the transmit command, he spoke with a shaky voice. "Space Control, this ... this is Turtle One, over."

"Turtle One, this is Space Control. We've had a ... uh ... situation develop."

"Roger, Space Control, we see it," Richard said, nodding at Jake.

"Turtle, a few minutes after you passed out of radio range, an unscheduled and unknown fleet exited parallel-space approximately fifty thousand miles above the planet. All attempts to contact them have gone unanswered."

While Captain Allison reported, Jake shrunk the image, bringing Earth's surface into the display. The fleet was closer to the planet. He pointed at the *Turtle's* red walls. "Tell them about that."

Richard nodded. "Space Control, be advised, the *Turtle's* computers have identified the fleet as hostile!" Richard reported, stress cracking his voice. "And, judging by their external appearance, I have to agree."

"Roger, Turtle One. As soon as we saw the first pics, we came to the same conclusion. The President has been notified."

Studying the planet through the view-wall, Jake felt his adrenaline ratchet up another notch. Turning to his fellow airmen, he said, "They're heading toward North America!"

"Turtle One, radar reports the formation is splitting up. Can you confirm?"

Jake turned back to the hologram. Reaching in, he magnified the image. The fleet differentiated into individual ships. He studied the image for a moment. "They are." With each ship on a slightly different vector, the alien formation was fanning out. "Not quickly, but they have moved apart."

Richard forwarded the confirmation.

"Captain Allison, this is General Tannehill. Thanks for your reports. They're still not replying to our calls. So, based on the *Turtle's* reaction, and what we're seeing on the front of those damn things, the President has agreed with the Joint Chiefs' recommendation that we attack while the alien formation is still grouped together." The general paused. "I suggest you hold back for the time being."

Jake couldn't believe how quickly the situation was devolving. In the space of a few minutes, they'd gone from sightseeing over the Moon to all-out war with an unknown alien race.

Frustration joined the myriad emotions coursing through Jake. "I wish this thing was armed!"

Richard nodded. "Me, too." He neutralized the *Turtle's* velocity, parking it a quarter of the distance from Earth to the Moon. Hopefully, far enough out to remain unnoticed yet close enough to permit safe observation of the coming events.

Above the night side of the planet, Jake saw the thin, arcing trail of a missile rising from central North America. A moment later, multiple missile signatures lifted from points all over the globe. Like yearning, skeletal fingers, numerous rocket plumes reached for the approaching alien fleet.

"Here they come," Victor said with an expectant, breathless awe.

While he watched the missiles rise toward their targets, several blindingly bright threads of light bore into the alien formation, yanking Jake from his veneration.

With dawning realization, he cheered. "Go, Star Wars!"

Goose bumps rose as he witnessed the deployment of a top-secret space-based laser defense system. Officially, Clinton had killed

Reagan's Strategic Defense Initiative or SDI in the nineties. However, the blazing beams originating from numerous points in space and burning into the alien fleet proved that assertion false.

"I didn't know it had been deployed," Victor said.

"Me neither," Richard said.

Jake returned his attention to the ballistic attack. He pumped his fist, willing the missiles toward their targets. "Come on!"

As they neared, his elation faltered. Even from this distance, Jake could see the laser beams stopping short of the asteroids. Terminating against some kind of force field, each laser strike illuminated a sphere around the targeted ship. The asteroidal vessels sat unmolested within the bubbles.

A brilliant light flooded the *Turtle's* cabin.

"Shit!" Jake screamed. He threw an arm across his face in a belated effort to block out the blinding nuclear blast.

"It's ok, it auto-dimmed," Richard announced.

Lowering his arm, Jake tried to blink away the after-image of the nuclear inferno. He helped Vic up from the floor.

Several more flashes strobed through the darkened view-wall as dozens of nuclear warheads slammed into their targets. Eerie silence belied the ferocity of the attack.

"Thank God for auto-dimming. We'd be three blind mice without it," Jake said. *Should have anticipated that,* he chastised himself.

Not able to see much through the view-wall, Jake turned to the holographic display. However, it had dissolved into a distorted storm of colors. Apparently, interference from the nuclear pulses rendered it useless. Looking for the fleet, Jake turned his attention outside. As the nuclear maelstrom's luminosity subsided, the view-wall slowly reverted to its normal clarity.

Shattering the silence, the radio crackled to life. General Tannehill's voice, full of anticipation, echoed through the ship. "Turtle One, do you have a visual on the target? Can you give us a damage assessment?"

Jake toggled the comm panel. "Roger, Control. We're trying to see through the afterglow now."

"Good, copy, Turtle One. We're standing by."

Jake studied the surreal scene. Earth filled the left half of the view-wall. On the right, like a tiny, new sun orbiting the planet, a roiling plasma ball had replaced the enemy fleet.

Over several seconds, the apparent diameter of the radiant sphere shrank to the size of the enemy formation. The three of them cheered, pumping their fists. It looked like all that was left of the alien fleet was a brightly glowing cloud of debris.

Jake actuated the comm panel. Excitement raising his voice an octave, he shouted over Victor and Richard's cheers. "Control! It looks like—" He cut off mid-sentence as the dimming cloud resolved into individual glowing spheres. Within each sat an undamaged asteroidal ship.

Each force field dimmed as the fleet continued unabated toward the planet.

Now too far apart to be attacked en masse, the ships continued to fan out, heading to all corners of the globe.

Deafening silence fell across the *Turtle's* cabin.

Jake shook his head. "Fuck!" He actuated the comm panel. "Control, the weapons were ineffective."

CHAPTER 17

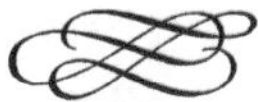

Sandy lay on the horn, narrowly avoiding the SUV that had pulled in front of her. The leaf-lined canyon walls formed by the tall, narrow trees that lined the approach to Nellis Air Force Base sped past in a green blur.

The words blaring from the radio broke through Sandy's shock. "More reports are coming in." The announcer sounded as astounded as Sandy felt. "Amateur astronomers are reporting an incoming swarm of asteroids." He paused, and Sandy heard shuffling paper. "This is incredible! The reports claim the asteroids are in an organized formation."

Sandy didn't know if that was true, although she had reason to believe it. In the early morning darkness, she pushed the Vette up to one hundred miles per hour. The street lights that illuminated the empty road flashed past. Her rapid progression through their glowing footprints created a rhythmic strobing effect inside the car.

An early morning call had woken her. Two seconds after answering, she was wide awake. She would remember the duty officer's words for the rest of her life.

"This is an emergency recall."

Throwing the covers back, she had leapt from the bed. "Emergency recall?" Instantly awake, she ran to her closet. Flipping on the light, she yanked down a flight suit. "Is it a terrorist attack?"

"Aliens and, no, I am not joking. Just get your ass to the squadron, ASAP!" Apparently remembering she was talking to a superior officer, the lieutenant on the phone belatedly added, "Ma'am."

Sandy froze. Mouth agape, she stared at the phone. A triple beep indicated the duty officer had hung up. She knew Lieutenant Janus well enough to rule out a prank. The woman had no sense of humor. Besides, a prank of that nature, utilizing official channels, would land her in extremely hot legal water.

Shaking off the trance, Sandy dropped her iPhone on the closet's carpeted floor and jumped into her flight suit. Five minutes later she had the phone back in hand and was on the road.

As she approached the Nellis gate, she heard more paper shuffling over the radio. "Are you sure?" the radio announcer said, apparently addressing someone in the studio. After a moment, she heard him whisper. "Holy shit." Without pausing to address the broadcasted expletive, he continued. "Folks, I've just been passed a report that some astronomers are reporting that the leading side of each asteroid has an alien face carved or ... sculpted into the rocky body."

Sandy activated her phone's voice dial feature. "Call Jake's mobile." Without ringing, her call went directly to voicemail. Terminating the call, she pressed the button again. "Call Asshole's mobile," using the name she had half-jokingly assigned to Richard's contact. It, too, went directly to voicemail.

"Shit!" *Where the hell are you guys?*

CHAPTER 18

"Charge the main weapon," Commodore Salyth ordered.

The shields surrounding the Forebearer's Retribution flared as another directed energy beam reached out from an Argonian satellite. He turned an irritated eye toward the attacking weapon. "Humans, earthlings, whatever these creatures want to call themselves—they're still Argonians—their pathetic nuclear weapons failed, yet they persist with these ineffective energy beams!"

He watched with annoyed satisfaction, as the ship's return-fire obliterated the offending machine.

However, the quick, resolute way these humans responded to his obvious intentions impressed him. He knew that had the Argonian defense forces responded as decisively, the Zoxyth's initial attacks would have failed, terminating the war to avenge the Forebearer's before its birth.

The shields flared again as the ship plowed into the atmosphere, leaving a roiling trail of superheated plasma in its wake. For hundreds of miles along the path to their primary target, a tremendous, supersonic shock wave blew over trees and structures.

Each of the sixteen ships headed toward the planet's largest and most strategically important cities. Major capitals topped the list. For Salyth's ship, this planet's most powerful capital lay ahead.

According to their intelligence, this country's government was the first the Argonians contacted. *And it will be the first the Zoxyth contact!* he swore.

CHAPTER 19

Like a scene out of a World War II movie, the pilots of Sandra's fighter squadron burst from their briefing room at a sprint. Running at full speed across Nellis Air Force Base's flight line, each pilot headed to their assigned fighter.

Sandy's head was spinning. She still couldn't believe what she'd just heard and seen. An hour ago, a fleet of alien ships had appeared in near space. They had not flown in or approached from the dark side of the Moon. They had simply popped into existence 50,000 miles above the Equator.

A Chilean telescope happened to be pointed at that part of the sky when the fleet had materialized. One moment, the astronomer was studying a star above the eastern horizon, the next it disappeared. At first he'd thought a sensor had failed. However, when he checked the telescope's systems, he found all in working order. Selecting a wide-angle lens revealed the obscuring body as one of a group of fuzzy objects. Changing the focal length brought the formation into perfect clarity.

Evenly spaced, it was not a naturally occurring collection of asteroids. However, with the exception of their forward section, an asteroid, or more accurately a collection of asteroids, is exactly what each of the sixteen objects looked like.

It was this military-like spacing along with the visage sculpted into the forward section of each of the sixteen asteroidal ships that had governments around the globe spooling up their weapons of Armageddon.

During the emergency prelaunch briefing, Sandy learned that the aliens batted away every attempt to fend off their advance as easy as a horsetail swats a fly. Even nuclear weapons had not slowed them.

Perhaps the most disturbing and incomprehensible part of the crazy events lay in the mouth of the sculpted alien face. While its curved-back, pointed ears, scaled skin, and razor-thin lips drawn back to reveal menacing fangs were obviously alien, the skulls clenched in their gnashing teeth were very terrestrial. Amongst the sixteen ships, observers had spotted slight variations in the stony alien visages, much like the subtle difference from one human to the next. The faces each had apparently been modeled after specific individuals within the aliens' race. However, the skulls occupying all sixteen mouths were unmistakably human.

Now one headed toward San Francisco.

How could a race we've never met hate us that much?

Arriving at her assigned F-22, Sandy scrambled up the boarding ladder. Levering against the stand's top rail, she gracefully slid feet first into the cockpit. Having climbed up behind her, the crew chief helped with the harness, helmet, and oxygen mask.

Sandy rushed through the starting checks. All the systems were already online. The ground crews had each fighter hooked up to a ground power unit. The fighter's computers had completed all preflight built-in tests. Having passed their BITs, each system displayed a green status. Finishing the few remaining pilot-initiated tests, Sandy gave her crew chief a thumbs-up. "Ready to go, Sergeant Feroni."

The tech sergeant responded with his own thumbs-up signal. Even with much of his facial features obscured by the headset's mouth-covering mic cup, the sergeant looked as nervous and confused as Sandy felt. He extended his right index finger. "Engine one clear to start, Captain Fitzpatrick." His voice was uncharacteristically shaky. The senior non-commissioned officer, a veteran of many combat deployments, was the unit's rock. No matter the situation, Sergeant Feroni always kept those around him calm through his measured, purposeful approach. His obvious shock at the current developments drove home the direness of their situation.

"Roger, Sergeant. Starting number one." In moments, she had the first engine started. She moved to the second engine. "Starting two."

"Clear on two!" Feroni said, his usual uninflected tone reasserting itself. Going through the regimented procedures had centered him.

The air rippled behind the rest of her unit's fighters as her fellow pilots fired up their fighters.

Sandy activated the second engine's starter.

Nothing happened.

"What the hell?" She toggled the switch several more times. Still no response.

"What happened, ma'am?"

"Nothing! It's not responding." Sandy had a sinking feeling. "Shit! Not now, please, not now!" Then, as she'd feared it would, the number two engine's BIT status shifted from green to red. "Damn it!"

"Let me guess, full FADEC failure?" the sergeant said.

Sandy nodded.

"Fuck!" the sergeant said, mirroring her frustration. "You know what to do ma'am."

Sandy did. After selecting the tactical radio, she toggled the mic. "Dragonfly Six, this is Five. Number two won't start, I'm going to have to go black." As she spoke, she ran through the shutdown checks. Her fingers flashed across the fighter's panels, toggling switches, depressing soft keys, and turning dials.

This sporadic problem had manifested after installation of a new piece of avionics for flight testing. Once the engine's computer latched the failure code, only a full reboot could reset it. Normally she'd be happy to discover this type of fault. It was part of the Testing Group's mission to find and identify system integration issues before they were widely distributed to the field. However, this was not the time for delays.

"So, the contractor's fix didn't fix a damn thing."

"No, sir."

Her fighter group, the Twenty-Eighth Test Squadron, was on a precise timeline. In thirty minutes, they were to link up with a vast, offensive task force assembled from every combat-ready fighter and attack aircraft within a thousand miles of the West Coast. Intended to overwhelm the alien ship's defenses, the assault's planned timeline placed each asset on the target simultaneously.

Sandy knew what was coming next.

"Dragonfly flight, this is Dragonfly Six," Major Donaldson called to his remaining fighters. "Five is gonna be delayed. Four, you'll move to my wing. One, Two, and Three form up as briefed. Captain Fitzpatrick, get that piece of shit restarted and catch up as fast as you can."

"Yes, sir. Sorry."

"No, Captain. It's my fault. I knew the contractor was full of shit, but I wanted them to figure it out. Anyway, I know you'll be right behind us."

While the major and his remaining four fighters maneuvered for takeoff, Sandy finished the shutdown procedures and turned off the battery. All instrument lights extinguished as the cockpit went black. Working with modern aircraft was not unlike working with a glitchy personal computer. When Control-Alt-Delete didn't work, you had to reboot.

Outside, Sergeant Feroni disconnected the external power. This particular glitch seemed to happen less frequently during self-starts, when energized by the on-board auxiliary power unit. While the glitch was rare, it had only happened when the GPU supplied aircraft power.

Unfortunately, the APU consumed the aircraft's on-board fuel supply. Normally it was considered negligible. However, for this rapid deployment, they had wanted to save every drop possible for the battle.

Having completed the pre-start checks, Sandy had the APU online and all systems ready for engine start. "Clear two?"

"Two clear!" shouted Sergeant Feroni.

Skipping straight to the problematic engine, she hit the start switch for number two and smiled at the high-pitch whine of its engagement. The engine rapidly accelerated to idle.

Sandy and Feroni both cheered, pumping their fists in the air. "Yes!"

The other engine started without incident. Sandy completed her before takeoff checks and received her taxi clearance. Arriving at the approach end of the active, Sandy taxied her fighter onto the runway.

"Dragonfly Five, this is Nellis Tower." The controller's voice quivered with nervous excitement. "Clear for takeoff from Runway Zero-Three." After a short pause, he added, "Good luck, ma'am."

CHAPTER 20

As he guided his space fighter from the lowest level of the Area Fifty-One underground hangar, Colonel Zach Newcastle finished his pre-flight checklist. The large elevator lifted the last four of his squadron to the surface. Zach twisted his head against the spacesuit helmet liner in a vain attempt to smooth a bunched-up tuft of his closely trimmed salt-and-pepper hair. *Damn cowlick.*

Because of their distinctive flight characteristics and the fiendish bat emblazoned across the unit's logo, the few who knew of the squadron's existence had taken to calling it Vampire Attack. The nickname stuck.

Manned around the clock for multiple contingencies, including the current one, the Vampires occupied the lowest, most secret level of Groom Lake's underground hangar.

As the four ships joined the twelve already above ground, Zach opened a private channel to General Tannehill at Space Control. "Space Control Actual, this is Vampire Six. First Space Fighter Squadron is ready for departure. Talk to me, Brice."

"Vampire Six," General Tannehill said, relief evident in his voice. "Your squadron may be our only hope. The lead ship is heading straight for D.C."

"Roger, Space Control," Colonel Zach Newcastle replied, his East Texas drawl stretching out the words.

Damn it, Brice, I wish you would've launched us sooner. Those lost minutes may cost us D.C.

Apparently reading his thoughts, General Tannehill said, "Sorry we didn't release you sooner, Zach. The President didn't want to risk triggering an attack, and once the nukes were launched ... well, you know."

"Brice, I think the human skull pretty much said it all," Colonel Newcastle replied. His weathered face leered through his spacesuit's visor. "Hell, we could have hit them long before they got within missile range." Anxious to get underway, he shook his head. "But I know your hands were tied. We'll make the best of it. Just hang in there, amigo. The cavalry is on the way."

"Godspeed, friend," General Tannehill wished him.

The rest of the Vampire ships signaled their readiness.

"Commander Yaakov," Zach said to the Russian Commander of Bravo Wing's eight ships. "Take your flight, and attack the ships approaching Europe and Asia. I'll take Alpha Wing, and we'll deal with the ships approaching this hemisphere."

"Roger, comrade," replied the Russian commander with his thickly accented voice. "Good hunting, my friend."

A moment later, Bravo Wing shot explosively westward, a quick blur the only clue to their departure vector.

Alpha Wing's eight fighters followed suit, launching east, into almost certain death, Colonel Newcastle reckoned. *But not before we take a few of the bastards with us.*

"Is the weapon charged and ready?" Salyth growled.

"Yes, Commodore, on your order," replied the weapons officer.

Ahead, the abhorrent city rose into sight. Its green expanses, geometric white structures, and unnatural layout sickened him.

The Argonians had forced the Forebearers into the same organized culture, a societal grain that abraded Zoxyth nature. A nomadic culture, they rose to the top of their galactic neighborhood by imposing their own organized disorganization upon their conquered foes.

The organization and social equality espoused by the hated Argonians were the fodder of the peasant working class. In Zoxyth culture, societal hierarchy reigned supreme. Just as genetic superiority had lofted him to this station, so should it lift Zoxia to the seat of galactic power.

He raised a heavily muscled arm and extended a gleaming, steel-clad talon toward the weapons officer. "Activate the main weapon as soon as we reach the assigned coordinates and altitude."

~

"What the hell is that?" Victor asked.

Jake tore his eyes from the lead ship's meteoric atmospheric entry.

Lieutenant Croft was pointing at several green holograms rising from the Nevada desert.

Utilizing one of his macro-zoom gestures, Richard magnified the formation.

The hologram resolved into sixteen small ships. Eight headed west while the rest blazed east at an incredible rate of acceleration.

The hologram's green color brought a glimmer of hope. Manipulating the display, Jake magnified the lead ship until it was the size of a basketball.

Stunned silence filled the *Turtle*.

As he had with the enemy ship, Richard made a twisting gesture. He added a nudge, and the holographic rendering continued a slow rotation. After studying the full three hundred sixty degrees, they exchanged confused glances.

"That looks like—" Vic started.

"Yep," Jake interrupted.

"Please, God, let them be armed," Richard prayed.

~

Groom Lake blurred as Alpha Wing lifted above the Nevada desert. Continuing their extreme acceleration, the ships climbed through the ever-thinning atmosphere.

Like a time-lapsed sunrise, the rapid ascension changed the sky from black to violet and then orange and yellow to white. The transition from night to day passed in mere seconds.

As Newcastle's fighters cleared the atmosphere, his ship's holographic display showed the alien vessel closing on D.C.

"OK, gentlemen, implement attack scenario three. We've been through it a million times in the simulator. Now we'll find out if these things work as advertised."

From the edge of space, somewhere over Colorado, he activated his comm panel. "Space Control, this is Vampire Six. ETA your location sixty seconds."

Washington, D.C., came into view. Zach no longer needed the hologram. Like a new mountain thrust from Earth's core, the alien ship hung over the city.

Turning to investigate a line of smoke, he gasped. "Oh my God!" A burning trail of charred earth ran south, disappearing over the horizon.

"Space Control, it looks like they've already attacked."

"Negative," replied General Tannehill. "That's the trail their atmospheric entry left. The blast wave caused catastrophic damage. We've lost contact with a huge swath of the Eastern seaboard. We're estimating casualties in the millions."

Colonel Newcastle's morale plummeted. Casualty was a military euphemism for deaths.

"They've settled over the city," General Tannehill reported. "The damn thing is only a few hundred feet over the Washington Monument, and it still won't respond to any of our calls." General Tannehill paused. When he spoke again, it was across Space Control's general frequency. His voice cracked with strain. "First Space Fighter Squadron, the President has authorized full weapon utilization. You are cleared to engage with nuclear bunker busters."

The weight of the order slammed home. His weapons were never intended for use in the atmosphere, certainly not this close to the surface, much less over their capital. "Understood," Colonel Newcastle replied grimly.

"We're ... hang on ..." Still depressing the transmit button, General Tannehill paused. Zach heard shouting in the background. After a moment, Brice continued. "We're detecting an unusual energy signature coming from—"

A brilliant flash of light exploded from the strange ship.

Zach keyed the mic. "My God, are you seeing this, General?"

Only the static of a dead radio answered.

With the alien ship at its center, a perfect sphere of light charged across the surface, its boundary racing inexorably across cityscape and countryside.

As the bubble reached for his fighter, Newcastle doubled over, racked by a powerful wave of nausea. It wasn't an emotional reaction. Somehow, the light was affecting him.

Through his grimace, he saw the other fighters waver as each pilot succumbed to the same effect.

"Keep your spacing," Colonel Newcastle ordered through the torment.

Then the brilliant sphere vaporized, its afterglow fading like a camera flash, taking the nausea with it.

A powerful foreboding washed over him.

"Space Control, this is Vampire Six, over."

Nothing.

"Space Control, come in," he tried again.

Nothing.

A new voice bleated into his helmet. "Vampire Six, this is Turtle One, over."

The Turtle? What the hell are they doing up here?

Newcastle checked his holographic display. "Turtle One, I don't see your location. Who is this, and where are you?"

"This is Captain Richard Allison. Space Control has us parked about fifty thousand miles out." He paused. "Do you know what that light was?"

"Captain Allison, I know of you. Listen, I think we've lost D.C. and then some. I know you haven't been briefed about my squadron, but I obviously don't have time to go over it right now. Just stay where you are, and stay clear of those ships."

"Roger, we'll stay out of your way. Good luck, Six."

Returning to the squadron frequency, Newcastle addressed his team. "The enemy ship is moving off to the northeast. We'll hit it while it's over Chesapeake Bay. That should minimize ground casualties." He released the transmit key. "If there's anybody left to save."

A few seconds later, they reached the computer-designated release point. "Proceed to your individual initialization points. Once at the IP, engage your tactical autopilots. The computer will control your ingress. Just concentrate on getting your weapons on target. Good luck, gentlemen."

CHAPTER 21

Glowing under the night's brilliant half-moon, the last of the snow-covered Sierra Nevada mountains glided serenely past Captain Fitzpatrick's right wing. With escalating impatience, Sandy watched the last peak's maddeningly slow passage. Having departed late due to engine difficulties, she pushed her fighter to its limit. Even on full afterburner, her progress felt glacial.

From the radio traffic, she knew squadrons from all over the West Coast were already harrying the massive alien ship that hovered over San Francisco. The combat communication net was on fire. She heard squadron commanders screaming reports and receiving orders.

In the two minutes since it parked over the city, the enemy ship had remained motionless and silent.

However, all hope for alien benevolence had evaporated when their meteoric atmospheric entry and its resultant shock wave had laid waste to a vast swath of the West Coast. Cities and countryside from Tijuana, Mexico, to just south of Monterey, California, were reportedly blasted and burned. As she departed Nellis, one of the air traffic controllers told her that large, superheated chunks of rock had spalled off of the asteroids that formed the massive ship. Extending the destruction beyond the area devastated by the giant ship's atmospheric shock wave, the trail of impact craters and fires left by the red-hot falling debris led all the way to its location over San Francisco.

The news hit Sandy especially hard. Her parents lived south of Monterey, near the boundary where the devastation of the atmospheric shock wave gave way to that of raining debris. The knowledge that they and millions of others might lie dead or dying in the hellish aftermath of the ship's passage crushed Sandy.

Struggling to focus on her duties, she studied her tactical display. The external viewpoint generated by its three-dimensional exocentric image combined lateral and vertical tactical information into a single presentation. The computer rendered Sandy's fighter near the bottom of the image as it would appear from the perspective of a camera looking down on her from behind and overhead. The display's over-the-shoulder point of view afforded F-22 pilots incredible situational awareness. The addition of pan and zoom functionality allowed her to see the position of every friendly asset within the theater of operations in real time. Each represented aircraft had a unique symbol or code. Units like fighter squadrons or bomber groups had discrete colors.

Just east of the swarm of symbols over San Francisco, the seventeen green icons representing the rest of the Nellis F-22s neared the battle. On the right side of the formation, the five fighters of the Test Squadron, designated as Dragonfly Flight, were a brighter version of the same color.

Panning the display's point of view, she magnified the San Francisco area. Like angry bees swarming a hive-raiding bear, squadrons of fighters filled the skies around the enemy ship.

Air Force, Marine, and Navy fighter squadrons from all over the West Coast were attacking en masse. To the east of the large symbol designating the alien ship, she noticed a group of nearly stationary icons. "Those must be the Army choppers." A squadron from the Army's Texas-based Sixth Cavalry Brigade—in California on a training exercise—maneuvered to engage the alien threat. As she watched, several blinked out of existence. Then she heard it over the tactical command net. "They've fired on the helicopters."

She watched with mounting horror as symbols for the squadron's eighteen AH-64D Apache attack helicopters blinked out in rapid succession. Stunned, and knowing those fading photons represented the deaths of thirty-six fellow aviators, Sandy stared at the display. "Oh my God."

Another pilot screamed over the radio. "Holy shit, they vaporized the entire Sixth Cav!"

Then a fighter symbol followed by a second, and a third, disappeared. Grunting under extreme G-loading, a panicked pilot transmitted over the tactical net. "They're firing on—" With an electronic sound like a lightning discharge, his voice cut out mid-sentence.

Devolving from organized mayhem to complete chaos, all semblance of tactical order disappeared. Before the enemy had fired, symbol colors showed a clear segregation of units along organizational lines. Grouped purple symbols in one sector and orange in another represented the coordinated attacks orchestrated by various squadrons. Now the display was a confused mix of colors. Several additional targets vaporized. Ingressing or egressing made no difference. Attacking or fleeing, fighters blinked out of existence.

Sandy tried to push her fighter faster, but the firewalled throttles refused to budge. With them at their max setting, and with the massive amount of fuel her fighter was consuming on full afterburner, this was a one-way trip. Whatever the results of the battle, she would be landing somewhere near San Francisco.

Over her flight's assigned frequency, she heard Major Donaldson, her flight commander, shout orders. "Direct your fire at the top of that alien head. It looks like a bridge to me."

Knowing she should be next to him, Sandy's frustration rose another notch. As the flight's second in command, she should be flying next to Major Donaldson as his wingman.

Another familiar voice broke squelch. "Six, this is Four. I haven't seen any missiles get through. The damn thing has shielding of some sort. Nothing's hitting the sons-a-bitches!"

It was her and Jake's friend, Captain Chuck Stanhem. After his Afghan tour and with Richard still recovering, Jake had received orders to attend the F-22 qualification course. Fortuitously, Sandy had orders to attend the same class. During training, they'd befriended fellow classmate, then-Lieutenant Charles Stanhem. It was a time she remembered fondly. Reunited for the first time since flight school, and without Richard's distracting persona, it was when she and Jake had fallen in love.

Sandy keyed her radio and called Major Donaldson. "Dragonfly Six, this is Dragonfly Five, over." She checked her GPS, 150 miles to go. Having just passed the Sierra Nevada mountain range, she saw the city lights of Merced ahead. Entering California's Central Valley region at Mach two, she was still six minutes away from the Bay Area —an eternity in battle.

"Dragonfly Five, where the hell are you?" said Major Donaldson. Before Sandy could reply, he transmitted again. "Dragonfly Three and Four, attack from the south. Dragonfly One and Two, I want you to attack from the north. I'll come in from above. Maybe our combined force can punch through this shielding or whatever the hell it is." Apparently remembering Sandy, he called, "Five, what's your ETA?"

"I am at least five minutes out, sir."

"All hell has broken loose here. I know the delay wasn't your fault, but I can't wait any longer. Get here as quick as you can." Again, before she could reply, he continued. "Dragonfly Two and Four, the three of us are the only ones with bunker busters. So, Dragonfly One and Three, I want you to lead with your Sidewinder and Maverick missiles. Two and Four, wait until your wingman's missiles impact before firing your bunker busters. Hopefully, it'll soften up their shields. With any luck, our busters will knock a chunk off these bastards."

"Six, this is Three. Sir, we don't stand a chance against that thing. It's ... huge! I can't even see the top. If nukes didn't stop it, what chance do we—?"

"Lieutenant, there are a few million people down there praying you'll do your best. We don't know that the nukes had no effect. For all we know, they could be ready to fall out of the sky if a fucking pigeon flies into 'em."

In the images taken just after the failed nuclear assault the ship had looked like hammered shit, but that might be its normal appearance. Its ability to hover that much mass above the city told her it would take a lot more than a flying rat to knock it down. However, she knew Major Donaldson was right. Considering the stakes, they had to exhaust all efforts.

A new voice entered. After a moment, Sandy realized it was coming from the command net. "I repeat, we've lost D.C.!"

Sandy's hastily eaten breakfast of greasy fast food threatened to come back up.

An authoritative voice came over the radio. "Last station calling, say again." It was General Pearson, the Nellis Air Force Base commander.

"Roger, Nellis Actual. We've lost all contact with Washington. Satcom is reporting a brilliant energy discharge over the city, possibly nuclear in origin."

After a slight pause, General Pearson's now grim voice returned. "I want all units attacking that target right now. Hit it with everything we have."

Major Donaldson transmitted on the flight's frequency. "You have your orders."

Sandy listened as the fighter pilots acknowledged. In their oxygen mask-muffled voices, she heard fear and nervousness.

He added, "We may only get one chance. Make it count."

Trying to will her fighter faster, Sandy pounded the engine levers. "Come on!" Looking up from the throttle quadrant, she froze, her breath catching in her throat as the alien ship finally came into view.

Having descended to 10,000 feet, her F-22 broke through a layer of haze and began skimming across the top of widely scattered billowy cumulus clouds. Finally visible, the alien ship dominated the distant horizon, extending above the Bay Area like a floating mountain. The lower half of the asteroidal vessel faded into atmospheric murk. Illuminated by thousands of street lights, the visible portion of its bottom glowed orange. Extending well above the cloud tops, the moonlit upper half stood in stark clarity. Its jagged gray edges contrasted sharply against the backdrop of scintillating stars.

As evidenced in the photos she'd seen during the briefing, the ship was a collection of asteroids strung together with a patchwork of trusses and plating. However, the pictures hadn't conveyed the true scale of those structures. They were huge. Even from more than 100 miles, the criss-crossing beams that stitched sections together were visible while the buildings of San Francisco's downtown skyline were too small to see, even if the air had been crystal-clear.

Sandy saw her flight's five bright green symbols split into two pairs and one solo. As planned, Dragonfly One and Two diverted south, while Three and Four went north. Flying straight up, Major Donaldson maneuvered his ship to attack from above the target.

Reaching their initialization points with well-practiced synchronicity, the fighters turned inbound as one.

"Dragonfly One, fox one, fox two!" Lieutenant Palmer shouted as he fired Sidewinder and Maverick missiles at the enemy ship's apparent bridge.

Sandy saw missile icons streaking from his fighter's symbol.

"Dragonfly Three, fox one, fox—"

Targeting Dragonfly One and Three, two green lasers burned through the night air. An instant later, rapidly expanding vapor clouds were all that remained of Lieutenants Jackson and Peters and their fighter jets.

"Jesus!" Sandy's friend, Captain Stanhem, yelled.

"Chuck!" she cried, involuntarily squeezing the transmit button.

"See you on the other side Sandy," Chuck said. Then he yelled, "Dragonfly Four, fox one!"

Simultaneously, the other two bunker buster armed fighters, Dragonfly Two and Six, also fired their missiles.

Three green lasers, one for each fighter, burned through the night sky.

Of the Twenty-Eighth Test Squadron's six F-22 symbols, only Sandy's remained. However, icons for three GBU-28 bunker busters stilled raced toward the alien ship.

Tears streamed under her clear visor. Refusing to turn back, Sandy armed her missiles.

Four tiny flashes signaled the arrival of the first wave of missiles. As they struck the target, a translucent blue sphere strobed into existence. It appeared to encase the entire enemy ship.

With no way to know if the barrage of Sidewinders and Mavericks had weakened those shields, she could only wait as the bigger missiles closed on the enemy ship.

She checked her GPS: 110 miles to go.

The bunker busters appeared to pass through the shield's barrier. An unrecognizable voice shouted over the tactical command frequency. "They're getting through!"

Then all three GBU-28s slammed into the enemy ship. From more than a hundred miles away, Sandy saw the flashes of impacts. Seeing the ineffectual size of the detonations, her momentary elation evaporated. The alien ship's sheer magnitude made the powerful explosions look tiny.

The blasts were bigger than those created by the smaller missiles. Even considering that most of a bunker buster's destructive power manifested below the surface, the scale of the asteroid rendered the damage inconsequential.

Sandy shook her head. *We may as well be the tiny people of Lilliput shooting arrows at giant Gulliver.*

Then the ship detonated. A bright sphere of light blossomed from its center. Watching the unexpected explosion radiate from the ship's heart, she wiped a tear and grinned. "You did it, guys!"

Studying the growing sphere, she realized it contained no fire. Also, it was spreading too symmetrically. Expanding at a consistent pace, the energy wave raced across the ground. Centered on the asteroidal ship, the blindingly bright bubble also grew vertically, reaching for space. Absent fire, the incredibly intense light wave grew in all directions. Rushing toward her, it soon filled her field of view.

As it approached, Sandy felt an internal fluttering. In two seconds, the flitting ramped up from an odd sensation to body-racking torment. She clutched her stomach against the mounting pain. Sandy rocked forward as an abdominal spasm threw her against the ejection seat's shoulder harness. Pressing against the straps, she clenched her fists in agony. "Oh God!"

Through pain-squinted eyes, she saw the wave closing on her. Its silent advance unrelentingly enveloped hills, farmland, and then a city she belatedly realized was Merced.

Like a million cockroaches trying to dig their way out of her abdomen, the boiling sensation overwhelmed Sandy.

Like the surface of a small sun, the energy wave's advancing front now filled her field of view, so big that its curvature was no longer evident. Along the vertical plane—above, left, right, and below her—the expanding sphere of energy created new horizons. For a moment, it generated the impression Sandy was tunneling straight up from some dark depths to emerge into a white-gold sky. Then the illusion reversed. It appeared she was plummeting nose first into a star's surface.

When the intensity of the light grew unbearable, Sandy threw an arm across her face. The ubiquitous light rendered flesh translucent. Even with her eyes squeezed shut, the shadows of her right forearm bones were clearly visible.

Air Force Captain Sandra Fitzpatrick screamed in horrified agony.

CHAPTER 22

In an instant, the all-consuming light and its attending agony vaporized. As if cast from an x-ray binary's brilliant star into its paired black hole, Sandy plunged into impenetrable darkness. In the radical reversal of sensations, she felt as if she'd fallen into a sensory deprivation tank.

A scream echoed through the black void.

Sandy gasped for air, and it stopped. Panting, she probed her surroundings. Her right hand fell on hard surfaces familiar to her touch. No longer masked by her screams, the surreally normal sounds of her fighter's cockpit reasserted themselves. Blinking furiously, her eyes darted left and right in a desperate search for visual input.

A moment before, she'd flown toward a blindingly bright energy wave. Now she couldn't see. Sandy's elation at still being alive ebbed as a new horror gripped her soul.

Am I blind?

A few panicked seconds later, the cockpit's instruments and then the city lights below came into focus. "What the hell was that?" A quick scan of the instruments showed all aircraft systems functional. She still rocketed toward the enemy ship at Mach two.

Sandy looked down. Without realizing it, she'd placed a protective arm over her abdomen when the wall of light had approached. Somehow, she knew the baby was okay. She didn't know how she knew it, but she did.

After a moment, she lifted the arm and manipulated the tactical display. On its surface, symbols of hundreds of her fellow aviators still rocketed in every direction. However, something was wrong. All communications had ceased. The previously manic radio chatter had evaporated.

Knowing she would receive no reply, but needing to check anyway, Sandy tried to reach one of her flight members. "Any Dragonfly assets, please check in."

Nothing but deafening digital silence.

She wiped a tear from her cheek. *Damn it! Chuck, Major Donaldson ... I'm so fucking sorry I couldn't help you.*

After a moment, she changed to the command network. This time, the snake of fear slithering up her spine worked its way into her words. "To any aircraft in the vicinity of San Francisco, this is Dra-Dragonfly Five. P-please come in, over."

Nothing, silence.

She swallowed, reining in her fear. After a calming breath, Sandy continued. "TacCom Forward, this is Dragonfly Five. Come in, over."

Still nothing. Only the normal clicks and ticks generated by cosmic rays and the secure radio's frequency-hopping algorithms came through her helmet speakers.

She looked at the tactical display again. It still showed hundreds of aircraft over San Francisco.

Looking outside, she glared at the giant alien ship seventy-five miles ahead of her fighter. Even from this distance, it was huge.

"What the hell did that light do?"

A yellow flicker drew her attention. On the ground, near the bottom of the mountainous ship, the bright flash of a small explosion blossomed along her line of sight. Checking the tactical display, she saw a purple icon disappear before she could read its identifier.

No laser had fired. It looked as if the aircraft had simply flown into the ground.

Scanning her instrument panel, Sandy's tear-muddled eyes kept gravitating to the tactical display. Something was odd, she couldn't put her finger on it. Except for the ones lost in the lead-up to the light, hundreds of aircraft symbols still flooded her display. Represented by every color of the rainbow, all the ships continued on various vectors.

"Vectors?" The word triggered something. Sandy felt an insight trying to percolate to the surface.

She jumped as the hauntingly silent radio sparked to life. "TacCom, this is Nellis Actual. What is your status? Over."

Again Sandy recognized the voice as General Pearson's. He was calling from Nellis Air Force Base's command center. The general received the same silence that had greeted her efforts.

"TacCom, this is Actual," General Pearson said with irritated impatience. "What is your status? Your data stream has flat-lined."

"Flat-lined!" The word triggered an epiphany. Sandy looked at the myriad fighters flying across the tactical display. The elusive oddity snapped into perfect clarity. Its message struck Sandy like a slap in the face.

"Oh God," she whispered.

After a hard swallow, she selected the tactical command frequency and toggled the mic button. "Nellis Actual, this is Dragonfly Five, over."

"Dragonfly Five, what in the hell is going on over there? Have any missiles hit the enemy ship?"

"Nellis Actual, the target was successfully engaged with at least three GBU Twenty-Eights."

"Great! How'd they work?"

"I was still pretty far away, sir, but they looked ineffectual. We may as well have thrown firecrackers against a tank."

The general paused, apparently taking in what she had said. When he spoke again, the impatience had returned. "Roger, Dragonfly Five. What happened after that? Why can't I raise TacCom?"

"Sir, when our missiles hit their ship, I think they fired some kind of ... main weapon. Something we hadn't seen before."

Closing to within fifty miles, the alien ship now towered above the horizon, its top obviously higher than her fighter.

"I think we lost everyone."

"Everyone?" The general sounded dubious. "Dragonfly Five, I'm not talking about your squadron. I mean TacCom. Why have all the data streams flat-lined? Why can't I get a hold of anybody?"

"Sir, I don't mean my unit. I think we lost *everybody* within a hundred miles."

After a moment, she realized she wasn't getting any closer to the alien ship. Even at Mach two, it appeared to be shrinking. Checking her tactical display, she realized the ship had already moved north of San Francisco Bay.

The general was still chewing on her ear. "What in the hell would make you think that?"

Sandy ran a hand across her abdomen. "General, whatever that weapon was, it almost killed me, too, and I was still over a hundred miles away."

"Dragonfly Five, I said the data had flat-lined, not died. I'm still getting feeds. They're just not doing anything. Everybody hasn't been blown from the sky. I don't know what you think you saw, but I still have a few hundred aircraft out there, and I need to talk to them!" He shouted the last part, the staccato sound of a hand slapping a desk accompanying each word.

General Pearson had touched on the oddity that had tugged at her subconscious. "Sir, when our aircraft lose all pilot input, they default to straight and level flight. If you check your data stream, you'll see that all of them are now doing just that."

After a pregnant pause, the general said, "Oh my God."

The enemy ship was gaining speed. Even at this distance, she could see it shrinking in apparent size. "Nellis Actual, the alien ship is moving north."

Falling behind at Mach two, Sandy cut the fighter's afterburners. Retarding the throttle, she set the autopilot to maintain 250 knots. Looking northwest, she watched in horrified amazement as it plowed through the atmosphere. A supersonic shock wave haloed the massive ship. A few seconds later, the monstrous vessel disappeared over the horizon.

A computerized voice snapped Sandy out of her trance. "Traffic, traffic!" On the tactical display, a blue symbol was dead ahead. The target's six hundred-knot airspeed combined with her own generated a closing speed in excess of eight hundred knots. Sandy had a split second to avoid a head-on mid-air collision.

A flick of the wrist sent her fighter into a ninety-degree right bank. A metallic flash followed by a shock wave marked just how close the plane had passed.

A quick scan of the tactical display showed that the other aircraft was a navy F-18 single-seat fighter. Clicking on its icon, she discovered its call sign, Blackjack 22. Switching to guard—a frequency monitored by all military aircraft—Sandy transmitted. "Blackjack Two-Two, this is Dragonfly Five on guard."

Nothing.

"Blackjack Two-Two, this is Dragonfly Five." Sandy's voice took on a desperate tone. "Come in, please."

Nothing, only deafening silence.

Banking hard to reverse course, she checked the display. Blackjack 22 still headed east, its altitude and heading apparently unperturbed by the near miss. While working to close the gap between the two fighters, she returned to the TacCom frequency. "Nellis Actual, this is Dragonfly Five. Still no contact on all frequencies, but be advised, the enemy ship disappeared over the northern horizon." Not waiting for a reply, she continued to transmit. "I just had a near miss with a naval F-18, Blackjack Two-Two. He's not responding on guard. I've turned to intercept. I'll try to visually verify the pilot's condition."

"Roger, Five. We monitored the ship's departure. That's a good plan. I need to know what the hell happened to our people. Check out the F-18 and report back. Nellis Actual, out."

"Roger, sir. Five out."

She was already closing on Blackjack 22. In tactical mode, it was running dark with position and anti-collision lights off. However, her forward-looking infrared scope had no problem picking out the small, twin-engine aircraft. Locking onto its IR signature, she programmed in an intercept vector. Taking over, the autopilot guided her fighter into gun range. Designed to keep the fighter's nose oriented on a potential foe, the system commanded the autopilot. Using fire-control computer data, coupled with the target's infrared signature, and fine-tuned with laser ranging and predictive algorithms, the system only required an F-22 pilot to pull the trigger to engage a tracked object. While the auto-lock feature wouldn't bring her into formation with the F-18, it was bringing the navy fighter into gun range. She had no intention to fire on the fighter. However, the resultant position would expedite the night link-up.

Indicating target in range, the symbols bracketing the F-18 changed from red dashed lines to solid green. Silhouetted against the snow-capped Sierra Nevada mountains, the fighter glowed in the monochromatic light of the half-moon. Sandy turned on her landing lights. The beams were invisible in the arid desert atmosphere. However, the sleek, gray, twin-engined fighter looked white in their brilliance. Hoping to get the pilot's attention, Sandy toggled the lights on and off several times.

"Blackjack Two-Two, this is Dragonfly Five. Please come in, over."

Nothing.

Wondering what horror awaited, Sandy shuddered as a chill ran down her spine.

The landing lights didn't work as a searchlight. She wouldn't be able to slew them sideways to inspect the fighter's cockpit. To preserve her night vision, she killed the lights.

Moving her fighter forward, Sandy narrowed the gap. Approaching the naval F-18 from the left rear, she studied the airplane's moonlit surface. Its iconic, slanted twin tail fins emerged from the darkness. Stenciled on the nearest vertical stabilizer, an uppercase S sat above an uppercase D. As she drew alongside, the wing and the rest of the gray fuselage came into view. Just forward of the cockpit, 22 was stenciled on the left side of the F-18 nose. In a flowing font, the pilot's name adorned the area below the canopy's bottom edge: "*Major Gregory Stillson.*"

Studying the fighter's transparent bulbous canopy, she shook her head. "What the hell?"

The moonlit far horizon glowed clearly through the transparent enclosure. Nothing occupied the space between the ejection seat and the instrument panel. Held up by seat belts and shoulder harnesses, even an incapacitated pilot should be visible.

She keyed the mic. "Blackjack Two-Two, Major Stillson, this is Dragonfly Five. Come in, over."

Still nothing.

"Shit!" From this angle, there wasn't anything to see. No helmet, body, blood, gore, grinning skeleton, or any of the myriad encounters she'd feared greeted her. It was clear she'd have to find another way to inspect the fighter's cockpit.

After a moment's consideration, she pulled a flashlight from its bracket by her right leg and switched it on. Pulling off her oxygen mask, she stuck the back-end of the flashlight in her mouth. To ensure she had all the light possible, she pre-positioned the map-lights that sat over each shoulder.

With a final glance at the moonlit F-18, Sandy grabbed the F-22's throttles with her left hand, and the stick with her right. Making sure not to disturb the navy fighter, she flipped her airplane over. A quick snap of her wrist accompanied by an appropriate power adjustment rolled her fighter on its back. Maneuvering cautiously, she positioned her jet over the F-18.

Sandy's heart pounded. She'd never been this close to another aircraft. *This is crazy.* Panting around the flashlight, she stole a quick overhead glance. *Crap! Still too far.*

Partially obscuring the moonlight, her F-22 cast a wedge-shaped shadow across the gray fighter. The exposed portion of the F-18's wings glowed in stark contrast to the darkened fuselage.

Concentrating on keeping her hands steady, she eased her fighter closer.

Sandy glanced overhead again. The map lights only illuminated the top of the other fighter's instrument panel.

She was too forward.

Palms sweating through her flight gloves, drool running down the flashlight clamped in her teeth, and hanging inverted from her ejection seat's restraints, Sandy struggled to rein in her body's physiological responses. She took in a deep breath. After holding it for a moment, she slowly released it as a long sigh.

Retarding the throttles a shade while applying enough forward stick pressure to maintain their separation, she allowed the F-22 to drift aft.

Finally, the ejection seat came into view. With the light still in her mouth, Sandy tilted her head back.

"Oh my God!" she gasped around the metal cylinder clamped in her teeth, almost dropping it.

Its lower half still encased in a G-suit, the pilot's empty flight suit sat on the seat. His upside-down helmet and oxygen mask rested on top of the piled garments. The helmet's inner liner, visible in the wan light, showed no sign of damage. Sandy saw nothing of Major Stillson. The garments and equipment formed the rough outline of the pilot. However, nothing else remained, no body or any part of it.

Shattering her shocked trance, a computerized voice shouted with programmed urgency. "Terrain! Terrain! Pull up! Pull up!"

This time, Sandy did drop the flashlight. Wide-eyed, she looked forward. An upside-down, snow-covered mountain was dead ahead. Still inverted, she jammed the stick forward, sending her fighter rocketing up. A split second later, a blinding explosion illuminated her cockpit as the F-18 slammed into the Sierra Nevada mountain range.

Rocky outcroppings, followed by streaks of snow-covered surfaces, flashed past her inverted canopy. Under the extreme negative G-forces, every beat of Sandy's racing heart pumped more blood and pressure into her upper extremities. Threatening to rob her of consciousness, blood pooled in her head. There was no time to maneuver. It was all she could do to keep her fighter off the rocks. Unable to flip the plane, Sandy pushed the stick harder as a cliff came into view. Pinned to the canopy's underside, the dropped Maglite danced like a trapped bumblebee. Grunting against the pain building in her head, she watched as the rocky surface passed a few short feet beyond the vibrating flashlight.

Then the mountain was gone. Her fighter rocketed straight up, the whizzing rocks replaced by a disorientingly motionless backdrop of stars, the half-moon filling the front of her canopy.

CHAPTER 23

"Space Control, this is Turtle One, over."

No reply.

"Come in, Space Control," Victor repeated, stress cracking his voice.

Exchanging glances with Richard, Jake shared Lieutenant Croft's despair. Whatever it turned out to be, he was sure the alien energy sphere portended a dark evil.

Wanting a closer view, Jake repositioned the *Turtle*. Swinging in well behind the mysterious squadron, he brought it to a stationary hover five hundred miles above central North America.

On the hologram, he watched Colonel Newcastle's squadron bear down on the alien ship. Having wreaked its havoc over D.C., it now moved northeast. As Jake watched it slide over Chesapeake Bay, a crushing realization hit him. "Oh my God. It's heading to New York!"

"Shit!" Richard and Vic replied, both as pale as Jake felt.

He placed his right hand back into the flight controller. "We need to find out what that ship did." Seeing a protest forming on Vic's lips, Jake held up a hand. "I want to know what they plan for New York."

Nodding, Richard panned the hologram, centering it on their current location. He brought his hands together in a macro-zoom-out gesture. The ground fell away, and the enemy ship shrank. All of North America entered the field of view. The red pulsing holographic renderings of two additional enemy ships slid into view. One glided over Central America. Over California, the other accelerated northbound, a trail of destruction and the San Francisco Bay Area in its wake.

With a grim face, Richard pointed at the other two ships. "And the rest of the world, for that matter."

Jake barely registered the comment. The image of the West Coast destruction and the apparent attack of the San Francisco area hit him like a freight train. All this time, he'd been too engrossed in the events over the East Coast to consider what Sandy might be doing. Now she was all he could think of. Had she and her squadron been thrown at that ship? No fighters had attacked the first ship, but that might have been a timing issue. He looked to the west. Was she still alive?

Victor's anxious voice snapped Jake from his thoughts. "Are you sure that's a good idea?" Victor asked. "There could be radiation and God knows what else waiting for us down there."

Jake's patience evaporated. "Damn it, Vic! That's a chance we'll have to take! Millions, fuck that, billions of lives are at stake! Unless we know what we're dealing with, we don't stand a chance!" Jake paused, casting a forlorn look at the ship plowing through the atmosphere over Chesapeake Bay. "Hell, even that probably won't be enough." He faced Victor again. "But, damn it, we have to try."

Looking like a scolded dog, Vic backed off. "Sorry."

"Jake is right. We need to get in there and find out what happened," Richard said.

Not waiting for Vic's reply, Jake actuated the controls. The ship rocketed toward D.C. In less than a minute, they were blazing through the atmosphere over Western Maryland.

"Look, there's still traffic moving in this area," Richard said, pointing at an ant-like line of vehicles streaming along an unknown interstate.

Jake slowed their approach. Progressing east, they continued to descend. In the course of a few miles, the traffic along the interstate tapered off, finally dropping to zero.

"There are no cars here, moving or not," Richard said.

Victor pointed farther up the highway. "Look up there."

To the east, a huge traffic jam capped off the long expanse of an empty roadway. Smoke billowed from several points. Ominously, beyond that, all activity ceased: cars, buses, trucks, everything sat dead still.

"Whatever it was, it ended there," Jake said, pointing at the leading edge of smoking cars. "Everyone outside of its influence kept driving."

"That would explain the long stretch of empty interstate we're passing over," Richard said.

Mute, Victor stared east through the view-wall.

Passing over the smoldering vehicles, Jake brought the ship to a high hover. Studying the orientation of them, he saw a pattern. The pileups congregated at curves and intersections, while straight-line sections of the road were relatively clear.

A glint of movement caught his eye. Scanning for its source, Jake made a shocked double take. "Hey, look there!" he screamed, pointing off to their left. Flying much lower than the *Turtle,* a large passenger jet was skimming across the ground at treetop level. It was north of them. Moving opposite their approach, it headed west.

Vic followed his line of sight and froze. "Oh my God." Then he smiled. "It looks like some people made it through. That had to have come from D.C."

Jake saw little puffs of smoke coming off the fuselage and wings as it started clipping treetops.

"Oh no," Richard whispered.

Vic's smile collapsed. "Why aren't they pulling up?" he screamed.

The impacts accelerated its descent, slamming the passenger jet into the ground. The plane burst into a racing ball of flame. The conflagration consumed everything for the next half of a mile.

They all stood in quiet shock.

After a few moments, Richard broke the silence. "I don't think there was anyone still alive or conscious to control the plane."

"Me neither," Jake said.

"That can't be," Vic protested.

Richard pointed through the view-wall. "Vic! Look at the cars and trucks. I don't see one person moving. Not a single car, truck, bus, or van is trying to get through the streets."

Lieutenant Croft studied the surreal scene in silence and then dropped his head in capitulation.

Jake realized his junior wingman was trembling.

"That's why I didn't want to come here," he whispered. When Vic looked up, tears fell from his eyes. "My mom was visiting D.C. this week. I didn't want to know this. I didn't want to lose hope."

Jake and Richard stood in shocked silence. Richard's face looked like Jake felt.

"Oh shit, I'm sorry—" Richard started.

"Don't worry about it," Vic snapped, shaking his head. As he stared through the view-wall, a range of emotions paraded across the lieutenant's face. Jake was shocked to see a sardonic smile in the mix. After a moment, Victor seemed to collect himself. His voice took on a steadier tone. "Let's just go find out what the hell happened."

Nodding, Jake turned back to the view-wall. Seeing D.C. on the eastern horizon, he guided the *Turtle* toward it. "We need to talk with Space Control. They'll have a better idea of what's going on. Hundreds of feet of earth and stone protected them. The weapon must've fried their aboveground radios. Since we can't reach them that way, we'll just have to go visit them."

Moments later, they were on final approach to the Pentagon. Jake activated the landing gear and brought the ship to a high hover. As they descended vertically toward its expansive central courtyard, he had a flare of hope and optimism. He halted the *Turtle's* descent and pointed northeast. "Look!"

Across the river from them, over the lake in front of the Jefferson Memorial, flocks of birds were coming in to land.

As he scanned the surrounding area from their high hover, Jake's hopes faltered. No one walked within the marina to the northeast. The repeated lift and drop of a security gate was the only movement in the northwest parking lot. Hitting the hood of a stalled car, the gate lifted. A moment later, it dropped onto the hood again, repeating the cycle.

Aside from the pattern of crashes he'd noticed earlier, there was no rhyme or reason to the placement of the various vehicles left strewn throughout the city streets. Some were in the middle of intersections, others had run up onto the curb.

Jake rotated the *Turtle*. Just south of the Pentagon, a huge collection of smoldering vehicles filled a curving section of I-395. Piled up on the outside corner of the turn, it appeared the drivers had forgotten to follow the curving white lines.

He and Richard exchanged worried looks.

"Let's go find out what the hell is going on," Jake said. Rotating the *Turtle* to face north, he lowered it into the Pentagon's center courtyard. A moment later, they landed in a clearing between the Ground Zero Café and the northern courtyard entrance.

Shutting down the ship, Richard secured all of its systems. Each lost in thought, they wordlessly proceeded to the airlock and exited the ship.

Passing through the outer door, an unexpected air of normalcy struck Jake.

"Do you hear that?" Richard asked. "I don't know what I expected to hear, but it wasn't this."

Jake nodded. To his surprise, everything sounded and looked perfectly normal. Over the ever-present sound of urban machinery, he could hear birds chirping, the sound periodically dampened by rustling leaves as a light southerly breeze blew through the trees. Somewhere, elevator music droned from a loudspeaker.

"Look, by the entrance. Are those bodies?" Vic asked. He started jogging toward the north end of the courtyard.

Exchanging confused glances, Jake and Richard followed.

With mounting unease, Jake studied the dark shapes scattered about the stairs. "Something doesn't look right."

They arrived to find small piles of clothes, each grouping arranged as if the person wearing it had vaporized. The garments had dropped in place, socks still in shoes, ties still wrapped around collars.

In a surreal moment of disconnected reality, a new tune, an orchestral waltz, blared from the overhead speaker as Victor searched through a pile at the top of the stairs. He stood up, holding a ring.

Jake saw the single-star rank insignia of a US Army brigadier general on the uniform's epaulets.

After studying the ring for a moment, Vic handed it to him. "It's a West Point class ring."

Jake turned it over in his hands. "Class of 1986."

Richard stood from his investigation of a separate pile. "There's nothing. They're just ... gone."

Like an icy snake seeking a warm shelter, a shudder slithered up Jake's spine and wrapped around his heart. Turning from the two, he walked to the main doors of the north courtyard entrance. "Let's get down to Command."

They passed into the foyer. As they moved beyond the range of the courtyard's surreal, melodic cacophony and into the silent interior, their footfalls echoed off the walls.

Walking down the long corridor, they checked each office. Collections of uniforms, dresses, and suits congregated below every exterior window.

Jake nodded at a particularly large pile in front of a wide briefing room's window. "They must have been watching the ship hovering overhead."

The other two nodded in reverent silence.

Turning from the room, they continued the emotionally onerous search. Jake felt overwhelming despair tugging at his chilled heart. *What happened to everyone? Where did their bodies go?*

Victor slipped, arms flailing as he fought to catch his balance. Water sprayed from his surging feet. Grabbing a door jamb, he arrested the fall.

Over his panting, Jake heard the sound of splashing water coming through the doorway Victor was clutching.

Seeking the source of the sound, all three peered into the room. It had vending machines along one wall and a kitchenette along the other. It was a break room. Half-eaten meals sat on the room's two dining tables. The same mixed groups of clothes lay in crumpled piles in front of the exterior window, although these sat in a pool of water.

Turning to the source of the noise, Jake saw a blouse draped over the edge of the kitchenette's sink, its arm hanging over the faucet's lever. A skirt, undergarments, and heels sat beneath the miniature waterfall cascading over the sink's front. Having flooded the entire break room, the water now flowed into the hallway. Victor walked to the sink and shut it off, staunching the flow. He stood there unmoving, head down, studying the blouse.

Standing in the doorway, Richard gave Jake a meaningful look.

Jake nodded. Walking up to Lieutenant Croft, he placed an arm around his shoulders. "Come on, buddy, we have to get—"

"They're all gone," Victor said, crumpling to his knees on the flooded floor. "They're all dead!" he screamed through his hands, voice cracking with the weight of it.

Knowing Victor was thinking of his mom, Jake squatted next to him. "We don't know that, buddy. Who knows, maybe they've just been ... moved ... or transported away. Hell, maybe your mom wasn't even here. For all you know, she got sick and headed home early."

"I don't think so," Victor said through his hands. "She never got sick."

In spite of Vic's words, Jake heard a slight change in his tone as he appeared to consider it. "Honestly, I don't know either. But we have to get some answers," Jake said. Standing, he placed a hand under his wingman's elbow. "Come on, Vic. Let's go find out what we can."

Wiping a sleeve across his face, Victor nodded and stood. Again Jake glimpsed a fleeting sardonic grin on the young lieutenant's face. Appearing to collect himself, he cast a contrite glance at the two of them. "Sorry."

"It's ok, we understand," Richard said, not quite hiding his impatience.

Jake turned to him. "How much farther to your wing?"

Richard pointed back into the hallway. "Just around the next bend."

~

"Nellis Actual, this is Dragonfly Five. SitRep, over."

Nellis Air Force Base commander, General Pearson, returned her radio call. "Dragonfly Five, send your situation report."

"I intercepted Blackjack Two-Two."

After narrowly avoiding the mountain, she had leveled off at 20,000 feet. Now, heading west over California's Central Valley, she set her fighter's altitude preselect for 5000 feet and programmed the F-22's autopilot to descend. "The pilot, Major Gregory Stillson, was … gone." Sandy paused, struggling with what to say.

Before she could continue, the general interrupted. "Gone? Was he dead?"

"No, sir. Gone, as in no longer in the cockpit."

"So, he ejected," the general stated as a matter of fact.

Sandy grew frustrated with the direction of the conversation. "Negative, sir. The cockpit was intact. The canopy was still in place." Not wanting to allow time for more questions, she continued. "His flight suit and G-suit were still there too. They were still in the shape of the pilot, but empty, and Major Stillson's helmet was sitting on the ejection seat. Hell, sir, his oxygen mask was still attached. I even saw inside it for a second before I … it …" Sandy paused.

Apparently digesting her words, Pearson didn't interrupt.

After all she'd been through, Sandy didn't care to mince words. Far beyond worrying if she would anger the general, she didn't pull her punches. "Anyway, there was nothing left of him, nothing! From what I could tell, his clothes weren't even wet. For Christ's sake, there wasn't even any blood." Stress cracked her words. Mercifully, the general didn't interrupt. She batted away another tear and took a deep breath. Calmer, she keyed the mic again. "I know it sounds crazy, sir, but I think those fuckers may have vaporized every human in the Bay Area."

A long silence greeted her report. To her surprise, when his voice returned, Sandy heard a shade of sympathy.

"I understand. I can't imagine what you've been through and seen.

Thank you for your report ... and your candor. Good work, Captain Fitzpatrick. There's nothing else you can do there. Return to base. Nellis Actual, out."

"Negative, sir," Sandy said. "I don't have enough fuel to make Nellis. I'm heading to San Francisco Airport."

After a brief pause, the general returned. "Roger, Captain." He sounded exhausted, as if Sandy's report had taken a physical toll. "I'll instruct Omaha Four-Four to coordinate your arrival with SFO air traffic control." The general took a deep breath. "Hopefully, there'll be someone there to answer."

"From your lips to God's ears," Sandy said without transmitting.

"In the meantime, I see you're already descending into the Bay Area. Give me a report before you land." After a brief pause, he added, "Once you're safely on the ground, let us know what you're seeing there too."

"Will do, sir. Dragonfly Five, out."

Studying the hundreds of ships scattered across her tactical display, Sandy shook her head. Some were heading out to sea. Many symbols had already drifted off-screen. Ahead, illuminated from below, a cloud bank glowed with the orange radiance of a city's worth of sodium-vapor street lamps. As she descended through 10,000 feet, the first fingers of the wispy cloud tops reached for Sandy's F-22.

Passing in and out of their amber, diaphanous obscuration and still east of Oakland, Sandy thought about her parents. To her survivor's guilt, she added remorse for worrying about them when so many millions may lie dead beneath her. A haunting epiphany sent a chill slithering down her spine. Considering what she'd seen, or not seen, in Major Stillson's cockpit, there were likely no bodies below her. Only a vast ghost town awaited.

Turning her head right, she glanced down, casting a forlorn look at the intermittent glimpses of countryside. "Mom, Dad, Chuck, Major Donaldson ... damn it!" She wanted to cry. She wanted Jake. Sandy struggled not to cry. "Where are you, baby?" Returning to the tactical display, she studied its myriad symbols. *Please don't be one of those.*

In spite of her determination not to shed another one, Sandy felt a tear trickle down her right cheek. Angered at feeling so hopeless, she brusquely batted it away and snapped her oxygen mask back in place. Sandy selected the radio frequency for Omaha Four-Four. Popularly called AWACS, the Airborne Warning and Control System aircraft was easily recognizable with the black and white disc-shaped radome rotating over its fuselage. Having been in a high-altitude holding pattern between Nellis and SFO, it should be safe and operational.

"Omaha Four-Four, Dragonfly Five, over."

Apparently waiting for her call, the military air traffic controller answered immediately. "Dragonfly Five, this is Four-Four. Go ahead."

"Roger, Four-Four, Dragonfly Five requesting clearance to SFO or handoff to San Fran Center."

"Uh ... Five." The male controller sounded confused. "We haven't been able to reach anyone at San Fran Center, Approach Control, or even the tower. Hell, ma'am, I can't even get the flight service station guy to pick up. I tried them on everything. Nobody's answering."

Sandy felt a knot form in her throat. It matched the one taking up residence in her stomach. Her thoughts returned to her parents in Carmel Valley. "Have you tried Monterey Approach?" The last word came out as a squeak.

After a long silence, Sandy was about to ask again when the controller returned sounding more confused. "No joy on Monterey either, Captain."

Her heart sank. *Mom? Daddy?* Another tear threatened to spill down her cheek. Sandy had been just over a hundred miles out and had survived. She tried to picture how far Monterey was south of San Francisco. She thought it was about that far. However, she had no idea where the exact line fell.

Sandy loved her mother, but she had always been a daddy's girl. She had grown up hanging around his hangar. Back then, he ran a small flight school at Carmel Valley Vintage Airfield south of Monterey. All of her best childhood memories centered around that hangar. She'd grown up there. As an eight-year-old, she'd held an airplane yoke for the first time. That first flight had hooked her for life. Many an afternoon she had hovered over her daddy as he overhauled an airplane engine. Remembering how he used to dab black grease on her button nose, she unconsciously raised a hand to touch it. As it landed on the oxygen mask, she could hear his laugh. It was a sound that always made her smile, but now it only served to deepen her dread.

Looking at the F-22's moving-map display, she focused on the coastline south of SFO. Even though the airport had closed just as her daddy retired—about the same time Sandy had left for Stanford—they still lived on its abandoned perimeter.

Not portrayed on her military map, the old airport fell within the represented area. She knew it was somewhere under the myriad symbols covering the area just south of Monterey.

Please let them be okay.

"Dragonfly Five, we do have contact with Fresno Approach. Would you like radar vectors?"

Sandy cast a wary glance at her fuel gauge. "Negative, Four-Four. I barely have enough fuel to make SFO." Between her afterburner-assisted sprint to catch up with her flight and intercepting a 600-knot Blackjack 22, she was already well into her emergency fuel reserve.

Finally breaking through the bottom of the clouds blanketing the Bay Area, Sandy gasped. Interspersed with the city lights, a spattering of fires littered the landscape. Descending through 6000 feet, she looked down on a crowded interstate as it streamed through her line of sight. While the inbound lanes were lightly populated, the outbound easterly lanes were full. However, no traffic moved.

Pileups marked each bend in the highway.

Is everybody dead?

She looked at the cityscape. The unending scenes of calamity scrolling beneath her fighter fit only one possibility. Simultaneously, everyone had either been killed or incapacitated ... *or vaporized.* With no one left to control the vehicles, they had crashed at the next turn or intersection. She'd been holding out hope that the aliens had only vaporized the attacking pilots, but now even that self-delusion faded.

Sandy jumped as her radio blared to life.

"Dragonfly Five, this is Omaha Four-Four. Turn to heading two-seven-zero. This will be vectors for ILS Runway One-Nine-Left."

Then an anxious, computer-animated voice demanded her attention. "Check Fuel!"

Keenly aware that, one way or another, her flight would end in ten minutes, Sandy punched a button, canceling the alert.

Knowing the instrument landing system's extended approach path would take her too far off the direct route to the airport, Sandra keyed the radio transmit mic. "Negative, Omaha Four-Four. I need to proceed direct to the approach end of the runway. I don't have enough fuel to fly the entire procedure."

"Dragonfly Five ... I still don't have contact with San Fran Approach," the controller said, with evident frustration.

"I understand, Four-Four." After a calming breath, Sandy continued. "Listen, I'm clear of the clouds, and it looks like I will be all the way into SFO. I'll maintain visual separation with any and all traffic."

Consulting her display, she didn't think that would be a problem. In the twenty minutes since the enemy ship had disappeared, the Bay Area's once full skies now seemed devoid of all traffic. Not that her display was empty. Hundreds of icons still populated its screen. However, maddeningly, they continued toward what she now believed would be their ultimate demise. Having cleared the local airspace, all persisted straight and level. Half were heading out to sea. Scanning east, she saw another icon blink out of existence as it too met the tightly grouped contour lines of the Sierra Nevada's western slope.

"Roger, Dragonfly Five. Turn to heading two-four-six. That should set you up nicely for a left base into Runway One-Nine-Left."

"Thanks, Four-Four. I'll take it from here."

Swapping frequencies she tried to call the airport directly. "San Francisco Tower, this is Air Force Seven-Niner-Zero-Papa, over." She tried several more times, but utilizing her aircraft's FAA registration number yielded no better results than had her tactical call sign.

The little voice of dread that she had, thus far, managed to keep tamped down blossomed into full horror. Crossing Oakland and approaching the east side of the bay, the same scenes of carnage played out in every direction.

The thought reminded her about the general's last instructions. Selecting the tactical radio, she keyed the mic. "Nellis Actual, this is Dragonfly Five, over."

Sounding worried, the general's gruff voice came back instantly. "Talk to me, Five. What are you seeing out there?"

Sandy described the unending scenes of abandonment and destruction scrolling outside her canopy. "Also, sir, I'm bingo fuel. I'm only a couple of minutes outside of SFO. I'll try to contact you once I'm on the ground."

The general relayed his personal mobile number. "Recon the ground situation and give me a call. Good luck, Captain Fitzpatrick." Still transmitting, he paused. "Don't take any chances. If you can't assure a safe landing on a damned clear runway, then point that fighter toward the bay and eject over the airport. I don't want to lose anybody else today."

"Yes, sir. Dragonfly Five, out."

Like a black void, the inky waters of San Francisco Bay passed beneath her F-22 fighter. Brilliant light flared over her right shoulder. Snapping her head in that direction, she watched a fireball rise into the night sky from behind Mount Diablo. An apparent firestorm raged on its far side, illuminating the atmosphere and silhouetting the dark mountain with an eerie, orange glow while the city lights beneath it reflected off the bay waters with surreal tranquility.

Sandy dragged her eyes from the scene. "San Francisco Tower, this is Air Force Seven-Niner-Zero-Papa calling in the blind." Using the standard radio procedure for suspected loss of communication, she continued the advisory call. "Mayday, Mayday, Mayday! Air Force Seven-Niner-Zero-Papa is declaring a fuel emergency. Any traffic in the vicinity of San Francisco Airport, I am five miles to the east, on a left base for landing to the south on Runway One-Nine-Left." Her voice cracked as she eyed her nearly depleted fuel level. "Any traffic, please advise."

Scanning the skies over the rapidly nearing airport, Sandy saw no aircraft lights. Nothing moved against the stationary backdrop of nocturnal cityscape. Blindingly bright and peppered with fires, the city beyond the airport perimeter contrasted starkly against the relative darkness of the airport's maneuvering area. The night vision-preserving dim lights of the runways and taxiways made the field only slightly brighter than the surrounding bay waters. Ahead, the ocean of twinkling city lights crashed against the peninsula's night-darkened central ridge line, their steep sides only sporadically interrupted by errant lights.

Turning her attention back inside, Sandy felt her stress ratchet up another notch as the last sliver of yellow on the number one engine's fuel gauge faded to black. A moment later, the other engine's fuel gauge also tripped empty.

Outside, the airport's runway started to come into alignment. Being careful not to slosh the tanks and risk an early flameout, she started a smooth left turn. "San Francisco Tower and any traffic in the area, Air Force Seven-Niner-Zero-Papa is turning left base to final for Runway One-Nine-Left, over."

Suddenly her fighter's engine noise halved as blossoming red and yellow lights and screaming horns announced the obvious. Her number one engine had flamed out.

"Oh crap!"

Looking at her last engine's empty fuel gauge, she was reminded of an ancient aviation axiom: An airplane can fly over gross, it'll even fly out of center of gravity limits, but it can't fly without fuel.

Not for long, anyway.

As the bay waters scrolled under her fighter, the runway slid into alignment. Sandy breathed a sigh of relief. From this position and altitude, she could glide to a landing if needed. She eyed the landing gear lever. Dropping the gear would decrease that glide distance. With so little margin for error, she was loath to extend them just yet. With one engine running, she could still lower them with the utility hydraulics. However, if the second engine flamed out, she would have to activate the emergency blow-down lever.

A new light yanked Sandy from her internal debate. Dead ahead, in the bay waters between her fighter and the runway, a flame flickered to life. In the fire's rapidly growing light, she discerned the aft half of a large jet protruding from the waves. A wing, cracked open midspan like a leg bent at the knee, jutted from the left side of the fuselage. Lightning-fast, the fire spread from the jet's right side to its left. Then a blinding, roiling fireball exploded from the airplane.

Sandy yanked her fighter hard left, narrowly avoiding the hellish conflagration. The horrible silence of a second engine flameout rewarded her efforts. Passing the expanding fireball, but now out of alignment with the runway environment, she set her flaps for max glide distance. Uttering a short prayer, she fingered the ejection handle. Reconsidering, she released it and gripped the fighter's control stick with one hand and the landing gear lever with the other.

"I'm not done with you yet!"

Passing over the seawall and panting, she watched the runway's near left side slowly slide toward her fighter while the ground grew closer. Her breath hitched as, directly in her flight path, twisted wreckage of two airplanes loomed out of the darkness.

"Oh shit!" She yanked the control stick left and slammed the emergency landing gear actuator. Three squibs detonated. Their report and the high-pitched whistle of streaming, compressed air along with the mechanical actions of the gear were uncharacteristically loud against the deafening silence of the dead engines.

Only a few short feet separated her fighter's belly and the airport's sod. Just as the near edge of the runway's left side rolled under her F-22, the two main landing gear indicator lights shifted from red to green. She rolled wings level, and the rear two wheels barked in protest of a rough landing.

Roaring down the runway at incredible speed, Sandy held the nose of the fighter off the ground, buying time for the aircraft's longest landing gear strut to complete its extension. She looked at its indicator light. The bulb formed the top of a triangle of three. Fortunately, the main gear's lower two lights remained solid green. However, indicating it had not reached the lock-detent, the nose gear light stubbornly remained red.

"Come on!"

Losing speed, the aircraft's nose started falling. Futilely pulling against the aft control stop with all her might, Sandra tried to hold it off the runway. However, the tail was in full stall. The drop accelerated. She cringed in anticipation of the gear's imminent collapse. Falling from the unusually nose-high attitude, the gear slammed into the runway with a loud, jolting crash. To Sandy's amazement, it held, the indicator shifting to green.

Miraculously, the fighter was directly over and in line with the runway's centerline lights. However, they were still flashing by too fast. Like a meth-fueled Pac-Man, the fighter's pointed nose gobbled up the streaming luminous dots. Sandy deployed the fighter's emergency drogue chute. The runway's edge lights were already red. Less than two thousand feet remained.

Looking ahead, she sought the thousand-foot marker, the section where the alternating red and white centerline lights also shifted to solid red. However, they weren't there. The lights appeared to come to an abrupt end at a rapidly closing point. With renewed horror, she realized the background stars and clouds were being blotted out by the looming nose of a giant aircraft parked over the far end of the runway.

Captain Fitzpatrick jammed in full right pedal, but the fighter didn't respond. Inexorably, it persisted on its collision course with the huge airplane.

"Shit!" Realizing the problem, she smacked the drogue chute's jettison lever. Released from the device's inline drag, the fighter shot diagonally off the runway, narrowly avoiding the double-decker Airbus A380. Its nose gear and then its left engine passed just off her left wing.

The last of her momentum carried her across a strip of sod and fortuitously onto a section of tarmac. Pressing the toe brakes with all her might, she finally brought the F-22 to a full stop, nose-to-nose with a stationary Learjet.

"Holy shit!"

CHAPTER 24

Following the weapon's deployment, Commodore Salyth scanned the displayed surface images, verifying the weapon's effect. The results mirrored those seen during the test against the Argonian refugees. Exposing dripping fangs, a dark grin spread across his face. *Lord Thrakst will elevate me above all others.*

On his command console, he watched the planet's radio traffic spike as panicked communiqués raced to every corner of the globe. "These Argonians are sniffing their fate," he gloated.

Yanking him from his exultations, the weapons officer yelled across the bridge. "Commodore Salyth! We have several ships inbound from port!"

"Don't bother me with trivial intelligence, idiot. Just destroy them!"

"But Commodore, they have the maneuvering profile of Argonian ships—"

Cutting off the officer, Salyth gesticulated toward the main display. "They're all Argonians!"

The weapons officer opened his mouth to speak.

Salyth's temper flared. Blood boiling, he closed on the obstinate officer. Towering over the hatchling, he placed a razor-sharp forearm talon against his neck.

To his surprise, the officer stood his ground. Slowly extending an arm, he pointed toward his display. "*Galactic Defense Force* Argonian ships, Commodore."

Salyth froze.

The officer continued. "Their trajectory originated from the surface."

After a moment, Salyth allowed his talon to slide into its recess. With a final glare at the officer, he turned to face the front of the bridge. "Put them on the main display!"

Without the commodore's attention, the monitor had returned to its default. It now showed an image of the bay waters ahead of the ship. The weapons officer changed the feed, and it morphed into a formation of eight fighters as they approached from the left side.

Studying the unexpected ships, Salyth stepped closer to the display. There was nothing Argonian in their appearance. "Those are not Galactic Defense Force ships," he growled at the officer. "They're on straight-line trajectories! I see nothing to ind—"

Salyth cut off mid-word. In an instant, all of the ships changed heading, shooting into eight separate vectors.

"Battle stations!" Salyth roared. He turned and ran to his command post. "How long until the weapon is charged and ready to deploy?"

"Thirty-eight zyxn, Commodore."

"We don't have time for that," he roared. "Engage them now!"

"Lord, the build-up of the weapon's quantum field can't be rushed. I can't fire it now. It won't—"

"Curse the gods!" Salyth roared. He blazed across the bridge. His steel-reinforced talons gripped the floor's stony surface, leaving a flurry of sparks in his wake. A ferocious blow sent his weapons officer flying across the room. A wet smack echoed through the cavernous bridge as his partially decapitated, lifeless body crumpled against the far wall.

Standing over the weapons console, he activated the hull-mounted defense systems. Eight energy beams shot out, one for each ship. Salyth's dread grew tenfold. As he'd feared, each ship instantly repositioned out of the beam's path. Their movement was so fast, it looked like the small ships disappeared from one spot, and reappeared in another—a ghostly blur, the only evidence of the transition.

The form of the ships confused him. They obviously weren't Argonian, but somehow these humans had mastered the same inertial control that had eluded Zoxyth for untold millennia.

"These devolved Argonians will not block my ascension!" he growled.

Activating all weapons, Salyth sent a barrage of beams at the enemy ships.

CHAPTER 25

Feeling the pressure of their rapid descent, Jake pinched his nose and popped his ears. The elevator chimed and slowed. With a final lurch, it came to a stop at the bottom of the deep shaft. The doors slid open and revealed the familiar stainless steel-trimmed onyx walls decorating Space Control's deep underground entrance.

Jake felt his last shred of hope evaporate. A pile of clothes and a discarded weapon lay where the guard should have been. Checking Victor, he was thankful to see the young lieutenant successfully fending off the dread hovering just behind his eyes.

Reaching the vacated guard station, Richard activated the security panel. It still worked just as the one above ground had. Once they passed the computer's security checks, the door opened, affording them their first glimpse into Space Control.

They silently walked into the large room. Jake wished everyone would pop out of their hiding places and shout: *Surprise*! Instead, he saw a broken coffee cup in the middle of the floor next to another pile of clothes. An unfinished email was visible on a computer near them. Empty shirtsleeves lay strewn across its keyboard.

"Oh shit," Vic said, looking at the far wall's large monitors.

A separate monstrous alien ship filled each display.

"They must've set the satellites up to track them automatically," Richard said.

Jake nodded. He counted six unique enemy ships. Four of them hovered over major cities while the other two glided across the surface, one over water while the other traversed a mountainous area. With compounding dread, he wondered what the other ten ships were up to.

Richard pointed at the alien ship on the top right monitor. "That looks like Paris."

"Yeah, that's the Arc de Triomphe on the right," Jake said.

"Look," Victor said excitedly. "Cars are still moving—" He broke off with a choked scream as a sphere of light blossomed from the hideous ship. Racing across the surface, it quickly filled the satellite's field of view.

"Oh God," Richard said.

Jake felt his heart sink.

As if trying to hold himself together, Vic wrapped his arms around his own shoulders. His eyes unfocused, he kept repeating the same words. "Oh God. Oh God ..."

Knowing they needed something to focus on other than the televised hell filling Space Control's walls, Jake moved to stand between his wingmen and the monitors. Placing a hand on Vic's shoulder, he tried to shake the young officer out of his catatonic state. "Listen, guys. Let's get out of here."

Richard tore his eyes from the displays. After a moment, he nodded.

Jake nudged Victor again. Sluggishly, he focused his eyes and also nodded.

"We have to figure out the weapon's range. Whoever is left in charge will need to know where to send aid. We need to know how far it went and what happened to the victims not at the epicenter. Maybe people were just incapacitated farther out." Jake pointed around the room. "This weapon isn't stopped by soil or rock, but we don't know what happens to it over distances."

Something on one of the displays drew Richard's attention.

Jake turned to see what had distracted him.

Richard pointed at the top left monitor. "Look at the ship over the water. It must be the one that attacked D.C. You can see those small ships closing on it."

"You're right," Jake said. Glimpsing his first clear image of them, he studied their shape on the high-definition display. "They look like smaller, low-profile versions of the *Turtle*."

"Yep, like a fighter version," Victor said.

Suddenly, a barrage of laser beams shot out from the alien ship. Somehow, the fighters evaded them. A few seconds later, an intensified laser attack streamed from points all over the enemy ship. Fired in an enveloping strategy, they appeared to cage each fighter in brilliant beams. Again the small ships dodged the attack, each leaping out of the path of the laser aimed at their central mass. However, one jumped into the path of another beam, instantly transforming into a brilliant vapor cloud.

"No," Vic whispered.

"Look!" Jake said, pointing at the screen. "The lasers won't be enough. They're almost to the ship's shields."

Richard nodded. "I hope they have a way to get through, otherwise ..."

Jake's optimism sprang anew as the ships made another rapid hop, safely emerging within the alien ship's force field. "Yes!" He pumped his fist. "Get some!"

"Who are these guys?" Victor wondered aloud, a glimmer of optimism edging the dread from his words.

A moment later, a familiar voice blared from a radio speaker.

"We're in, gentlemen," Colonel Zach Newcastle said to his space fighters. "Let's not waste Major Pell's sacrifice. Make it count. Go to your attack vectors. Launch your weapon at the assigned time. Once it's away, get the hell out of there. We'll rendezvous just as we've trained, assess the situation, and God willing, move on to the next targets."

He looked down at the narrowing bay, wishing it was open ocean. He never imagined a scenario where they deployed these dreadful weapons this close to the planet, much less a population center.

The weapon, a secret asteroid buster, was a two-stage double nuclear penetrator. A special chamber encased the first-stage nuke. For the initial nanosecond of its detonation, the energy from the exploding atom bomb focused in one direction, generating an intensely powerful x-ray laser beam. Even though the nuclear detonation obliterated the device a fraction of a millisecond later, the initial powerful beam disrupted molecular bonds deep into the target. To preserve the integrity of the second nuke, the same focusing physics diverted a significant portion of the first nuke's energy away from the trailing stage's hardened nuclear weapon.

Shedding sacrificial layers of carbon steel, the second nuke bored through the resultant blast and into the tunnel of plasma-state matter. Even without the nuclear laser assist, the second stage slammed into the target with enough kinetic energy to go through one hundred twenty feet of reinforced solid concrete. Theoretically, the combined effect could drive the second nuclear device ten times that depth, up to twelve hundred feet, into solid rock. Set prior to launch, a collapsing-capacitor timer detonated the second nuclear device when it reached the center of the target.

It was rumored the design came from a weapon initially drawn up as a bunker buster for use in an all-out nuclear war. However, this will be the first full-scale aboveground deployment of the device.

When General Tannehill called with a brief description of the alien ships and the apparent threat portended by their silence and appearance, Colonel Newcastle had framed a quick battle plan. He decided to attack the first two targets—one in D.C., and one in Moscow—with eight simultaneously fired missiles. Depending on their success, he would further divide their forces, attacking the rest of the alien fleet before more cities were lost.

Each ship only carried four missiles, so they had to maximize their effectiveness.

Colonel Newcastle's fighter raced along its assigned vector. In less than two seconds, all seven of the remaining fighters reached their designated initialization points and turned inbound on their attack trajectories.

~

"It looks like they're spreading out, surrounding the entire ship," Richard said as they watched the scene develop.

Jake studied the evil-looking alien visage. "I see some structures on top of the head. I hadn't noticed them before. It almost looks like a ... bridge."

"That thing is huge," Victor said. "Those fighters look like gnats. They don't stand a chance."

"Obviously they think they do, and considering they're apparently our last hope, we better—"

Suddenly, brilliant light haloed the enemy ship. In an instant, its intensity grew too bright for the camera. The satellite's video feed washed out.

~

The ship's huge size amazed Colonel Newcastle. They were inside its shields, but they were still a mile from their target. Even at this distance, the ship filled his forward screen.

Thank God our theories on how the drive would penetrate a force field were right. Otherwise, this would have been the shortest counter-attack in the history of warfare.

What happened next was so quick the human eye could not truly appreciate or capture it. If you filmed the event with a high-speed camera and slowed the playback, you would see the ships simultaneously dart at the alien ship from seven discrete attack angles. In a millisecond, they reached the desired speed and released their missiles. Then the ships instantaneously changed course ninety degrees. Shooting straight up, they rocketed out of the area with enough speed to outrun the ensuing nuclear shock wave.

Colonel Newcastle's helmet visor auto-darkened as a brilliant light enveloped the wing's seven remaining fighters. Reaching the relative safety of space, he turned to observe the effectiveness of the attack.

CHAPTER 26

"Oh God, we lost them," Vic cried. His plaintive words echoed in the control room's cemeterial silence.

As the brilliance faded and the video feed resumed, a second explosion ripped through the giant ship. Glowing with dazzling internal brilliance, hundreds of fissures spread across the ship's component asteroids. Then it blew apart. Huge pieces of various sizes plunged into Chesapeake Bay.

They stared at the screen in shocked silence, then all three men screamed with joy. Richard wrapped Victor in a bear-hug. The small lieutenant's feet left the ground. Jake laughed, then he heard the radio crackle to life. "Wait, listen."

"... Wing, this is Vampire Six, over."

Richard set Victor down. "It's Colonel Newcastle."

"They made it," Vic whispered.

"This is Bravo Wing," replied a voice with a thick Russian accent. "We're three minutes from engaging the bastards that just hit Moscow."

The news slammed Jake. "Oh, fuck."

"Damn it! I'm sorry, Vlad."

Jake heard his shock mirrored in the colonel's voice.

"They hit D.C. too," Colonel Newcastle said, his East Texas drawl heavy with the news. "We don't know what the weapon did, but I'm pretty sure it ain't good." The colonel's voice took on an urgent tone. "Anyway, we don't have much time, so I'll make this quick. We hit them en route to New York. The tactic worked. The enemy ship was destroyed. As briefed, divide your wing into four pairs. Attack the remaining ships in teams of two. I'll split up Alpha Wing, and we'll do the same."

"Comrade, I know we discussed this, but are you sure a pair of ships can handle one of these things? It is huge."

"Believe me, friend. Two will be enough. We hit it with seven." The colonel paused, chuckling menacingly. Sharing Newcastle's apparently vengeful elation, Jake imagined him staring down into the steaming, partially submerged remnants of the shattered enemy ship. "It was destroyed ... completely, serious overkill."

"Da, Vampire Six. My wingman and I will attack this one. Thank you for the news, comrade."

"Make 'em pay, Vlad."

"Oh, I will," the Russian commander said with an ominous tone. "Bravo Wing, out."

Jake dug a headset from the uniform piled in front of the radio. Sliding it over his head, he detected the faint scent of the previous user's aftershave. Looking down, he saw a name tag:

TANNEHILL

"Oh shit," he said.

Seeing the same thing, Richard bowed his head. After a silent moment, he lifted an angry glare to the enemy ships on the large monitors. "He was a good man."

Undoubtedly thinking of his parents, Vic had a sickened expression.

Jake placed a reassuring hand on his shoulder. "They may have been out of town."

Shaking his head, Victor's gaze shifted from wall to floor. His expression transitioned from glare to lost stare.

Frustrated, Jake shook his head. "There's nothing we can do for anyone here. Let's focus on what we can do for those left." He keyed the mic. "Vampire Six, this is Turtle One calling from Space Control, over."

"Roger, Turtle One ..." said Colonel Newcastle with evident confusion. "You're in Space Control?"

"Yes, sir. I wanted to find out what happened."

"Is this Captain Giard?"

Jake paused, looking at the mic. *This guy is well informed.* "Uh ... yes, sir, it is."

"Okay, good job, Captain. What is our situation on the ground?"

Jake swallowed hard. "Sir, D.C. appears to be a complete loss."

A long silence followed Jake's words. "Thanks for your report, Captain. I'm sure he's on the horn with the President, but I need to speak with General Tannehill. Please call him to the radio."

Jake cast a forlorn glance at the general's name tag. "I'm sorry, sir. It reached here too."

Another pause. "That deep underground?"

"Yes, sir."

"General Tannehill?"

"Gone, sir."

Silent, Jake stared at the radio, giving the colonel a moment to digest the news. When the pause started to feel too long, he reached for the mic then stopped as the speaker crackled to life.

"What happened?"

He looked from Vic to Richard. "Honestly, sir, I don't know. Structurally, everything is intact. Buildings, trees, and equipment are all still standing. Even machines and electronics still work, but all the people are ... gone."

"Gone?"

"Yes, sir. It looks like they ... vanished. All we've found is piles of clothes left where they dropped. We haven't found any bodies, even down here."

Deafening silence streamed through the radio speaker. "Gentlemen, I need to know the range of that weapon."

Jake gave Richard a meaningful glance. "Yes, sir. We were already working on a plan to do just that."

"Good. This thing must have a recharge time. I can't imagine they would've let us within its range if they could've simply activated the weapon and vaporized us. So, if my fighters are going to be successful, we need to know how far to stand off when they're about to activate it."

Jake hadn't thought of that. He was impressed with how fast the colonel accepted the disastrous news and shifted back into strategizing.

Newcastle continued. "We'll work out the timeline, but I need your team to find its range."

"Roger, Vampire Six," Jake said. "We saw some activity in Western Maryland. We'll head that way. I'll report back to you on this frequency."

"Good, copy, Turtle One. I've split my wing into three groups. We're heading to our next targets, so get me that data ASAP."

"Roger, Six, Turtle One out," Jake said, pulling off the headset. He turned to see Captain Allison and Lieutenant Croft already heading for the door. After a quick glance back at the alien ships on the monitors, he turned and followed.

Captain Sandra Fitzpatrick's steady rhythmic breathing, a technique born through years of cardio training, belied the horror gripping her soul. *The teddy bear, oh God, the teddy bear.* An image she couldn't shake, the vision would haunt her for the rest of her days.

Earlier, while jogging toward the distant terminal building, Sandy came across a still idling airport transfer bus. Hoping to use it to expedite the crossing, she peered into its closed glass doors. In spite of the eastern glow of the coming sunrise, she couldn't discern details through its dirty windows. However, the bus looked empty.

Jamming her fingers into the rubber gap between the panels, Sandy tried to pry the split glass doors apart. After a fruitless, half-minute struggle, she finally noticed a backlit, recessed emergency-release button left of the door. Activating it, Sandy heard a short blast of compressed air. She jumped as the doors popped two inches out of their opening and then parted, each sliding in opposite directions.

"Hello?"

No reply rose above the bus's droning diesel engine.

She took a tentative step into the opening. "Is anybody in here?"

Standing half in the doorway, Sandy screamed as two strong hands, squeezing from both sides, grasped her shoulders. Another blast of compressed air burped from under the bus, and the door trying to close on her retracted.

"Shit!" Sandy kicked the right panel of the retreating glass door and shook her head. *Keep it together, Captain Fitzpatrick.* She stepped all the way into the bus, and its doors slid closed. Air-conditioner blower noise replaced the engine's. Getting over her skittishness, she stepped into the driver's compartment. In the dawn's wan light, the seat looked empty. Groping in the darkness, Sandy worked her way closer. A few awkward seconds later, she finally dropped into it.

Something was wrong with the seat. It felt like someone had left a towel or cloth on it. Running her fingers across the material's loose, rippled surface, Sandy froze, remembering what she saw while peering down into the empty F-18's cockpit. An uncomfortable hard object dug into her right thigh. Wide-eyed in the dark, she leaned left and pulled it out from under her leg. Breathlessly holding the object up, she studied its angular silhouette against the deep turquoise hue of the early morning sky. A round ball on one end and a long rod on the other, it felt metallic. With her opposite hand, she blindly searched the instrument panel for a light switch. A huge windshield wiper arm sparked to life, its dry, rubber blade chattering against the dirty glass. Another switch later, the bus's cabin lit up like an exam room. Sandy blinked and squinted as the sudden blast of light burned her dark adapted eyes.

Finally able to see, she squinted at the device in her hand. Struggling not to scream, Sandy dropped the artificial hip. Jumping to her feet, she looked down to see a bus driver's uniform strewn across the compartment. While the driver's shirt was on the floor, the pants, belt still buckled, lay in the seat. She saw several shiny objects littering the interior of the pants. Bending, she looked closer. In a sudden epiphany, she recognized the parts as titanium screws.

What the hell could do that? She looked from the strewn articles, to the screws, and finally to the artificial hip where it had landed next to her right foot. *Why isn't there any blood?*

Backing away in shocked dismay, Sandy stumbled. Regaining her footing in the bus's central corridor, she looked aft and froze. Visible in the cabin's stark, white light, emptied articles of clothing littered the entire bus.

A glint of light drew her attention to one of the front left seats. A teddy bear's half-open, glass-bead eyes peered from under a vacated toddler's outfit. On the narrow bench, a little girl's tiny white and yellow dress sat between piled clothes of an apparent mother and father. Worn in anticipation of an early morning departure to some exciting destination, the tiny girl's yellow ribbons and pink bows now lay strewn about her emptied clothes.

Sandy had a mental image of the parents casting horrified glances at the monstrosity hovering overhead while they tried to calm their frightened little girl. But in Sandy's vision, she and Jake were the anxious couple. The child between them was the little girl with golden locks that she'd often imagined would grace their future. Unconsciously, her hand drifted to the point where the baby bump would soon show.

As a tear threatened to breach the levee of her lower eyelid, Sandy extended a trembling hand toward the stuffed animal. After a short hesitation, she caressed its furry belly.

The teddy bear's lifeless, doll-like eyes snapped wide open. "Are you my mommy?"

That was several minutes ago. She couldn't remember leaving the bus. The next thing Sandy knew, she'd been running across the tarmac with tears flowing down her cheeks, an agonized wail streaming from her throat.

Further investigation wasn't necessary. The scene in the bus told her all she needed to know about what had happened to San Francisco. She didn't think a search of the terminal or the city beyond would reveal anything new. Besides, she had no desire to subject herself to more of that imagery.

The same scenes of sudden abandonment were evident in every direction. Here, a truck's rear end protruded from a ditch. On her right, a tug towed a train of baggage trailers in a large, perpetual loop. She imagined the operator's empty shoe must be wedged in the accelerator pedal.

Sandy ran faster toward Gate Twenty-One. Focusing on the object drawing her in its direction helped stifle the shock. Winded in spite of her extensive cardio training, Captain Fitzpatrick finally arrived at her destination. Unable to hear anything over the scream of a nearby jet, Sandy placed a hand against the vehicle's thick, metallic skin. She was relieved to feel rhythmic vibrations pulsing through its chassis. Left in park with all of its lights on and flashing, the large fuel truck was still running.

Only fifty feet away, a massive pile of shattered safety glass surrounded the large, black tires of a Boeing 777 nose landing gear. Convulsing under the unrelenting thrust of its massive, screaming turbofans, the wide-body jet was jammed into the expansive glass wall of Gate Twenty-One.

A windstorm blasted across Sandy as she opened the driver's door of the fuel truck. Flowing across the cab from the open passenger window, air rushed to fill the void created at the turbine inlet only twenty feet behind her.

As Sandy climbed into the seat, a loose strand of blonde hair whipped across her eyes. She pinned it behind an ear and scanned the gauges. The tanker only had 600 gallons of Jet-A fuel.

"That will have to do."

The fighter's landing gear blow-down feature only works once. Afterward, the gear stays locked down until a mechanic resets the system, a process requiring tools and equipment not at Sandy's disposal. The resultant high drag and slow speed meant a flight to Nellis required more than 600 gallons. However, it was sufficient for the trip she had in mind. Sandy knew plenty of fuel waited at her next destination.

Depressing the truck's heavy clutch, she dropped its transmission into gear. Releasing the pedal caused the vehicle to lurch into motion. Running through the gears, Sandy coaxed the heavy truck up to speed, gradually pulling away from the noise of the Boeing's roaring jet engines. After a few moments, a new sound supplanted the turbine cacophony. Surreally, Barry Manilow's *Copacabana* blared from the truck's speakers. Following a cable extending from the radio's face, she found the music's source. The driver's iPod sat on the center console.

The sight reminded her about the phone in her flight suit's leg pocket. Digging it out, she pressed the power button.

Returning to Western Maryland, the *Turtle* screamed past the raging inferno of the crashed airliner. Jake pointed through the view-wall. "Keep an eye out. We're nearing the area now."

After making their way back to the *Turtle*, they had departed D.C., heading toward Western Maryland. Richard was at the controls. "I'm keeping it slow enough so we'll see if anything changes between here and the edge of the blast area. Hopefully, the weapon's effect drops off at a distance."

An unending panorama of carnage scrolled across the view-wall. Jake's horror mounted as every passing mile brought additional signs of sudden abandonment. Uncountable columns of smoke stretched to the horizon. Blazing pile-ups clogged corners and intersections. Homes burned as their untended heat sources found additional fuel. Shaking his head, Jake said, "It hasn't changed yet."

As they neared the Appalachians, dark shadows coalesced from the smoky haze to form the mountain range's foothills. Nestled amongst them, a small town materialized.

Pointing, Jake said, "That's the last place I remember seeing movement."

Richard slowed the ship. They crossed the town's eastern edge at a thousand feet above ground level. "You're right," he said, pointing to the community's far side. "From up here, I can see some activity on the town's west end."

Looking at the motionless urban scenery beneath the *Turtle,* Vic shook his head. "Yeah, but it's still dead on this side," he said somberly.

Jake gestured toward the grassy slope of an open-air park just east of the town center. "Let's land over there."

As Richard extended the landing gear, he said, "Good thing the locals haven't ventured over here yet, they'd take one look at this ship and assume we're the bad guys."

Jake's iPhone started ringing. Digging into his leg pocket, he said, "I forgot I had this." Pulling it out, he saw Sandy's picture on the screen.

A swipe of his finger connected the video call. For a moment, Jake couldn't tell what he was seeing. Then a light illuminated, and he saw Sandy's beautiful face. It looked like she was in the cab of a truck. Barry Manilow's nasal crooning erupted from the phone's speaker.

Copacabana? "Sandy?"

"Jake? Oh, thank God!" Sandy yelled over the crazy music. "Shit! Hang on." Barry's voice died mid-Copa. Then Jake heard her grunt as he saw her throwing something through the truck's open window. "Enough of that shit."

"Baby? Are you okay?" he said.

She looked into the phone's camera. "I'm a long fucking way from okay, but I'll live. What about you? Where are you?"

"I'm ... okay, so far. I'm with Richard and Vic." Turning to his wingmen, he mouthed, "Let's go."

With a final look at the panorama of carnage visible through the ship's view-wall, Jake turned and walked toward the airlock. "I won't be able to talk much longer, baby."

"Where are you?" she asked again.

After a quick glance at the alien ship's strange interior, Jake shrugged. Considering the day's events, the program's secret status was a moot point. "I'm in Western Maryland ... in a spaceship."

On the screen, Sandy's face froze as she stared unblinkingly back at him. After a few seconds, her eyebrows raised in a go-on gesture.

"A galactic government loaned it to us." She still didn't respond, so he continued. "It's part of what I've been doing since the ... uh, accident. Anyway, we're assisting the fighters that destroyed the enemy ship over Chesapeake Bay."

From across the continent, Sandy stared through the phone's screen as the news left her speechless. A diesel engine droned over the speaker. A moment later, she found her voice. "Oh no ... oh my God. One hit the East Coast too?" Then, apparently registering his last words, she raised sanguine eyes. "We killed one?"

"Yeah ... wait. Where are you?"

"I'm in San Francisco."

Joining the other two in the airlock, it was Jake's turn to freeze as fear gripped his soul. "Get out of there, Sandy!"

Richard and Victor swapped concerned glances. All three of them had seen one of the alien ships peel off the main formation and head toward the West Coast.

When Sandy's voice returned, Jake heard tremendous emotions straining her words. "It already hit here." She paused, looking down. When she looked up, Jake heard and saw the tears. "Everybody's gone."

Over the next couple of minutes, they exchanged stories. Sandy relayed a brief synopsis of her experiences, both in the air and on the ground. Jake told her what they'd seen over Maryland and inside the Pentagon.

The news that they'd also lost a huge swath of the West Coast hit Jake hard. On the video, he watched the same gut-wrenching emotions march across Sandy's face.

Then her expression morphed into anger. "What Galactic Government? Is that who is attacking us? Is this—"

"No," Jake interrupted. "I promise, these aren't the same aliens."

"But ..." She paused, apparently searching for the right words. "Why are they attacking us? What could we have done to them?"

"We can't figure that out either, baby. But thank God you had that engine problem. As far as we can tell, their weapon has some effect out to about a hundred miles. If you'd been any closer, I probably would've lost you too."

Holding the phone with one hand, she grabbed the fuel truck's single-point refueling nozzle. "Hang on." Sandy set the phone on the tarmac under her F-22's wing.

Looking up from the camera's grounded point of view, Jake watched as she wrestled the heavy fuel hose to the fighter's refueling socket. Grabbing the nozzle's two handles, she slammed it home. Throwing her whole body into the movement, Sandy wrenched it ninety degrees to the right, locking it into place.

Watching the nozzle, she picked up the phone and pointed at the tanker behind her. "There's enough fuel in this truck to get me to Monterey Regional." Sandy's gaze turned from her aircraft to stare into Jake's eyes with a meaningful look. "That's about a hundred miles south of here. I gotta check on my parents."

"Oh shit," Jake whispered.

"Yeah, they live a few miles southeast of the city." A tear ran down her face.

Jake stared into her beautiful eyes. Picturing the desolation spanning the hundred miles between D.C. and his current location, he looked into the iPhone's camera and lied to the love of his life. "I'm sure they're okay, baby."

"I can't lose them, Jake." She paused, shaking her head, then her lower lip trembled. "I can't lose my daddy." Before Jake could say anything, Sandy's expression hardened, banishing the scared little girl who had momentarily cracked through her brash façade.

She cast a look at the fuel truck. "All right, Captain Giard, this thing is almost done. I have to get back in the air and report to General Pearson."

"Yeah, we have to get going too. Colonel Newcastle is waiting for our report."

Sandy brusquely swiped a tear from her cheek, then she pointed at him. "Come back to me in one piece, Captain Giard."

"You too, Captain Fitzpatrick."

As her finger approached the screen, she mouthed, "I love you."

Jake mouthed, "I love you, more." The call ended. He stared at the blank screen for a moment then nodded to his wingmen. They proceeded through the airlock, emerging into Western Maryland's cool, crisp air. Standing outside the *Turtle,* they studied the surreal scene of rising smoke columns littering the eastern horizon.

"We've seen this, let's keep moving," Jake said. Turning to head toward downtown, he found himself staring into the cavernous muzzle of a very large double-barreled shotgun.

"Freeze, you sons-a-bitches!"

CHAPTER 27

Angered by her displayed weakness, Sandy batted away another tear. *I can't believe I let Jake see that!* Wrenching the empty fuel truck's nozzle free, she resisted the temptation to toss it on the ground. Sandy rolled it back into the truck and turned off the pump. Climbing into the vehicle, she stared at the western hills. Retrieving her phone and selecting her parents' home number, Sandy placed the call. After the fifth ring, it went to voicemail. Turning a desperate glance south, in the direction of Monterey, Sandy ended the call and closed her eyes. "Please be okay."

After a moment, she punched in the general's number, took a deep breath and placed the call.

General Pearson answered on the first ring. "Talk to me, Captain Fitzpatrick."

Taken aback, Sandy hesitated. Finally, she said, "It's bad, sir. Really bad."

She described the scene in the bus, leaving out the teddy bear. Also, she told him about her conversation with Jake. None of the news seemed to surprise him, including the downing of an enemy ship. After a brief pause, she told him of her Monterey plans.

"Okay, Captain. Go there and let me know what you see on the ground, but continue on to Nellis as soon as you get refueled."

Expecting this, Sandy countered. "Sir, on the ground, I can travel to the weapon's boundary and find out what's happening there."

"No, Captain." His tone brooked no compromise. "Colonel Newcastle is forwarding Captain Giard's reports. I won't discuss our plans on a non-secure phone line, but I need you and your aircraft back here."

Sandy's heart sank. Stunned, she was speechless.

Taking her silence as consent, the general continued. "Thanks for your report, Captain. Come see me when you get back to Nellis."

"Yes, sir," she said weakly.

The call disconnected, and Sandy mutely stared at the phone. After a moment, she dialed her parents again. This time, she tried each of their mobile phones as well. Maddeningly, each went to voicemail. With their cellphones, she'd expected as much. At night, they always turned them off. Hoping they might wake and receive them while she was airborne, Sandy left messages on each.

She took a deep breath and let it out in a long sigh. "Okay, Captain. Time to get to work."

After looking at the two jets still sitting nose-to-nose, Sandy dropped the truck into gear. Intending to inch it forward until the front grill contacted the leading edge of the Lear's left wing, she tried to slip the clutch. However, it refused to cooperate. The truck lunged forward. Sandy winced at the sound of metal scraping metal. Fortunately, the jet's brakes weren't set. Bouncing off the front of the truck, the aircraft rolled back a few feet. She nudged the Learjet a few more times, cringing and saying sorry after each impact. Several crunches later, Sandy finally cleared enough space to maneuver her F-22.

Hopping out of the truck, she sprinted to her waiting F-22. Without a boarding ladder, she used the fighter's built-in steps and hidden handholds to scramble into the cockpit.

In clear violation of regulations, Sandy left her phone turned on and clipped it to her approach plate chart holder. The position would allow her to see the screen should her parents call while she was en route. Sandy planned to stay at an altitude low enough to permit cellphone reception.

Finally buckled into the ejection seat, she ran through the start checks. A couple of minutes later, both engines were running, and all systems were online. Ready to taxi, Sandy pressed the F-22's right toe brake and eased the left throttle forward. Responding to the asymmetrical forces of differential thrust and braking, the fighter pivoted about its right main landing gear.

As the nose swung through north to point east, yellow light flooded her cockpit. The blazing sun was rising over the San Francisco Bay and the backdropping Oakland Hills. While the towering storm cloud hid the golden orb from direct observation, the calm bay waters acted as a mirror. From behind the cloud, the sun's reflection burned a fiery trail across the bay. Like spokes attached to a hidden hub, its radiating golden beams framed the cloud in wasted beauty. Ominously, a lightning bolt shot out, striking a grounded tanker ship. Sitting on a rock jetty, the badly listing vessel appeared to have broken open when it ran aground. Leaning to the right, or starboard, the massive ship sat in a spreading pool of crude oil.

Suddenly, light Sandy mistook for the lightning strike's afterimage blossomed into a rapidly growing fire. Its luminosity soon eclipsed the sunrise. Thick, black smoke roiled from the ship's surface. Within seconds, the water itself was on fire. It was insanity ... and utterly beautiful.

From the F-22's cockpit, Sandy watched in amazement. Craning her head left and right, she realized the entire horizon was dotted with columns of smoke. The burning jet at the runway's north end and the tanker to the east were only two of what appeared to be thousands of uncontrolled fires.

"San Francisco traffic, this is Air Force Seven-Niner-Zero-Papa. I am departing Runway Zero-One. Any traffic in the area please advise."

"Dragonfly Five, this is Omaha Four-Four on tactical."

Sandy selected the appropriate radio. "Go ahead, Four-Four."

"I copied your San Fran radio call. Be advised, we still have no traffic in your vicinity. All inbound commercial flights have been diverted. As before, I'll be your air traffic controller. What are your intentions?"

The controller's steady uninflected monotone voice was in stark contrast with Sandy's internal conflict and the apocalyptic panorama confronting her. Taking a deep breath, she willed herself into a calmer state. "Omaha Four-Four, I only have enough fuel to make Monterey Regional. I should be able to get more there."

"Five, be advised, I still can't raise Monterey Approach."

Sandy's thoughts returned to her family. She looked south again. *Daddy?*

"Dragonfly Five, this is Omaha Four-Four. Did you copy?"

"Yes, I copied," she said weakly, unable to keep despair from her voice.

Raw emotions melted through the controller's disconnected monotone. "What did they do?" The Air Force airman paused. Sandy could tell by the background noise that he was still transmitting. He still had his mic key depressed. "I'm from the Bay Area. I have a satphone, but I can't get anyone to answer. Is everyone all right? Are they ...?" He stopped, unable to finish the question.

Sandy was speechless. She'd been completely immersed in her potential loss and the apparent real loss of all the people who, a few hours previous, had occupied the clothes, buses, airplanes, terminals, West Coast, and East Coast. Now she realized, at a personal level, this would hit everyone.

If anybody is left alive.

Sandy had no reason to think the aliens would stop before every man, woman and child on the planet was dead. She didn't understand why they had attacked Earth without provocation. How could their hate for us be so ingrained that they would build massive ships with a plainly human skull depicted so grotesquely? While she couldn't understand the hate, it was overtly manifest in their ships and actions. Considering all of that, it was hard to imagine them not using a weapon this effective to its final conclusion.

"Five? Are you still with me?"

"Sorry, Four-Four. I don't have any good news for you. It looks like everybody is ... gone. I'm sorry, I have to get going, can't tell you more right now."

She took a deep breath, steeling herself for the work ahead. She would go to Monterey, get some fuel, and only stay long enough to verify the weapon's effect on the area. Colonel Newcastle's forces had proved the aliens could be defeated. She needed to get back to Nellis as soon as possible. An apparent plan was in the works. In the long term, the best hope for her parents and the rest of the world was for a military victory. She would try to call her parents again from the ground in Monterey. After that, she had to follow the general's orders.

Not waiting for more questions, Sandy called the controller, shifting back to standard radio protocols. "Omaha Four-Four, Dragonfly Five on Runway Zero-One, ready for departure. For a final recon, I'll make a low pass over the city before turning south for Monterey."

A long pause followed her radio call. The man's voice returned choked with emotion, but he resumed standard radio protocols. "Roger, Dragonfly Five. Cleared for departure. I have no other traffic in your area. Following your recon, cleared direct to Monterey Regional." Through a stifled sob, he added, "Godspeed, Captain."

"Thank you, Four-Four. Dragonfly Five copies cleared for takeoff. Will advise when I turn direct Monterey. Five, out."

Taxiing past the massive double-decker Airbus at the runway's south end, Sandy studied its inflated emergency slides. Encircling their bases, piles of clothes and bags marked the spot where each person had succumbed to the weapon's effect. Two widely dispersed trails of clothing streamed away from the aircraft. One led toward the bay to the east, the other toward the nearest terminal building. It looked like some people ran toward the nearest shelter, others appeared to have simply run away from the monstrous alien ship hovering overhead.

Sandy's eyes returned to the slides. She saw a civilian pilot uniform stuck on the nearest slide's yellow surface. Knowing the captain would've been the last to depart, Sandy realized the crew had shut down all systems and abandoned the plane with the passengers.

That's why I didn't see it sooner, there were no lights left on.

Clear of the Airbus, Sandy steered her fighter to intercept the runway's centerline. Ready to put the airport and its teddy bear behind her, Sandy firewalled the throttles. Pressed deep into her seat, she watched the withering column of smoke rising over the burned-out, partially submerged fuselage to the north. Judging by the fuel required for a fire of that intensity and duration, the wide-body 747 had probably been en route to Tokyo or some other Far East port of call. However, its journey had ended far short of that. The weapon's energy wave must have hit just as the pilots started an emergency takeoff. If not, the 747 would have crashed well beyond the departure end of the runway, perhaps hundreds, if not thousands of miles later.

Captured like a macabre snapshot by the energy wave's near-simultaneous eradication of all life, the positions of the A380 parked at the south end, and the burned-out 747 at the north end painted a picture of escalating chaos in the minutes before the hovering ship deployed its main weapon.

As her fighter accelerated through takeoff speed, Sandy applied aft pressure to the control stick. Her F-22 rose gently from the runway. Initially banking right to avoid the smoke billowing from the Boeing, she then banked left as the burning tanker, its fire still growing, passed to the right. Turning slightly left, toward downtown, Sandy throttled back, wanting to stay low and slow.

"Any traffic in the San Francisco area, Air Force Seven-Niner-Zero-Papa is five miles southeast. Will be crossing downtown at one thousand feet AGL. Any traffic in the area please advise."

As expected, the radio remained silent. With the exception of Omaha Four-Four's symbol, her F-22's tactical display was void of air traffic. The last of the empty aircraft had either crashed or continued flying straight and level beyond the sensor's range. As far as Sandy could tell, nothing bigger than a large bird was airborne within 100 miles of San Francisco Bay.

She wanted to check the city center. Reasoning the efficacy of the alien weapon might attenuate when the target's density rose above a certain level, Sandy hoped to see signs of life. If the weapon's effect could be overloaded by a dense population center, what better place to look than downtown San Francisco.

Crossing over the eastern edge of the area, she turned her fighter. Flying low in a left bank, she studied the motionless streets as Transamerica's iconic, thousand-foot pyramid passed on her left, its pointed peak rising higher than her current altitude.

Sandy strained to see through the exceptionally smoky air clogging the atmosphere over this part of the city. She gasped as the source of the obscuration came into view. The slopes of Telegraph Hill on her right, as well as Nob Hill and Russian Hill to her left, were ablaze. Reminiscent of photos she'd seen of the immediate aftermath of the great earthquake of 1906, whole blocks were involved. With no one to fight them, the fires were spreading from house to house. Flames leapt hundreds of feet above the homes, framing Russian Hill's crooked Lombard Street. Stacked at the bottom of the street's switchbacked section of road, several cars burned in a Detroit-fueled bonfire. Devoid of their controlling occupants, the cars had left a trail of destruction in their wake. As they careened down the steep hill, they had crashed straight across the center of Lombard Street's retention walls and flower beds.

Ubiquitous fires littered the scene. The speed with which untended technologies ran amuck amazed Sandy. She knew crashed cars caused many of the fires. However, flames also leapt from buildings in the middle of roadless blocks. She envisioned a flaming stove top with a spatula's plastic handle melted into a puddle. Completing the imagined scene, a wedding ring sat in the middle of the bubbling plastic, still lying where it had dropped from a vaporized hand.

Sandy shook off the unbidden vision. Ahead, Fisherman's Wharf emerged from the haze in stark clarity. A strong, northwesterly wind blew the smoke inland. Several businesses burned, but the onshore breeze quickly carried the smoke away.

Banking her fighter hard right, she circled back around. Extending her flaperons, Sandy slowed to a velocity just above the F-22's gear-down stall speed. In a few moments, the wharf was back in front of her. Craning her neck for a better view, she saw the movement again. Having grown up in Northern California, Sandy had visited the Bay Area on many occasions. So, when she saw the location of the moving bodies, she instantly realized what they were.

"How are you guys still alive?"

Somehow, the energy wave hadn't affected the famous Pier 39 sea lions. Apparently startled by the roar of her passing fighter, several of the sunbathing beasts rolled off their floating docks. Their huge mass cast jets of salt water onto the buoyant panels.

Additional movement on her other side drew Sandy's attention. She banked hard left. It was a horse-drawn carriage. Apparently panicked by the fires or Sandy's fighter, a frightened horse was galloping down a street bordering the waterfront. A loose collection of clothes was all that occupied the carriage's front bench.

How could it only affect humans? Angry and confused, Sandy shook her head. "Fuck it!"

Retracting the fighter's flaperons, she shoved the throttles forward and banked the fighter. Setting the GPS to Monterey Regional Airport, Sandy engaged the autopilot. As the aircraft climbed above the Presidio, she checked out the Golden Gate Bridge on her right. Another vehicular bonfire was growing on the nearside of the central span. A tanker truck on the edge of the conflagration suddenly detonated. Cars and debris shot in every direction as the mushroom cloud exploded skyward. Water fountains sprung up beneath the bridge as smoldering chunks rained down from above.

The apocalyptic scene mercifully faded to gray as her fighter rose through a cloud bank drifting in from the Pacific. No longer able to hold back the rising tide of emotions tearing at her soul, Captain Sandra Fitzpatrick sobbed uncontrollably.

Staring into the cavernous maw of a very large double-barreled shotgun, Victor froze mid-step, slowly raising both hands. Captains Giard and Allison did the same. From the other end of the cannon, a huge sheriff glared down the weapon's sights. "Who the hell are you?" he asked. Without taking his eyes or the gun off of Jake, he nodded toward the *Turtle*. "And where in the *hell* did that thing come from?"

Intelligent eyes peered from the deputy's confused face. The man had the haggard look Victor often saw in the eyes of pilots returning from Afghanistan. He thought it came from seeing more hell in a single deployment than most people experienced in a lifetime. The officer's eyes darted to Victor, then Captain Allison and back to Jake. Apparently registering their uniforms, his evident confusion doubled. "Well?" he demanded.

Richard held his hands in front of his shoulders, palms facing the deputy. "We're from the Air Force." Without lowering his arms, he pointed an index finger toward Washington, D.C. "We're trying to find out how far that weapon reached, and what it did."

Still aiming the shotgun at Jake's face, the deputy nodded toward the *Turtle* again. "That doesn't look like any Air Force ship I've ever seen."

Jake nodded. "Suffice it to say, the government still has a few secrets." Slowly, very slowly, he offered his right hand. "I'm Captain Jake Giard."

After a few tense seconds, the deputy relented, his expression and stance softening. Lowering the shotgun and shifting it to his left hand, he shook each of theirs. "I'm Sheriff Larry Biggs."

Fitting name, Victor mused as he glanced down.

His mother's voice chimed in. *I can't believe you didn't piss yourself.*

"Shut up," Victor muttered. All of the men looked at him. He shook his head. "Sorry."

After an awkward silence, Sheriff Biggs turned his confused look on Captain Giard. With an Appalachian accent thicker than Victor's, he said, "I sure hope you boys can clarify what the hell's been goin' on. The news on the radio is crazy. Stories of giant alien ships appearing over cities worldwide, and suddenly, they lose all contact with those cities."

Captain Giard shook his head and pointed southeast. "I wish I could tell you it was just the one, but the radio reports are right," he said. "There is some good news, though. Our fighters destroyed the ship that attacked D.C., and they've gone after the rest of them."

The deputy seemed to breathe for the first time. "Oh, thank God."

Jake nodded. "It's a start, but we need more information. Our fighters need to know how far the weapon reaches and what happens there."

The sheriff's face darkened. "I can show you what you're looking for. Ain't no use trying to describe it, though. Follow me," he said. Turning and breaking into a run, he shouted over his shoulder. "It's in Old Downtown."

After exchanging glances, all three pilots followed at a jog. A quick block and a half later, they rounded a corner onto a long street and found themselves in the crosshairs of a squad of the sheriff's deputies.

Almost falling, Victor slid clumsily to a stop. "Oh fuck," he whispered.

Slowing to a brisk walk, and still loosely holding the shotgun in his left hand, Sheriff Biggs raised his right and shouted, "All clear."

Up the street, the obviously edgy officers lowered their weapons. Fifty yards northwest of Victor and, therefore, fifty yards farther from the weapon's epicenter, the sheriff's men stood in front of a large group of nervous-looking civilians.

An apparent historical district, Old Downtown looked like a tourist haven. Blocking automobiles while permitting pedestrian traffic, large evenly spaced ornate stanchions guarded each end of the main thoroughfare. Nineteenth-century gas lamps decorated both sides of the cobblestone roadway, and antique awnings adorned the red-brick shopfronts.

This morning, many of the tourists had apparently started their shopping early. Deposited by vaporized shoppers on a busy morning, emptied articles of clothing littered the scene. Looking around, Victor realized they were everywhere. He pointed at the scattered piles. "Holy shit!"

Mounds of clothes lined both sidewalks, some propping open shop doors, others had dropped as their occupants vanished while crossing the street. Having spilled from dropped bags, their early morning purchases lay strewn amongst the scattered articles.

Scanning the street while proceeding northwest toward the group, Vic did a double take and stopped mid-step.

Seeing him, the sheriff nodded. "Yep, that's what yer looking for."

"Is that?" Vic started, then froze. "No ... no, oh my God." Breaking from his paralyzed epiphany, he ran to the corner of a nearby storefront, retching the whole way.

Pussy! His mother's disembodied voice chided.

"I didn't expect this," Richard said between his own nauseated chokes.

Victor stared at the gory panorama. Unable to accept the reality streaming into his eyes, he shook his head. "I never even *imagined* this."

Approaching the edge of the weapon's effect, Jake studied a collection of lumpy piles.

Standing unsteadily, Victor ignored his mother's unending rant and walked to Captain Giard's side, almost tripping on the way. Apparently, the energy wave struck a large group of shoppers standing in the middle of the road. In a day full of horrors, this was the worst. It was also the first blood he'd seen. Although Victor feared it wouldn't be the last.

Of varying thickness, blood-soaked piles of clothes formed a clearly delineated boundary. Immediately outside that line, partial bodies still occupied sleeves, pant legs, and skirts. Based on the missing parts, you could discern the walking direction of each victim. Seeping from cleaved bodyparts, vermillion rivulets flowed down the street. Adding to the calamitous milieu, the jagged red stripes that covered the scene looked like the work of a demented artist loosed on a blood bank.

A pale Captain Giard shook his head. Gesturing to the bloody streaks, he said, "I recognize this pattern. I saw the same thing after a terrorist attack in an open-air market outside Bagram Airfield. The arterial spray released by the suicide bomber's shrapnel painted the same design."

"Oh my God," Richard gasped as he dropped to his knees next to a woman's emaciated remains.

Apparently facing southeast, it looked like she had been walking toward ground zero. The weapon took the front half of her head, neck, and torso. Her right leg and left arm were missing as well. Soaked in blood, the woman's clothes were too flat in those areas. Except for the intact garments, it looked like a giant butcher's cleaver had bisected her midstride.

"As far as we've looked, the boundary line continues southwest and northeast. We sent several survivors to the emergency room with partial amputations," Deputy Biggs said, looking haggard again.

A new wave of nausea rolled over Victor. Bending over, he threw up the snack he'd scrounged as they left the Pentagon.

There's my boy, his bitter mother said sardonically.

Before Victor could say anything, more ham and cheese splattered the cobblestones.

Jesus wept!

Captain Giard gave Victor an appraising stare, then shook his head in disgust. Vic couldn't tell if it was directed at him or the scene.

The captain turned back to Sheriff Biggs. "How far from here to D.C., as the crow flies?"

One of the bystanders raised a hand. "I'm a private pilot. Before Nine-Eleven, I used to fly there from Cumberland Airport. Now it's too much of a pain in the ass, what with all the airspace restrictions." Seeing Captain Giard's impatient expression, the man shook his head. "Sorry." He pointed south. "Cumberland is just across the river in West Virginia. From there to Ronald Reagan Airport is ninety-three nautical miles or about a hundred and six statute." He scratched his head and added, "I'd say it's about the same distance from right here."

"Thanks for the info," Jake said, nodding to the stranger. He pulled Captain Allison to his feet.

Having seen more than enough, Victor turned away from the carnage. Feeling pale-faced and wiping a sleeve across his mouth, he stood next to the captains in the center of the street.

Captain Giard turned to Sheriff Biggs. "We need some weapons.

The ship we're flying is unarmed, and I feel totally naked in combat without my sidearm. I doubt we'll be in a position to need them, but I'd rather have them and not need them than vice versa."

Without hesitation, Biggs offered the captain his shotgun and nine-millimeter. He gestured to two of the other deputies who responded in kind after a slight hesitation, handing both Victor and Richard a pistol and shotgun as well.

"Thanks, gentlemen," Jake said, nodding to each.

With a final look at the carnage strewn across the otherwise peaceful city street, Jake turned and trotted back toward the *Turtle*.

Victor looked nervously at the pistol, then tucked it into a flight suit pocket. His sweaty palms had already stained both weapons. He shifted the shotgun to his trembling left hand. As he turned to follow Captain Giard, Victor heard a female's high-pitched cackle behind him. It took all his will not to look back.

Pussy.

CHAPTER 28

"Oh shit," Sandy whispered. Ahead of her fighter, a massive cloud she had mistaken for a huge thunderstorm resolved into a roiling smoke cloud. The churning black column extended tens of thousands of feet above the airport. At its bottom, the furnaces of hell appeared to be consuming the entire Monterey Regional Airport.

The sight brought a new fear. Approaching from the north and short of fuel again, Sandy saw no place to land. It appeared that flames completely engulfed both the general aviation ramp to the north of the main runway complex and the commercial terminal on the south side.

She decided to do a low pass recon along the airport's west side. As in San Francisco, the onshore breeze fed comparatively clear oceanic air into the western portion of the airfield. However, smoke from the multitudinous smaller fires dotting the city drifted across the field. So, clear was a relative term.

The airport's inferno was passing on Sandy's left. As she crossed the departure end of the east-west-oriented Runway Two-Eight Left, a gap in the smoke clouds came into view. Forming an atmospheric canyon, the onshore breeze was driving a river of clear air between the boiling black clouds.

That was when the source of the spreading fires came into view. It appeared that tank farms on either side of the east-west runway had ruptured and breached their retaining walls. The unrestrained spreading fuel had flooded the area. Everything was burning from the inside out.

While the chasm of clear air was in no way an optimal landing area, Sandy was out of fuel and options. As she'd expected, the flight from San Francisco had taken every bit of fuel she'd been able to scavenge from the chaos of SFO. She had to land here now or risk an ejection somewhere else later, and not much later at that. Ejections were a dangerous option. A not insignificant percentage ended in serious injury or even death. Considering the current situation, even something as simple as a broken leg could be fatal. Emergency medical attention wouldn't be available.

Sandy quickly realized her refueling plan was also going up in smoke. In a hellish cascading calamity, the conflagration had spread to every aircraft, fuel truck, and fuel system on the flight line.

The fighter's computer had already warned her several times about its low fuel status. Sandy needed to land, now.

Unfortunately, the scene here was worse than what she'd experienced at San Francisco airport. While it was daylight here, spreading smoke and fire cast dark shadows and faltering light. The onshore breeze wasn't enough to deflect the main fire's superheated smoke column from its heavenly aspirations. It shot vertically for thousands of feet to form the clouds Sandy had initially mistaken for a cumulonimbus thunderstorm. However, coupled with the smoke drifting in from the city, there were more than enough satellite fires of lesser intensity to spread smoke across the runways and city east of the terminal area.

Sandy's heart raced as she considered her options. She looked again at the relatively clear air streaming between the two blazing halves of the airport. *Land in that sucker-hole or punch out.* "Shit!"

"Omaha Four-Four, this is Dragonfly Five. It's bad here. The whole damned airport is on fire."

Apparently waiting for her call, Four-Four responded immediately. "Roger, Five. What are your intentions?"

"I'm out of options. I have to land here ... or eject. I think there's enough room on one of the runways." Sandy banked her fighter to circle around the airport's south side. To take advantage of the slower touchdown speed the onshore winds would afford, she needed to land to the west. "I'm circling to land on Runway Two-Eight Left. I'll give you a call when I'm safely on the ground."

"Roger, Five. I'll be standing by. Omaha Four-Four, out."

Finishing her long, looping turn, Sandy flew through the smoke drifting east from the southern fire. Emerging back into her chasm of clearer air and facing west, Sandy aligned her fighter with the runway. Day seemed to shift to night as her fighter passed into the space between the two conflagrations. It was almost claustrophobic as the walls seemed to be closing in on her.

On Sandy's right, a new massive explosion burst from the center of the black cloud. In the moisture-laden coastal air, a rapidly expanding vapor shield of a supersonic compression wave shot out from the smoky chasm wall. Sandy's aircraft and body shook with its passing. For a moment, her fighter rocked sideways. A quick correction leveled it just as she planted the F-22 on the runway.

The jet decelerated hard as Sandy activated maximum braking. From the direction of the new explosion, the roiling black cloud to her right bulged as if reaching out for her fighter. As the cloud shifted from charcoal black to brilliant gold, a forty-foot flaming object materialized. Rolling like a burning tire, one of Monterey Regional's massive fuel tanks, apparently blown from its foundation and set rolling on its side by the latest explosion, bounced out of the fire and into her path. It was too big and moving too fast to avoid. There was no time to react. Her fighter was on a collision course.

Sandy grabbed the ejection handles and yanked. In adrenaline-filled time dilation, she heard and felt each of the sequenced explosive charges fire in slow motion. As her fighter rushed to its doom, Sandy heard the canopy jettison. The leg arrestor's squib fired, reeling her boots from under the instrument panel.

Like a flat-sided bowl rolling on its edge, the approaching tank loomed, its top forming the bottom of the bowl. Too fast, it grew to blot out the sky ahead. Sandy recoiled, throwing her arms over her face as a protective shield as her fighter was drawn into the waiting monster's open maw.

Finally, the ejection seat's rocket motor hammered her spine. Sandy narrowly escaped being bisected by the tank's rigid lip. Shooting vertically out of the cockpit, she saw the squat cylinder's jagged metal edge flash past, just missing her legs. Had the ejection motor kicked in a thousandth of a second later, she would have caught the tank's upper edge in the middle of her body.

Below her, the F-22 and wayward fuel storage tank met in a tremendous explosion. The scant fuel remaining in the fighter's wings flash-burned. The tank rocketed forward, shooting ahead of Sandy and her still rising ejection seat. Fortunately, the tank's walls contained the explosion, shielding her from the shrapnel-like projectiles screaming from the impact.

Another rocket motor whooshed overhead as her ballistic parachute deployed. The combination of self-righting rocket boosted ejection seat coupled with a parachute that rapidly deployed under its own smaller rocket motor gave the F-22 a zero-altitude ejection rating.

Under her parachute canopy, Sandy drifted earthward. The onshore breeze carried her farther downwind, away from the burning lump of tank and fighter. Breathing heavily, she snapped her head left and right, studying the walls of fire and smoke bracketing the runway. *Thank God I'm not being blown into that.*

She was drifting away from the burning wreckage. However, debris littered the runway ahead of Sandy. Chunks of aircraft and tank littered the area where the parachute was taking her. Exacerbating the situation, she was facing the wrong direction. She was going to land downwind. The parachute was adding its forward airspeed to that of the tailwind.

Sandy looked left and right again. Unless she wanted to risk flying into a wall of fire, turning was not an option. The debris-cluttered runway rushed up to meet her. An exceptionally large, twisted chunk of unidentifiable metal lay directly in her path.

Sandy yanked the parachute's right riser. The chute responded to that side's additional lift and drag by swinging her away from a direct impact. However, the pendulous action reached its apex just before she struck the ground. At the last second, her body dropped sideways, slamming her left hip and shoulder into the runway's surface.

The impact knocked the breath from Sandy's lungs. She felt something give in her left knee. Then a burning sensation shot up her left arm. A few feet later, fighting to breathe, she finally slid to a stop.

From her curled-up position on the runway's skid mark-blackened landing area, Captain Fitzpatrick threw back her head, mouth agape, struggling to draw air into her burning lungs. After a seeming eternity, she managed to pull in a ragged breath. The acrid air sent her into a coughing spasm.

Battling her way upright, Sandy almost fell as the pain in her left knee blossomed into pure agony. Bent at the waist, struggling to balance on her right foot, she fought to maintain the hard-won vertical position. Rummaging through the debris littering the runway, Sandy collected a bent piece of aluminum strut that worked as a makeshift crutch. Turning back, she spotted a pool of blood. A trail led from it.

Looking from the puddle to the line of red drops, Sandy followed them to where they connected to a smaller puddle under her left arm.

"Oh shit!"

Grimacing, she pulled up the flight suit's sleeve. Blood streamed from a ten-inch slice running the length of her left forearm. Below it, dark red blood soaked her flight glove. Crimson rivulets criss-crossed the painted surface of the aluminum strut gripped in her trembling hand.

Sandy frantically scanned the runway for the ejection seat. She needed its first aid kit. Finally, her eyes landed on the tangled, burning mass of fighter and tank, realizing her seat must've dropped into it.

"Crap!"

Sandy hobbled to the fluttering, tangled parachute. A chunk of twisted metal held it on the runway. Finally catching a break, she almost felt lucky. Digging out her survival knife, she hacked out a long ribbon of silk. After a few minutes of tugging with her teeth and right hand, Sandy fashioned an effective pressure bandage out of the parachute's canopy.

Now for the knee.

Like unending thunder, the jet fuel-fed fire shredded the atmosphere. Whipped into a frenzy by the conflagration's insatiable demand for oxygen, the channel of air rushing down the runway flapped and tugged at the ensnared chute. Sandy used another strip to tie back her blowing blonde hair.

She found two short pieces of aluminum strut. Placing them on either side of her busted left knee, Sandy fashioned a splint by wrapping a long strip of silk around the whole thing.

Scrambling back to her feet, she made a quick assessment. While significant blood had soaked her forearm's pressure bandage, it appeared the bleeding had slowed to a trickle. Tentatively, Sandy transferred some weight to the bad leg. Fresh pain erupted, but it was manageable. She inventoried her equipment. In addition to the survival knife, her Beretta 9mm pistol still hung in its shoulder harness. Patting her leg, searching for the iPhone, she came up empty. Standing, Sandy looked at the burning wreckage of her F-22. "Shit." Left on the chart holder, it had gone up with the fighter. Pulling the emergency radio out of her survival vest, she studied its boxy form. "At least you're all right."

Sandy started coughing again as more smoke drifted over the runway. *I have to get out of here.*

The wind had blown her closer to the east end of the field. While she was still between the two raging infernos, she was at their eastern edge. The airport's boundary fence lay beyond the end of the runway. Sandy saw something embedded in it. Leaning heavily on the makeshift crutch, she limped eastward.

As she emerged from between the fires, the oppressive heat finally relented. Sandy allowed a little hope to creep in as she identified the object she'd spotted. It was an airport maintenance pickup truck.

A few minutes later, she hobbled to the truck's side. Inaudible over the din of burning airport, its engine was still running. Nosed into the chain link fence, its body panels vibrated as the still engaged motor struggled against the restraining perimeter barricade. A man's empty coveralls and work shirt lay in a heap under the steering wheel.

The driver had locked the door, but fortunately he had left the window rolled halfway down. Standing on her tiptoes and reaching through the opening, Sandy pulled the inner handle. The door popped open. A startled scream slipped past her lips as a hard hat fell out, landing on her right boot. Resisting the angry urge to sweep the pile onto the dusty ground, Sandy folded the clothes and respectfully placed them into a neat stack on the edge of the road, topping it with the boots and hard hat. The collection looked like an odd memorial. She supposed it was.

Sandy climbed into the truck. As she suspected, it was still in drive. Selecting reverse, she backed the truck away from the fence. Initially, it snagged the truck's front bumper. She pumped the accelerator, but the fence wouldn't let go. On the third attempt, it finally broke free. Being careful not to run over the airport worker's memorial, Sandy guided the truck back onto the perimeter road.

Ahead, paralleling the airport boundary, the road disappeared into the northern fire. Behind her to the south, the other conflagration obscured that end of the road. Hammering the truck's accelerator, Sandy spun the truck one hundred eighty degrees. Following the perimeter road south she crossed the runway's east end. Here the road disappeared into the southern fire.

"Shit!"

Sandy looked west. The runway was still a narrow canyon between two churning walls of fire and smoke. "Screw that!"

Looking left, she studied the fence and the down-sloping terrain beyond. She knew Highway 68 lay at the bottom of the scrub-covered hillside that formed the airport's eastern boundary. The road's southeast trajectory would take her farther from the weapon's epicenter. Had she still needed to find its range, Sandy would take that route. Also, it led to her parents' home. She could only hope they were outside of its reach. Along with a pang of worry, an epiphany blossomed, and a plan took root.

"That's it!"

With her aircraft destroyed, along with apparently every airplane at the airport, Sandy realized she now had a good excuse to check on her parents.

Utilizing her handheld emergency radio, Sandy contacted Omaha Four-Four and appraised him of her situation. Shocked to hear she had ejected, the controller kept asking if she was okay.

Glancing at her leg, she said, "I'm a little banged up, but nothing I can't handle." Since the iPhone likely was a melted bubbling lump, Sandy had the controller relay her plan to General Pearson.

A few minutes later, the Base Commander's response came through. "Sorry to hear about your fighter, but glad you're okay. I like your plan, Captain. I'll see you back here when you're done."

Smiling for the first time that day, Sandy tucked the radio into its holster. The truck rolled to a stop pointing due east, aimed straight at the field's perimeter fence. Sandy buckled her seat belt. After a few deep breaths and a short prayer, she floored the truck's accelerator.

The airport maintenance truck crashed through the fence. With the inertia of its thirty miles an hour velocity, the vehicle shredded the wire mesh. Now outside of the airport's perimeter, Sandy struggled to rein in the truck as it sped down the sharply sloping terrain. Braking, Sandy felt the tires slide across the hill's gravelly surface. Unsuccessfully, she tried to steer away from a doomed scrub bush. The impact sent leafless brown branches flying. The plant's root mound launched the truck, its tires momentarily leaving the ground. Sandy braced her hand against the cab's ceiling, glad she'd put on the seat belt.

Letting off the brakes, Sandy finally gained a measure of control. As long as she kept the tires rotating and didn't turn the steering wheel too sharply, she could maneuver around the biggest obstacles.

A horrifying minute later, the truck crashed through a wood rail and passed from the steep limestone onto the gently sloping grass of a small municipal park. Rolling to a stop, Sandy leaned against the headrest. Staring at the sagging dust-covered headliner, she slowed her breathing, willing herself to calm down. Another bout of coughing wracked her body.

She killed the pickup's engine. Grasping its handle, Sandy threw open the door. Spilling out of the truck's cab, she fell to the damp grass, crumpling awkwardly onto her side because of the splint on her left knee. She breathed deeply between coughs. While she was able to purge the airport's smoky air from her lungs, she knew she'd never purge the horrific visions of the last few hours.

Looking around, Sandy rolled onto her butt. Intermixed with the sweet aroma of freshly mown sod, the bitter smell of damp bird guano wafted from under a nearby tree. An asphalt jogging trail ringed the park. Scattered piles were all that remained of the early morning joggers present when the alien's energy wave struck. While the majority of the people in San Francisco had known of the menacing alien presence hovering over their city, many here had likely not been aware of their other-worldly presence. When the ship approached from the south, its catastrophic atmospheric entry had reportedly laid waste to a huge swath of Southern California. However, the ship had passed this area slowly enough to go unnoticed by most. They may have heard distant sonic booms, but many had likely written it off as something with a terrestrial origin and gone back to sleep.

Sandy saw plenty of evidence the Montereyans had been going about their normal morning rituals. A collection of three bicycles painted a tragic scene. Two lay on their side, while a third, smaller bike stood in the middle, its training wheels still holding it upright. Lying on its right side, Mom's pink-trimmed mountain bike led the way while Dad's black bike brought up the rear. His black biking gear and safety helmet, as well as Mom's pink gear and helmet, sat strewn around the bikes. The toddler's pink and lime-green shirt had fallen across her pink bike's handlebars. White handgrips, their red, white, and blue tassels fluttering in the wind, protruded from either side of the tiny shirt. Buffeted by the onshore breeze, the little girl's safety helmet rocked like an upside-down turtle in front of the small bike.

Sandy imagined the threesome pedaling in formation, the parents assuming their normal protective stations front and rear. In her mind's eye, Sandy saw herself on the front bike, looking back at Jake and then to a beautiful blonde girl with the same curly golden hair she'd had as a toddler. Then night turned to day as the onrushing energy wave filled the sky. All three froze in horror. As it neared, they screamed in agony. Deafening silence fell over the scene as the weapon's life-stealing wall of light passed. As if in slow motion, their empty clothes and unsupported bicycles drifted earthward.

Shaking her head, Sandy banished the disturbing imagery. To her left lay another tiny outfit, this one trimmed in blue. The bird shit-tarnished odor of toddler-trampled sod still hung in the park's air. However, all that remained of the little boy was the small, turf-stained shoes and clothes that had hopped, rolled, and tumbled with him through sandboxes, over climbing-timbers, and down slides.

Sandy looked down. Unbidden, her hand had gone to her abdomen again. She hadn't told Jake about the baby yet. She'd thought about it during their video call, but she wanted to tell him in person.

Standing, Sandy turned back to the truck with mounting anger. The park's scenery was too much. Everywhere she looked, signs of lost life screamed for recognition. Her hormonal state turned every loss personal. She couldn't help but see every tragic waste of human life from a first-person perspective.

Sandy placed both hands on her stomach. Her maternal instinct kicking in, she'd never felt so protective. Glaring at the northern horizon, in the direction the aliens had departed, she screamed, "Fuck you!"

Ready to put the scene behind her and get on with the mission, she turned and stepped toward the truck. An advertising flyer tumbled across the grass. It came to rest against Sandy's right calf. As she climbed into the truck, she grabbed the yellow sheet. Across the top, it read: "Buck's Sport and Fish." Under a long-handled fish net graphic, it said: "Open till 9:00 p.m. Saturday and all day Sunday for last-minute Father's Day shoppers."

Forlornly, she looked southeast. "Please be okay, Daddy."

With reverence, Sandy set the damp sheet on the seat next to her right leg. Wiping another tear from her wet cheek, she started the old truck's engine. Placing it in drive, she guided the vehicle across the park, turning to avoid running over any of the small piles of clothes or bicycles.

As the truck dropped across the curb onto Salinas Highway, Sandy turned it southeast. The tires squealed as she floored the accelerator. Slowly, it rattled up to sixty miles per hour. She pressed the pedal harder, but the pickup refused to go faster.

Behind Sandy, the park's disturbing milieu shrank. Dwarfing it, the airport's inferno painted a hellish panorama across the truck's rear and side-view mirrors.

She spent the next few minutes negotiating the highway's post-apocalyptic obstacle course. Several times Sandy had to veer to the shoulder and even off the road to maneuver around pileups. As she'd seen from the air, the wrecks were concentrated at intersections and bends in the road.

Finally, she approached the crossing highway that would take her over the ridge separating Salinas Valley from her parents' Carmel Valley. A burning heap of cars, SUVs, and tractor trailers blocked the entire intersection.

She bounced on the bench seat as the airport truck rode over the curb and into a bank's tree-lined parking lot. Picking her way around and through the confused mass of vehicles, she worked her way across the lot. Passing between a burned-out hulk she recognized as a Toyota Highlander and a still running, late model red Camaro, Sandy gasped and locked the truck's brakes. Something about the car made her do a double take. It was running, and the doors were open: something she'd already seen numerous times. However, in its ashtray, a wispy trail of smoke rose from a half-burned cigarette.

Sandy leaned across the cab and cranked the truck's right window halfway down. "Hello, is anybody there?"

For a moment, there was no response. Then she heard a commotion inside the bank. It was hard to tell over the combined noise of the truck and Camaro engines, but it sounded like someone was arguing. Unbuckling her seat belt, she slid across the bench seat. Sandy reached for the door handle, but before she could open it, a sallow face peeked out from inside the bank. The hollow-cheeked man was sporting a three-day beard partially obscured by the long, greasy hair dangling in his face. A look of anger and hate banished the nervous curiosity. Apparently, seeing the roof-mounted lights and the airport logo on the door, the man mistook the truck for a police vehicle. "It's the fucking pigs!" he yelled.

From nowhere, he produced a huge shotgun. Before Sandy realized what was happening, the truck's right mirror and half-open window exploded in a cloud of flying glass and metal. Sandy screamed. Sliding back in her seat and ducking, she floored the accelerator, the truck lurched and died. Cursing, she put the transmission in park and fumbled with the keys. Two excruciating seconds later, the engine fired up.

Glass shards rained down into her hair as another shotgun blast took out the rear-view mirror and driver's side window. Sandy couldn't believe this white-trash asshole was trying to kill her. "I'm not a fucking cop, jackass!"

The click-clack sound of the idiot pumping another round into the shotgun's chamber rewarded her communication efforts. Not willing to wait for improved discourse, she dropped the transmission into drive and hammered the truck forward, tires squealing as it raced away.

Sandy hazarded a peek over the truck's steering wheel just in time to avoid plowing into one of the trees lining the parking lot. Yanking the wheel to the right, she guided the pickup across the landscaping and onto the intersecting Laureles Grade Highway. She knew the road well as it had been the route her parents used to cross from Carmel Valley to Salinas Valley on their regular trips to and from Monterrey.

Panting through gritted teeth, Sandy stared ahead. Periodically, she cast nervous sideways glances into the left mirror that had miraculously escaped destruction. The truck lumbered its way back up to the agonizingly slow sixty miles per hour governed limit. The rising, winding road cut back and forth several times. Finally, it straightened for a mile. Reaching the far end, she allowed herself to relax as the red Camaro failed to manifest. Sandy hoped the road was well enough off the beaten path to dissuade the looters from veering too far away from the chain of gold mines that the Salinas Highway represented.

Slowly prying her white-knuckled fingers away from the steering wheel, she flexed the blood back into them. Sandy willed her respiration rate down, fighting to rein in her emotions. Now anger had rejoined the party. Except this time, the catalyst was terrestrial in origin. She was amazed that the situation had degraded to looting so quickly.

The realization brought in a whole new concern. With her parents at the periphery of the weapon's effective range, she now realized they were also at the advancing forefront of human society's darker side.

Sandra pressed the accelerator harder. Stubbornly, the pickup refused to break sixty.

Five minutes later, she crested the ridge and passed into Carmel Valley. Like undulating corrugated ribs, parallel lines of grapevines rose and fell as the unending panorama of the valley's ubiquitous vineyards unfolded.

Frustratingly, driving downhill afforded no additional speed. The old white and blue pickup rattled down the winding country road at a steady sixty miles per hour. On both sides, purple-accented, lush green vinery slid past at a glacial pace.

The scenery brought mixed feelings. As memories of her parents competed with worry for their safety, nostalgia and dread sat side-by-side in her heart. Cool, dry air whipped an unrestrained strand of blonde hair across Sandy's eyes. Annoyed, she tucked the wayward lock behind her left ear, then pounded the truck's steering wheel. "Come on, you piece of shit. Move!"

Ahead, where organized lines of vines gave way to open cow pasture, the road made a sharp turn. The rural highway swept left, but fresh wheel tracks continued straight, leading to a new hole in the pasture's barbed-wire fence. Beyond the breach, the rear bumper and spare tire cover of a black H2 Hummer protruded from a ditch.

Slowing for the curve, Sandy studied the scene. The rocky soil showed little sign of the vehicle's passage. A couple of scrub bushes had fresh damage. Dragged from their original upright positions, several fence posts on either side of the break in the barbed wire leaned away from the road.

As the pickup rounded the corner, the scene moved into the truck's right window. Taut as a guitar string, a single strand of wire stretched from the last upright post on the left side. Running through a broken post laying on the ground, the wire appeared to be tangled in the Hummer's undercarriage.

Something moved in Sandy's peripheral vision. Snapping her head left, she slammed on the brakes. "Shit!"

A black and white cow stood in the middle of the road. The truck slowed to thirty miles per hour, but it was still too fast. The surging anti-lock brakes wouldn't stop the pickup in time.

Sandy yanked the wheel right. With the road still curving left, the truck shot off the paved surface. She missed the beast, but the left mirror ran out of luck. Striking the bovine's left hip, it shattered and fell off the pickup.

Crossing the gravel on the road's right shoulder, Sandy spun the steering wheel left.

It didn't respond.

Blasting through the barbed-wire fence, the truck created another exit for any additional cows remaining within the field's confines.

As if hitting a surface covered with ball-bearings, the old pickup seemed to accelerate as the pasture's gravelly hardpan afforded the tires no purchase. To Sandy's horror, the Hummer-eating ditch passed under the sliding truck's front right fender. Then the vehicle's slow left spin threw the right rear tire into what Sandy now realized was a small washout.

The truck fell sideways into the gully, striking the wash's dusty floor with a bone-jarring impact. The collision threw Sandy across the cab, slamming her into the right door as the truck finally stopped on its right side, wedged between the narrow walls of the arroyo.

The impact knocked the wind out of her. After a few hard-fought ragged breaths, she lifted her head from the dirt floor, filling the blown-out right window. "Holy shit!" she growled through clenched teeth. Doing a personal inventory, she tentatively flexed her arms and legs. Finding no new injuries, Sandy gave silent thanks that it hadn't been the same side she'd injured when the last-minute parachute maneuver had slammed her into Monterey Airport's Runway Two-Eight Left.

From her crumpled position on the inside of the truck's right door, Sandy reached up and switched off the truck's ignition. The sputtering engine finally fell silent.

From the bottom of the sideways cab, the truck's interior felt like a skinny phone booth. Overhead, the left window looked impossibly distant. With her uninjured leg, Sandy kicked at the shattered windshield. On the third try, the whole thing popped out as a flexing mass. Another string of profanities followed as she scrambled through the opening. Glass crunched underfoot as she stepped onto the crumpled windshield.

As Sandy inspected herself for cuts, a new shadow crept across the gully. Throwing her back against the dirt bank, Sandy snatched the nine-millimeter pistol from its shoulder holster and pointed it at the shadow owner's head.

Apparently uninjured, the offending cow stared at her over the edge of the gully. Silhouetted against the deep azure sky, its backlit black and white ears twitched. Regarding her, the cow batted its ludicrously long eyelashes. Somehow, Sandy resisted the urge to put a bullet between those eyes.

"Stupid cow!"

The animal blinked again and licked its snout. After snorting its disapproval of her appraisal, the cow turned and sauntered out of view.

She pushed off the wall, returning to her feet. Holstering the Beretta, she scanned the wash for a way out. Here, the sides were completely vertical and ten feet tall. Looking past the pickup, she spotted the other vehicle fifty yards farther up the gully. There, the sides didn't look as steep.

Squeezing through the narrow gap between the truck's roof and the wash's west wall, Sandy walked up the small ravine toward the H2 Hummer.

CHAPTER 29

"All attack squadrons are to launch the instant we drop out of parallel-space!" ordered Admiral Thoyd Feyhdyak, Commander of the Galactic Defense Force's Third Carrier Group.

His massive command ship, the *Galactic Guardian*, headed the task force. Similarly named, and second only to the *Helm Warden* in mass, it shared the same grand design, history, and military capability. He was confident of a quick victory against the Zoxyth. *I just hope we're not too late.*

Thoyd watched the countdown in his EON's synthetic vision.

One of his staff read it out loud. "Three, two—"

A second early, the entire fleet snapped out of parallel-space. Unceremoniously, the Guardian and its formation of ships slammed into regular space. The forward star-field orb exploded to encircle the ship. Thoyd expected Earth's sphere to swell from a pinpoint and fill the view-wall. However, it barely expanded enough to differentiate from the background of stars.

As if a falling axe had cleaved half his mind, Thoyd's EON lost connection with his Omninet-based self. Judging by the reactions of his bridge crew, they had all experienced the same disconnect sensation. The schism of being cut off from his network-based id left him feeling vulnerable and oddly alone.

An epiphany rocked Thoyd. "Hold all fighters." Dropping out of parallel-space a second early meant tens of light seconds separated them from their planned deployment point. Even with the gravity drive's impressive speed, traveling that far was going to take some time. *So much for the element of surprise.*

Already knowing the answer, Thoyd turned to the officer manning the tactical console. "What happened?"

"A quantum disturbance is jamming our wormhole generator."

Thoyd nodded. "Someone's dropped a disruptor field around the planet." It made sense. The ability to enter and stay in parallel-space required the capacity to open and maintain a stable wormhole. Any technology capable of collapsing that powerful quantum field would easily collapse their zero-width communication wormholes as well. The thought opened up a hopeful possibility. To slow the Zoxyth approach, Admiral Tekamah may have dropped a disruptor in Earth space.

"Are you detecting any GDF transponder codes in system?"

Looking for other Galactic Defense Force ships, the tactical officer ran another sweep. After a few seconds, he looked at the admiral and shook his head.

"Then where the hell is it coming from?"

The officer bent over his console, his fingers dancing above its surface. "The effect is centered on ..." Pausing, he cast a confused look at the admiral. "Earth. It's coming from a body of water along one of the planet's continents."

Turning his attention back to his display, the officer froze, a look of horror banishing his confusion. "Sir! I'm also detecting a faint Zoxyth drive signature at that same location."

Frustrated, desperately wanting to report the development to Admiral Tekamah, Thoyd turned his inner eye to the inactive Omninet link. "How in the hell did Zox get disruptor technology?"

Wide-eyed, the officer looked up from his terminal. "It's not the only Zox ship, sir. I'm detecting fifteen additional ships spread around the planet."

CHAPTER 30

An unending, high-pitched squeal rang in his ears. After an eternity, his eyes fluttered and opened. Flashing amber and red beams swirled through the dark, misty atmosphere. He shook his head, and the ringing subsided, a cacophony of horns rising to supplant it.

Salyth's arm groped in the strobing darkness. Finding the helm, he fought to gain his footing on the slanted floor. Excess moisture was everywhere. With a mighty effort, he hoisted his large frame upright. Struggling to maintain the hard-fought gains, Salyth grasped the sides of the wet console like a drowning drycat lizard. He activated the emergency lights. Very weak, they didn't provide much illumination, but he could see his blood splattered across the console. The tilt of the floor told him the ship was pitched forward on its bow and badly listed to port. Inertial compensators were offline.

Shaking his head, he tried to clear the swamp-fog from his thoughts. "These Argonians will pay dearly for this!" Salyth swore, the words triggering another bout of coughs.

As he actuated the controls to reboot the bridge's computers, one of his officers stirred. "To your feet," Salyth growled, a gurgle rattling deep within his chest. Another wet cough spewed more of his blood across the control panel.

Computers restored, the bridge's artificial gravity re-exerted itself, and the inertial compensators came back online. After a wave of vertigo, Salyth felt the floor level. Although sensors showed the ship was still pitched forward and leaning left.

"I need to know what I have left," Salyth said weakly, this time fending off the cough.

"Yes, Commodore Salyth," the officer said. Struggling to his feet, the junior commander coughed up blood, as well.

While the officer evaluated his computer console, Salyth inspected the bridge. Now that the computers were coming back online, normal lighting filled the cavernous room. The rest of the crew members were dead. Broken bodies and severed limbs littered the bridge. Most of the control stations were black.

"Commodore Salyth, all passages leading from the bridge section have sealed. All communication links are gone. With the built-in redundancies, the only way we could lose all contact is if all other sections were destroyed," the bridge officer reported in a low, guttural voice. "We must be the only viable portion of the ship."

Furious, he wanted to walk over and send the officer to an early meeting with the Forebearers. Knowing he was already shorthanded, he decided to reserve his vengeance for the Argonians.

The officer's next report removed himself from Salyth's ire. "We have no shields, but the bridge section's drive system is coming online." He looked up with a toothy grin. "It appears to be ninety percent operational."

For the first time since regaining consciousness, Salyth felt a glimmer of hope. "Bring up the exterior display!"

"Yes, Commodore Salyth," the officer replied through another bloody cough.

The main display flickered to life. The point of view was from behind and above the bridge looking forward. They had fallen into an angry body of water. Rough, steam-filled waves crashed against the Forebearer's visage.

The bridge was the only recognizable section. Scraggy trusses reached out for missing structures, steam rising from their melted and distorted features.

As Salyth surmised, the bridge section was listing to port and pitched forward, resting on its lower bow. The image of the Forebearer's face buried in this alien estuary's muddy bottom enraged him.

"Get my ship off this filthy planet. I want to know the progress of my fleet."

"Yes, Commodore."

Salyth felt the floor shudder as the bridge section struggled to raise from its watery grave. Turning to the display, he watched the outside view as the ship leveled. It stopped for a moment, the muddy bed unwilling to release its prey. Then it broke free with a final shudder. Clear of the sea, it accelerated toward space. Unshielded from atmospheric friction, the muddy water boiled from its surface and burned up in the ship's meteoric plasma trail.

"Commodore, I have numerous targets entering Sector Sixty-Four!" shouted the officer. He paused for a moment, studying the display. Turning to Salyth with renewed energy, he said, "It's the Galactic Defense Force, sir."

Reaching the desired altitude, the remnant of the *Forebearer's Revenge* parked above the planet's curving surface. "Excellent! Instruct all ships to fall back and reform on my position," ordered Salyth.

CHAPTER 31

Jake toggled the comm panel. "Vampire Six, this is Turtle One, over."

Stepping up to the helm, Richard started bringing the ship's systems online. Vic carried the newly acquired weapons to the left end of the view-wall. As he approached, a rack with a slot for each weapon grew from the floor.

"I still can't understand how it does that," Vic said as he placed the weapons in their appropriate slots.

Richard impatiently shrugged as he grasped the flight controller. "Arthur C. Clarke once said, 'Any sufficiently advanced technology is indistinguishable from magic.' Guess you'll have to go with that."

The ship turned east while gently rising to an altitude clear of the buildings and the gathering crowd. After hovering for a moment, Richard said, "Let's get back in space so we can see what's going on." His arm tensed, and the outside world blurred as the ship rocketed skyward.

Jake activated the radio again. "Vampire Six, this is Turtle One. Come in, over."

The speaker crackled to life. "Turtle One, this is Vampire Six. We're setting up to attack the ship that just hit Mexico City."

Richard looked at him with shocked dismay. "Twenty million people live there."

The news struck Jake like a sledgehammer. "My God, there were sixteen of those ships. How many people have we already lost?"

Colonel Newcastle continued his transmission. "What can you tell me about their weapon's range? What did you find in Western Maryland?"

Swallowing down the rising bile, Jake activated the mic. "It's bad news, sir. It looks like we've lost everyone within ninety-three nautical miles of the weapon. Unfortunately, its effect doesn't fall off with distance." Pausing, Jake shook his head. "Jesus, sir. There wasn't even a drop of blood ... not until the edge, anyway." Recalling the scene in Old Downtown sent a shiver down his spine.

A long pause greeted his report. Finally, Newcastle said, "Almost a hundred miles and no drop off ... holy shit."

Richard said, "Yes, sir. We don't know how the weapon does it, but we've seen, very graphically, what happened to those on its periphery."

"Thank you, gentlemen," Colonel Newcastle said wearily. "I'll call you back after we kill these bastards. I want to take 'em out before they wipe humanity off another two hundred-mile swath of—"

He cut out mid-sentence. By the background noise, Jake could tell he still had his mic key depressed.

"What the hell," Colonel Newcastle whispered. "They're bugging out!" Hope blossomed in a voice that, only a moment before, had carried the weight of the world.

"Say again," Jake said, praying he'd understood.

"They're bugging out, leaving. They just vertically accelerated back into space."

"They must be falling back to regroup after your success over the Chesapeake," Jake said.

"I don't think so," Richard interrupted.

Jake shook his head. "What else could it—?" Turning toward Richard, he froze. Apparently, while he'd been talking with Newcastle, the hologram had come to life. Still rendered in red, the regrouping alien ships appeared to be gathering a couple of hundred miles above the North Atlantic.

Lieutenant Croft pointed at a small red dot that the alien ships were surrounding. "What's that?"

"I don't know, but look," Jake said. Both he and Richard pointed to the display's top left corner.

A new fleet of huge ships was sliding into view, their holographic color: green.

CHAPTER 32

Reaching the floor of the valley, Sandy guided the Hummer onto Carmel Valley Highway. Negotiating another smoking heap of burned-out cars, she turned left, heading south. After a few miles, a city limit sign came into view: Carmel Valley Village Population 4,704. It was the unincorporated rural community her parents called home and Sandy's favorite place on the planet.

Growing up, she'd witnessed the explosive growth of the region's vineyards and wineries. Stone-walled villas dotted the landscape. The lush green peaks of the surrounding hills and the corduroy carpet of vinery flowing across their lower climes looked like a slice of Southern France.

Sandy's concern for her parents deepened with the passage of every desolate mile. She was now just over a hundred of them from the epicenter. She'd been about this far away when the alien ship had fired its weapon. However, other than the looters, Sandy had seen no humans, alive or dead. The expectation of finding someone around each corner was drawing out the search. It was an agonizing never-ending cycle of optimism and dashed hopes.

Sandy's heart raced in anticipation as yet another blind corner loomed. Rounding the bend, she slowed the Hummer. Ahead, forming a T intersection, a secondary road dead-ended into the highway at the apex of the curve. Again she had to inch the vehicle over the curb and onto an empty parking lot to get around an intersection-clogging calamity. On Sandy's right, the back of a black Range Rover protruded from a winery's cobblestone-lined glass storefront. Its engine was still running. A thin wisp of fumes trailed away from its dripping exhaust pipes. Every few seconds, the rear windshield wiper swiped empty air. Apparently blown out by the impact, the blue glass pebbles of the SUV's shattered rear window had rained down onto the crushed cafe patio furniture that jutted from under its rear bumper.

Two obstacles later, Sandy steered clear of the last of the wreckage, guiding the H2 back onto the highway beyond the curving section of road. Her heart skipped a beat. A few hundred yards down the straight roadway, a line of police cars formed a roadblock, flashing red and blue lights adorning their roofs.

Reacting to her sudden appearance, a swarm of police officers took up defensive positions. In a matter of seconds, Sandy was staring down the barrels of several rifles, shotguns, and pistols.

Careful not to make any sudden movements, she allowed the Hummer to roll to a stop. As she'd been going less than twenty miles per hour, the truck halted in a couple of seconds, two hundred feet shy of the heavily armed roadblock.

Sandy killed the Hummer's engine and heard a nervous amplified voice: "—and step away from the vehicle. If you do not turn off the vehicle and show us your hands, we will be forced to open fire."

Sandy realized she was probably the first thing they'd seen emerge from the affected area. Shouting loud enough to be heard across the distance, she said, "Don't shoot! I'm an Air Force pilot."

Even from a couple of hundred feet away, she saw some of the officers visibly relax, the aim of their weapons shifting away from her. Sandy wondered what they'd been expecting to encounter, looters assuredly, aliens possibly. Although Hummer-driving little green men with blond hair seemed slightly less likely. Many of the weapons still pointed at her. Belatedly, Sandy realized she was likely invisible behind the glare of the mid-morning sun reflecting off the vehicle's windshield.

The loudspeaker crackled back to life. "Show us your hands, and step out of the vehicle."

Not wanting to tempt a trigger-happy deputy into firing, Sandy slowly slid both arms through the open driver's window. Grasping the exterior lever, she unlatched the door and eased it open. Swinging her legs out, she placed both boots onto the road's asphalt surface. With her arms still protruding through the driver's side window, Captain Fitzpatrick leveraged her forearms against the top of the door and pulled herself to a standing position behind it.

A few more weapons lowered. However, having shifted from the vehicle to point at her, several still aimed at Sandy. Evaporating her patience, the grainy red flicker of a laser sight's light filled her vision. "Lower your damn weapons, for Christ's sake! I'm one of the good guys!"

A portly, balding officer rose from his crouched position behind a police cruiser's front fender. "Sandy?"

Sandy squinted at the man and then smiled. "Uncle Bobby?"

"Holy shit!" He waved both arms in wide, downward arcs. "Lower your weapons. It's Johnny Fitzpatrick's girl!"

Finally, the last of the weapons veered away from her head. Sandy stepped from behind the door and limped toward the roadblock. Bobby did the same, meeting her in the middle of the impromptu no man's land.

He nodded at her left leg. "Are you okay?"

Sandy waved a dismissive hand. "I'll be all right." She studied his face. Not really an uncle, Bobby had been one of her parents' closest friends. While he wasn't a pilot, he had spent many an afternoon in her father's hangar sharing post-flight beers and war stories with Dad and his small collection of instructor pilots. She'd just seen Bobby a few months back. At the time, he'd looked like his usual self, youthful for his sixty years. However, today he looked bone-weary and haggard. The morning's events appeared to have aged him. Sandy placed a concerned hand on his shoulder. "What about you? You look like I feel."

"I don't know, Sandy." He shook his head. "Between missing bodies and rumors of aliens and the such, everybody's scared shitless. There was an explosion or sonic boom early this morning. Sue and I heard it, but I thought it was lightning. Then we woke up to blinding light and one hell of a burning stomach. Since then, we've had no TV or Internet. Hell, I can't even raise anybody on the radios or the phones. What the hell happened?" He paused, looking over her shoulder. "And where'd you come from?"

She told him about the aliens' arrival and her unit's deployment. Having apparently heard this news, he nodded. When she told him about the energy wave and what she'd seen between San Francisco and their roadblock, the man's face darkened, appearing to sag under the weight of the news.

"It goes on for a hundred miles from here?"

Sandy nodded. "Yeah, and a hundred miles to the north, as well. I've heard it went that far on the East Coast too."

Turning pale, he shook his head. "Oh my God, hun. That's gotta be millions of people."

Sandy nodded. "More like tens of millions." Remembering the San Francisco teddy bear, she shivered. "It's bad, Bobby, really bad."

"Hell, Sandy, I've been a cop for thirty years. Thought I'd seen everything, but I've never seen *anything* like this shit."

"Yeah, I still don't understand what happened to everybody. The way it left the empty piles of clothes is almost worse than finding a body."

Bobby shook his head. "No, hun. It's not the *empty* clothes I'm talking about." He pointed up the street, beyond the line of police cars. "Once you see that crap, you'll wish empty clothes were all you'd seen."

"What?" Sandy said. Her heart pounded with renewed fear. Her parents' home lay less than a mile in the direction he was pointing. "What is it? Are my parents okay?"

"Your parents?" He looked confused for a moment, then comprehension filled his eyes. "Oh, they should be fine. We've had a few reports of broken windows, even some structural damage. Shit, one wacko claimed a giant rock fell from the sky. I wouldn't worry too much, though." Shifting his arms, he pointed east and west. "They're not along the line."

It was Sandy's turn to be confused. "Line?"

"You don't know?"

She shook her head. "I'm supposed to find out how far the weapon reached." Sandy pointed at a pink and white jogging outfit sprawled ahead of a pair of pink-trimmed white sneakers. "But so far it hasn't even tapered off."

Bobby shook his head. "It doesn't."

"It doesn't what?"

"Taper off."

"What do you mean?"

He shook his head again. "It's best you see for yourself." Gesturing for Sandy to follow, he turned toward the line of police cars. Passing between the two closest at a fast pace, he continued talking. "It took us a while to figure out what happened. Hell, I still don't understand it or what exactly *it* was. At first, we thought the aliens had nuked us." He pointed at the Starbucks they were approaching. "But there's no amount of radiation that could do this."

Studying the scene, Sandy saw nothing unusual—at least under the revised definition the day's events lent the word. Like misplaced dirty laundry, a man's suit, draped half in the doorway, lay in a drying latte puddle. Lying where the vaporized hand had dropped it, an empty paper cup rolled back and forth in the morning breeze.

Being careful not to step on the articles, Bobby opened the coffee shop's front door and waved for Sandy to enter.

She stepped over the black suit. "I agree. It can't be radiation, not the kind nukes put out, anyway." Looking at the suit's yellow tie, she pointed down. "But, this is the same thing I've seen since—" Sandy stopped mid-sentence as the rank stench of raw death assaulted her senses. "Oh my God!" It was a smell she hadn't encountered since a particularly bad day in Afghanistan. Holding a hand over her nose and mouth, she retched involuntarily.

Wide-eyed, Sandy looked around the shop's interior. A local artist's flowery offerings hung on one wall. An easel near the door held a small blackboard. A rainbow of chalks spelled out the day's specials.

In colors forming a sickening parody of those adorning the chalkboard, intestines and various other spilled organs traced lines across the floor where they'd run from the middle of a line of bisected bodies. It appeared the weapon had maintained full strength up to its periphery. Unfortunately, the line to wait for service paralleled the weapon effect's outer circumference.

A mix of suits, both athletic and business, formed a fifteen-foot line from east to west. Still partially filled with half-vaporized remains, they lay in uneven mounds. No longer contained by abdominal walls, the innards of many victims had spilled across the coffee shop's floor.

Lying on the tiles behind an empty dress-suit, the front half of a head was all that remained of one customer. Like a swimmer emerging from the depths, a woman's agony-contorted face sat in a crimson halo of blood. Her glazed-over dead eyes glared at the ceiling. The lady apparently kept her dark brown hair pulled back in a ponytail. However, missing its back half, every strand ended at exactly the same point. No longer held tight to the skull, the blood-tipped hair blossomed like an inverted flower, ringing the face in a mane-like mushroom cap.

Sandy looked at Bobby. "This continues east and west?"

"As far as we've checked, anybody that was clear of the line lived." He pointed to her side and shook his head. "On or inside it ... not so much."

Chewing on her lower lip, Sandy nodded. Silently, she scanned the scene. Relief granted by the knowledge that her parents' home lay outside the line brought its own guilt. Wondering if this was what Jake had found in Maryland, she multiplied pi times the two hundred-mile diameter of the weapon's effective range. A quick estimate told her its boundary cut a three hundred-mile arc of carnage across the state. Crossing the beach just south of where Carmel Valley met the ocean, she envisioned the curving line running a hundred miles inland before bending back to rejoin the coast the same distance north of San Francisco, probably around Anchor Bay.

A detail she'd missed earlier drew Sandy out of her thoughts. Conspicuous against the ubiquitous arterial blood streaks littering the scene, one trail led from a gap in the customer queue and out the adjacent exit. Sandy pointed at it. "It looks like there's a missing body."

Grimacing, Bobby pointed through the side door. "That was Hank Stewart. Told me he'd been grabbing a sandwich out of the cooler when it hit. It's a sad day when you count a man lucky for only losing a left hand and part of his ass."

"Where is he?"

"He's headed to the hospital. Farther down the line, we found a couple of people with similar injuries. I packed all three of them into an ambulance. We were going to send them into Monterey, but couldn't raise anybody on the phone. I was worried they'd been hit too. Guess we know for sure now. Anyway, they went south to the ER over in Templeton."

"How many more did you find like this?"

"Not many. Most people were either on one side or the other. Several couples were separated ... permanently." He shook his head. "I don't mind telling you, if I never see this morning's heartache again, it'll be too soon."

Sandy considered the long, arcing trail of carnage. "I hope they can get in."

"Huh? Who?"

"Hank and the others." She pointed east and then curved her hand north. "This continues on for at least three hundred miles. You might as well write off all the hospitals in there. So, that means every hospital within driving distance of the line is probably being overrun."

Bobby looked dejected. "Oh shit."

Sandy stepped to the portly older man and hugged him. "Hey, you did the right thing. Hell, it was the only thing you *could* do, and you probably sent them in the right direction sooner than most."

As he opened his mouth to reply, a new voice crackled to life. Mid-sentence, an anchorman's live image chased away the static test pattern displayed by the cafe's sole television: "...much of that area was devastated by an apparent low-altitude nuclear engagement."

Sandy and Bobby exchanged nervous glances.

The talking head continued. "Not much information has come from the area since the explosion. However, this video just came in. Reportedly, it came from the Chesapeake Bay area. As you know, we've received several reports of a large section of the ship rising from the bay. We cannot confirm the authenticity of this video, but it does match the descriptions we've received." As he spoke, a grainy video replaced the anchorman. Apparently filmed with a camera phone, the image shook unsteadily. In the foreground, tree-covered hills sloped toward a distant body of water that Sandy guessed was Chesapeake Bay. Churning sea fog obscured the bay's far bank. As if whipped by a hurricane, the waters closer to the near shore churned with mad intensity.

The scene reminded Sandy of the damage wrought by the massive waves that rushed inland after Japan's tragic 2011 earthquake. She stared in shocked horror at the near shoreline. It looked like a massive tsunami had stripped the land. From the water's edge to a line a few hundred feet up the hills, a colorless band of exposed soil stretched the full width of the image. The foreground's lush green hills contrasted sharply against the long, gray pile of splintered trees, unidentifiable debris, and chunks of buildings marking the farthest uphill reaches of the tsunami's devastation.

New movement over the far side of the bay drew her attention from the hillside's devastation. The churning fog obscuring those waters bulged upward and darkened. The activity ebbed for a moment. Then a solid black mass broke the fog's surface. Initially, it looked like a basalt rock formation was growing from the bay's floor. The ebony mass slid inexorably from the fog. It soon became obvious that most, if not all, of it had been below the surface. Its height above the cloud bank far exceeded the fog's thickness and still more slid into view.

Sandy's suspicions proved correct when the nostril slits came into view. A massive, shattered alien face broke the fog's surface. White wisps clung to the slowly rising scaled face. Tendrils of vapor streamed from the slits and its reptilian eyes. Oriented toward the camera, the charred and back-tilted head appeared to glare down on the observer, its horrible human trophy still clamped firmly in its jaw.

Rising slowly, the massive alien visage clawed its way into the sky. Its swept-back, horn-like ears dragged streamers of fog into the clear blue atmosphere. Then, under tremendous acceleration, the ship exploded skyward. While it wasn't the physics-defying instantaneous velocity change described by Jake, it was shocking nonetheless. In seconds, a conical, supersonic shock wave haloed the face's advancing front as brute power shoved the non-aerodynamic, chiseled asteroid through the speed of sound. The resultant sonic blast knocked the observer onto his back, blue sky filling the picture. The trees in the image's periphery rocked violently. Many surrendered to the shock wave, falling away. The top of a downslope tree flashed into the image, slamming down only a few feet to the observer's right. The video blurred and then cut out.

Slack-jawed, Bobby turned to her. "What the hell was that?"

"One of the alien ships that attacked us today. Well ... part of one anyway."

He pointed at the TV. "That thing was huge!"

Sandy nodded. "And that was the smallest part of it."

"Holy shit ..." Bobby said under his breath.

Sandy touched the shocked man's arm. "Uncle Bobby, I need to get going."

Dragging his eyes from the frozen image of the sculpted alien head, he turned back to Sandy and hugged her. "Thanks, hun." Stepping back, he nodded toward the north. "Based on what you've seen between here and Monterey, I'm going to send my boys back to their families." Then he placed both hands on her shoulders and gave her a meaningful look. "You found what you told your general you were looking for. Now go do what you really came here to do. Make sure your parents are okay."

Sandy opened her mouth to protest her innocence. She had

another viable reason to visit her parents. She also thought about warning him about the looters, but they'd been pretty far northeast of here. Considering the day's events, his men needed to be with their families more than they needed to guard the dead zone. She closed her mouth and smiled. "Thanks, Uncle Bobby."

~

As Sandy guided the Hummer around Ford Street's last corner, she glimpsed her parents' small neighborhood. Something massive obscured the view of their end of the block.

"Oh, no ..." she gasped.

The size of a four-story office building, a smoking boulder sat across the road. Most homes still stood on the left side of the street, although two appeared to have been crushed under a wall of heavy earth. On Sandy's right, several houses along the west side of the road had disappeared under the rock and displaced earth. Like a tsunami frozen in mid-break, the heaved soil formed a steep embankment around the asteroid. In front of her, the road curled up the face of the wave. The right half of the pavement had folded back on itself, leaving a large slab of road lying upside down at the wave's base. Like a finger pointing skyward, the left side of the street jutted ten feet into the open air above the crater's rim.

The mounded soil and smoking asteroid blocked the line of sight to her parents' home. Sandy sincerely hoped the width of the mountainous rock exceeded its depth. Otherwise, there wouldn't be anything left of them or their house. She didn't want to think what horror awaited discovery if the destruction extended as far behind the crater rim as it did from her left to right.

Sandy slowed the Hummer as it neared the area where the road curved up the leading edge of heaved earth like a ski jump. The horrific scene Uncle Bobby had shown her had been deeply disturbing, but it had also cracked opened the door of hope. Now the giant boulder towering over her slammed it shut.

As it approached the nearside of the crater, the Hummer started up the ramped pavement. Sandy stopped the vehicle and killed its engine. To her left and right, a few people with minor injuries milled about in shock. Otherwise, the street was eerily silent.

In the homes still standing, every window appeared to have been blown out. On the rim's right edge, a disconnected chunk of roof gable lay on its side. Sandy recognized the metal rooster-shaped weather vane jutting sideways from its peak. Since childhood, she had used it to judge the wind direction. Visible from her backyard, the rooster-clad gable had been on the back of their next door neighbor's house. The home belonged to her parents' best friends, Jim and Betty Sanderlin.

There was no way around the mound. Earth, homes, and disassociated chunks of both blocked her on each side of the street. She stepped from the vehicle. Again the surreal silence of the scene struck Sandy. Not for the first time, she felt as if she'd stepped into a nightmare.

A startled jolt ran through her entire body as a frail, feminine voice came from immediately behind her. "Sandy?"

She spun around. "Momma!" Throwing her arms around the slight woman, Sandy hugged her trembling mother tightly. "Oh, thank God you're all right! I've been so worried about you and Daddy."

The shuddering increased at the mention of Sandy's father. The reaction stoked the fires of dread. Pulling back, Sandy placed both hands on her mother's shoulders. She stared into her mom's blue eyes. Like the walking wounded, she too had numerous cuts and abrasions. From her left temple to her jawline, a long, shallow cut ran across her left cheek. As if she'd been hung upside down, a trickle of dried blood ran upward from each auditory canal, ending in small, crusty puddles at the top of her ears. Careful to avoid the injured area, Sandy ran her fingers through the silver highlights of her mom's blonde mane. The similarity of facial features and hair always made Sandy feel as if she were staring into a time-shifted reflection.

"What happened, Momma?"

"I don't know, honey." A confused look filled her face. "The last thing I remember is being in my truck."

"Your truck? Where? Was Daddy with you?"

"No, he never wakes that early. I was heading to my yoga class."

"I don't understand," Sandy said as she searched the road. "Where's your truck? How did you get back here?"

"I never made it off the street. I remember pulling out of the driveway and starting up the road." She paused, rubbing her head. "I heard a huge rushing sound ..." Her voice trailed off, a confused look clouding her face.

"Then what happened?" Sandy prompted.

She shook her head. "I don't remember anything after that whooshing sound."

"How did you end up here?" Sandy looked around again. "Where's your car?"

"It's over there." She pointed at the home to the right of the Hummer. "Behind Susan McClatchy's house. I woke up a few minutes ago hanging upside down. I was still buckled in, but the Suburban was on its roof. It took me a couple of minutes to climb out." Her voice rose an octave as she spread her arms apart. "All the windows were blown out, just ... gone!"

There was a car-sized chunk of roof ridge missing from the McClatchy's home. Seeing where Sandy was looking, her mom pointed at the hole. "I must've hit that. When I was climbing out, there were shingles and splintered chunks of wood all over the place." She ran a finger along the cut on her left cheek. "I think some of it scratched me."

Sandy hugged her. "Thank God you're okay, Momma." Pulling her to her side, Sandy wrapped her right arm around the shorter woman and turned her southward. "Now we have to find Daddy."

"Yes, dear. Let's go," she said with a resolute nod. She started walking, then stopped and pointed at the giant boulder. "Hun, what is that thing? Where did it come from?" She paused and turned to Sandy, fresh confusion twisting her features. "And how did you get here so fast?"

Sandy realized her mother didn't know about the aliens, San Francisco, or all the people who'd vanished.

Picking her way through the carnage, Sandy told her about the strange alien ship and how parts of its asteroidal hull had broken off as it moved toward San Francisco.

"Oh my word! Aliens?" her mother asked. She scanned Sandy's face, apparently looking for a sign that she was joking.

Sandy nodded.

After a moment's consideration, she too nodded and started walking again. Climbing up the mounded earth, her mother looked at the broken houses on each side. A fresh tear streaked through the dust covering her face. "Do you think they've hurt anybody else?"

Sandy couldn't bear to deepen her worries. Helping her over a piece of debris that jutted from the heaped earth, she held her mother tightly and lied. "I don't know, Mommy."

They stepped over a still smoking rock that appeared to have broken off the larger section. Her mother cast a nervous glance at the huge boulder ahead. "I thought an asteroid this big was supposed to make a much bigger crater." She looked at Sandy. "Remember when we visited that big old hole in Arizona?"

"Yes, Mom. That was Meteor Crater."

She nodded. "Yep, that was it. Remember how the guide told us that the whole thing had come from a rock no bigger than half a football field." She pointed at the asteroid. "This thing is at least that size." Spreading her hands, she asked, "Where's the big hole?"

Reaching the top of the mound, Sandy paused and looked down into the crater. It was indeed very shallow. However, the asteroid still blocked the view of her parents' property. Frustrated, she scanned the tortured earthworks for a safe way around the giant boulder. After a few seconds, Sandy spotted a path.

She turned toward her mom and saw her lower lip trembling. Apparently, the conversation had been distracting her mother, keeping her mind from her worries. Sandy's silence had snapped her back to the present. Grabbing her frail, wrinkled hand, Sandy gave a reassuring squeeze and continued the conversation. "Well, Mom, the one in Arizona was going thousands of miles per hour. This one only fell a couple of thousand feet. You heard something because it was traveling less than the speed of sound. Otherwise, you never would've heard it coming."

The lip firmed as her mother seemed to consider this. "I guess you're right, honey." She cast a knowing glance at Sandy. "Now quit worrying about me, and let's go find your father." Then, not waiting for Sandy's guidance, she stepped over the next rock.

"Yes, ma'am," Sandy said. Still tightly grasping her hand, Sandy was yanked forward. It was good to see her mother's fire re-establish itself. As far back as she could remember, her mom had always been full of piss and vinegar, in spite of her diminutive size.

Leading the way, her mother followed the same path Sandy had intended. While avoiding smoldering chunks of asteroid, they climbed over uprooted tree trunks and terrestrial boulders. Each time one of them tripped over hidden roots or slipped while traversing loose gravel, the other's hand gave support.

Several exhaustive minutes later, their end of the street slid into view. They both froze mid-step.

Her mother's free hand flew to her mouth. "Oh, John!"

Sandy cried, "Daddy!"

The front half of the house, including the entire garage, was gone. While the main body had missed it, a separate van-sized chunk of asteroid sat in the center of a crater occupying the space that had previously been garage, living room, and entrance foyer. The rest of the home was wrenched and twisted. Forming a parallelogram, the normally square angles of walls and roof leaned right.

A small section had burned, but a still geysering broken water main appeared to have quenched the flames.

"Come on," her mom said, breaking into a jog down the back of the crater rim.

Snapping from her trance, Sandy followed. Slowed by the knee she'd injured during the aborted landing in Monterey, she struggled to keep up with her reinvigorated mother. Sandy felt the first hint of hope swim to the surface. The house hadn't been pulverized as she'd feared. However, the fact he hadn't been on the street searching for her mother was still worrying.

Crossing into the remnants of their front yard, her mom called, "John?"

Only the sound of water spraying from the broken main answered.

Going around the smaller crater formed by the asteroid fragment, they moved toward the back of the house. Arriving at the side gate first, her mother fought with the sticky latch. "I've been telling your father to fix this damn thing for years."

"Let me." As she'd been doing since childhood, Sandy gave the handle a yank while applying upward pressure. The gate's cedar planks racked, and the latch popped out. Its hinges squealed their protest as she swung it open.

"If that man spent a tenth of the time on this house as he does on that stupid plane, this wouldn't happen."

Sandy knew the complaints served to deflect her mom's thoughts from what might await their discovery in the minutes to come. Her mother had always complained about her father's constant tinkering with the grounded decertified airplane parked in his hangar. Situated behind their house and overrun by weeds, grass and dirt, the hangar and adjacent runway were the last remnants of the long-defunct Carmel Valley Vintage Airport, the home of so many of Sandy's memories.

Fully opening the gate, Sandy gestured into the backyard. "I know, Mom. Let's go."

Looking down, her mother started crying and trembling. "I'm afraid. I can't lose him, Sandy. He's all I, I ..." She seemed to melt before Sandy's eyes. The strong, rock-solid firecracker, as her dad always called her, cried uncontrollably.

Sandy hugged her. "I'm sure he's okay." Holding her tightly, she added, "Why don't you wait here. I'll go check inside—"

"No!" she interrupted, shaking off Sandy's embrace. Taking a few deep breaths, she steadied herself, apparently quelling the tormenting emotions. The firecracker façade reasserted itself, making the woman appear much taller than her diminutive five feet two inches. "Let's go find the old coot." Waving a dismissive hand at the chaotic scene behind them, she added, "That man is way too stubborn to let this shit knock him down."

Not for the first time, it occurred to Sandy that this is where she'd acquired what Jake jokingly referred to as her *colorful vocabulary*.

Her mom pointed to the sky. "And, if those sons-a-bitches hurt my Johnny, they'll have me to deal with!"

Wiping away a tear of her own, Sandy smiled in spite of the dire situation. "I know that's right, Momma. I know that's right."

CHAPTER 33

"Admiral, the squadrons are away," reported a bridge officer.

"Very well," Thoyd replied.

The long inbound flight from the edge of the disruptor's field had been excruciatingly slow. Counter-intuitively, the Zoxyth hadn't used the extra time to affect their escape. He had assumed that the Zox commander had deployed the disruptor to buy time for a tactical withdrawal should the GDF arrive. Instead, they had used the period to take up a defensive position over one of the planet's oceans.

It also appeared the Zoxyth had yet to attack the planet. Aside from blast patterns consistent with hypervelocital atmospheric shock waves, they saw no sign of attack, no use of Zoxyth weapons.

After another inward glance at his synthetic vision's dead Omninet icon, Thoyd turned to his tactical officer. "Colonel, where do we stand?"

After activating the bridge's holographic display, the officer pointed at the gathering enemy ships. "They're still forming over the planet, sir."

Admiral Feyhdyak studied the collected rocky vessels. "That's not their standard attack formation. It's purely defensive." Accessing the display with his EON, Thoyd magnified the enemy fleet. The point of view flew into the rocky formation as would a closing fighter.

His tactical officer nodded. "Yes, sir. It appears they're moving to support a smaller ship."

Continuing to zoom in, the hologram's moving point of view flew between the outer ships, closing on the center vessel until its image filled the three-dimensional display.

Thoyd shot to his feet. "I thought you said we had no other ships in sector?"

"I did, sir. We're the first Galactic Defense Force on station."

"Are you sure?" the admiral pushed.

Confused, the officer scanned his console again. After a moment, he shook his head and looked at the admiral. "I'm positive, sir."

"Then who or what did that?" he asked, pointing at the decimated Zoxyth bridge section.

The tactical officer shook his head, then paused, studying his console. "Admiral, I'm receiving reports of new ships lifting from the surface."

With his EON, Thoyd adjusted the holographic display, bringing Earth's surface back into view. Chasing some of the Zoxyth dreadnoughts from the surface, several small, gray holograms lifted from points around the globe.

He sat back in stunned admiration. "Looks like these earthly Argonians have a little bite in them."

"But, sir, there's no Zoxyth weapon's signature over any of the planet's continents."

"I'll wager there's at least one sign of non-Zoxyth nuclear attack."

"Uh ..." The officer paused, taking a moment to study the readings. "Yes, sir. There are several gamma source points near North America's East Coast." Then he looked up, amazed. "It's the remnant of a Zoxyth dreadnought."

The admiral nodded, sharing in the officer's amazement. Shifting his gaze outside, he studied the planet below. This was his first visit to Earth. He thought it was beautiful and could understand why lost colonists would choose it. The Zoxyth ships were gathering high over one of its oceans. A quick EON access of the planetary database identified it as the Atlantic. Clearly visible on the day side, North America bordered it on his left, Europe on the right.

"How in the hell did they defeat a Zoxyth dreadnought?" Admiral Feyhdyak wondered aloud. "And prior to it attacking, no less."

On the display, he watched his attack squadrons maneuver. Each eighteen-ship squadron had three wings of six Firebird light-attack ships. The computer used color codes and symbols to represent the various squadrons and subordinate wings. The holographic representation of the attack squadrons formed a multicolored sphere encircling and tightening on the Zoxyth fleet.

Representing a peace-loving government, the Galactic Defense Force's policy dictated they not shoot first.

"Remind our squadron commanders that we're on a weapon's hold status. They are to continue their box-in maneuver but are not to fire unless fired upon," Thoyd ordered. "The Zoxyth haven't attacked. We may yet bring this to a peaceful solution."

The communications officer nodded and EONed the command to the fighter squadrons.

Thoyd reviewed the tactical implications of the Zox position. According to EON-supplied demographics, a nuclear electromagnetic pulse radiated from the location and altitude of the Zoxyth formation would fry the primitive electronics of the planet's leading technological societies.

The admiral turned to the helmsman. "Position the carrier group between the Zoxyth and the planet's surface," he ordered. "If they try a diversionary attack, our shields will protect the surface from enemy nuclear weapons and E.M.P."

Utilizing his EON's dedicated combat communications channel, the helmsman shared the plan with his opposite within each of the carrier's complement of fourteen battlecruisers. Simultaneously, the massive formation turned toward the planet. Per protocol, six cruisers led the way. A quartet formed a defensive halo around the carrier, and the remaining four dropped into rear cover.

Normally, the fleet would occupy a region of space the size of

Earth's Moon. However, the compactness of the Zoxyth formation and its proximity to the planet's surface dictated a significantly smaller defensive arrangement.

Studying the EON-generated graphics superimposed over his real-world view, Thoyd eyed the inactive Omninet link. Disconnected from his main consciousness, he felt like an island of humanity. He turned to the communications officer. "Can we take out that disruptor field?"

The portly, bald officer shook his head. "Not without an all-out assault. And, with all the shielding his surrounding ships are providing, that won't be an easy task, sir."

Admiral Feyhdyak shook his head. "They haven't attacked anybody, yet. Enemy or not, I'm not going to wipe out thousands of them just to re-establish communications."

Thoyd walked into the center of the expansive bridge's hologram and stood face-to-face with the three-dimensional alien head at the formation's center. The rendering cast a red glow across his countenance. Staring into its burning eyes, he said, "What the hell are you up to?"

~

"Those are Argonian ships!" Richard said excitedly, then hesitated. "But ... something is wrong."

"What?" Jake said.

"I'm not sure, but it looks like they dropped out of parallel-space farther away than normal. A few months back, we met with one of their large ships on the far side of the Moon. They didn't want to be seen from the planet. So, they dropped back into real-space at the exact coordinates specified for the meeting. It was incredible. One second, there was nothing, the next: a huge ship popped into existence." Richard pointed at the green formation and shook his head. "Now flying into combat, they're approaching from way beyond the Moon's orbit ... under normal propulsion." He looked at Jake. "They've crapped away the element of surprise."

As additional green ships slid into the holographic display, Jake reached into it and magnified the largest Argonian vessel. It was a thing of beauty. The spaceship's soft curves and flowing lines made the enormous vessel look as if it could fly through the atmosphere or float on an ocean.

"Take the flight controller," Richard said, stepping to the display.

Jake moved to the control panel. After evaluating the relative position of the enemy and Argonian ships, he said, "I'm going to park us south and well above the enemy formation. That'll keep us out of the way and out of their weapon's range."

"Sounds good," Richard said as he studied the holographic display. "Plus, that'll give us a good perspective on the battle."

"I'm sure one is coming," Victor said.

Jake nodded, wondering why it hadn't already started. Toggling the comm panel, he called, "Vampire Six, this is Turtle One, over."

Richard manipulated the display, positioning a hologram of the largest Argonian ship next to that of an enemy ship.

Jake marveled at its apparent size. It dwarfed the aliens' city-sized asteroidal vessel.

"Oh my God," Vic said, his jaw hanging open in unbridled amazement. "They're beautiful ... and *huge*!"

"It is," Richard agreed. A look of wonder temporarily displaced his ever-present sardonic smirk.

Colonel Newcastle's reply echoed through the ship. "Turtle One, this is Vampire Six. Got you loud and clear. My holographic display shows the enemy forming on a smaller ship. We're maneuvering to press the attack."

"Negative, Vampire Six. You need to stand off," Jake said.

"No, Captain. Timing is of the essence. We need to attack before they can redeploy their weapons," Colonel Newcastle replied, misinterpreting Jake's concern. "With the speed of their attacks and subsequent movements, we've only managed to take out the one ship we killed over the Chesapeake. From the timing of their attacks, we've determined they have a forty-five-minute recharge time."

"It's not the weapon, sir. Our display is showing a new fleet."

A long pause followed Jake's report. Finally, the colonel said, "I don't see it, but my hologram is a reverse-engineered copy of yours. It doesn't have the range of the Argonian sensors. What is it displaying?" Newcastle asked, then added, "Please tell me they're green."

Colonel Newcastle's comments answered one question. Jake looked at Richard. "Reverse-engineered? Guess we know where they came from, then."

Richard nodded. "Apparently, we weren't the lowest level in the hangar."

Jake keyed the mic. "Yessir, very green. It's an Argonian fleet."

"Hot damn! The cavalry is coming," replied the colonel, excitement breaking through his battle-weary tone.

"They're advancing on the alien fleet," Jake said. Watching Richard manipulate the hologram, he added, "And you're right about the enemy ships, sir. They are regrouping around a smaller ship."

Jake refocused on the events unfolding outside. Something was raising alarms in his mind. "Hey, Richard, I'm guessing they've never brought a force of this size to Earth space."

"No, never. They have very strict non-interference rules." Pointing at the display, he added, "A fleet that size doesn't go unnoticed."

"That's what I thought. They must've received intel these aliens were coming. Right?"

"I'd say that's a safe assumption. I just wish they would have gotten here a few hours sooner."

"No shit," Victor said.

Jake nodded and pointed at the enemy formation. "So, the weapon these assholes attacked us with can't be new to them?"

"No. The Argonians are the most technologically advanced race in the galaxy."

Jake persisted. "By my count, that's two major assumptions we've made in the last sixty seconds. Normally, I don't like making *one*."

Richard raised his hands in surrender and returned to the console. "You're right. I'll try to raise them."

Activating a new section of the panel, he spoke in the Argonian tongue. "To the Galactic Defense Forces in Earth space, this is United States Air Force Captain Richard Allison, over."

They stared at the silent radio.

"Argonian fleet entering Earth space, this is Captain Allison of the US Air Force. Please come in, over."

Still no reply.

"GDF Fleet this is—"

"Captain Allison," interrupted an annoyed Argonian voice. "This is the Executive Officer of the *Galactic Guardian*. As you may have noticed, we are a little busy at the moment. Please clear this frequency."

"Roger, Galactic Guardian. I just wanted to make sure you were aware of the enemy's weapon—"

"Captain!" the snide officer said, cutting him off again. "I assure you, we are fully capable of dealing with these Zoxyth dreadnoughts. Now please clear this frequency."

Activating the radio transmitter, Richard growled through clenched teeth, "Roger. Captain Allison, out." Releasing the key, he added, "Asshole!"

Amazed at the Argonian's response, Jake shook his head. "Some things never change."

"Guess there are assholes in the future too," Vic said, shaking his head.

"Well, now we know the name of those fuckers," Jake said as he pointed at the enemy fleet.

"Speaking of," Richard said, walking back to the display. "Let's see what these *Zoxyth* are up to." He magnified the enemy formation. The small ship at its center grew to fill the display. They all took a shocked backward step. In spite of the extensive blast damage, the evil visage was easily recognizable. Now twisted and partially melted, the human skull still sat in the alien's clenched teeth.

Jake snapped from his shocked trance, quickly toggling the radio. "Vampire Six, it looks like part of the ship you attacked over the Chesapeake survived."

"Part of it?" the colonel asked incredulously.

"Yes, sir. It's the section we've been calling the bridge. The part carved into an alien head somehow survived, and now it's back in space."

After a brief pause, Newcastle said, "Son of a bitch! All right, Captain Giard. Thanks for the info. General Tannehill and I thought it was the bridge too, and considering it attacked the US capital, I believe that was their command ship."

"Roger, sir," Jake said. "The way the ships are circling the wagons, it looks like they're trying to protect it."

"So, what's the cavalry up to?" Colonel Newcastle asked.

Richard zoomed out the display. "Look at that!"

A swarm of small ships streamed from the largest of the Argonian ships, their maneuvering patterns unmistakable.

Victor said, "Those are fighters!"

Richard nodded with an enthusiastic grin. "First time I've seen them."

Jake knew he should be excited as well. However, something still gnawed at him. Something didn't add up.

Richard toggled the comm panel. After informing Newcastle of their conversation with the GDF executive officer, he added, "The *Galactic Guardian* just deployed its fighters. It looks like they're moving toward the Zoxyth dreadnoughts."

"Good, copy, Turtle One. I can see part of their formation at the edge of my hologram. We just parked a couple hundred miles east. I have you on my display as well. Looks like you're in a good spot. Keep me updated. Vampire Six, out."

"Wilco, Six. Turtle One, out."

Jake watched the swarming fighters divide into individual groups. Pointing into the display, he said. "They're splitting into attack wings."

Richard and Vic nodded their agreement.

While the formations were recognizable, the choreography differed from anything Jake had seen. Not limited to an atmosphere nor tied to any sense of up or gravity, the fighters maneuvered in all three dimensions and sustained attitudes that would be impractical for an atmospheric fighter.

Simultaneously, the attack wings shot apart like an exploding Fourth of July missile, each group rocketing away from the center on a discrete vector. Reaching a predesignated initialization point, the wings turned inbound as one. In a matter of moments, they enveloped the Zoxyth fleet in a menacing and tightening sphere of fighters, each pointing toward the center of the enemy formation.

Jake refocused his attention on the larger ships. As they, too, neared the amassed enemy ships, the alarm ringing in his head raised another notch.

CHAPTER 34

Holding hands, they stepped around the back corner of the house. Curtains billowed through the patio's blown-out sliding glass door. Blasted across the rear deck and into the backyard by the impact's pressure wave, shards of pebbled safety glass sparkled in the morning sun.

Knocked down by the blast, some of the patio cover's rustic roof timbers had fallen. Its far end propped up on the patio's back wall, the front of the ridge's massive central beam had fallen to the floor, its tilted end disappearing under the curtain.

Below that, Sandy spotted a dark puddle. It had flowed around some of the tiny cubes of safety glass. The light reflected off them took on a crimson hue. Sandy stopped. Pulling her mom back, she pointed. A gust flipped the curtains back to reveal her father's prone body.

"Daddy!"

At the same time, her mom screamed, "Johnny!"

They ran to his side. Laying on his back, his legs protruded through the opening. Draped across the empty threshold, it appeared the blast had blown him halfway through the sliding glass door. He had hundreds of small cuts from the exploding glass, but the blood she'd seen had come from his right leg. The patio cover's massive ridge timber had crashed down on his right thigh, pinning him to the floor.

Sobbing, her mother knelt, hands over her mouth. "Oh God, the blood ... There's so much of it."

Stepping through the opening, also crying, Sandy dropped to her good knee by her father's right shoulder. She extended a hand, intending to check his neck for a pulse. She hesitated, afraid it would only confirm the worst. His usually tanned skin was ashen, not much darker than the old white tee shirt under his blue denim overalls.

Sandy closed her eyes. "Daddy ... Oh, God please, no."

"If you two hens don't stop clucking, I'm never gonna get any sleep."

Sandy's eyes flew open.

Her father's loving crow's-feet-lined eyes, eyes that had a smile all their own, were shining at Sandy. Weakly, he said, "Hi, Pumpkin."

"Daddy!" Tears of joy sprang from her eyes. Throwing her arms around his shoulders, she hugged him. Sobbing into his neck, she said, "We ... I ... I thought we'd lost you."

Her father chuckled. "I told your momma a long time ago that she's stuck with me."

Pulling back, Sandy ran her fingers through his silver hair. Her mom put a trembling hand on his chest.

Turning to her, he said, "Hey there, Firecracker. You ain't gettin' rid of me that easy."

Smiling through her tears, her mother cast a nervous glance at his crushed leg. Then she gestured toward his overalls. "I thought you were still in bed." In mock admonishment, she added, "You were heading out to tinker with that stupid airplane, weren't you?"

"Guilty as charged," he whispered. His weak laugh morphed into coughs. Reaching for the timber crushing his right leg, he screamed in pain between each hack, the spasms generating fresh waves of agony.

Sandy saw the tourniquet he'd fashioned from his overalls' denim belt. The jolting coughs had loosened it. Fresh arterial blood spurted from the point where the end of the massive beam sat on her father's right thigh. By the shape of the upper leg, Sandy could tell his femur was broken. She grabbed the tourniquet, giving the large pocket knife he'd used another twist to tighten the belt. Considering how long he'd been pinned here, Sandy knew he would almost certainly lose the leg. However, if she couldn't keep him from losing more blood, that would be the least of their worries.

"Momma," Sandy said. "Get me one of your big wooden spoons."

Wordlessly, her mom jumped to her feet and ran to the kitchen.

Studying his leg, Sandy asked, "Daddy, how long have you had this tourniquet on?"

No answer.

She looked up. Her father's eyes had closed. A check of his neck revealed a weak pulse. His massive chest rose and fell with each raspy breath.

Her mother ran back into the room. Seeing her husband's deteriorating condition, she froze. "Is he ...?"

"No, but he's lost a lot of blood, Mama." Sandy held out her free hand. It was soaked in her father's vital fluid. "Spoon!"

Her mom popped it into her hand. Sandy pushed the pocket knife out of the tourniquet and dropped it into one of her flight suit's leg pockets. Sliding the wooden spoon into the empty loop, she retightened the tourniquet. Significantly longer than the pocket knife, the utensil allowed greater leverage. She gave it a couple of extra turns, completely staunching the flow of blood.

"Hold this."

Her mother took a position beside her. Grabbing her mom's hand, she placed it on the twisted knot of denim belt wrapped around the spoon. "Keep pressure right here, and don't let it spin!"

With both hands free, Sandy tucked the spoon's handle under the edge of the tourniquet. "This should hold it in place."

Her mother nodded. "What are we gonna do now?"

Sandy looked at the beam. The far end still rested against the top of the patio's partially collapsed back wall. Milled from a massive tree trunk, the twenty-foot-long rough-cut timber was almost two feet thick from top to bottom and more than a foot wide. Almost all of the log's massive weight dug into her father's leg.

As she loosened the straps around her makeshift splint, she said, "I have an idea." Positioning herself under the timber and bending at the waist, Sandy pressed her lower back against its bottom. Legs bent, she slid sideways toward her father, the gap between the beam and the floor narrowed. When it closed enough to afford optimum leverage, Sandy pushed her lower back hard into the bottom of the beam. She held a hand against her injured knee. Under her boots, the patio's wooden deck creaked, but the log didn't budge. With her legs shaking under the strain, she gave a primal roar and tried harder. The floorboards groaned, but the log still refused to move.

The grunt devolved into a scream as she surrendered. "Fuck!" Breathing heavily, she stepped back and studied the angle.

"It's too heavy, honey," her mother said.

"Hang on. I have another idea."

Still under the beam, Sandy rolled onto her back and placed both feet against its bottom. "When it lifts, pull his leg out."

Her mother nodded.

Sandy took a few quick breaths and then shoved with all of her might. She could feel the boards bowing under her back. The timber shuddered. Sandy took another quick breath and redoubled her efforts. A scream of agony burst from her lips as her injured leg erupted in pain. Clutching the left knee, Sandy rolled onto her right side. Curled up in a ball, she pounded the floor with her right fist. "I can't move it!"

Her mother's soft sobs banished Sandy's self-pity. She squeezed her eyes shut. *Come on, Fitzpatrick, pull it together! Think, think!* With a sudden realization, she opened her eyes. "I know what to do!"

Her mother's cries stopped as she looked at Sandy through tear-filled, bloodshot eyes. She'd never seen her mom look so frail and vulnerable.

"I'll be right back, Momma. I have to get something out of Daddy's hangar."

She only nodded. Sitting with her husband's limp hand grasped in one hand and the other firmly clamped over the tourniquet knot, her mother looked on the verge of giving up all hope.

Sandy gave a reassuring smile. "He's going to be okay, Momma. I promise. I know what to do now. We'll have him out of there in no time."

"Okay, hun," she said. She gave a wan smile, doing her best to put on a brave front. The quiet desperation lurking in her eyes made Sandy's heart ache.

She pointed toward the closed airfield behind their backyard. "Does Daddy still keep the hangar key in the same spot?"

Her mother nodded.

"Okay." Sandy held up a finger. "I'll be right back."

CHAPTER 35

Watching the last of his dreadnoughts slide into position, Salyth swiped at the blood dribbling from his lower jaw. With great anticipation, he savored the developments. His fangs dripped in expectation of the coming victory. The Argonians will see his fleet's formation as a desperate ploy to guard their damaged command ship. Watching for one wrong move, they'll come in nice and close.

"It's critical we maintain this altitude. Do not allow their ships to draw us higher. Let them approach. No one is to fire!" he growled to his subordinate.

"Yes, Commodore Salyth," the officer replied. Hunching over his console, he forwarded the reminder to the fleet.

Outside, the small Argonian Firebirds encircled his formation. Employing their standard box-in maneuver, the fighters trained their deadly weapons on his ships. Focusing on the larger vessels of the carrier group, Salyth barely noticed. The GDF battlecruisers and their central carrier ship drew closer.

His black tongue flickered, lapping the dripping saliva. Through his bloody maw, he grinned menacingly and growled, "That's right, come into my cave."

CHAPTER 36

Jake's dread mounted. The Argonians were getting too close. However, their biggest ships still hovered outside the range of the Zox weapon.

He keyed the mic. "Vampire Six, how much time before one of the enemy ships can fire that weapon?"

"I was just calculating that. All of the ships fired their primary weapon at least once ... several twice." The colonel's voice cracked, the gravity of the news the words conveyed apparently weighing on him. After a brief pause, he continued. "The ship with the longest time since weapon activation is the one that took out Moscow. That was thirty minutes ago. So, we have fifteen minutes." Colonel Newcastle finished.

Jake's blood ran cold, *More than sixteen of our biggest cities gone. We've lost so much today.*

"Look!" Richard said, pointing at the large ships. They had been outside of the enemy's weapon range. Now the fleet maneuvered to take up a defensive position between the planet and the alien formation.

A crushing realization hit Jake. He checked his watch. "Oh, shit!"

Richard and Victor looked at him.

Jake slammed his hand down on the comm panel and screamed, "Vampire Six, it's been more than an hour since the ship over D.C. deployed its main weapon! It's an ambush, a coup de main! We have to warn them!"

Jake saw comprehension on Richard's face as his combat wingman leapt to the GDF section of the comm panel. Vic looked confused. Turning to him, Jake said, "These aliens attacked us to lure the Argonians into a trap. It's the only thing that makes sense."

Richard activated the GDF radio. He started shouting into it in the Argonian tongue.

Jake continued. "The unprovoked attack, no demands, just their systematic elimination of city after city, it's all been designed to draw the Galactic Defense Force. This must be a new weapon. If the Argonians knew of its capabilities, they wouldn't be positioning themselves this close to their fleet."

"Surely they have shields," Vic said.

"Maybe, but if hundreds of feet of earth and rock didn't protect Space Control, I doubt shields will do any better."

Behind him, Jake heard the *Galactic Guardian's* executive officer berate Richard.

Lieutenant Croft's face turned ashen as a powerful shudder racked his body. "If they destroy the Argonians, we'll—"

"We're not going to let that happen!" Richard interrupted. Turning back to the radio, he continued transmitting. "I don't care what you think. I need to talk to your commander! It's imperative. I believe the Zoxyth are drawing you into a trap!"

"Captain Allison," replied a very authoritative voice. "This is Admiral Thoyd Feyhdyak. Let me assure you, there is nothing these Zoxyth have that our weapons and shielding cannot defeat."

Through clenched teeth, Richard said, "Admiral, they've already wiped out several of our cities, totally vaporizing every man, woman and child within a hundred miles of their ships!"

"Vaporized?" the admiral responded.

Jake heard the first hint of concern in the Argonian's voice.

Not waiting for a response, the admiral continued. "Aside from a reading over North America's East Coast, we've detected no sign of fission reactions."

Maddeningly, the Argonians continued to mass their forces between the Zoxyth and the planet.

"No, no!" Richard said, pounding the control panel. "No nuclear weapons were used on us. They're using a weapon that only affects humans."

"They've attacked you with chemical or biological weapons?"

"No, sir! Some kind of energy wave bursts from their ship!" Richard said, still pounding on the control panel to emphasize his words. "It vaporizes every human within a hundred miles! It doesn't affect structures or plants or animals. It only kills humans! In case you don't understand a hundred miles, that's *millions* of us vaporized every fucking time they've fired that goddamned weapon!"

After a brief pause, the admiral returned, a tone of pure horror supplanting his condescension. "You're describing a gene disruptor weapon. They've been banned for millennia, the technology is a closely guarded secret. I'll explain more in a moment. Stand by."

Space beyond the view-wall burst into brilliant fire. Jake threw a panicked arm over his eyes. For a terrifying moment, he thought the Zoxyth had deployed their weapon.

The *Turtle's* view-wall auto-dimmed, damping the brilliance down to a bearable level.

"Holy shit!" Victor whispered.

Outside, the Zoxyth shields glowed like miniature suns under a tremendous onslaught of brilliant laser beams. The force fields overlapped like a collection of luminescent soap bubbles, completely obscuring the ships within.

In the face of so much violence, the silence within the *Turtle* was surreal.

The Argonian radio crackled to life. "For now, we need to keep them under attack. A gene disruptor weapon will penetrate a shield, but it cannot be fired by a shielded ship," Admiral Feyhdyak finished.

"Gene disruptor?" Richard asked.

"Yes, it's a focused quantum phase disruptor. They target a single species. Designed to shift all material within their sphere of influence to a higher energy state, they are tuned to a specific DNA strand's sympathetic frequency. Essentially, the targeted bodies are moved into a dimension incompatible with life."

"It's a genocide weapon," Richard replied.

"That's why it's banned technology," Admiral Feyhdyak said.

A pulse caught Jake's attention.

"Look, one of their shields is failing," Vic said.

"Turtle One, this is Vampire Six. What the hell is going on?"

Richard switched radios. "Colonel, I'm on the horn with the Argonian commander. We were right, this is a new weapon, although apparently not unknown. Their commander says the aliens won't be able to deploy it while under fire."

The strobing shield flashed then failed. A barrage of lasers converged on the unprotected ship. It exploded like a scene from a movie, a radiant shock wave signaling its demise.

CHAPTER 37

Launching through the patio's blown-out rear wall, Sandy hobbled across the backyard. Even limping, she traversed the freshly mown lawn at a respectable pace. Reaching the rear property line, she stepped onto prone cinder blocks. Knocked over by the shock wave, the eight-foot block wall lay on its side. Now only eight inches high, it barely slowed her. Emerging onto the closed airfield, Sandy angled left, heading straight to the old T-shaped hangar.

Seeing the structure elicited a flood of childhood memories. This was where Sandy had grown up, where she'd spent her summer breaks and school holidays. She had loved the sights and sounds, even the smells. Sandy could almost see Tom Flannery's old LTD next to the hangar and smell the ever-present cigar smoke that followed her father's friend and fellow instructor pilot. As if rooted in the man's bushy mustache, a thin stogie always hung from Tom's lips. He, along with a cadre of polyester-clad fellow pilots, had been permanent fixtures at that hangar.

Over the years, her father, with help from the self-proclaimed *Lounge Lizards,* taught her everything from how to change a spark plug to how to recover a spinning airplane. The seed of her love of all things aviation germinated grew and flowered in this very spot.

Carmel Valley Vintage Airport closed over ten years ago. After a decade of neglect, soil and sod partially obscured the derelict runway, though long sections of pavement still spanned the gaps. However, in her mind's eye, Sandy could still see all of it as it had appeared in her childhood.

The rear property lines of the homes on her parents' side of the street ran parallel to the airfield's sole runway. As the neighborhood's southwestern most property, her parents' house sat at the field's southeast corner, less than a hundred yards from Dad's old T-hangar. Having earned their name from an airplane-conforming shape, the T-shaped buildings were the country's most popular type of general aviation hangar.

Limping through knee-high weeds, she continued toward the maroon corrugated metal building. Sandy veered away from the central main doors. Instead, she headed to the front left edge.

Arriving, Sandy leaned on the building's corner. Grimacing against the pain shooting through her left leg, she fought to catch her breath. Dropping her head, she looked down on a dusty flagstone. "There you are." Bending at the waist, Sandy lifted the flat rock, revealing an ancient lozenge tin. Picking it out of the dirt elicited a metallic rattle. Lifting the hinged lid, she grabbed a well-worn bronze key and unceremoniously dropped the small box onto the ground. Reconsidering, she bent over and gently set the tin back in place, then repositioned the flagstone.

Standing, Sandy registered movement at the airfield's northeast corner. A dust cloud expanded behind a vehicle. It appeared to have just entered the field from the subdivision's far north end. When she'd first encountered the asteroid blocking her path, Sandy had considered doubling back to that end of the neighborhood to approach her parents' house from this side. However, that plan had evaporated with the appearance of her mother.

Still a couple of thousand feet away, the vehicle formed a tiny dot at the middle of an expanding ochre dust cloud. An inverted image reflected off the tarmac's shimmering heat waves. Morphing the car into the central disk of a surreal flower, the symmetrical likeness paraded an ever-blossoming halo of rippling pedals. It appeared to head straight toward Sandy. Disquieted by the vehicle's sudden emergence, she studied it for a moment, then shook her head in self-reproach. *Stop being a paranoid jackass. Get what you came for.*

Tearing her eyes from the distant car, she crossed to the hangar's side door. Thoughts returning to her father, Sandy grabbed the ancient lock hanging in its rusty hasp. Well maintained, the padlock accepted the key without resistance and easily opened. She removed it and threw open the door.

Morning light burned a hole through the hangar's darkness. Spilling through the opening, the light revealed a white wing tip. It was the right wing of her father's airplane. He'd had the four-seat high-wing Cessna 172 since Sandy had been a toddler. She'd grown up climbing in and on this airplane. It was also the first plane Sandy had ever flown.

Stepping through the opening, she ducked under the wing. Knowing exactly where to find her quarry, she didn't bother with the light switch. Tripping over clutter wasn't a concern. When it came to this hangar and his aircraft, her father was the ultimate perfectionist. Mom often joked that Wikipedia's page on Obsessive-Compulsive Disorder featured a picture of her father standing in this hangar.

Reaching the back wall, Sandy dropped to her good knee. Groping in the darkness, her hand immediately fell on the item she sought. "There you are." Grunting under the load, Sandy picked up the heavy floor jack.

The mixed aroma of aviation gasoline, oils, and cleaning supplies reinforced her sense of nostalgia. With no time to reflect, Sandy hurried back to the door. Walking outside, she heard the throaty sound of an idling V8 engine.

Stepping off the hangar's entry stoop, Sandy froze. Parked a hundred yards away, a familiar dark red Camaro sat along the airfield's eastern boundary. Strung behind it, the ghost of its dust trail still hung in the air.

"Oh shit," Sandy whispered. Without turning, she reversed directions, cautiously extending her foot back toward the stoop's three-foot-wide concrete pad.

Suddenly, a hand clamped onto her right arm, and a raspy voice issued from behind her right ear. "Hello, Blondie."

Sandy dropped the jack and grasped for the pistol hanging under her left arm. However, another hand was already pulling the Beretta from its shoulder holster. Sandy clutched at it. A hard object jabbed her left ribs.

"Uh-huh-huh," taunted a second voice from her left rear. "I'll take that."

As the pistol slid from its nest and out of her grasp, Sandy quit struggling and tensed. "What do you want?"

"It's the end of the world, bitch," the voice in her right ear whispered. Like an ashtray dumped on two-day-old road kill, the hot, dank breath on her neck reeked of rot and stale cigarettes.

Stepping around her right side, a short, rail-thin man moved to stand in front of Sandy. Pointing an intricately engraved, nickel-plated forty-four magnum at her face, he glared over the iron sight of the cannon's twelve-inch barrel. Bloodshot, his sole visible eye leered between matted strands of greasy, shoulder-length black hair. Blinking furiously, it sporadically trembled side-to-side. Having extensively travelled through inland California—or Calabama, as many called it—Sandy recognized the eye twitch as a side effect of crystal meth abuse.

With the pistol shaking in his left hand, the meth-head pointed a yellow-nailed right index finger at the man behind her left shoulder. "Me and Leroy figure it's time to take a little back from this here world."

"You got that right, Buck. Get while the gettin's good," Leroy said from behind her.

Buck chuckled. "As a matter of fact, my brother had just said how unfortunate it was these aliens hadn't left any bitches layin' around. Then your fine little ass shows up."

Leroy laughed hysterically at that. Stepping from behind her, the same greasy-haired Calabamaian white trash she'd seen looting the bank joined Buck in front of her. The younger of the two, Leroy had a massive burn scar distorting the left side of his face, something she hadn't noticed during their first encounter.

For a moment, the two stood grinning stupidly. Leroy's manic eyes, as well as Buck's single visible one, greedily scanned up and down her body, lingering on her crotch and breasts. Like misaligned hundred-year-old tombstones, the gray-edged yellowed teeth of their grinning meth-mouths sent a chill down Sandy's spine.

Leroy lifted the shotgun's muzzle from her midsection. Resting its barrel on his right shoulder, he kept his right index finger on the trigger.

Buck hooked a right thumb at his brother. "Dumb ass thought you were the cops. Good thing ol' Leroy ain't exactly a crack shot with that thing."

Leroy laughed. "When I told Buck how hot you were, he said we had to find you."

Buck pointed at the Camaro. "But, by the time we got that thing past all the wrecked cars, you were long gone. When we found your crashed truck, I thought you'd gone to ground. Then ol' Leroy spotted that Hummer at the bottom of the valley."

Leroy nodded with idiotic pride. "Yep, I saw you turn left on the highway."

"Then we almost stumbled into that damn roadblock. I don't know what you told them, but after you left, they folded up camp. Thanks for that. I thought we'd have to give up the chase."

Impatient with thc idiots, Sandy cast a nervous glance toward the back of her parents' house.

Buck caught the look. "Is that where the old lady went?"

Sandy looked away too quickly. "Who?"

"We saw the two of you scrambling round that rock."

"Yeah," Leroy said through his crazy, machine-gunning laughter. "She was F-I-N-E fine."

Buck shot an annoyed glance at Leroy and then turned back to Sandy. "Hell, we woulda followed you then." He pointed his free hand toward the neighborhood. "But, there were too many assholes walkin' around." Shifting his arm, he pointed at the still idling red Camaro. "We stole that fucker fair and square, and I'll be goddamned if some jackass is gonna take it from me."

His nervous energy boiling over, Leroy giggled and said, "So, we went around to the—"

"We found another way," Buck interrupted, apparently impatient with all the talk.

"So, where is she?" asked Leroy, not catching his brother's aggravation. "She looked pretty fine! I'd like to—"

Buck smacked the back of Leroy's head, shutting him up. Shaking his head, Buck turned his attention back to Sandy. "You'll have to forgive Leroy. He has a thing for ladies with ... a few more miles on the old odometer." Exposing the dingy remnants of his wrecked teeth and gums, he grinned and winked at Sandy. Glancing right, he added, "Don't worry, brother, we'll save the best for last." Turning back to her, Buck's lust-filled eye crawled down Sandy's flight suit-clad body. "But we're gonna fuck this one first."

Sandy's heart raced: she wasn't worried about herself. However, fear for her mother's safety now boiled up to mix with the dread she already had for her father.

Buck stepped forward. The gun in his white-knuckled left hand trembled. However, the muzzle never veered from her face. The weapon's cavernous maw looked big enough to drive a truck through. His right hand reached for her left breast.

Sandy batted it away.

From under the mop of hair, anger flared in Buck's visible eye as it snapped up to lock onto Sandy's. "Fucking cunt thinks she's too good for us!" Pulling back the silver revolver's hammer, he cocked the massive weapon. Raising its end, he jammed the cold, steel muzzle against her forehead. Pressing her head back, he gestured to his right. "Now Leroy doesn't much care if you're alive or dead. He's what you might call an equal opportunity lover."

Leroy's manic staccato laughter sent another chill running down Sandy's spine.

As his brother's fit passed, Buck continued, the fire of his anger at her rebuff still burning brightly in his cycloptic eye. "As for me ... well, I like mine a bit *hotter*." He emphasized the last word in a way that made Sandy's blood run cold.

Leroy stopped laughing. Absent-mindedly, he fingered the left side of his face, tracing the twisted lines of scar tissue. "I know that's right," he said in a faint voice.

Ignoring his brother, Buck pressed harder, digging the muzzle into her forehead. "So, unless you'd like me to end it right here and let my brother have his way with your chilling corpse, I suggest you take on a more ... cooperative disposition."

Pressing her lips into a thin line, Sandy nodded her head.

"Good, now that we have that settled, let's take this inside."

"But what about the old lady?"

"She'll still be there, jackass." Buck said dismissively. "You can fuck her all you want when I'm done with this one."

"Don't call me that, Buck," Leroy said in a whiny tone. "You know I don't like—"

"Shut up, jackass."

Shoved backward through the door, Sandy tripped, landing hard on her butt and biting her tongue. The coppery taste of blood filled her mouth. Light chased away the hangar's inky blackness as Buck, close on her heels, easily found and flipped on the light switch. He kicked the door shut behind him.

"What the fuck, Buck?" Leroy yelled through the door.

Looking down on Sandy, Buck chuckled. "That never gets old." Then he shouted over his shoulder. "Just watch the goddamn door! I'll be out in a little while." Holding the gun on her, he scanned the hangar's interior. Apparently spotting his quarry, he stepped to the back left wall.

Seeing what he picked up, Sandy whispered, "Oh fuck."

Leroy called through the door. "Okay, Buck, but don't burn her yet. I want my turn."

The can of gasoline in Buck's hands confirmed her worst fears. Sandy closed her eyes. She knew, if these animals had their way, not only would she die a horrible death, but her parents would too. With every ticking second, Sandy felt her father's life slipping farther into the abyss. While it might be a silent passing for him, it would be anything but for her mother.

"Stand up, cunt!"

Sandy opened her eyes and did as he had instructed. The forty-four's muzzle never left her face. She looked into Buck's eye. "I like the way you take charge."

His cycloptic expression shifted from hot anger to wary confusion. Still aiming the gun at her head, he set the can on the floor and fumbled with her flight suit's front zipper.

"Here, let me," she said, giving him a nervous smile. As she slowly slid the body-length central zipper down, his look shifted from distrust to hope. Shoving the two sides of the flight suit apart, her large tee shirt-clad breasts fell through the zipper opening. No longer compressed by the flight suit's confines, they now heaved with each breath.

The meth-addicted cyclops stared with unbridled fascination.

Sandy moved closer. The gun finally wavered from her face. As she pressed her body against him, he moaned, his rank breath boiling over her.

Stifling a gag, she asked, "You like that?"

His moan morphed into a hissed word. "Yes."

Sandy smiled. Sliding the one-piece flight suit over one shoulder and then the next, she slowly turned around. As she faced away, her smile melted into a grimace of pure hate and revulsion.

With the uniform sliding past her waist, Sandy slowly bent over.

Buck scrambled to undo his ragged jeans.

As the flight suit spilled to the floor around her ankles, its left side caught on the splint she'd fashioned for her knee. Undeterred, the pig grabbed her bare hips. Grinding his pitiful crank-shrunk junk against her thong, he moaned again. No longer pointed at her, the side of the forty-four Magnum pistol dug into her left hip.

"Yeah, baby," Sandy said. Still bent over, she reached between her legs. Grabbing the jeans bunched up around the top of his dusty boots, she drew him in tight.

He moaned even louder.

Sandy said, "How do you like this?" Like a long-snap pro-football center, she whipped her arm up as fast and as hard as she could. She felt a sickening but very satisfactory popping sound as the six-inch blade of her father's Buck knife sank to the hilt in the bastard's crotch. Bouncing off the inside of her forearm, his severed penis fell to the floor.

Having slipped the knife out of her flight suit's leg pocket as she'd bent over, she now released it, leaving the blade buried in Buck's groin.

Convulsing, the man let out a high-pitched squeal.

Outside, Leroy laughed. Apparently mistaking Buck's scream for hers, he shouted, "Fuck her good, Buck!"

Wrenching the gun from the shrieking man's left hand, Sandy fell away from him. Spinning, she landed on her back and said, "You scream like a girl." She pulled the trigger. The massive gun jumped in her hands and shattered the air.

Buck's girlish scream died with him. The top of his head disappeared as a crimson mist haloed a geysering cloud of brain and skull. Reaching its apex, the gore reversed direction and rained down on Sandy. Then the lifeless body fell on her. She struggled under its weight for a moment. Finally, a grunting shove cast the thin man off her.

"What the fuck, Buck?" Leroy yelled apprehensively.

Sandy decided that Buck had been wrong. That shit *did* get old. Still lying on the floor, she quietly slid her gore-soaked flight suit back into position and zipped it.

"Don't burn her yet. I want my turn with the bitch."

Prone, Sandy aimed the hand cannon toward the voice and pulled the trigger three times. Twice the gun leapt, belching fire from its muzzle. Like white lasers cut through the hangar's wall, two new beams of sunlight burned through the smoke-filled atmosphere. The third trigger pull generated a click as the hammer fell on an empty cylinder.

Against the ringing in her ears and her echoing breath Sandy tried to listen for evidence one of her rounds had struck home. After a few tense seconds, she received her answer. A new shaft of light burned through the smoky air. A blast of shotgun pellets dug into the hangar's concrete floor mere inches from her head.

"Fucking bitch, you nearly killed me."

Sandy rolled right, away from the line of fire. In desperation, hoping to find another live round amongst the revolver's six cylinders, she again aimed toward his voice and pulled the trigger several times.

Echoes of the hollow clicks bounced off the metal building's walls.

Apparently tracking the noise, Leroy fired again. A volcano of pain erupted in Sandy's abdomen. Unstoppable, a scream escaped through her clenched teeth. Like a deer caught in the headlights, Sandy lay between the twin beams of sunlight the shotgun had carved into the hangar's atmosphere.

The crunch-crunch sound of Leroy pumping another round into his shotgun passed through the openings.

Paralyzed by the pain burning through her, Sandy closed her eyes, waiting for the third and final blast to cut through the wall and her head.

The shotgun roared again.

Her ears rang against the deafening silence that followed the blast. Sandy's eyes flew open. There wasn't a new hole in the side of the hangar. No new light beam had joined the other two. She did a quick physical inventory. Other than the fire still burning through her right side and her aching left knee, she was intact.

"Sandra?"

"Mom?" Sandy's heart raced with terror. "Run away, Momma. He's a sick bastard! He's—"

The hangar door swung open.

Sandy's heart sank as the muzzle of the psycho's shotgun slid into sight.

CHAPTER 38

Through a rarely utilized fleet-wide EON command, Admiral Thoyd Feyhdyak ordered, "We have a Level One threat. All ships, commence firing immediately!"

Without hesitation, every GDF ship opened fire.

Thoyd turned to his tactical officer. "We have to destroy these Zoxyth. I want the *Galactic Guardian's* main batteries to fire on any enemy ship that lowers its shields. There can be no hesitation."

"Yes, Admiral," the colonel replied and forwarded the command.

As he finished debriefing Captain Allison, one of the Zoxyth's shields started to fail. Several of the *Guardian's* batteries focused their fire on the failing shields. A moment later, the shield winked out. Under the onslaught, the ship instantly dissolved into bright red molten slag.

No longer held in place by a drive system, the debris surrendered to Earth's gravity, raining down on the carrier group. It bounced harmlessly off their shields, then accelerated toward the ocean two hundred Earth miles below.

"Have the rear battlecruisers take care of that," Admiral Feyhdyak ordered. "If those largest blobs make it to the ocean intact, we'll have massive waves devastating coastlines around the planet."

Concentrating on the biggest targets, the assigned battlecruisers fired their laser batteries into the falling debris.

The diverted laser attack impeded the destruction of the Zoxyth fleet.

"Damn it!" he yelled. Feeling the trap closing around his throat, he slammed his fist down.

The colonel looked up. "Do you want me to order a withdrawal, sir?"

Admiral Feyhdyak shook his head. "No." In a normal firefight, they could outmaneuver the Zoxyth ships—a tactical advantage the Galactic Defense Force had exploited to turn back the enemy's early victories. Thoyd now realized their gene weapon nullified that advantage.

The Zoxyth advance into Sector Sixty-Four and their defensive posturing following his arrival was all designed to draw the GDF into this very position. Thoyd shook his head again. "And I fell for it."

"Excuse me, sir?"

"No, hold position. We're faster than they are, but not enough to clear the weapon's range. A retreat will diminish our counter-fire and open an opportunity for them to deploy the damn thing. Our only hope is a massive, overwhelming counter-attack."

An idea flashed into his mind. Activating his EON's communication link, he transmitted, "Captain Allison, I require your assistance."

CHAPTER 39

"He's a sick bastard, Momma!" Sandy repeated. Tears of dread flowed down her cheeks.

In the hangar door, her mom stepped into view. Silhouetted in the opening, her tiny mother cut a long shadow across the hangar floor. Held across her body, the massive double-barreled shotgun had thin wisps of smoke wafting from its twin muzzles.

"He's a *dead* bastard, honey," she said from the door opening. Apparently unable to see in the relative darkness of the hangar's interior, she said, "Sandy?"

"Oh, Momma. Thank God! I'm over here," Sandy said through clenched teeth. The pain in her side still burned intensely. However, probing the area tentatively, Sandy could feel the pellets just below the surface. She'd only caught a couple of them. Judging by their depth, they had been slowed enough by contact with the wall, and maybe even the floor, to stop them from cutting into her abdominal cavity.

Moving a hand to her belly, she found no other injuries. Fresh relief washed over her. She gently caressed it. *Someday, you and I are going to have a lot to talk about.*

Turning to the sound of Sandy's voice, her mother stepped into the hangar and out of the bright pool of light spilling through the doorway. Seeing Sandy lying on the floor, she froze.

"Oh my God, Sandy!" Forgotten, the shotgun fell to the floor as both hands flew to her mouth. Fresh tears welled from her mother's bloodshot eyes as she tried and failed to stifle the sobs.

"Daddy? Did Daddy? Did he ...?" Sandy couldn't finish the question.

Her mother's red but still soft eyes shifted from horror to confusion then compassion as she knelt next to Sandy and placed a comforting hand on Sandy's right shoulder. "No, dear. He's awake." Tears streamed down her cheek. "But what about you? You're hurt bad, hun."

Sandy shook her head. "It hurts like hell, Mom, but it didn't go very deep." She lifted her blood-soaked right hand away from her side, exposing the area hit by Leroy's shot. "I'll survive."

Her mother gestured toward her flight suit. "Then where did all this stuff come from."

Wincing at the pain in her side, Sandy struggled to sit up. The effort had her sweating profusely in the hangar's hot smoky atmosphere. The sleeve wiped across the sweat pouring from her brow came away covered in gore. Looking down at her blood-spattered uniform, Sandy realized what had freaked out her mom.

Sandy pointed at the blood and noodle-shaped gray bits of brain splattered across her flight suit. "This isn't from me." She nodded at the lifeless body a few feet to her left. "It's from him."

Horror returned to her mother's eyes. "There was a second one?" She looked around nervously. "Are there any more?"

"No, just these two, and they're both dead now." Grimacing, Sandy stood. "We need to get Daddy to a hospital." Holding her side, she limped through the door into the bright sunlight. Squinting against the brilliance, she looked down into Leroy's scarred and very dead face. Larger in the front than in the back, a gaping hole cut through his abdomen. The double blast of twelve-gauge buckshot had nearly cut the man in half.

Sandy pulled her Beretta nine-millimeter pistol from where Leroy had tucked it into the top of his jeans.

Returning to the hangar entrance stoop, she tried to pick up the floor jack. Covered with dust and splattered with blood, it still sat where Sandy had dropped it when Buck and Leroy had ambushed her. She tried to lift it, but couldn't. It had been difficult enough when she only had a knee injury to deal with. Standing, she cast a worried look toward the patio. "Damn it!" Something squealed and rattled behind her. Sandy spun, pistol at the ready.

Pushing a wheelbarrow, her mother strode from behind the building. Transported across the rocky soil, the shotgun chattered in the cart's metal belly.

After casting a disdainful glance at Leroy's corpse, Sandy's mother turned and smiled. "I think this should help."

A few minutes later, having successfully lifted the beam and loaded her daddy into the cart, they rolled back into the rear yard. The barrow's wheel squealed and groaned its protest. Sandy winced as it bounced over another obstacle. The backyard soil had always been rocky. Between shattered asteroid fragments and broken bits of building, it was practically impassable now.

Her father's head lolled back. "Would it kill you to miss one of those?" Before Sandy could protest that she was doing her best, he winked. "Thanks for coming for us, Pumpkin."

Mom picked up where she'd left off earlier. "If you spent half the time working on this yard as you do on that stupid airplane, you'd be getting a smoother ride, mister."

Propped up in the wheelbarrow, her father raised his eyebrows. "Woman, quit your bellyaching. If I hadn't kept *ol' Betsy* in tip-top condition, we'd be driving to Nevada."

Sandy smiled. It was good to hear them return to their playful bickering.

"I never understood why your father still maintains that thing. The Feds retired him and that plane years ago."

Sandy knew she was right. If it had been anybody else's airplane, she'd be concerned. However, her father, the ultimate perfectionist—at least with all things aviation—had maintained *ol' Betsy* impeccably.

"And," her mother continued undeterred. "They closed this field over ten years ago." Feigning indignation, she added, "Considering he lost his medical about the same time, I thought we'd finally get some quality time together."

Her father rolled his eyes and grinned at Sandy. "So, now you know why I spend so much time in the hangar." He chuckled, but it quickly morphed into another coughing fit.

The two women exchanged concerned glances. Her mom's hand went to his shoulder.

As the coughs passed, he took her hand in his. "Don't you worry, Firecracker. I told you, you're still stuck with me."

After lots of grunts, heaves, and more than a few yelps, they made it through the yard, over the collapsed block wall, and into the aircraft.

Sandy closed the plane's right door. From his position in the back right seat, her dad gave a weary thumbs-up. Sitting next to him, her mother smiled nervously and raised a tentative thumb as well.

Walking around the front of the plane, Sandy scanned the airfield. Other than the still-running Camaro, the scene was tranquil and quiet. Having already opened the left side of the hangar's main door, she swung the other wide open. Sandy hurried back to the plane and climbed into the front left pilot's seat. To her right, her father's splinted right leg rested on the back of the folded-down front seat. The tourniquet, still held tight by Mom's wooden spoon, seemed to be doing its job. Sandy knew the standard practice was to release it a couple of times per hour. However, considering the quantity of lost blood, she decided it wasn't worth the risk.

Through the airplane's automotive style rear-view mirror, Sandy made eye contact. "Everybody ready?"

Side-by-side and holding hands, they nodded. Ghost-white, her daddy looked on the verge of passing out, but he smiled and gave her another thumbs-up. "You have the controls, Pumpkin." Mom, usually the outspoken one of the two, simply smiled and nodded again.

Running through the start, taxi, and before takeoff checks by memory, Sandy soon had the plane out of the hangar and roaring down the remnants of Carmel Valley's aptly named Vintage Airfield. Closed more than 10 years, the runway was anything but ideal.

She steered the small, single-engine plane down the smoothest available section of runway. However, an involuntary screech slipped between her father's clenched teeth each time the plane hopped and bounced across an unavoidable knot of grass or pothole.

"Sorry, Daddy."

Two yowls of pain later, his rigid posture went limp. In the rear-view mirror, she saw his eyes roll back as the pain and blood loss overwhelmed him. He was unconscious. A few agonizing and bone-jarring seconds later, *ol' Betsy* finally clawed her way into the sky.

"Sandy."

"I know, Mom. We'll get him there."

The atmospheric shock wave generated by the enemy's arrival had decimated most of Southern California. Sandy also imagined the injuries she'd seen on the north side of Carmel Valley Village extended along the entire periphery of the weapon's effect. Every operational emergency medical facility this side of the Sierra Nevada mountain range would be overwhelmed. Her father's best chance lay farther east, in the capable hands of Nellis Air Force Base's emergency medical staff, many of them freshly returned from combat tours in Afghanistan.

Thanks to strong tailwinds and her father's power plant modifications, the plane made the trip faster than she dared hope.

"Roger, Nellis Tower, Seven-Zero-One Mike Delta, clear to land Runway Zero-Three," Sandy transmitted.

"Be advised, the ambulance you requested is standing by in front of Base Ops."

"Thanks, Tower."

Sandy turned the small plane onto the final approach course. Vacated of all aircraft, the usually crowded expansive ramp running parallel to Nellis Air Force Base's main runway was a concrete desert.

At its north end, in front of the Base Operations terminal, she saw an emergency vehicle's flashing lights.

The empty ramp gave Sandy an idea. "Nellis Tower, Seven-Zero-Three requests permission to land directly to taxiway Foxtrot." Over eight thousand feet long, the eastern edge of the tarmac, designated as taxiway F, was longer than many runways, easily four times longer than what she needed right now.

"Uh, I'm not sure I can approve that, Seven-Zero-Three."

Casting a nervous look at her still unconscious father, Sandy shook her head. She shifted the plane's track left, toward Foxtrot.

"Sorry, Tower. You're coming in broken and unreadable. I think this old plane's radio is going Tango Uniform. If you can read this, I'm shifting to land on Foxtrot abeam Ops. Over."

"Uh ... Roger, Seven-Zero-Three," he replied in a resigned tone.

Landing as close as feasible to Base Operations, Sandy set the plane down on Foxtrot's north end. Keeping her taxi speed as fast as she dared, she sped toward the waiting ambulance. Many other vehicles sat parked around it. Sliding to a stop in front of the group, Sandy killed the engine. Setting the parking brake, she jumped out.

Gesturing to the two corpsmen standing on either end of a rolling litter, she ran to the plane's right side. Throwing open the door, she waved them in. Unmoving, the medics stared open-mouthed at her blood-covered flight suit. "Hurry, goddamn it! He's lost a lot of blood."

Snapped out of their trance, the medics scrambled to comply. "Sorry, ma'am," the lead one said. He pointed to her especially bloody right side. "What about you?"

She shook her head. "Don't worry about me, Sergeant. Just take care of my father, please."

"Yes, ma'am. We'll do our best."

The other medic had already climbed into the seat vacated by her mom. The sergeant said, "How's that I.V. coming?"

The airman nodded. "Just about there."

"Good." The sergeant produced a unit of blood from the large red bag hanging on his right shoulder. Handing it to the medic, he turned back to Sandy. "Captain Fitzpatrick, you're certain he's O-positive, right?"

Sandy nodded.

The sergeant nodded, too. "Good, we'll pump as much into him as we can." He opened his bag to her.

Sandy was relieved to see several I.V. bags of blood nestled in its confines.

Five eternal minutes later, the first unit of blood was half-depleted. With the help of several waiting security police, they extricated him from the plane's cramped quarters onto a backboard and finally onto the waiting litter.

As they rolled her dad into the back of the ambulance, a voice came from behind her. "Captain Fitzpatrick?"

Sandy turned. A female in full dress uniform stood alone. Twenty feet behind the major sat a Hummer with the markings of an Air Force two-star general. Sandy saluted General Pearson's aide. "Yes, ma'am, I'm Captain Fitzpatrick."

Seeing Sandy's condition, the major's arm wavered mid-salute. "Holy shit, Captain. Are you okay?"

Sandy held up a finger. "Hang on, I'll be right with you, ma'am." Not answering the question or waiting for the major's reply, she turned to her mother. "You ride with Daddy."

Her mom watched the medics work on her husband in the back of the ambulance. "Thanks for coming for us, hun. I would've lost him."

"You saved me too, Mom."

The slight woman shuddered as a sour look crossed her face. "Those A-holes deserved a lot more than that." Pulling her eyes from the ambulance, she looked at Sandy with burning intensity. "Don't you worry about us." Her mother nodded toward the general's Hummer. "I know you have work to do." Then she pointed a middle finger at the sky. "Now go give those other A-holes hell."

It was good to see her mom's brashness return. During the flight from Carmel Valley, Sandy told her all she knew about the alien invasion. Considering what she was going through, Sandy hadn't wanted to burden her with the news. However, once they'd climbed to altitude, her mother witnessed the widespread devastation first-hand.

"I'll check on the two of you in a little bit. Make sure they take good care of Daddy."

Her momma hugged her. Wincing, Sandy returned it. Moving her hands to cradle Sandy's face, she looked into her eyes. "Be careful, honey." Pulling her head down, her mom kissed Sandy's forehead and then waved a dismissive hand toward the ambulance. "Don't you worry about your daddy." She winked at Sandy. "He's survived forty-nine years of my nagging. The stubborn ol' coot'll survive this."

Having finished prepping her father for transport, the medics were ready to depart. Sandy helped her mom into the back of the ambulance.

"I'll make damn sure these boys take good care of my Johnny."

Sandy smiled and gave her hand a reassuring squeeze. "I know you will, Mom. I know you will." Almost feeling sorry for him, Sandy gave the sergeant an apologetic nod. "Take good care of my parents."

He saluted her. "Yes, ma'am."

Sandy closed the ambulance's door and smacked the vehicle's side twice. Siren blaring and engine roaring, the truck sped off.

CHAPTER 40

Salyth seethed. Attacking first, the Argonians had broken protocol, leaving his plan in ruins. He pounded a fist into the rock ceiling as two more of his ships imploded under the onslaught.

"Commodore, our dreadnoughts are being wiped out. Ship commanders report all available power is being diverted to their shields. They're unable to complete weapon recharging. We have no gene weapons to deploy."

"Has our weapon finished charging?"

"Almost, Commodore. I've been charging it since we brought the computers online. However, maintaining our shield strength, coupled with the reduced power available, is slowing the process."

Salyth roared in frustration. "Have the two closest ships extend their shields. Once they're covering us, divert all power to charge the gene weapon." As he gave the order, another ship's shields collapsed. Instantly, it detonated under an intensified barrage of energy beams. Chunks of ship and molten asteroid rained down. Bouncing harmlessly off the Argonian shields, it fell toward the planet below.

The GDF battlecruisers diverted more of their firepower at the falling debris, slowing their destruction of his fleet. The sight spawned a spark of hope. "The fools are so concerned with protecting their brothers on the planet, they're giving us the time we need to assure their destruction!"

His momentary elation faltered as another ship's shield failed in a spectacular explosion.

"Commodore, even at this rate, our fleet may be completely wiped out before the weapon fully charges."

Salyth roared. Blazing across the bridge, he struck as Lord Thrakst had during the first test of the gene disruptor weapon. However, Salyth did not retract his forearm's razor-sharp talon. The officer's blood flew across the bridge. He fell to the floor, gurgling and clutching at his slashed throat.

Kicking aside the convulsing body of his last officer, Salyth took over his station. "You go tell the Forebearers it can't be done. I'll stay here and make it happen!"

The dead eyes of the now motionless body accusingly stared into Salyth's soul. *It's your fault, Commodore! We're all dead because of your ineptitude!*

"Shut up, coward!" Salyth snapped. He kicked the dead officer. The body rolled, coming to rest with its back to him. Maddeningly, the partially decapitated head lolled back, its dead eyes staring at Salyth.

White light filled the bridge. The commodore tore himself from the hatchling's dead, accusatory eyes. Outside, a supernova appeared to flare from within two of his ships. Surrendering to the nuclear holocaust, they shattered, spraying molten stone and metal against the extended shields protecting his vessel.

Argonians don't use atomic weapons.

Remembering the ships that had nearly destroyed him, Salyth shook a fist at the ceiling. "Forebearer's damnation! Once I finish with your ancestors, I'll feast on your human bones!"

Turning to the blood-covered control panel, he pounded the weapon's status display. "Charge, you cursed weapon! *Charge*!"

~

"Stand by, Captain Allison. My other fighters are rejoining," Colonel Zach Newcastle said.

"Roger, sir."

Having completed their first attack run on the reorganized enemy fleet, Vampire Squadron's Alpha and Bravo Wings reunited east of the battle. Superimposed over Earth's curving blue sphere, Vlad's ship pulled alongside his. "Bravo Wing checking in," Commander Yaakov reported through a thick Russian accent.

"Roger, Vlad," Zach said, saluting him through his fighter's canopy. "Good shooting, comrade."

Commander Yaakov returned the salute, his mirrored helmet dipping in a nod. "As well to you, my friend."

Nodding and dropping the salute, Zach returned to the Space Control frequency. "That's great news, Captain Allison. I'll brief my squadron. Then we're heading back in. Keep feeding me the updates."

"Will do, Colonel. Turtle One, out."

At Admiral Thoyd Feyhdyak's request, the squadron had rejoined the battle. The Argonians had diverted most of their strong lasers to vaporizing the massive chunks raining down from the conflagration. Because of the suspected hot enemy weapon and the ongoing laser barrage, Admiral Feyhdyak asked Vampire Squadron to abandon their previous close-combat tactics and deploy their bunker busters from a greater distance. He said the combined effect of the squadron's nukes coupled with the Argonian's lasers would speed up the destruction of the Zoxyth while limiting the unit's exposure.

Zach knew they owed the Argonians a great debt of gratitude. He figured some of the GDF ships could get away if they made a run for it. However, that would leave the planet undefended and lighten the barrage, potentially opening a window for the enemy to drop shields long enough to deploy their weapon. The Argonian ships were holding station in a heroic effort to save the planet.

He returned to the squadron frequency. "Good job, Vampires. Our first attack helped destroy all but the last two enemy dreadnoughts."

A chorus of cheers filled his helmet.

After a quick inventory of the squadron's remaining missiles,

Colonel Newcastle continued in a somber tone. "Those two enemy ships are all that stand between us and what's left of their command ship. It's time to finish these bastards. Only nine of us still have missiles." He nodded to his right. "Commander Yaakov, in addition to your two missiles, I count one each in three of your fighters. Take your armed fighters and hit the far ship with four missiles."

Vlad nodded.

"Major Jakobson, I'm going to bring up the rear with my two missiles. You and three of your wingmen have one missile each. I want you four to hit the near ship with four missiles as well. I'll take care of the command ship. Stagger your weapons. If the first one weakens the shield, the second or third might get through. At any rate, the combined effect should give the Argonian lasers an opening to finish this."

Commander Yaakov's thickly accented voice came across the radio. "Comrade, by my count, we have eleven missiles left. No?"

Newcastle nodded. "Da, my friend. I want to keep a couple in reserve. You and I will hold onto one missile each."

Vlad nodded again.

Zach punched a series of numbers into his fire-control computer. "I'm uploading the attack sequence into each of your FCCs." Two seconds after pressing the send key, he received an automated confirmation from each fighter.

Saluting his squadron, he said, "Good luck, gentlemen, I'll see you on the other side."

Each returned the salute.

Heart racing—as it always did just before joining the battle—he watched the computer countdown. At the designated time, Alpha and Bravo Wings accelerated to their initialization points. Reaching their assigned vector, each turned and rocketed toward the back of an Argonian fighter.

With an eye on his clock, Zach flexed his gloved fingers over the fighter's flight controller. *Three ... two ... one ... now!* He shoved the stick forward. The fighter shot west, toward the battle, quickly narrowing the two hundred-mile gap.

Ahead, Alpha and Bravo Wing's missiles started streaming toward their targets. Launched at their programmed intervals, they looked like a staggered line of fiery-tailed arrows. Each flew straight toward the back of the friendly Argonian fighter assigned to block its approach from enemy observation. At the absolute last second, when Zach was certain it was doomed, each fighter darted out of the missile's path. The tactic hid the Vampire fighters' egress and their missile's ingress until each had accelerated to a velocity that left the enemy no time to react.

On cue, the Argonians unleashed a fresh onslaught, providing cover for the egressing fighters.

Reaching his approach vector, Colonel Newcastle's ship turned and accelerated toward the back of his assigned Argonian fighter. One hundred miles from the enemy ships, he launched his missile. An instantaneous course reversal snapped his ship outbound. Flying backward, he watched the first group of missiles approach their targets.

His canopy auto-dimmed as a strobing chain of four brilliant nuclear detonations blossomed above the bracketing enemy ships. Not penetrating, the nukes exploded against their shields.

The hourglass shape of the overlapping glowing shells looked like a massive amoeba frozen in the act of cellular division. Completing the illusion, the ships within formed nuclei. The right half of the amoebic shell flickered and collapsed. As the others had, the shield released its energy in a storm of dissipating lightning bolts.

"Come on!" he screamed, heart racing.

Adding to the assault, the few Argonian lasers not tasked with debris vaporization still drilled into the trio. The fifth nuke detonated against the far ship's shield. Still extended to encapsulate the enemy ship remnant, it flared like a teardrop-shaped miniature sun, but somehow it held against the nuclear assault.

"Damn it! Come on," he growled, willing the last shield to collapse.

The sixth and seventh missiles slammed into the unprotected near ship. For a millisecond, it looked like a star had been born within the vessel's rocky confines. Glowing with internal brilliance, a network of hundreds of fissures suddenly criss-crossed its surface. Then the dreadnought disintegrated in a nuclear holocaust.

Newcastle pumped his fist. "Yes!"

Turning from the roiling plasma cloud, he watched the eighth missile close on the last enemy dreadnought. Following close behind, his missile bore down on the ship remnant.

Eyes narrowed with focused hate, Newcastle glared at the bastard that had wiped out D.C. "Die, you son of a bitch!"

Another blinding flash came from the right of Salyth's ship. Checking that sector's video feed, he saw the unmistakable roiling fireball of another fission bomb. Its shields weakened by the barrage of focused energy weapons, the starboard dreadnought succumbed to the renewed nuclear attack.

The blast slammed the remains of The *Forebearer's Revenge* into the ship on its left. The impact overloaded the inertial compensators. Thrown across the bridge, Salyth crashed into the far wall with bone-crushing force. Fighting to his feet, he scrambled back to the weapon control panel. Through the blood covering its surface, the *Charging* icon still pulsed red.

Outside, brilliant light blossomed again as another fission bomb struck his final dreadnought. The last protective ship's force field flickered, threatening to fail. His ship rocked under the shock wave, knocking him to the deck again.

Pulverized and bleeding profusely, he clawed his way back up to the control panel. Knowing his death was only moments away, Commodore Salyth feared he had failed the Forebearers.

The tremendous battle played across the *Turtle's* view-wall. Only the ship remnant and its two protective dreadnoughts remained.

Jake felt a hint of hope struggling to cast off some of the day's overwhelming dread and horror. The three Air Force pilots watched in shocked trepidation as Vampire Squadron's nuclear bunker busters slammed ineffectually into the Zoxyth shields. Like an insane disco-strobe on hyperdrive, the rapid-fire detonations and subsequent auto-dimming painted the *Turtle's* cabin in surrealistic stop-frame animation.

Two blinding flashes later, the right dreadnought ruptured with the brilliance of an internal nuclear detonation. Under the combined assault of the Argonian's laser barrage and Vampire Squadron's nuclear bombardment, its shields collapsed in a spreading electrical discharge and the asteroidal ship detonated, a blinding fire blasting from a spiderweb of fissures.

"Yes!" Jake screamed.

Their stop-animation celebration froze when the third missile detonated against the left cruiser's shields which flickered but appeared to hold. Their final hope rested on the last two missiles bearing down on the remaining two targets.

"Please," Victor whispered.

Collectively holding their breath, all three pilots stepped up, placing their hands against the view-wall. Willing the missiles into their targets, Jake whispered through clenched teeth, "Go ... go ... go!" He pushed against the clear wall with each chant.

At the last moment, the two Argonian fighters who shielded their approach darted aside. An eternal second later, just before the left missile struck, the last force field collapsed. Passing through the expanding web of lightning bolts, the missile slammed into the final enemy dreadnought and it exploded with wonderful internal brilliance.

Jake's heart raced as the final missile closed on the Zoxyth command ship. "Time for you to die!" he shouted. The view-wall auto-darkened as the missile struck the ship remnant with a brilliant flash.

Salyth could feel his strength waning. His blood now ran freely across the console. Checking the flickering tactical display, he saw two missiles bearing down. The final one had the *Forebearer's Revenge* in its sights.

The radio crackled to life. "Commodore Salyth, I've failed you. That last missile drained our shields to five percent. We won't survive the next."

As the final dreadnought commander's transmission ended, a mad laugh echoed through the cavernous bridge.

Salyth looked at the severed head. The obstinate dead officer's eyes seemed to glare accusingly. The commodore feebly kicked at it and yelled, "Shut up!"

Again the speaker blared. The commander's words echoed off the rock walls. "It's been an honor, Commodore. I'll see you with the Forebear—" His sentence died unfinished as the blinding flash of the next fission bomb flared across the bridge. Its shock wave shoved Salyth sideways.

The nuclear inferno of the burning dreadnought wrapped around his unprotected ship. In the brilliance flooding the bridge, Salyth turned back to the control panel. Barely visible through the radiance, a new light shone through the vital fluid puddled on its glass top. With a tremendous effort, Salyth swung a heavy arm across the console. An arc of blood sprayed from its surface. Rubbing his massive hands across the panel, he squinted, trying to read the display. Finally, the wavering letters came into focus: WEAPON CHARGED.

Commodore Salyth tilted his head back and roared. With the last of his failing energy, he hoisted both arms toward the ceiling. "The Forebearer's are avenged!" Then his body collapsed. Falling through the white-hot light flooding the bridge, his arms thrust toward the weapon's actuator.

CHAPTER 41

Sandy followed the general's aide down a long, featureless corridor. The razor-sharp creases of the woman's uniform, lack of jewelry, and jet black, tightly drawn hair gave the senior officer a severe look. The female major slowed as she reached the end of the hallway. "In here, Captain."

Sandy nodded to her and passed through the double steel doors the officer had indicated. The placard on the wall above the entry read: Combat Control Center. Usually referred to as C3, the room was full of computer consoles and displays. A layman could easily mistake it for NASA's Mission Control. From here, Air Force Command staff monitored deployed forces around the planet in real time.

Stopping to stare at the room's main display in open-jawed amazement, Sandy realized the capability also reached into space. An incredible scene played out across a large display dominating the room's back wall. Like a cinematic space battle, hundreds if not thousands of ships filled the screen. Some flew about in total chaos, while others hovered in a stationary formation too big to fit in the image. Extending above and below the satellite's narrow field of view, the scope of the engagement made it difficult to tell one side from another. The disparate collection of ships, multicolored laser beams, and flickering curtains of energy painted a confused mural across the large display.

Utilizing the same gravity-defying ability demonstrated over San Francisco, the stationary vessels in the battle hovered over a large body of water. The conflict was obviously taking place in space. However, she had no way of deducing the location or altitude. Holding their position, the alien ships slowly shrank as the terrestrial satellite providing the video feed maintained its orbital velocity. Every second brought additional ships into the expanding view. A land mass slid into the bottom of the screen's right side. The curving shoreline formed familiar lines that Sandy belatedly recognized as Spain's southwest coast when the iconic Strait of Gibraltar also glided into view. Looking backward and slowly receding from the space battle, the spy satellite continued its southeastward track, bringing North Africa and the Sahara desert into the image's lower left side.

As the point of view drew farther away, the full battle finally came into sight. Arranged in a large sphere, hundreds of sleek, wedge-shaped ships formed a cocoon with several dark structures at its center. Like spokes of a wheel, scores of laser beams attached the outer shell of ships to the bulbous energy curtains encasing the central targets. As if choreographed to an unheard musical accompaniment, the beams oscillated and randomly pulsed off and on. Sweeping around the formation, incidental patterns generated by simultaneous volleys seemed to race around the sphere like a hyperactive music visualizer.

A new barrage of lasers drew her attention. Burning from various points within the glowing orbs, fruitless violet lasers blazed through empty gaps in the encapsulating formation. As another flurry of beams shot through the shell, Sandy caught movement. They weren't firing at empty space. Each beam had targeted a specific vessel. However, as if prescient, the sleek wedges skipped aside, instantaneously dodging each beam.

The scale of the image slammed home when the shielded objects revealed themselves during a lull in the attack's intensity. Sandy recognized the central small irregular edifices as a collection of the giant asteroidal enemy vessels. Judging by those proportions, and the relative size of the continental land masses below, it looked like a few of the enemy ships had been trapped in a desperate defensive formation a couple of hundred miles above the Atlantic Ocean.

In a sudden epiphany, Sandy realized the encompassing fleet must belong to the galactic government Jake had described. Unrelentingly, the short-duration laser beams continued to burn from the nose of each of the encircling ships. Studying their form, Sandy decided the wedge-shaped vessels must be a space-based alien analogue of a fighter jet. As she examined them, several new, larger beams joined the assault, burning into the shields of the enemy formation.

Following the new lasers to their source, Sandy spotted several dark shapes sliding into the satellite's ever-expanding field of view. Arranged in an expansive grid, a fleet of massive ships hovered below the sphere of fighters. As if absorbing all light, their profiles appeared to cut black holes into the backdropping azure atmosphere. The flowing lines of the beautiful crafts contrasted sharply against the irregular angularities of the antagonistic alien's asteroidal ships. Dwarfing the enemy vessels, the largest of the sleek, black ships easily exceeded five miles in length.

Barely discernible against the ocean below, a shimmering halo surrounded each. When one of the entrapped enemy vessels fired its own laser down into the flat formation, the faint shimmer blossomed into an opalescent sheet. Sandy realized it was a force field similar to that employed by the enemy ships. The overlapping shields of the massive black ships created a huge, circular plane between Earth and the enemy fleet.

While the encapsulating fighters continued to pour fire into the entire enemy formation, all the lasers reaching up from the fleet of huge, sleek vessels burned into one object. The targeted asteroid's force field glowed like a white egg, completely obscuring the shrouded enemy vessel from view. Oscillating luminosity created a dizzying strobing effect as the force field appeared to weaken under the continued assault. Then its opalescent shimmer faded to a lambent grid of sheet lightning. Unrelenting brilliant beams of energy continued pouring into it. The bubble flared blindingly white and then collapsed, discharging its energy in an enormous flash of Saint Elmo's fire. The force field surrendered in a death knell of dissipating lightning bolts that leapt from ship to ship, dancing across every vessel in the conflict. The last of their energy spent, the fingers of blue plasma finally flickered and died as they passed into the void beyond the attacking ships.

In the same instant, the giant asteroid started dissolving under the continued assault. With unimaginable power, the lasers rendered the city-sized rocks into molten slag. Some sections detonated, casting glowing orange blobs in every direction. Trajectories curved into graceful hyperbolic arcs as their sub-orbital velocities proved insufficient to keep the molten rocks from falling into Earth's gravity well. Like a live-action version of Salvador Dali's surreal melting clock, the rigid protuberances of the asteroidal ships drooped. Under the continued laser assault, the sagging ship's energetic glow ramped up to white-hot. Now flowing like lava, the melted ship, no longer supported by its drive, surrendered to Earth's gravity and poured down on the vessels below. The small fighters in its path slid aside. When the hellish rain passed, they snapped back to their previous position, all while continuing to pour laser fire into the remaining enemy ships.

The molten rock fell onto one of the large vessels below. To Sandy's amazement, it bounced off the much larger ship's force field. Like mercury seeking low ground, it puddled in a depression in the formation's overlapping shield bubbles. The enormous, sleek black ships didn't even shudder under the impact. However, the entire grid seemed to sag until a gap opened, allowing the liquefied rock to slip past.

Sandy gasped as the mountainous glowing glob raced toward the

Atlantic Ocean. Then all the large ships turned their lasers and fired into the falling debris. The powerful beams broke the melted minerals into their constituent atoms. Freed of molecular bonds, the liquefied rock evaporated into a gaseous plasma. Like a comet passing too close to the sun, the plummeting molten sphere grew a fiery tail.

"Holy shit," Sandy whispered.

Renewed activity at the conflict's core drew her attention. Like an hourglass laid on its side, the overlapping shield bubbles protecting what was left of the enemy fleet fluoresced under the unyielding onslaught. Between flares, she glimpsed two ships within the double-bubble. A smaller, third entity appeared to occupy the area between the two. Then the linked orbs opaqued in a spasm of opalescent light fluorescing under the continued laser assault of the encapsulating fighters. A brief lull in the bombardment revealed the third object as the blasted ship remnant that had risen from Chesapeake Bay.

Sandy turned a nervous eye toward the planet below. "What are they doing about the other ships?"

"What other ships?" the major asked.

Sandy pointed at the two and a half vessels hovering at the center of the image. "There were sixteen of those assholes. I assume that's the one that came out of the Chesapeake. It and those two, along with the one they just shot down, only accounts for four of them." Prying her eyes from the incredible scene playing out on the display, Sandy turned to the female major with a questioning look. "Where are the other twelve?"

The major pointed at the Atlantic. "Sinking to the bottom of the ocean." For the first time since meeting Sandy, the stark officer smiled. "What's left of them, anyway."

Before she could ask the myriad questions elicited by the answer, movement at the top of the display drew her attention. New, disc-shaped ships darted into the image.

Sandy had observed combat operations from this room in the past. Like her fighter's tactical display, the command center's computers normally superimposed an icon over each asset in theater. Whether manned fighter or remotely operated drone, each aircraft had a computer-generated icon following its every movement. Likely due to the lack of tracking telemetry, neither the antagonistic aliens nor the apparently malevolent forces garnered a symbol. However, computer-generated icons tracked each of these new vessels.

Now four more ships shot into view, bringing the icon count to eight. Moving incredibly fast, the octet of thin, silver discs diverged. With instantaneous course changes, they turned onto eight discrete paths. It appeared each vessel's approach angle would ultimately converge on the enemy fleet. However, a wedge-shaped fighter-analogue in the spherical formation appeared to block the inbound path of each silver disc. Just as Sandy recognized the threat to the apparently allied ships, the approaching discs reversed direction. Not believing what she'd just seen, Sandy blinked her eyes. One moment, they'd been screaming toward the battle, the next they blasted away from the formation in an instantaneous course reversal.

Sandy recognized the fighters from Jake's description. Pointing at the icons, she turned to the major standing next to her. "Are those the fighters that shot down the ship over Chesapeake Bay?"

The major nodded.

The two groups of four ships were labeled *Vampire Alpha* and *Vampire Bravo*. The emblems rushing outbound passed a new solo icon labeled *Vampire Six*. Heading inbound, it passed between the eight symbols of Alpha and Bravo Wings. An instant later, it too reversed course, following the other ships upward, away from the formation.

Several new icons popped into existence. Trailing thin, fiery tails, a chain of silver missiles rushed inward. Labeled *BB22* through *BB29*, the eight icons each flew straight toward the back of an allied fighter. A ninth symbol joined the onslaught. Labeled *BB31*, it too rushed toward the back of an allied fighter.

Sandy turned to the female major again. "Those have to be the nuclear bunker busters! Why are we shooting at the good guys?"

The general's aide held up a finger. "Watch."

As each of the lead missiles reached the back of the formation, the imperiled alien ship darted out of the way. As the missile passed, the ships slid back into position. Finally understanding, Sandy nodded. "The Argonians are hiding their approach until the last possible moment."

Again the major nodded. "Our fighters can avoid their lasers, but the missiles can't."

Rocket motors added to the incredible velocity the Vampire fighters had imparted upon the missiles. In the short seconds it took them to bridge the gap, every fighter in the ball-shaped formation continued to pour laser fire into the glowing oblong double-bubble.

The image flashed bright white as the first missile impacted the right side of the enemy formation. A split second later, three more nuclear detonations struck in short intervals. Overdriving the satellite's visual sensors, the strobing nuclear blasts completely washed out the image.

As the nuclear conflagration faded, Sandy saw the final fighter dart sideways, allowing the last missile, *BB31,* to pass.

The image flickered as the still receding satellite increased magnification. In an instant, the round formation of sleek, black wedges blossomed from the center third of the display to completely fill it.

The right half of the glowing hourglass pulsed, then collapsed in another lightning storm of discharging energy. A second later, it disintegrated under a nuclear barrage as the sixth and seventh bunker busters slammed into it.

Sandy felt hope blossom as the sole ship's shield flickered. Still encapsulating the ship remnant, it had taken on a teardrop shape. Then it collapsed completely as the eighth missile passed through it and into the massive ship. The final vessel disintegrated in the fire of the bunker buster's double nuclear assault.

While the final missile bore down on the last target, a hazy film slid across the image. As the satellite receded farther from the battle, the planet's curvature pushed the atmosphere into its field of view.

Just as the horizon of the Sahara desert started obscuring the bottom of the battle, the missile slammed into the ship remnant. Like the sun rising from behind an ocean of sand, a brilliant arc of golden light exploded from the enemy ship.

As the satellite's inertia carried the scene out of view, the Combat Command Center personnel broke into cheers, hugging and high-fiving one another.

Silently watching the golden orb set behind the western horizon, Sandy placed a hand on her abdomen.

CHAPTER 42

To Captain Giard's horror, light raced from the missile's point of impact without dissipating. Debilitating nausea and abdominal pain hammered Jake. To his side, Richard and Victor spasmed in obvious pain.

Jake placed an open palm against the view-wall. Through clenched teeth he whispered, "God, please. No!"

His prayer for divine intervention went unheeded. Expanding at a preternaturally steady pace, the energy wave blazed across the battlefield. Inexorably, its abhorrent effulgence wrapped ship after ship in its vile embrace, quieting weapons, and setting vessels adrift.

Wide-eyed, Jake watched it reach for the Argonian Carrier Group. At the last moment, its battlecruisers tried to dart away from the advancing wave. However, the effect's speed eclipsed their drive's capability. Encapsulating the entire Argonian fleet, the wave reached its maximum range and faded to black. Minus their masters, the jumping battlecruisers lost all semblance of organization, each starting a slow tumble.

As the last plummeting molten asteroid disintegrated under its laser barrage, the massive carrier's beam fell silent, dying with the crew of its ship. Having stood its ground till the last, the huge Argonian carrier sat stationary, as if in silent vigil.

Beyond the *Turtle's* view-wall, surreal calm fell across the apocalyptic panorama. At its heart, the inexplicably intact grinning alien bust glared from the center of its attendant swarm of ghost ships.

PART III

"O war! thou son of hell,
Whom angry heavens do make their minister,
Throw in the frozen bosoms of our part
Hot coals of vengeance! Let no soldier fly.
He that is truly dedicate to war
Hath no self-love, nor he that loves himself,
Hath not essentially but by circumstance
The name of valour."

— William Shakespeare

CHAPTER 43

On his knees, Victor bent over and retched, then wrapped arms around himself. Staring at the floor, the junior officer started rocking back and forth, repeating the same word. "No, no, no ..."

Grimacing against the fire burning through his body and struggling to breathe, Jake leaned against the view-wall. He didn't want to accept the imagery streaming into his eyes. However, as if confirming the new reality's solidity, an abandoned Argonian fighter tumbled past. Apparently tossed from the battle, it narrowly missed colliding with the *Turtle.* Jake watched its slow-motion summersault in shocked silence.

Well beyond its target, the last bunker buster rocketed toward Earth's southwestern horizon, then flickered and disappeared, apparently self-destructing in a non-nuclear detonation.

"Damn it!" Richard growled as he punched the view-wall.

Dragging his eyes from the fighter, Jake looked at him. Glaring at the miraculously intact remnant of the enemy command ship, Richard shook his head. "Those fuckers need to die!"

As the weapon-induced nausea eased, Jake straightened and did a head-shake, trying to banish the mind-fogging shock. Blinking, he said, "Yes, they do."

Still kneeling, Victor continued his chant.

Clutching his gut, Richard looked at the lieutenant with evident disgust. Returning his attention beyond the view-wall, he pointed at the enemy ship. "Looks like Colonel Newcastle missed."

Jake shook his head. "He couldn't have. The missile was heading straight at it. Hell, I saw it hit." He traced the missile's fading smoke trail back to the enemy's command ship. It appeared to pass directly through the center of the alien visage.

Turning his attention back to his wingmen, Jake watched Richard look through the view-wall. Many of the emotions contorting his old flight schoolmate's face mirrored his own. Below him, Victor ceased his chanting and looked up. "I can't believe they're dead."

Richard's face hardened. "Well, they are," he said in a flat monotone.

Jake patted his shoulder. "Come on, Vic."

Taking the offered hand, the young officer stood. "What are we going to do now?"

"We're going to fuck them up, that's what!" Richard snapped.

Lieutenant Croft flinched, then asked, "How are we—?"

Richard spun on him. Eyes burning with anger, he looked ready to pummel Victor. "Goddamn it, Lieutenant! Stop your—"

Jake placed a hand on both men's shoulders. "Let's figure out what happened to that missile."

Victor looked back and forth. After a few seconds, Richard sighed and turned away.

Jake stepped to the holographic display and magnified the enemy ship. Vic watched in nervous silence as the alien vessel expanded. Rotating the display, Jake found his quarry. "Oh shit."

Richard turned from the wall. "What?"

Jake slid the holographic rendering between them and looked at Richard through the hole the missile had bore through its center.

"It went right through," Vic whispered.

They stared in shocked silence. Then all three flinched as the radio shattered the cabin's cemeterial silence. "Turtle One, this is Vampire Six. Please tell me y'all were clear of the blast zone."

Richard toggled the radio. "Roger, Six. We're ..." He stopped and looked outside. Jake saw anger and worry mixed with self-loathing. Richard hated weakness, couldn't tolerate it, especially in himself. Ever since flight school, the man had been impatient with anyone that he felt didn't measure up. Closing his eyes, Richard took a deep breath, held it for a moment and let it out in a long exhalation. Eyes opening, he continued. "We're here, sir."

"Hang in there, Captain," Colonel Newcastle said, sympathy softening his Texas drawl. "We still have a job to do. This isn't over yet."

Jake patted Richard on the shoulder and stepped to the radio. "Sir, we're looking at a magnification of the enemy ship. Your missile punched right through."

Colonel Newcastle sighed. "I was afraid that might happen. It must be too hollowed out. We have two more bunker busters. I'll change the nuke's settings and take it out."

Jake checked the dead Argonian fleet. The sight of its ships drifting farther apart generated an epiphany. "Colonel, if that thing falls into the ocean, tsunamis will flood Europe and the Eastern seaboard. Plus, your nuke's EM pulses will fry half the world's financial networks."

After a long pause, the colonel said, "You're right, but if those bastards get anywhere near the surface, millions of lives will be at stake. We have to use the nukes."

Jake looked at the enemy ship. It appeared to glare at him. Below, the massive carrier still maintained its silent vigil. Jake toggled the radio again. "But, sir, if that thing drops into the ocean intact—"

"Damn it, Captain!" Newcastle interrupted. "I'm aware of that, but we're out of options here. So, unless you have a better idea—"

"I do, sir."

"You do what, Captain?"

"Have a better idea, sir."

Richard and Vic looked at him. The radio speaker crackled. "I'm all ears, Captain."

After another look outside, Jake took a deep breath and toggled the radio. "The ship hasn't moved since the attack. Everybody onboard might be dead. At the very least, they have to be seriously degraded. Between your attack over the Chesapeake and the pummeling they've taken here, they must be cooked and battered." Jake looked at his wristwatch. "Sir, we have forty-one minutes before he can fire his weapon again. Let us probe the ship. If we can find a way on-board, we can sweep through and mop up any survivors."

Richard smiled, but Victor's face was a study in abject horror.

"Captain, I appreciate your out-of-the-box thinking, but last I checked, the *Turtle* is an unarmed ship. Besides, how do you propose to get on that thing?"

"Actually, sir, we procured some weapons in Maryland."

"Okay, Captain." The colonel sounded less dubious. When he again asked how he planned to get on-board, Jake thought he heard hope creeping into Newcastle's voice.

Jake manipulated the hologram. The Zoxyth ship already filled most of the display, but he was interested in a specific part. After a quick adjustment, he stood back and pointed into the hole left by the unexploded bunker buster.

"Sir, your missile cut a tunnel all the way through the enemy ship. Let us investigate it. If we can't find our way on-board before time runs out, we'll back off and let you nuke it."

Still hugging himself, Victor paced back and forth. Smiling predatorily, Richard nodded his agreement.

After a long pause, Newcastle's voice returned with a tone of admiration. "I like how you think, Captain. For now, we'll move in hot with cannons and conventional missiles. While we attack from the front, you and your team move in from the rear. The *Turtle* will keep you safe. It has the same maneuvering capability as the Argonian fighters and should have no problem evading enemy laser fire, should it come."

"Yes, sir."

"We'll buy you as much time to recon as we can, but, if it comes down to it, I'll use the nukes." After a meaningful pause, he added, "Whether or not you and your team are still on-board."

Staring at the floor, Vic took a deep breath. Then, apparently reining in his fear, he looked at Jake and nodded. Richard nodded, as well.

"Roger, Six. We'll reconnoiter and report back to you as soon as possible."

"Make it less than forty minutes, please."

"Will do, sir."

"Good hunting, gentlemen. Vampire Six, out."

The holographic display showed his fighters splitting into pairs. The formation rocketed past the enemy ship. Setting up well to its front, they turned inbound.

Jake looked outside and saw them fire their smaller missiles, pinpoints of light racing toward the enemy ship. Unfortunately, lasers fired back at the space fighters. In the hologram, he watched them easily evade each shot.

Jake reached into the flight controller. "Ready, gentlemen?"

"Ready boss," Richard said.

He turned to Lieutenant Croft. "Hanging in there, buddy?"

"Yes, sir. I'm ready," he managed nervously.

Jake nodded and turned his attention outside. Before hesitation allowed doubts to creep in, he activated the controller and the *Turtle* blasted toward the enemy ship.

"Curse these Argonians!" Salyth screamed, firing again. Once more, the targeted ship darted out of the beam's path. Without the rest of the ship's weapons, he couldn't send the full barrage needed to overwhelm the annoying tactic.

He hadn't expected to live long enough to cherish his victory over the Galactic Defense Force. Following his activation of the gene weapon, a tremendous crash had shaken the ship. He had closed his eyes, expecting that when he opened them he'd be surrounded by the Forebearers' grateful faces. Instead, when the weapon's luminosity faded, only the traitorous officer's dead eyes greeted him.

A quick review of available systems showed a path of destruction cut through the ship's center. The missile assigned to send him to the Forebearers had passed completely through his asteroid. Bulkhead doors had preserved the atmosphere. Power supply still worked, but a surge had knocked part of the drive system offline. While it still countered the planet's gravity, its stalled motivator left him dead in the water. Given enough time, it could be brought back online. Also, the gene weapon was recharging, but he didn't think he'd survive long enough to use either.

Salyth fired another volley at a pair of incoming ships. They darted out of the beam's path. The commodore roared with frustration. "Don't toy with me! Kill me, you backwoods Argonians! I've fought with honor, now send me to the Forebearers."

A rumble passed through the ship. He braced for the end, but it still didn't come. Confused, he looked around the bridge.

Then a voice echoed through the room, *You're not worthy.*

Seeking the source of the rebuke, Salyth's head whipped from side to side. Locking eyes with the lifeless, partially decapitated weapons officer, he roared, "What did you say, coward?"

No answer.

"That's what I thought," Salyth said, turning to the tactical display. On its screen, he watched another pair of fighters unleash a volley of shots. "They're firing projectile weapons?" The realization sent him into stunned silence. After a moment, he burst into a fit of gurgling laughter that morphed into gore-spewing coughs.

Spitting blood at the officer's body, he taunted, "They're out of nuclear missiles. The Forebearers have more work for me."

Searching space, he found a target. Tumbling pilotlessly, the closest Galactic Defense Force's Phoenix Fighter begged for his attention. Activating his starboard weapon, Salyth fired an energy beam at the drifting ship. After several seconds it exploded.

More gurgling laughter and coughing echoed through the bridge.

The dead officer's voice still taunted. *Coooommodoooore...*

Salyth tried to ignore it. He knew that, when subjected to extreme trauma, Zox often succumbed to psychosis.

Coooommodoooore...

He slowly turned to the weapons officer's lifeless eyes.

You lost an entire fleet, Coooommodoooore! Lord Thrakst will curse you!

Salyth, eyes burning bright with insanity's cold fire, turned on the dead officer. "Coward! I don't need your insolence!" He kicked the corpse again. The vicious blow finished the decapitation, sending the severed screaming head rolling across the bridge.

You killed... Clunk-clunk. ...*us all!* Clunk-clunk.

He watched wordlessly as the head wound to a slow spinning stop in the middle of the floor. Finally grinding to a halt, its accusing, glazed-white eyes burned through him.

"I wiped out the Argonians!" Salyth roared defensively.

The dead officer stared through him.

Dragging his eyes away, he fired at another drifting ship. As it exploded, Salyth turned to the drive system's status board. "If these feeble *Humans* can't send me to the Forebearers, maybe I can send a few more cities to theirs."

As sardonic laughter echoed through the bridge, Salyth cast a wary glance at the disembodied head.

"Bravo Wing, concentrate your fire on the upper bridge section. I see light coming from that area. See if you can punch through. Maybe we can open it to space. In the meantime, my fighters will go after those lasers."

"Roger," Commander Yaakov replied.

Turning to his wing's frequency, Colonel Newcastle continued. "Alpha Wing, our first pass was ineffectual. We need to defang this ship." As the toothy alien visage passed under his fighter, he winced at the incidental pun. His ship juked as another enemy laser reached for it. "He can't hit us, but we need to take out that laser battery before they start taking pot-shots at the unmanned fleet. Follow me to the initialization point. When we roll in from the IP, I want all conventional weapons brought to bear."

The damaged ship had two remaining laser batteries, one tucked into a fold on each side of the alien bust.

"We'll attack the left one first," he said as they turned inbound from the IP. "Fire, fire, fire!"

He opened up with the fighter's thirty-millimeter cannon. Firing a Maverick missile designed for use in the vacuum of space, he watched as the munitions closed on the target. Thousands of depleted uranium rounds peppered the side of the ship. They spalled small pieces of asteroid, but none made it into the laser emitter's fold.

"What the hell?"

His missile, followed by those of his wingmen, slammed into a small, invisible force field. Striking a bubble of shielding that only protected the laser, they detonated above the target in a haunting miniature replay of the first futile attacks on the enemy fleet.

Colonel Newcastle growled in frustration. *It's like shooting a BB gun at an elephant.*

A laser beam shot past his vessel. Snap-rolling the fighter, he realized it wasn't aimed at him. He turned his ship in time to see the intended target, an Argonian ship, detonate in a brilliant flash.

"I hate it when I'm right."

Because the aft section of the enemy ship remnant had received the heaviest damage, Jake reasoned it would have the biggest blind spot. While he steered to a vector that would bring them in from its rear, two beams reached for their ship, and each time its self-defense system instantly yanked it out of the laser's path. Now heading straight at its rear, Jake applied maximum acceleration. The *Turtle* closed the hundred-mile gap in less than a minute. No additional lasers fired at them.

Closing to within a few miles, Jake watched as First Space Fighter Squadron's attacks proved ineffectual. Small explosions wrapped around the enemy ship's upper bridge, but as Bravo Wing zipped past, their wake revealed it as undamaged.

Richard shook his head in frustration. "Shit! That section has the same secondary force field. They can't hit the lasers or the bridge."

Jake nodded, frowning. "They're tearing up the areas they can hit, but the ship is just too big. They'll deploy their gene disruptor before we can make a dent in it."

A laser beam blasted another empty Argonian fighter.

Jake shook his head. "Damn it!"

Victor still looked nervous. "We can just fall back when the recharge time ends. Let them fire the weapon. We'll stay out of its range, nobody'll get hurt. Newcastle won't even have to fire the nukes. Then we can find another way to stop them. Hell, maybe we can get some assistance from the surface."

Richard spun on Victor. "Come on, Lieutenant Croft, think! If we fall back, they'll continue picking off the Argonian fleet, one ship at a time."

"We'll just move back in as soon as they fire the weapon."

Jake spoke up. "Vic, they won't fire. They'll hold us off with the threat of it. All while continuing their destruction of the Argonian ships."

"So?"

Jake took a calming breath, then pointed at the enemy ship. "Vic, do you think that's the last Zoxyth dreadnought in the galaxy?"

Lieutenant Croft froze in shocked silence.

"If any more of them show up and find this, they'll wipe us out." Jake gestured at the vacant fleet. "We may need those ships."

Vic's face brightened. "But more Argonians will come."

"Maybe, maybe, but we can't count on that. Playing devil's advocate, if I was launching an ambush against an enemy force of that size," Jake said, pointing at the empty Argonian fleet. "You can bet your ass, I'd find a way to tie up their backup forces. At any rate, there's too much at stake to assume reinforcements will show. What if that thing heads for another city."

"I thought you said ..." Victor paused, then shook his head. A myriad of emotions flooded the young lieutenant's face. He looked down. "You're right."

Another Argonian fighter blew up.

After giving Richard a meaningful glance, Jake looked at the enemy ship. The lieutenant was right to be scared. Hell, Jake was scared shitless, himself. He knew they probably wouldn't make it out of this. Shifting his gaze to the beautiful blue panorama below the swarm of ghost ships, he said, "A lot of people might be counting on us."

CHAPTER 44

Looking like a true asteroid, the dark, cratered back of the sculpted alien head filled most of the *Turtle's* view-wall, leaving a thin margin of stars at its periphery.

Victor scanned the nearing enemy ship with mounting horror. A shiver ran down his spine. He looked at the floor, shaking his head. When he looked up, Captain Giard was giving him that same appraising stare. Vic tried to smile. "I'm okay."

Jake nodded and turned his attention back outside.

Chiming in, his mother's ever-present voice berated him. *They know you're a fraud. It's beyond me why you had to run off and join the Air Force. I told you—*

"Shut up, mother," he muttered.

Captain Allison's head snapped toward him, eyes narrowed. "What was that, Lieutenant?"

"N-nothing," Vic stuttered.

After glaring at him for another second, the captain turned forward again, shaking his head.

Captain Allison always seemed to see straight through him.

Of course, he does. Everybody can see what a wussy I raised. You're such a waste of—

"Let's hold here," Captain Giard said. He turned from the view-wall. "It's time to get dressed."

Victor looked up. "What?"

Shaking his head, Jake walked toward the center of the ship. "Captain Allison, watch the helm for a moment. Lieutenant Croft, I don't have time to play twenty questions with you." Stepping into the circle, he rose to the second floor.

Victor broke his paralysis and followed.

Reaching the upper level, Captain Giard disappeared through the opening.

After a hesitant step into the lift's circle, Victor flinched as it gripped his lower legs and hoisted him toward the ceiling, depositing him next to the captain. He watched Jake activate the spacesuit section of the center pedestal. Like a rewinding time-lapsed video of a melting ice sculpture, the spacesuit lockers grew back out of the floor.

"Captain Allison didn't show us how these work," Vic complained shakily.

From below, Richard yelled, "You'll need to take off all of your clothes."

Jake shrugged. "There you go."

Victor froze, stealing a self-conscious look at his flight suit. *That's right, little boy,* his mother chided. *Time to show everybody your shriveled, hairless balls.*

"Shut up, Momma!" Vic said, subvocalizing this time.

Disrobing, Jake said, "Richard, tell me if I get this wrong."

"I'm all ears."

"Everything on this ship has been very intuitive, almost idiot-proof."

It ain't Victor-proof, his mother said through a sardonic laugh.

Captain Giard continued. "I can't imagine these'll be any different." Naked, Jake approached the closest locker. Each was big enough to hold a large man. When he touched the front of the cabinet, its face dissolved, generating the now familiar white noise.

Looking over the captain's shoulder, Victor looked through the man-sized opening. The interior looked like a locker with a glowing ceiling and a floor featuring two flashing footprints.

Speaking loud enough for Richard to hear, Jake said, "Looks like I just stand in the footprints. I'll bet a dollar to a doughnut it'll take care of the rest."

"That's right," Richard shouted. "But I should warn you, it can be a little ... unnerving, but there's no pain, and it only takes a couple of seconds."

Turning back to Vic, Jake smiled. "See, can o' corn."

Victor nodded, trying to look confident, knowing he failed.

Captain Giard gave him a hard look. "Are you going to be all right, Lieutenant?"

Victor raised a thumb. "I'm fine."

Liar. Jesus, what a pussy. Unnerving, ha. My little boy is going to piss himself as soon as those little machines start crawling across his skin.

Jake stepped into the machine. Turning to face Victor, he stepped on the glowing icons and winked. Then the sound of static filled his ears and the locker's opening turned solid, sealing the captain within its coffin-like confines.

A few seconds later, he stepped out, clad neck to toe in a flexing, metallic skin. "What the hell?" Vic said. "That looks more like tights than a spacesuit. There's no room for air."

Captain Allison's disembodied voice drifted through the opening in the floor. "The suit uses mechanical compression instead of air pressure."

After a moment's consideration, Vic nodded warily. He pointed at the captain's neck. "There's a ring at the top. Looks like a base for a helmet." Looking over Jake's shoulder, he scanned the locker's interior. "But I don't see one."

"I'm sure it'll be there when I need it," Jake said. He gestured to the adjacent cabinet. "Next."

With a reluctant nod, Victor finished undressing. Self-consciously covering his privates, he stepped through the opening. Turning around, he placed both feet in the outlined area. He gave Captain

Giard another shaky thumbs-up. White noise shredded the air and metal filled the opening, sealing him in the locker.

Vic held his breath. After a two-second pause, his heart leapt as a film peeled away from the inner wall. Seeking his unprotected, naked skin with snakelike undulations, it billowed across the intervening open space. Victor began hyperventilating as the nanobots slithered across his body with a creepy, tingling sensation, only ceasing its flowing undulations once it had fully encapsulated his entire body in its constricting grip.

Swallowing hard, he stifled a scream. The wall dissolved. Outside, Jake gave him a concerned look. Vic smiled weakly. "Unnerving, my ass," he said as he stepped from the locker.

Jake patted him on the shoulder and chuckled. "I hear you. Thank God it didn't cover my face. I probably would've lost my shit."

Vic looked at his right arm, flexing it, he was surprised what little resistance the suit provided. Starting to relax, he realized the pressure against his skin felt similar to what he'd experienced wearing a drysuit during immersion survival training. He felt it firmly supporting *everything* below the neckline. Flexing his fingers, he studied its milky, metallic skin. Like elastic armor, it perfectly conformed to his hand.

Captain Giard inspected Victor's neck ring. "Looks like it's made from the same material as the rest of the suit." Vic studied Jake's. It tilted forward and was thicker at the back than at the front.

The captain pointed through the opening in the floor. "Let's head back down." He stepped over the hole, and the gravity field lowered him to the flight deck.

Vic looked at his discarded flight suit. Puddled around his combat boots, it reminded him of the multitude of emptied garments decorating the Pentagon. A shiver ran down his spine again. Dragging his eyes from the disquieting mnemonic, he stepped to the opening. As the lift lowered him, his mother broke her momentary silence, her vitriol floating down through the hole in the ceiling.

Pussy!

~

"Jesus!" Jake said, seeing Richard.

"Hey, it's called efficient time-management." Already naked, he stepped from behind the control panel and jogged to the lift. "I'll be right back."

Jake shook his head. "There's some shit you can't unsee."

Vic's nervous chuckle dwindled to a withering sigh as he looked outside.

In less than a minute, Richard returned. "Ready." He took a sip from a small tube extending from inside his neck ring.

"What's that?" Jake asked. Exploring the inside of his suit's collar, he found an identical line.

"It's a drinking tube."

Nodding, Jake started pulling weapons from the rack, handing each of his wingmen a pistol and a shotgun.

"Where does the water come from?" Vic asked. Pulling out his own tube, he placed it in his mouth.

Jake removed the last weapon, and the rack melted back into the floor.

"It comes from you," Richard said.

Taking his pistol and shotgun, Vic spit out his straw. "What?"

Richard shot him an annoyed glance. Impatiently, he said, "These suits are like miniature processing plants. They take everything your body excretes—and I mean *everything*—and process it, breaking down the solids and separating the water. The liquid flows through capillaries in the suit's skin." Pausing, Richard took several long draws from the straw. After an exaggeratedly refreshed sigh, he said, "It provides temperature control and doubles as a potable water supply."

"How did you already get enough for a drink?" Vic asked.

Captain Allison shrugged. "Well, when you gotta go, you gotta go."

Jake shook his head.

After making a sour face, Victor looked down at his smooth suit. Holding up his pistol, he asked, "Where do I put this?"

"You don't want me to tell you where to put that," Richard said under his breath. After a warning look from Jake, he raised his voice. "Just hold it against the suit's skin for a couple of seconds. The nanobots will understand your intentions and grip it." Demonstrating, he held the pistol against his right hip. When he let go, it stayed, making him look like a space-age cowboy. "That'll work for anything you want to carry."

Vic and Jake did the same.

"Where are the oxygen tanks and power supply?" Jake asked.

"There are none. Every time you move an arm or leg, you're displacing millions of nanobots. They convert the movement to electricity and store it in the network of nanoscale capacitors powering the suit. For air, another class of bot harvests oxygen from the water while scrubbing carbon monoxide from your breath."

Slipping his wristwatch on, Jake checked the time. "We have thirty-five minutes left." Stepping to the console, he toggled the radio. "Vampire Six, this is Turtle One, over."

"Go ahead, Turtle One," Colonel Newcastle replied.

"We're prepped for EVA. Right now, we're parked in the ship's blind spot, but I'm about to maneuver us around to the head's left side and approach the tunnel."

"Thank you, Captain. I'd volunteer to join you, but our suits don't have an extended EVA capability. What can we do to assist?"

"I've been thinking about that. They haven't fired at us in a while, but I'm not sure what'll happen when we poke our heads around the corner. As much as possible, I need you and your fighters to keep them looking the other way, sir."

"Will do, Turtle One." Newcastle paused. "Listen, Captain, if you can't finish them off in a half-hour, get your asses out of there. I can't hold off. From a hundred miles out, the missiles will never make it to the target. We don't have the Argonian fighters to hide their approach. They'll just pick them off with their lasers. We *will* fire our missiles in exactly ... thirty-three minutes."

"Understood, sir."

"Again, good hunting, gentlemen."

"Thank you, sir. Turtle One, out."

"Vampire Six, out."

Jake turned his attention to the holographic display. The two fighter wings came together between the Zoxyth ship and the Argonian fleet.

"They're making it look like they're protecting the empty Argonian ships," Richard said.

"Hope that keeps them looking the other way," Jake said, grasping the flight controller. As he guided the *Turtle* closer, the ship remnant, still the size of a basketball arena, swelled to fill the view-wall, blotting out the rest of the star field.

"It makes the Moon look positively festive," Richard said.

Jake nodded. Except for a smattering of distorted structures, conduits, and cables protruding from its surface, this side looked like a normal asteroid, albeit charred and melted.

Closing on the asteroid, Jake stopped the *Turtle*, its nose only a few feet from the ship.

"Whew," Richard whispered. "No lasers so far." He looked around the interior. "There's never a piece of wood to knock on when you need it."

"I'm going to slide left. We'll work our way around to the missile's exit hole."

Jake saw wavering reflections of the *Turtle* as they glided over sections of rock melted glass-smooth in the nuclear furnace of battle. As the *Turtle* rounded the asteroid's back left corner, the Argonian fleet slid into view. Nearer, the horizon of the rock's lifeless surface contrasted strikingly against Earth's azure biosphere.

"There it is," Jake said, pointing at a small crater. Silhouetted against the Atlantic Ocean, it protruded from the rocky surface. Having entered the sculpted alien head aft of the right temple, the missile's path cut downward diagonally from the top right to the bottom left, exiting just behind the chiseled alien jaw.

Richard studied the ship's surface. "Look at all the melted metal and craters. I can't believe there's anyone still alive in there."

Jake stole a sideways glance at Vic. The lieutenant put up a brave façade, but obvious dread hovered just below the surface. Breathing heavily, the slight officer's chest rapidly rose and fell. Jake elbowed him. "Hang in there, buddy. We'll kick their asses. It'll be nice to get some payback."

The last comment seemed to strike a chord with Vic. He lifted his chin and nodded. "I'll be all right."

Jake felt his own adrenaline ramping up as the extraordinary prospect of close combat with an unknown alien species neared reality.

Beyond their destination and still clamped in the alien's jaw, the left side of the pitted and charred human skull slid into view.

As they closed on the crater, the opening appeared. Starting as a dark sliver, it quickly expanded into a full circle, revealing the tunnel's smooth walls.

"Now we find out how accurate the hologram was," Jake said, slowing the *Turtle*.

As they drew closer, the tunnel stretched deep into the ship, a small star-field materializing at its far end.

"Yes," Richard whispered.

Jake stopped the *Turtle*. "Why are you whispering?"

Richard did the Area Fifty-One salute.

Jake chuckled nervously and looked at the tunnel's five-foot diameter. He pointed to the side. "I'll park us right there with the airlock exit pointing at the hole."

"Once we're in position, activate the autopilot position-hold ... here," Richard said, pointing out the control.

"Yeah," Vic said through a manic laugh. "It might be a little difficult to leave if our ship isn't here waiting for us."

Jake considered ordering him to remain in the *Turtle*, then decided against it. Stopping the aliens was all that mattered. Deleting a pair of eyes to leave a man on lifeboat guard duty was a luxury he couldn't afford.

Jake pitched the *Turtle's* nose up and extended the landing gear. As it gently touched down, all three sat in breathless silence. When nothing happened, Jake exhaled and activated the position-hold. Picking up his shotgun, he pumped a round into the chamber, wincing as its click-clack sound echoed loudly through the silent

Turtle. Turning to his two wingmen, he whispered, "Gentlemen, any final requests?"

Richard grinned and pumped a round into his shotgun. "Guess it's too late to ask for that steak dinner."

"Yep."

Vic cocked his shotgun too. A slight shiver cracked his brave façade.

Jake didn't blame him. Judging by his own pounding heart, enough adrenaline coursed through Jake's veins to give a rhinoceros a coronary.

"Richard, you take point. Vic, you take the middle and watch our sides. I'll watch our rear. Any questions?"

They shook their heads.

As they entered the airlock, the helmet issue resolved itself. One grew from each suit's collar. Undulating like flowing water, a clear membrane propagated vertically from the ring. Meeting at the top, it solidified into a perfectly smooth dome with a small fixture at its peak.

Victor looked at Jake's helmet. "What's that on top?"

As he turned to look at the lieutenant, light poured into his eyes from Victor's fixture. Jake squinted. "Thanks, bud."

Victor narrowed his eyes against the light shining from Jake's helmet. Realizing he was blinding him, Vic turned away. "Sorry."

Jake heard him over a speaker in his suit.

Victor turned his head and looked up, watching the spot track his line of sight. "Cool, the light shines wherever you look. These guys thought of everything."

Richard nodded. "It's all pretty intuitive."

Each man attached a shotgun to the outside of his left thigh. The smart-suit held it like Velcro. Experimentally, Jake peeled off the weapon. It released with moderate effort. It even sounded like Velcro. Pressing it back in place, Jake took a deep breath and exhaled, then took a long drag on his waterline. "Let's do this."

They turned toward the *Turtle's* outer skin. A fading hiss echoed through the chamber. Then the wall vanished, exposing the airlock to space.

Jake's heart raced. His ears rang with an adrenaline-fueled rush. Swallowing hard, he stared through the opening at the fissured surface of the alien ship. With all the handholds the cracks provided, the transit would be easier than he'd feared. "Use the cracks to pull yourself over to the opening." Looking across the enemy ship's surface, he saw the Atlantic Ocean two hundred miles below. "Watch that first step, it's a doozy."

Richard stuck a tentative foot through the opening. "The *Turtle's* gravity field ends right here," he said, pointing at the edge of the airlock's floor. "Feels like zero-Gs beyond."

Peering over Richard's shoulder, Victor looked at the distant ocean. Through another nervous chuckle, he said, "That's good. Otherwise, that really would be a big step."

The lieutenant's words triggered a realization. Jake hadn't considered how far outside the asteroid's surface the alien's gravity bubble might extend. Thankfully, Richard had already confirmed that it reached at least a few feet. Jake wondered how much farther it protruded.

Richard crouched. Reaching for a crack in the asteroid's surface, he eased his head through the opening.

As his body passed through, Richard's respiratory rate doubled. In a surreal gravitational disconnect, he floated weightlessly, only five feet from where Jake stood in normal gravity. Like an underwater swimmer gliding just above pool bottom, Richard drifted hand over hand across the surface.

Dislodged by his passage, a rock drifted up from the asteroid. Roughly the size of a baseball, it tumbled as if in slow motion, gradually rising. Answering his wonderings, it suddenly fell earthward when it reached eye level. "Holy shit," Jake whispered.

Victor's head snapped around. "What?"

"Oh." Jake waved dismissively. "Nothing, it's just an awesome view."

The lieutenant gave him a queer look, then shook his head. Breathing heavily, he turned and crouched to follow Richard. Looking across the ten-foot gap between the airlock and the crater, he asked, "Could you have parked any farther away?" A nervous edge crept back into his words.

Vic reached for the first crack and started to pull himself through the opening. When his head exited, Jake saw his body convulse. Throwing his other hand into the fissure, he pulled himself tight to the surface. "It feels like I'm falling!"

"You're doing great, buddy," Jake said, trying to encourage him. "You're just feeling the zero-Gs."

Richard reached the crater rim. Grabbing it, he pulled himself head first into the five-foot opening. Disappearing for a moment, he re-emerged with his head and shoulders protruding from the hole. Waving impatiently, he said, "Let's get moving, ladies."

After a moment, Vic pried one paw from the rock face. Extending a trembling hand, he desperately grasped the next crack and shifted forward. Maddeningly slow, he crept toward the opening.

Jake followed close behind, only allowing himself a brief moment to realize this was his first taste of weightlessness. Before he was fully through the door, he heard a panicked voice over his suit's radio.

"Shit ... *Oh!*"

Jake looked up to see Vic flail as a piece of asteroid crumbled under his death grip. In a panicked swing of his arms, the lieutenant tried to grab the surface. Finding no purchase, his hands struck the rock, only accelerating his drift into space.

"Oh God!" Victor squeaked. His spasming body was three feet up and rising. Two feet above him, the rocks he'd launched reached the edge of the gravity bubble and fell earthward like homesick granite.

Still clad in her stark military dress uniform, the dark-haired female Air Force major strode into the Command Center and approached the two people standing in front of a large wall map of Central California. "Sorry for the interruption, sir, but I think you'll want to see this."

Having just finished debriefing the base commander, Sandy looked from the general to the excited aide.

With a somber shake of his head, the general turned from the long, red arc Sandy had drawn on the map. Closing his eyes, the older man ran grizzled fingers through his short, gray hair. After letting out a long breath, the general looked at the thin, dark-haired officer. "What is it, Major?"

The aide placed a hand on the shoulder of a young female sergeant sitting in front of one of the room's consoles. Pointing at the Center's main display, she said, "Bring up video feed sixteen."

The major turned back to the general. "We have one of the new Keyhole spy satellites coming into position, sir."

The large display flared to life, Earth's beautiful horizon chasing away the blank blue screen. Arcane digital location data churned through a gray bar spanning the bottom of the display. Most of the numbers made no sense. However, Sandy did recognize the first four digits: KH-12.

This was a live feed from the National Reconnaissance Office's newest spy satellite. Recently launched, it had optics and sensors better than the Hubble Space Telescope.

"The battle was at a higher altitude than the satellite's orbit, so we had to turn it away from the planet."

In amazed fascination, Sandy studied the ultra-high-definition display. Earth's gently curving surface filled the left half. On the right side, a majestic field of stars shone like diamonds scattered across space's black velvet void.

Far exceeding the video feed supplied during the battle, the image created by combining the KH-12's clarity with the ultra-HD display's pixel density was breathtaking. It looked like a twenty-foot-wide portal to outer space had opened in the room's main wall.

Looking forward this time, the satellite drifted toward North America's cloudless East Coast. Curving out of view at the bottom of the display, Florida's peninsula extended south. Ahead, sunlight reflected off the Atlantic Ocean. Even visible from this altitude, the long south-to-north swath of decimation wreaked by the alien ship's calamitous atmospheric entry matched the destruction Sandy had seen extending south of Monterey, California.

"The techs are fighting with the system's software," the major said. "They said the change in orientation and focal length is playing hell with their control algorithms. For now, they're using the wide-field optics."

"Have we heard from Colonel Newcastle yet?" the general asked.

The major shook her head. "No, sir."

Sandy looked at Earth's scrolling horizon. In the few minutes that had elapsed since they'd watched Colonel Newcastle nuke the last enemy ship, they'd been unable to get a status update. The video feed wasn't the only thing supplied by the previous satellite. It had provided the telemetry data and radio relays. So, when the battle disappeared behind the horizon, those went with it.

The aide pointed victoriously as a charcoal speck peeked above the distant horizon. "There's the debris field!"

For the second time in twenty minutes, the room's occupants broke into cheers and applause.

"Debris field?" Sandy asked. The question went unheard in the loud room. Eyes furrowed, she studied the slate-gray dot with mounting disquiet. There shouldn't be anything left. The ship remnant should've fallen and been vaporized like the rest of its fleet.

The screen flickered as the satellite increased its magnification. The dark point blossomed to fill half the display. The object hovering in stark clarity silenced the room.

Unease morphed into horror as Sandy stared breathlessly.

General Pearson's head snapped back as if he'd been slapped. "What the hell?"

Like a satanic sunrise, the malevolent, sculpted alien face Sandy had first seen rising from Chesapeake Bay now slowly rose from behind the planet. It was still very much intact.

In the magnified view, Earth's distant horizon partially obscured it. However, gradually revealed by the planet's rotation and the spy satellite's faster orbit, the sneering, rocky visage appeared to slither up through the planet's murky atmosphere. As if blackened in hell's fiery furnaces, the sculpted bust looked like a scorched horror movie prop. Finally rising clear of the obscuration, and still clutching a human skull in its fangs, the pock-marked and blackened alien ship remnant appeared to glare down on the room's occupants.

The image flickered and the pitch-black bust shrank as the satellite decreased its magnification. In the wider field of view, Sandy saw several of the much larger ships also rising above the atmosphere. According to General Pearson, they belonged to the defense forces of the galactic government working to integrate Earth.

Barely discernible in the blackness of space, the ships no longer maintained an ordered formation. Sandy's horror now blazed white-hot as the dreadful reality struck home. All but one of the GDF ships were slowly tumbling. The sole stationary ship sat dead still.

"Oh my God!" She blinked away the tears threatening to breach the dam of her lower eyelids. "Jake was right," she croaked through a tightening throat.

The general had been unsure of the *Turtle's* current status. However, during her short debrief, he had described the minutes leading up to the battle she'd witnessed upon arriving at the Combat Control Center. Sandy had been surprised to discover the integral part the *Turtle's* crew had played. Finding out that we are descendants of the galactic rulers had been a big shock in a day chock-full of them.

"Excuse me?" the general said.

Sandy shook her head and pointed at the drifting ships. "They're all gone."

"What do you ..." The general stopped mid-sentence as the battle's apparent outcome struck home. "Oh fuck ..." His voice trailed off as he dropped into a chair. As if deflated by the news, the general appeared to age before Sandy's eyes. Turning from the man, Sandy stared at the horrible scene filling the room's wall.

After a few moments, the base commander's tired voice ruptured the silence. "The Argonians were too ... humane!" After shaking his head for a moment, he pointed at the reptilian head. "And the goddamned lizards used it against them." He looked at Sandy and nodded. "If Captain Giard hadn't figured it out, they would've vaporized them first and then turned their attention back on us. Vampire Squadron would be trying to nuke these fuckers as they skipped from one holocaust to the next."

A pair of sleek silver ships sped through the image.

The general's eyes brightened with relief. "Speak of the devil."

"Vampire Squadron?" Sandy said.

The general nodded. "I thought we'd lost them too." Pumping his right fist, he yelled, "Get 'em Zach!"

Glinting flashes stitched fiery lines across the giant, sculpted alien head. Blasting away the scorched surface and revealing the rock's underlying natural color, the relatively small explosions of the fighter's ineffectual cannon fire sewed a line of small, orange craters across the blackened asteroid.

Emitted from the sides of the rocky face, a pair of laser beams chased the two fighters. To Sandy, they looked perfectly aimed. However, the lasers had missed.

Two more Vampire Attack fighters strafed the alien ship with similarly ineffectual fire. General Pearson studied the scene with a look of consternation. "It's like pissing on a goddamned forest fire. We're never going to get anywhere like this."

A moment later, the aide pointed at something creeping from behind the mountainous rock. "We have a new player here."

Looking at the image, Sandy felt her pulse quicken. She moved closer to the display. Squinting, she studied the squat disc-shaped object. While it looked much thicker from top to bottom, the new ship was a little longer than the Vampire fighters. Its round top matched the description Jake had given her when they'd spoken during her San Francisco ordeal. *Is that you, Jake?*

Tapping the sergeant on the shoulder again, the aide pointed at the new vessel. "Zoom in on that."

A few keystrokes later, the screen flickered and the alien head filled the display again.

General Pearson confirmed Sandy's suspicion. "Holy shit! That's the *Turtle*."

Like an insect skittering across a boulder, the relatively small vessel proceeded down the alien ship's side. Apparently finding what it was looking for, the *Turtle* turned its flat bottom parallel to the surface. Sitting motionless, it looked like the disc-shaped vessel had somehow parked itself on the side of the asteroid.

Sandy stared longingly at Jake's ship. *Come back to me, baby.*

Something stirred in the small gap under the *Turtle's* belly.

The aide stepped closer. "Is something moving in there?"

Watching in stunned, frightened fascination, Sandy gasped and her heart skipped a beat as something next to the *Turtle* flared white.

The point of view gradually shifted as the spy satellite continued to close the gap. With an orbit that carried it under the asteroid, the KH-12's camera now looked up at the alien ship. In the left and right margins, an unending conveyor of scintillating stars scrolled across the display. Nearing its alien perigee, the spy satellite's point of view zoomed closer with every second. The proximity revealed the bright white object to be one of the crew members emerging from the *Turtle's* shadow. Sandy pointed at the spacesuit fluorescing under the direct sunlight as it wiggled across the alien ship's rocky surface. "One of them just crawled out."

The aide pointed at more movement in the *Turtle's* shadow. "Is that the other two?"

General Pearson squinted at the screen. "What the hell are they doing?"

One of the room's many radios crackled to life. "Nellis Actual, this is Vampire Six, over."

After staring at the image for another moment, General Pearson broke from the monitor. Stepping to the console, he snatched up the mic. "Go ahead, Vampire Six. This is Actual." The general turned his narrowed eyes back to the display. "What's going on up there?"

"We've got a problem, sir."

"Considering I'm still looking into the eyes of that goddamned alien rock, I'd have to agree."

"Yes, sir. We're just as frustrated up here. My bunker buster passed right through it."

Shaking his head, the general stared at the display. "Shit." He keyed the mic. "How many more do you have, Zach?"

"We're down to two, sir. I sent four of our fighters back to rearm with our last missiles, but they won't make it back in time to make a difference." After a static-filled, pregnant pause, the colonel continued. "However, there's another problem."

Looking stricken, the older officer slid the chair from under the communications console. Collapsing into it, he looked like a cancer patient bracing to receive bad news from an oncologist. General Pearson toggled the mic. "What is it, Zach?"

"*If* we can get a missile to detonate, a double EM pulse will hit North America and Europe."

With obvious agitation, the general sat bolt upright. "Screw the goddamned EMP, Zach. I want that thing taken out now!" He smacked the console's laminate top. "Hell, fire the missiles in opposition if you have to. That ought to do the trick. If it fries a few networks, we'll deal with it later." The general pointed at the alien bust filling the screen. "*After* that city buster is taken out." The general leaned back in the chair and lowered his voice to an empathetic tone. "I appreciate all you've done, Zach. Let's get the *Turtle* out of there and wrap this up."

Sandy nodded her head. Jake's proximity to the alien ship had her heart racing. She thought the general was right about firing the missiles in opposition. With two remaining, they should be able to engage from both directions simultaneously. The impact generated when the missiles met head-to-head should be more than enough to set off one, if not both, of them. It would be easy enough to coordinate the attack if the space fighter's fire-control computer had capabilities approximating those of her F-22.

"Uh ... well, sir, my biggest concern is the debris."

Standing up, the general reddened with mounting frustration. "Damn it, Zach." Pausing in an apparent effort to rein in his anger, he released the mic key. Before he could continue, Colonel Newcastle interrupted.

"Captain Giard might've come up with a way to end this, sir. We might not have to risk either problem."

Hearing Jake's name sent Sandy's heart into orbit. It raced with joy at knowing he was still alive and pounded with renewed fear for his confirmed proximity to the enemy ship.

Head bowed, General Pearson leaned over the console with his two fists digging into its laminate top. Sandy was surprised the mic still clutched in his right hand wasn't crushed.

After a moment's consideration, he appeared to calm, his anger ebbing. Standing upright, he lifted the mic to his mouth and keyed it. "I'm listening."

"I've placed him in charge of a boarding operation."

Mouth ajar, the general leaned back, studying the display with renewed curiosity. "Boarding operation? Last I checked, the *Turtle* was unarmed. Hell, it's just a technology demonstrator. The bastards in that rock are still firing at you." Driving the point home, another laser beam reached out for one of Colonel Newcastle's fighters. "So, unless it's an automated defense system, there's still someone manning that S-O-B. What the hell is Giard going to do, throw rocks at 'em?"

"Apparently, they picked up some weapons when they reconned Maryland for me."

The major pointed at the screen. "The first one just disappeared!"

Sandy stared in wide-eyed disbelief. *What the hell are you doing, Jake?*

Colonel Newcastle was still talking. "They're trying to get in through the hole my missile punched."

After staring at the screen for a few silent seconds, the general turned to Sandy. "Your boyfriend's a ballsy bastard." Turning to his aide, he pointed at the enemy ship. "How much time do we have before they can fire that goddamned weapon?"

The major checked her watch. "Thirty minutes, sir."

Sandy turned back to the display. Emerging from the small ship's shadow, a second person drifted into the light. Cycling to a higher magnification, the image flickered again and the *Turtle* filled the screen. Sandy's heart raced as she watched the new man float jerkily across the rocky surface. As his legs trailed in the zero-G environment, the unknown officer proceeded haltingly from one handhold to the next.

More white light flashed as the third man's helmet emerged into the sunlight.

"The third one is coming out too," the aide said.

Sandy watched in silence, holding her breath. A helmet appeared to grow from the rock in the same area where the first man had disappeared.

Apparently buoyed by the prospect of progress, General Pearson seemed to brighten. Pointing with excitement, he said, "The first one *is* inside. That's his head poking out of the hole."

Sandy realized he was right. There was a hole there. However, it was impossible to see it at the oblique angle of the satellite's point of view. Only a few feet of scorched asteroid separated the opening in the *Turtle's* belly and the hole. Halfway between the two, the middle man flailed, his arms swinging wildly as he lost grip.

An involuntary scream broke through Sandy's clamped lips.

General Pearson twitched. "Oh shit!"

Bending at the waist, the drifting man's hands clutched desperately at the rocky surface. To Sandy's horror, the panicked swipe accelerated his drift away from the asteroid.

The aide's brisk façade cracked, her hands flying to her mouth. "Oh my God!"

Sandy screamed, "Jake!"

CHAPTER 45

Jake reached out to grab Lieutenant Croft and missed. "Shit!" Hooking his heels on the edge of the *Turtle's* airlock door, he stretched out and snagged the man's ankles. However, the lieutenant's upward inertia dragged them in a slow arc. Like a couple of trapeze artists, they swung toward the edge of the gravity field.

Jake looked up, wide-eyed. "Oh fuck!" Earth's gravity was about to pull them into its waiting arms like a two-man human roller coaster cresting the world's tallest hill. Jake dug the back of his heels into the opening's edge. With a mighty heave, he pulled their combined inertia toward the *Turtle*. Completing the trapeze analogy, Jake bent his knees and hooked his calves over the lip.

Through his heavy breathing, Vic said, "Thank you! I thought I was a—" His words dissolved into a scream. Croft's inertia suddenly converted to weight.

Jake's body shook with the effort of holding up the lieutenant. "Shit!" As their arc reached its zenith, the weight quickened the return swing. Their velocity accelerated radically. Victor whipped back out of the planet's gravity field. However, at this rate he'd slam into the surface and bounce off. Jake had only one option. Judging the distance and the timing like a quarterback trying to lead a crossing receiver, he released the lieutenant.

"What are you doing?" Victor screamed.

"Richard! Catch him!"

Flailing his arms, Lieutenant Croft flew across the intervening space in a diagonal that carried him straight at the tunnel's opening.

Jake's inertia swung him into the airlock and back into the *Turtle's* gravitational field. He crashed to the floor on his back, the impact knocking the wind out of him. Struggling to draw breath, he looked up in time to see Vic bounce off the near rim of the crater. His arms ineffectually batted at the surface, sending more rocks flying to their doom. Heading back out to space, he flew over Richard's head. The captain grabbed the spasming lieutenant. His inertia started dragging Richard from the hole, but the captain's toes apparently caught on a lip and they came to a halt.

Croft still waved his arms.

"Stop fucking moving, Lieutenant!" Richard yelled. "I've got you."

"Oh, thank God," Vic whimpered.

Careful not to dislodge his toehold, Richard eased them into the tunnel.

"Thank you," Vic said between gasps.

Panting and heart racing, Jake stood. "I don't know about you two, but I've got plenty of drinking water now!"

Vic laughed nervously. "Yeah, I think I pissed myself about a gallon of it."

Richard glared at him, then shook his head. Turning to Jake, he waved. "Come on, Captain. We're burning daylight."

Bent over, Jake nodded. After a moment to catch his breath, he passed through the airlock and proceeded hand over hand to the opening. Richard waited with an extended arm, Vic floating at his side.

Jake grabbed the crater rim and the offered hand, sliding head first into the tunnel. Finally inside the smooth-walled hole, he noticed a slight gravity.

Richard nodded his head. "You feel it too?"

"Yeah, I bet it gets stronger farther in."

Starting to think he'd made a mistake, Jake studied Vic's panting face through his fogged helmet.

Apparently reading his expression, the lieutenant made a visible effort to center himself. Eyes closed, he took a couple of calming breaths. Opening them, he put on a brave face and nodded. "I'll be okay. Let's go get the fuckers."

Richard turned and pulled himself deeper into the ship. Vic and Jake followed close behind. Gravity increased with every foot they progressed. Having felt neutral in the no-up-reference of zero-G space, the tunnel began to feel and look like it was running uphill. After a few more steps, the gravity leveled off at just under one-G.

Jake stood. When he looked back toward the opening, the tube appeared to run steeply downhill. "Don't slip. It looks like you'll slide down the tunnel and shoot out into space." The thought sent a shudder down his spine.

Apparently appraising his weight, Richard did a couple of deep knee bends. "Thank God these aliens didn't come from a bigger planet." Turning to look up the tunnel, he added, "Doubling our weight might have slowed us a bit." Richard paused, then whispered, "I see an opening ahead." He crept a couple of feet farther up the black tunnel. Resting his hands on a ledge, he scanned the darkness beyond.

Unable to see from the back, Jake turned to check their rear. Finding nothing at their six o'clock position, he asked, "What do we have?"

"It's a small room." As Richard scanned its interior, the helmet light tracked his movements. "It's clear, I'm going in."

Jake watched as he hoisted himself onto the ledge. "Is that a floor?"

"Yep, come on up," he whispered.

Richard's arm extended from the darkness and helped Vic up to the ledge.

Walking toward the opening, Jake made another quick check of their rear. Reaching the ledge, he hoisted himself onto the floor. The room was dark and dank. The light from his lamp reflected off walls covered with flash-frozen algae. Before exposure to the vacuum of space, it looked like a perpetual thin layer of moisture had coated the walls.

The other two officers studied a panel with a pulsing red square. It was next to a half-open metallic door leading deeper into the ship.

Pulling his pistol from his hip, Richard stepped to the door and placed his hand on it. "It's vibrating like it's trying to close." After a quick scan of the room beyond, he said, "All clear," and passed through the opening.

Next, Vic drew his weapon and disappeared into the darkness.

Drawing his pistol, Jake walked back to the tunnel. Scanning left and right, he verified their six was still clear. Returning to the jammed door, he saw why it hadn't closed. A rock had lodged in its track.

He stepped through. The other two were twenty feet away studying a door on the far side of the room. "What do you have for me?" Jake asked as he looked around. His helmet's spotlight fell on machines and pipes of indiscernible purpose. The ubiquitous frost and patches of frozen algae persisted through this room too.

"There's another panel to the right of this door," Richard whispered. "But, instead of a pulsing red square, this one has a steady green one. There's a button just below the panel. Should I push it?"

"Yes."

Signaling for Vic to move to the left side of the door, Richard aimed his nine-millimeter at the door's right side.

Pistol at the ready, Vic stepped to the left.

Jake stood off to one side. He didn't think anything would happen, but better safe than sorry.

Richard pressed the button. The door didn't budge, but the green square flashed red twice then returned to steady green.

Jake looked back at the half-open door. "Try it again."

"Okay," Richard replied. When he hit the button on the far door, the light on the half-open door shifted to steady red for a couple of seconds and then resumed flashing.

Jake described what he'd seen. "We're going to have to gamble that, once this door closes, the computer will let the other door open. I think they've programmed them to work like an airlock in the event of a hull breach."

"No, let's just go back to the tunnel and find another way!" Vic begged. "If you're wrong, we'll be stuck in here."

Jabbing at his wristwatch, Richard shook his head. "Damn it, Lieutenant! We only have twenty-one minutes left before we need to be done or heading out. Besides, he's right. This'll work." Turning to Jake, he said, "Do it."

Jake kicked the rock blocking the door's track. On the second attempt, it broke free and the door slid closed, silently locking into place in the room's vacuum. After an agonizing couple of seconds, the light turned green.

Jake turned to look at the far door. Richard was pushing the button. The light on its panel was still green, but nothing else happened.

"Shit—" Vic started, but cut off mid-sentence when Jake raised a hand.

"Just a second, can you hear that? It sounds like—" To Jake's horror, his helmet retracted. Ice-cold air struck his face. The sound he'd heard must have been the atmosphere flowing back into the room. The smart-suit had obviously detected it. He took his first tentative, icy breath. The air had a musty, humid feel and taste, but seemed to have adequate oxygen.

He saw horror then relief cross his wingmen's faces. Their lights had moved to the neck ring. Turning his head, he saw his had relocated as well. Its white spot followed his line of sight, briefly shining in Rich and Vic's eyes.

"All right, we're in now. Next time you press that button, it'll open. We need to go into full tactical mode. Remember your combat survival training, move and cover, move and cover. We need to make our way to the upper level. We'll breach each door we come to with crossing fields of fire. Richard, you stand to the right of the door, covering the left sector. Vic, you stand to the left, covering the right sector. I'll stand back a few feet and cover the center field of fire. Any questions?"

They both shook their heads, wordlessly moving into position. Returning the pistol to his hip, Jake drew the shotgun and dropped to a knee seven feet back. Raising the weapon to shoulder, he aimed at the door and nodded to Captain Allison. When he reached for the button, Jake was surprised to see Richard's hand tremble.

He pressed it.

To Jake's relief, the door slowly slid open this time. The room beyond was a dimly lit cavernous space. Its soft light slivered through the gap, creating a widening shaft of illuminated dank air in their makeshift airlock.

Captain Allison and Lieutenant Croft both gave the all-clear sign.

Seeing no movement or evidence of life, Jake gave the same sign. In the dim light, he reached down and touched his lamp. It extinguished, melting back into the ring.

The other two did the same.

Jake pointed to Richard and gave the advance sign.

He nodded. After another quick scan, Captain Allison stormed through the door and took cover. A moment later, Lieutenant Croft did the same. Once the two of them were in position, Jake followed, leaving the door open to allow for a quick retreat.

As his eyes adjusted to the room's ambient light, he realized they were in a cavernous cathedral. The large assembly area's ceiling vaulted fifty feet. Having entered from a side room, they crouched behind a row of stone bench seats. Shattered rock littered the floor. Apparently cast about by the battle, several broken benches lay on their backs. Before being disturbed, it looked like they had formed arcing rows. Like an amphitheater, each seat faced an elevated table or altar to Jake's left.

Jake's breath hitched in shock. Behind the altar stood a thirty-foot-tall backlit statue of what must have been a Zoxyth. With its head lifted toward the ceiling and its mouth open in an apparent victory roar, the beast had broken chains dangling from shackled hands and feet. Raised toward the ceiling, the left arm had a sickle-shaped, razor-sharp appendage protruding from its forearm.

Tearing their eyes from the monstrous beast, all three men stared in shocked horror at the scene above the altar. Extending forward, the demon's right arm hovered over it. Clutched by their hair, two severed human heads hung from its clenched fist.

"These guys *really* don't like humans," Richard whispered.

Vic nodded. "Ya think? Look at those claws."

Gripping a handful of human hair, razor-sharp talons extended from its three fingers. Palm down, the right hand's opposable thumb was on the outside, opposite of where it would be on a human hand. The Zox's lower leg sported another knife-like appendage. It protruded from the back of the alien's calf. Similar to the hand, and again anatomically opposite from a human, the biggest talons on the creature's foot extended from the outside.

Scanning the rest of the cavernous room, Jake looked right. Standing like giant, macabre Academy Award Oscars, a backlit headless Argonian statue adorned each side of the cathedral's main entrance. Cracked across the top of its bound knees, the left human form had tipped across the top corner of the opening, its truncated neck precariously balanced against a glowing sconce centered over the entranceway.

They would've been twenty-five feet in height had their heads still been attached.

Victor looked back and forth between the Zox and human sculptures. "If they're to scale, these bastards must be at least eight feet tall," he whispered.

"I'm sure shotguns will kill 'em just as dead," Jake said, hoping he sounded more confident than he felt.

Casting nervous glances at the pistols in their hands, Richard and Vic returned them to their hips and drew the shotguns. All three officers cringed as a sound similar to peeling Velcro echoed across the silent room.

When nothing happened, Jake pointed toward the back of the cathedral. "Let's keep moving." Turning to Richard, he pointed two fingers at his own eyes and then through the opening, giving the signal to advance and cover.

Richard nodded and squat-ran down the side to the back wall.

Creeping toward the opening, he scanned the area beyond. Reaching the right side of the entrance, he took up a defensive position and nodded, giving the all-clear signal.

Jake waved Vic forward.

Lieutenant Croft nodded, took a deep breath, and scrambled along the side to the back wall. Scurrying left, he stopped next to Captain Allison.

After a quick check of their rear and another glance at the horrible icon behind the altar, Jake ran to the third row from the back. Using the benches for cover, he scooted toward the center, stopping just shy of the aisle. Shotgun at the ready and his back to the altar, he sat propped against the smooth stone face of a fallen bench.

His suit glistened with condensed moisture. The stone bench seats, as well as the walls and floors, were soaking wet. An unending staccato of drips echoed through the room.

Aiming the shotgun toward the opening, he leaned into the aisle, scanning the entrance and beyond. About twelve-foot-tall by nine-foot-wide, the entryway afforded a broad view of the area beyond. Across a twelve-foot gap, an apparent hallway's damp rock wall extended left and right out of sight.

Peering over the benches, he gave the all-clear and signaled for Richard to advance.

Richard nodded, signaling for Victor to cover him.

Vic nodded.

Richard darted across the opening, coming to a stop with his back against the left side with his shotgun aimed down the hallway to the right. His scan faltered as he lowered the weapon an inch, studying something on the floor beyond Jake's line of sight.

After a moment, he raised the weapon and finished the scan. A cutting motion across his throat and a quick point indicated the presence of a dead enemy body in the hallway.

Jake and Vic nodded.

Placing a finger over his lips, Jake signaled for Vic to move into the hall.

After a reluctant nod and a deep breath, he stepped through the opening and took position on the other side of the wall. Shotgun aimed, he scanned down the passage to the left, making the same double take as Richard. He turned and gave the hand signals for another dead alien.

Jake advanced to Richard's side, gravel crunching lightly underfoot.

Richard pointed through the opening and whispered, "Dead bogey."

Jake nodded, motioning for the two of them to stand-fast. He peered out, scanning left and right, then darted across the hallway, pinning his back to the wall, weapon at the ready.

Two bloodied corpses bracketed the cathedral's opening. Judging by their placement and ornate robes, Jake guessed they were ceremonial guards. The extent of their injuries was incredible. Their bodies had been pulverized.

"Green blood," Vic whispered.

Both bodies lay in pools of it. Additional green splatters on the walls and ceilings marked the impact points where the guards had met their demise.

"Hopefully, the rest of the crew is in the same condition," Vic whispered.

A distant guttural roar echoed from an opening to Jake's right.

They froze.

The roar continued for a few seconds, rising and falling in pitch, but sounding no closer. The distant sound emanated from a point along the wall a few feet to Jake's right.

Lieutenant Croft looked ready to bolt.

Jake extended his hand in a bouncing, settle-down gesture. "It's not coming," he whispered.

He counted their blessings. From the outset, he hadn't believed they'd make it this far or long without a firefight. He still felt they'd be lucky to survive the day. However, he also knew that perhaps no battle in Earth's history carried the import of their actions today. Failure was not an option.

After a few calming breaths, Victor seemed to settle down.

They were in a long passageway. Its slimy stone walls floor and ceiling looked more like a cave than a hall.

Inching along the wet wall toward the source of the sound, Jake came to a familiar structure. The distant screeching roar erupted again. Drifting through the ajar and crooked oversized elevator doors, the sound morphed into an impossibly deep voice ranting in an unrecognizable language.

An intermittent ceiling light flickered inside the elevator car stuck in the bottom half of the opening.

Jake realized the shaft must lead to the bridge. *I hope there's some type of ladder.*

With a signal from Jake, Richard took position on the other side of the opening.

Jake moved across the hall. Bracing against the far wall, he dropped to a knee and aimed his shotgun up the shaft. Vic moved to cover the elevator's right side.

Jake gestured to Richard, pointing to the watch on his wrist.

Richard held up ten fingers.

Ten minutes! Damn, this had better work.

Jake stepped to Vic, motioning for Richard to join him. Grabbing both of their arms, he pulled them close. "This should lead us directly to the bridge, but it'll also make a perfect sound conduit. Be very quiet, not a peep if we want to live through this."

They nodded.

Richard stepped to the opening.

Jake held Vic's arm a moment longer, studying his eyes. The lieutenant appeared to be managing his fear. Leaning closer, Jake spoke in his left ear. "That night, before we encountered the UFO, I told you your training would kick in. You're doing a great job. I'm proud of you, Lieutenant."

Looking uncomfortable under Jake's appraising stare, he mouthed, *Thanks.*

Jake turned and gave Richard the go-sign.

Richard began to climb through and then slid out of sight, quicker and more graceful than Jake would have guessed possible, considering his old knee injury. While Jake continued to cover the cave-like passageway, Vic haltingly followed him through and then disappeared with the same speed and finesse Richard had displayed.

Jake slid through the opening. The farther he progressed, the lighter he got. Once fully in, he floated weightlessly next to his comrades. The shaft had no gravity. Belatedly, Jake realized it made perfect sense. If you were generating artificial gravity, you wouldn't create it inside a shaft where you'd have to expend energy to counter it.

Like three kids floating in a pool, they each held onto a stone ledge. Jake looked up the long vertical shaft—though, in the no-up-reference of zero-G, it looked more like a tunnel than a shaft. At the far end, a slim bar of light from an unseen source cut through the damp, hazy air.

Jake pointed in that direction, placing an extended left index finger against his lips to re-emphasize the importance of silence.

Both men nodded.

Shotgun at the ready, Richard pushed off the support, starting a cautious, steady drift toward the far end of the shaft.

Vic followed him.

Jake made a quick check of their rear, still amazed and thankful they hadn't encountered any resistance.

He watched Vic, knowing his younger wingman's adrenaline had to be maxed out. Hell, Jake's ears still rang with all the adrenaline coursing through his veins. He hadn't felt this much of it since his first combat sortie.

He pushed off the support beam, starting his own drift toward the far end of the shaft. Above him, Richard had already covered half the distance.

Grabbing one wet structural member after another, Captain Allison slowed his ascension. Jake and Vic did the same, silently decelerating.

The source of the light drifted into view. To his relief, the shaft's upper elevator doors were jarred half-open. Without the need for hand signals, Richard and Victor took up their positions, the captain below and left, the lieutenant below and right of the opening.

Richard drifted up, moving his head slowly into position to scan his field of fire.

Jake saw the thin shaft of light illuminate his right eye.

Richard froze with a shudder, horror evident in his face. He slowly pulled back out of the light and gave them a signal.

There was one live bandit in his field of fire.

Nodding, Jake turned to Victor and gave him a thumbs-up.

After a brief hesitation, he nodded. Eyes closed, he took a calming breath. Opening them, he slowly drifted up and slid his head into position. His left eye passed into the beam of light. Scanning left and right, he paused twice. Sliding back out of the light, Vic gave them the hand signals for two dead bogeys.

Giving the stand-fast signal, Jake drifted up, his entire head passing into the shaft of light. He felt totally exposed. The room beyond appeared to be the bridge. Multiple control panels lined its walls. Other stations were dispersed across its floor. Some flickered with energy, but most were dead. A large display covered the left side of the far wall. A computer-rendered targeting reticle locked on a drifting Argonian fighter. Alien digital characters scrolled next to the image.

Looks like a countdown.

Off to one side, at least two bodies lay in a tangled mess, so mangled that all points of reference were lost. He couldn't tell where one ended and the other started. At the center of the bridge, gore trailed from the neck of a disembodied Zox head.

Scanning farther right, he discovered the source of Richard's horror. Across the room, a massive Zoxyth stood with its back to them. Lieutenant Croft had been correct, the beast was at least eight feet tall. Green blood covered its dark scales. Jake hoped the monster had lost a lot of it. Resuming its ranting diatribe while pounding on an apparent control panel, it roared and spoke with an impossibly deep voice. Jake could feel its sub-aural frequency vibrating his insides.

Some movement to the beast's left drew a fresh roar. A mixture of a growl and screech, the howl devolved into a gurgling cough.

Jake shifted to see what had drawn its ire. Displayed on the bridge's large screen, he saw Vampire Squadron make another pass.

Thank God they're still keeping it occupied.

Jake and his wingmen needed to get closer. Forty feet was too far for a shotgun engagement, and he thought pistols would just piss it off.

The monstrous alien went into a fit of rage, renewing its pounding. Then it froze.

Fearing the Zoxyth had sensed their presence, Jake held his breath.

The beast slowly turned left toward him and the open elevator doors. However, his gaze dropped to the floor. Silently, the monster stared at the disembodied head.

Beating again, Jake's heart pounded so hard he worried the demon would hear it.

As its scaled chest heaved, the monster's rattling breath echoed through the sudden silence. Razor-sharp lips peeled back from huge, dripping fangs. Angled back like horns, his long, swept-back, pointed ears twitched.

Jake couldn't look away from its eyes. They held an insane rage. A madness the cathedral's sculpture hadn't conveyed.

Erupting into a fresh rant, the monster screamed at the head and stormed toward their elevator.

Jake's blood turned to ice.

However, reaching the head, the Zoxyth stopped and scooped it up. Turning away, he raised it and glared into its unseeing eyes. After a moment, he roared again and started shouting into its dead face.

With the beast's renewed din echoing off the bridge's walls, Jake decided it was time to make their move. Knowing they had none to waste, he pushed back from the opening. Drifting rearward, he pointed to himself, held up one finger, and mouthed, *I'm going.* Pointing to Richard, he held up two fingers: *Second*. To Vic he held up three fingers: *Third*. His back reached the far wall of the shaft.

Without waiting for their acknowledgment, he pushed off, lunging through the center of the opening, timing his entry into the gravity field so that he landed on his feet.

Slamming his massive fist onto the control panel, the beast continued its tirade. Turning the severed head to face the display screen, they both watched as another empty Argonian space fighter exploded under the Zox's laser assault. Turning the face back to his, the beast renewed his rant, as if taunting the lifeless head.

Shotgun trained on the monster, Jake took cover behind a stony control panel a few feet from the elevator. He motioned for Captain Allison.

Richard drifted through the opening, landing feet first just inside the bridge. The alien's unending diatribe masked any noise Captain Allison generated. Quickly crossing the open space, he took up position on the other side of the console from Jake.

Looking to Vic, he gave the all-clear and turned to watch the Zox. At first, nothing happened; Vic just sat there. Then, in his peripheral vision, Jake saw him climb through the opening to crouch just inside the bridge.

Knowing Vic was exposed, Jake waved for him to cross the open area and take cover behind him.

Lieutenant Croft nodded and stepped into the no man's land between the elevator and the console.

The brute chose that horrible moment to finish his rant.

In the sudden silence, Vic froze, stopping dead in his tracks.

The beast still had its back to them.

Jake waved for Vic to continue.

Lieutenant Croft didn't see him. As if in slow motion, he was turning to look at the Zox.

Jake waved frantically.

Vic gasped.

It hadn't been much, but to Jake's horror, it was enough.

The monstrous Zox's head snapped around, green blood flying from its scaly face. For a surreal, frozen moment, both the beast and the severed head seemed to glare at Lieutenant Croft.

At the sight of an intruder on his bridge, the Zoxyth unleashed a monstrous, howling screech.

Maddeningly, Vic stood frozen like a deer caught in the headlights, the shotgun hanging limply in his hands.

The beast charged, closing the forty-foot-gap with impossible speed.

Jake and Richard popped up, their roaring shotguns adding to the cacophony, both hitting center of mass.

Barely slowed and otherwise unfazed by the twin shotgun blasts, the Zoxyth turned, redirecting his considerable might and insane rage toward the two nearer targets.

Holy shit, he's fast! Jake chambered another round as the beast closed on Richard, who had just re-cocked his weapon.

The monster batted away Captain Allison's shotgun with a roar, raising a scaly arm to strike.

CHAPTER 46

Alone in the shaft, Victor watched Captain Allison scramble into position. His heart raced. It pounded in his ears, even eclipsing his raspy, hyperventilating breaths.

As Richard kneeled opposite him, Captain Giard signaled for Victor to advance.

He hesitated. Never missing an opportunity to berate her disappointment of a son, his mother chided him. *Move, pussy! You're pathetic.*

"Shut up, Mother."

Undeterred, she persisted. *I can't believe I wasted nine months and gave up my good body to birth you. Just sit there, then.*

"Shut up!" he growled. Not as sure-footed as the captains, he climbed through the opening. Finally on the bridge floor, he stood shakily. Captain Giard waved for him to cross.

Suddenly, the monster fell silent.

Victor froze. Slowly he turned toward the beast. Seeing it for the first time, he gasped.

The demon and the head in its hand turned toward him.

Paralyzed with fear, Vic couldn't even raise his shotgun.

That's my boy, his dead mother sardonically chided.

Seeing him, the monster roared. With explosive speed, he dropped the head and rocketed straight at Victor.

Captains Allison and Giard jumped up, both firing their weapons. Hit by both shots, the beast changed course, his re-energized roar eclipsing the twin shotgun blasts.

Of course! Just stand there, pantywaist.

Victor couldn't take it anymore. Raising the shotgun, he shouted, "Shut up, bitch! You're dead!"

As it closed on Richard, the beast extended its sickle-shaped forearm appendage. Knowing it wouldn't be enough, Jake raised his weapon. Suddenly, Victor screamed, "Shut up, bitch! You're dead!" Charging the monster, Victor fired his shotgun into the Zox. "Get the fuck away from him!" Pumping his shotgun, he fired again. Jake tried to fire, but Vic stepped in his path.

Struck right of center, the beast spun away from Richard. Jake saw fresh green blood erupt from where Victor's second shot had hit him.

The monster turned its ire back on Vic. As the lieutenant pumped a third round into the chamber, the Zoxyth warrior used the centrifugal inertia imparted by the shotgun strike to accelerate the swing of his right arm. It zipped past Victor's neck with blinding speed.

Blasting rock from a control panel, Lieutenant Croft's weapon fired wide. Victor froze, red mist exploding from his neck. The shotgun clattered to the floor. A confused look took over his face, and then his eyes glazed over. A moment later, his head rolled from his shoulders and fell to the floor. His lifeless, decapitated body stood for a second, then collapsed.

Screaming with shocked rage and horror, Jake fired point-blank into the Zox's chest. The impact spun the beast halfway around but didn't knock him down.

Richard fired into the Zoxyth's side, spinning him backward toward Captain Giard.

Jake brought his freshly cocked shotgun to bear, but the Zoxyth dived through the open elevator doors, bending and racking them farther apart. He quickly disappeared down the shaft, a trail of green blood droplets left floating in his wake.

After a sorrowful glance at his fallen wingman, Jake lunged head first through the opening. As he passed into the zero-G shaft, he shot toward the far end, kicking off the same structural member as had the Zoxyth. At the bottom, the demon disappeared into the lower hallway.

Jake's anger erupted like a volcano. The brutal death of his young friend coupled with the day's loss of so many people had Jake's blood boiling. "You're dead, fucker!"

Near the bottom, he grabbed a structural member, flipped around and aimed feet first for the open elevator doors. Hitting it perfectly, he flew through the opening and landed on his feet, shotgun extended, ready for battle.

The beast ran into the cathedral.

Chasing it, Jake ran through the opening.

Heading for the altar, the monster was halfway down the center aisle.

With a primal roar, Jake ran up the passage firing his shotgun.

Scales, flesh, and fresh green blood erupted from its back. The beast stumbled and then continued inexorably toward the altar.

"Die, fucker! Die!" Jake screamed. He closed the gap to ten feet.

As the Zoxyth reached the steps, Jake saw a stone block the same width as the tile covering it, rising under the altar. The tile slid back to expose a concave Zoxyth palm print.

Jake aimed at his spine and squeezed the trigger. Fire belched from the muzzle. The blast's roar echoed off the cavernous room's damp walls as green tissue and blood geysered from the wound.

With a yowl of agony, the Zoxyth fell to his knees. Still struggling for the altar, it crawled up the steps, extending an arm toward the elevated block.

Jake realized it must be a self-destruct button. Crossing the last few feet and pumping the shotgun, he placed its muzzle against the back of the beast's head.

He screamed, "Die!" and pulled the trigger.

Click.

The monster roared with something that might have been laughter. Its arm flashed backward, striking Jake center of mass. The breath exploded from his chest as he flew halfway down the aisle, landing hard on his back.

Forgetting the self-destruct mechanism, the beast climbed back to its feet and advanced on Jake.

Sprawled on his back and struggling to pull air into his seized chest, Captain Giard tried to scramble from the monster. In a moment, it was on him. Bending over, the Zox lowered its scaled face, stopping mere inches from Jake's. Its putrid hot breath spilled over him. Then it roared, spraying Jake's face with a mix of spittle and green blood.

"Hey!"

The monster looked up.

Dragging his eyes from the beast, Jake tilted his head back. Richard stood in the entrance, aiming the shotgun over the demon.

"Get the fuck off him!" Fire spewed from the weapon.

The Zox flinched.

Jake covered his face against the anticipated spray of green gore, but none came. Instead, he heard the rattle of stone chips rain down behind the altar.

Had Richard missed?

The monster spun toward the sound.

Still struggling for breath, Jake lifted his head, seeking the source of the falling gravel. A portion of the Zoxyth statue's midsection was blasted away.

Richard had shot it.

The Zox's head snapped back, eyes flaring with insane rage.

"Come get me, you son of a bitch!" Richard screamed. He pumped another round into the chamber.

Forgetting Jake, the beast charged with renewed energy.

Richard fired point-blank into the monster's chest. It didn't slow.

Head tilted back, watching the scene upside down, Jake saw the Zoxyth snatch the shotgun from his hands with his left claw while a blow from its right launched Richard backward. Flying through the entrance like a rag doll, he crashed against the hall's far wall, his limp, unconscious body crumpling to the floor.

With a victory roar, the Zoxyth snapped the shotgun in half, throwing the two pieces against the cathedral walls.

Jake struggled to his side, finally rolling onto his belly: he still fought to breathe.

Richard moaned.

With both fists raised, the sickle-shaped appendages slid from the brute's forearms. Head tilted back and launching into another rant, the monster closed on Captain Allison's limp body.

He's going to kill Richard too.

Jake pulled the nine-millimeter from his hip. Futilely aiming the pistol at the back of the Zox, he fired, the weapon jumping in his hand.

The demon continued undeterred.

Something over the Zox's head drew Jake's attention. Shifting his aim, he pulled the trigger. The weapon leapt again as another shot rang out.

The sconce over the Cathedral's entrance exploded.

No longer supported, the tilted, massive stone Argonian body fell toward the Zox. The monster leaned back. As if trying to catch the tons of falling rock, he raised his hands. However, unimpeded, the human statue slammed across the beast's body. Crushing the Zoxyth's abdomen under its bulk and pinning his arms, it launched an arcing spray of black and green entrails across the far wall of the cathedral.

Dust and debris rained down. As his arms gave out, Jake's face dropped to the floor. Blood trickled from his lips, mingling with the dust under his left cheek. As quiet settled over the room, he watched as a lone shell from Richard's ruptured shotgun bounced and rolled to a stop against his hand.

Fighting to hold onto consciousness, he groped for the shell, finally gripping it on the third attempt. Sliding a knee under his belly and pushing off with his hands, he struggled to stand. Leaning against a toppled stone pew, he began to catch his breath.

The mortally wounded Zoxyth writhed under the human sculpture.

Dazed, Jake limped toward him. Almost tripping over something, he looked down to find his empty shotgun lying in the middle of the aisle. Fighting not to pass out, he bent over and picked it up. Fending off vertigo, he stood and started limping toward the monster.

Finally reaching the entrance, he turned to face the beast while leaning against the prone statue. Jake was certain this was the enemy commander, the catalyst for the day's death and destruction.

Loading the lone round into the shotgun's empty magazine, he pumped it into the chamber and pointed into the demon's face.

Seeing him, the Zoxyth unleashed a fresh screeching roar.

Jake jammed the muzzle into its gaping maw.

"This is for Victor!"

He pulled the trigger.

The roar of the shotgun silenced the beast's howl. An explosion of green brain matter sprayed the floor, finally ending the monster's reign.

CHAPTER 47

Bone-weary, Jake struggled to stand. The shotgun's recoil had knocked him back into the prone statue, buckling his knees and dropping him hard on his ass. A final shove brought him back to his feet. Working his way around the sculpture, he limped to Richard's side.

Coughing and pulling himself to a seated position, Richard looked up at him. "Nice finale."

"Hey, somebody had to do the work. You were just lying around," Jake said, plopping down next to him.

Jake's chuckle died as his thoughts returned to Victor.

Apparently reading his face, Richard said, "There's nothing you could have done to prevent it. It's not your fault."

"There's always another way. Maybe I could have—"

"You can *maybe* yourself to death," Richard interrupted. "Or, you can know you did the best anyone ever could, in such an insane situation. Hell, I'm the one that was an asshole to him." Somberly shaking his head he added, "If it weren't for that crazy little fucker, I'd be dead." He stopped and checked his watch. "Not that it matters much. We'll be joining him in another sixty seconds."

Jake nodded. "Guess we both knew this would be a one-way trip."

"Yeah, once that door slid shut, I figured we'd never find a way back out before time was up. Too bad we don't have a handheld radio. If we had a way to tell Newcastle it's our ship, we could wave him off."

"Yeah, it's our ship all right." Jake looked around. Spreading his arms he sang, "And you could have it all ..."

"My empire of dirt," Richard finished with a wry smile. "Love me some Nine Inch Nails."

Jake shook his head and looked down. Then, rocked by an epiphany, he sat bolt upright. "Holy shit!"

As he checked his watch again, Colonel Newcastle's heart sank. He couldn't wait any longer.

"Commander Yaakov, we have the last two bunker busters."

"Da comrade."

"I think the force fields protecting the bridge and lasers will provide sufficient resistance to detonate our missiles."

"The thought occurred to me also, comrade."

"I'm sending your fire-control computer the coordinates. I want you to hit the left laser's force field. I've programmed your attack vector so that if it breaks through, but doesn't detonate, it'll still take out both lasers."

"Understood."

Colonel Newcastle continued, responsibility weighing heavily on his words. "I'll hit the bridge."

Hearing the strain in his voice, Vlad said, "Comrade, we have done all that can be done. They understood the risk. Now we must do our duty."

Zach shook his head with frustration, but knowing he had no choice, he called back. "Thank you, my friend. Now let's be done with it."

"Da."

Colonel Newcastle actuated his flight controller. The ship rocketed toward the initialization point. For the first time, Zach found himself lamenting its extraordinary speed. Turning inbound from the IP, he armed the weapon. The tactical computer showed Commander Yaakov's fighter doing the same.

The ship remnant expanded, his finger hovered over the trigger. Closing his eyes, he whispered, "God forgive me." He fired the missile.

Opening his eyes, he saw it accelerating toward the ship's bridge. Through one of its portals, Zach saw a white light cycling between short and long flashes.

"Oh shit!"

In the over-the-shoulder point of view provided by the new satellite, the back-end of Colonel Newcastle's fighter floated superimposed over the alien ship.

Sandy clenched her fists. *Come on, Jake!*

The radio crackled to life. "I can't wait any longer, sir."

After a forlorn glance at Sandy, the general closed his eyes and lifted the mic. "Roger, Vampire Six ..." The microphone drooped as he struggled with his next words. After a moment, he shook his head. "Fuck!" The handset rose to his mouth again. "Colonel Newcastle, this is General Pearson. You are cleared to engage the target with nuclear munitions."

"No!" Sandy screamed.

The aide placed a sympathetic but firm hand on her shoulder, trying to gently guide Sandy toward the door.

She shoved the senior officer's hand away. "No! I'm staying."

The major cast a questioning look at the general. He nodded, and the aide relented.

Blinking furiously, Sandy stared at the display through tear-filled eyes. She stifled another scream when a golden-tailed black rod flew from the fighter. Instantly, a blue icon popped into existence. Labeled *BB32,* it raced toward the target. Sandy knew another missile, blocked from view, was burning its way inward from the opposite direction.

She focused on the area they'd identified as the alien ship's bridge.

Holding her left hand to her abdomen, Sandy extended her right. *I love you, baby. I—* A flashing white light broke her thoughts. In an instant, she recognized the pattern.

Sandy spun on General Pearson. "Abort the missiles! Abort the fucking missiles!"

"I can't—"

Cutting him off, Sandy pointed at the flashing white light. "That's an SOS!"

"Oh God!" Jake screamed. He quickened the rhythmic tapping on his suit's spotlight. "They've launched!"

"I've got one on this side too!"

"Keep signaling them!" Watching in horror as the missile, a black dot in the center of a budding flower of fire, accelerated directly at the bridge, he added, "It's been an honor, Richard."

"Same here, friend."

Jake looked toward the western horizon. "I love you, Sandy."

Closing his eyes, he braced for the end.

A brilliant light shone through his eyelids.

CHAPTER 48

"Abort, abort, abort!" Colonel Newcastle screamed. He hammered his missile's self-destruct button.

"Commander Yaakov, abort your missile!" It was useless. The asteroid was blocking his radio's line of sight.

Newcastle's weapon flashed. Horror shifted to hope as the non-nuclear detonation of its explosives shredded the missile's components.

"Commander Yaakov, please reply—"

Just as the shattered remnants of his bunker buster splashed across the alien bridge, a brilliant flash blossomed from the ship remnant's far side, casting the profile of the beast's visage in a macabre silhouette. To Zach's immense relief, the conflagration faded just as quickly.

Striking both sides simultaneously, burning missile debris splashed ineffectually across the ship remnant's small force fields.

A moment later, Yaakov's fighter darted from behind the asteroid and Zach's radio sparked to life. The Russian commander's voice was full of dread. "We failed, comrade."

Confused, Colonel Newcastle stared at his radio.

Before he could reply, Yaakov continued. "This time, our missiles didn't punch through. The aliens found some way to activate its self-destruct."

Now Zach was truly confused. "I thought you self-destructed it."

"Me? No, Colonel. Why would I do that?"

A new voice joined the discussion. "No, Colonel. That was me," said an unfamiliar female voice. "Now sir, if you don't mind. Could you please go get my boyfriend off that goddamned rock?"

A roar followed the bright light. *I shouldn't have heard that. It should've been flash, then blaring trumpets and Pearly Gates.*

Jake opened his eyes. He and Richard faced each other, wide-eyed.

"Holy shit!" Richard said.

"We're alive!" Jake screamed. He grabbed Rich, crushing him in a bear-hug.

"Easy there," he said grimacing, a hand to his ribs.

"Sorry." Jake set him back down. "I can't believe it worked."

"You're a genius," Richard said, clapping him on the shoulder.

"You're the one that gave me the idea."

"Huh?"

"I was actually singing the Johnny Cash version of *Hurt*."

Richard looked more confused. "How hard did that fucker hit you?"

Jake shook his head and smiled. "When you mentioned Nine Inch Nails, I pictured their famous acronym. It's my favorite three-letter palindrome."

"Palindrome?"

"Yeah, it's the same forward or backward."

Comprehension blossomed on his face. Nodding, he said, "Just like SOS."

"I just added *Save*. You called it *Our Ship*."

"Still, the idea to use our suit lights to send an SOS was a stroke of genius."

Both captains jumped as something flashed in Jake's portal. Seeing its source, they erupted into relieved laughter.

Two sleek Vampire Attack fighters floated outside, one rhythmically flashing its landing lights.

Jake read the code: S-T-A-T- U-S.

He tapped out a quick reply on his suit lamp: *Ship secure. All enemy KIA.* After a brief pause, he added: *Croft KIA. Will find exit and report from Turtle. Over.*

After a moment, Newcastle's fighter started flashing again.

Jake read it out loud: "GOOD JOB, MEN. STANDING BY."

CHAPTER 49

"Vampire Six, this is Turtle One, over."

A relieved voice greeted them. "Turtle One, thank God. I was starting to wonder if you'd ever find a way out. What's your status?"

Physically and mentally exhausted, Jake dropped into the chair rising from the ship's floor. "Mission complete, sir. There was only one alien left alive. He's been ... terminated."

"Outstanding work, gentlemen! I'm proud of you."

Jake shook his head. "No, sir. I lost a man in there. I should've—"

"Son, we've all lost friends today. I know it's especially hard when it's someone under your command."

"Yes, sir. I just keep thinking that if I would've done things a little different, maybe Lieutenant Croft would still be alive."

"We are our own worst critics—it's a commander's burden—but you'll be the only voice of doubt. In the face of impossible odds, you and your team prevailed. Had you done anything different, that outcome could've been jeopardized."

"Thank you, sir," Jake said. Looking at Victor's shrouded corpse, he silently hoped the colonel's words might one day allow a measure of self-forgiveness.

"The world owes you all a great debt of gratitude. Unfortunately, you'll have to wait a while to cash it in."

Jake and Richard exchanged confused glances.

"I'm placing both of you under my command. Welcome to the First Space Fighter Squadron, or as we're called by the few that know of us, Vampire Attack."

"Yes, sir," they replied in unison.

"I have assignments for both of you. What's your physical condition? Did you sustain injuries during your engagement?"

Jake looked at Richard and received a thumbs-up.

Aside from a couple of cracked ribs, bumps and bruises, they had emerged from the battle relatively unscathed.

Jake nodded and keyed the mic. "Nothing we can't work through, sir."

"Okay, here's what we're looking at. As I see it, our first two priorities are securing the Argonian fleet and gathering sufficient pilots and commanders to staff it."

"Yes, sir," Jake agreed.

"The fleet is still drifting apart. Some of the ships are getting dangerously close to entering the atmosphere. They won't burn up. They're not at orbital velocity, but before they start getting scattered by the four winds, we have to find a way onto that main ship."

"Good, copy, Vampire Six. What about boarding the fighters closest to the atmosphere? If we can move them to a higher altitude, it'll buy us more time."

"Already tried that. No obvious means of entry. Our only option is to gain access into the carrier ship and remotely recall them."

"Additionally," he continued. "I want commanders and pilots ready to move into position as soon as we gain access. If more of these alien bastards show up, I want to have a big surprise waitin' for 'em."

"Roger, Vampire Six," Jake replied. "How can we assist?"

"Captain Allison, you're more familiar with the *Turtle's* capabilities. I need you to take it back to Nellis Air Force Base in Vegas. I want you to link up with General Pearson, the base commander. I've already briefed him on our status. I'll update him, and let him know you're coming."

Richard reached over and toggled the comm panel. "Yes, sir."

"He's putting together a group of naval commanders for the bigger ships and pilots from all services for the fighters. Once you've debriefed the general, you're to begin ferrying personnel and supplies."

"Good, copy. Will do, sir."

Jake toggled the panel. "And for me, sir?"

"First, Captain Fitzpatrick sends her regards."

Jake sat upright. "Sandy?" He toggled the radio. "How did she ... is she okay? Are her parents ...?"

"I'm told it's a long story, Captain. Suffice it to say, she and her parents are safely back on the ground at Nellis. As a matter of fact, your still being alive is in no small part because of her actions."

Dumbfounded, Jake wordlessly stared at the radio.

"Anyway, Captain Giard, you can get the rest of the story from her later. I'm sending the rest of my squadron back for rearming. In the meantime, you and I are going to link up and find a way into that carrier."

"Good, copy on all, Zach. Sorry to hear about Lieutenant Croft. Please pass on my thanks to Captains Giard and Allison. Nellis Actual, out."

Colonel Newcastle's voice echoed through the command center's reverent silence. "Roger, General. I'll pass it on. Vampire Six, out."

Torn by the dichotomous news, Sandy struggled with her emotions, unsure whether to smile or cry. While she'd never been close to Lieutenant Croft, she'd always liked him. Having taken Victor under his wing, Jake had seen the junior officer as a little brother.

Apparently reading her mixed emotions, General Pearson's brusque features softened, his steel-gray eyes actually looked sympathetic. "I'm sorry for your loss. I understand the young lieutenant was a friend to all of you." He turned toward the room's main display. On it, Colonel Newcastle's Vampire Space Fighter glided up to the parked *Turtle.* "All of you did great things today." Turning from the screen, he proffered his right hand.

Startled and speechless, Sandy took the hand in hers and shook it.

The grizzled old man's hard face softened further and his eyes sparkled with admiration. "Good job, Captain Fitzpatrick. I, hell, all of us, owe all of you a great debt of gratitude."

Sandy opened her mouth to tell him she hadn't done a thing, but he held up a hand.

"I know you think it was all them, but if you hadn't thought so quickly, we'd have lost your friends." He pointed at the alien rock. "And that ship, along with the secret of its weapon, would've crashed into the ocean, causing even more death and destruction."

"But, sir—"

The general shook his head. "I'm not finished, Captain."

Sandy nodded. "Yes, sir."

"Do you see all those?" He pointed at the drifting fleet of dark, sleek Argonian ships. Not waiting for her acknowledgement, he continued. "I need pilots to man them." He cast an apologetic look at her. "I mean staff them, or hell, whatever. You get the idea." Lowering his arm, the general gave Sandy a meaningful look. "Anyway, Captain, as much as I think we owe you and your fellow officers, I think we're going to owe you a lot more." He glared at the charred alien visage. "We may have won this battle, but I don't think the Zoxyth are done with us, and I know I'm not done with you."

Sandy's thoughts reeled with the implications of the general's plan, but her myriad questions went unasked as all that came out was another "Yes, sir."

General Pearson smiled. After a paternal pat on her shoulder, he turned and walked away.

Sandy placed a hand on her abdomen. Under her bloodied flight suit, she felt the edge of the bandages the medic had applied to her side. After a quick examination, he'd given Sandy and her unborn baby a clean bill of health. The sergeant, the same medic who had met her on the Nellis tarmac, had also informed her that, while her father had lost his leg, the doctors thought his prognosis was very good and they expected a full recovery. He'd also said the entire ICU staff had given her mother the honorary title of General Firecracker, one she had apparently taken to quite readily.

Looking at her future baby bump, she smiled. "Looks like you and I will get to have a little chat with your daddy, soon."

Jake stepped into the airlock and turned back to Richard. "Now don't forget—"

"Dude, I told you I'll talk to her and find out what happened. I'm just as curious about what Newcastle said as you are. I'll check on her and get word to you ASAP."

"Thank you," he said, then nodded toward the shrouded body in the ship's center. "Make sure Lieutenant Croft gets the recognition he deserves."

"Nothing but the best," Richard agreed.

A backward step took him deeper into the airlock. He saluted sharply. "Captain Allison, it's been an honor."

Richard returned the salute. "Same here, Captain. Be careful out there."

Lowering his arm, Jake said, "See you on the other side."

The airlock wall sealed.

As Jake turned toward the outer wall, his helmet's limpid visor flowed into shape, protecting him from the ensuing vacuum. The exterior wall evaporated, revealing a beautiful panorama of stars. At its center hovered a Vampire Attack fighter. Through its open canopy, Colonel Newcastle raised a hand to his spacesuit's helmet.

Standing in the opening, Captain Jake Giard returned the salute.

EPILOGUE

"I*n the midst of chaos, there is also opportunity.*"

— Sun Tzu, The Art of War

EPILOGUE

"Admiral Tekamah, all ships report battle-ready," said the Helm Warden's tactical officer.

The Galactic Defense Force's supreme commander, Admiral Ashtara Tekamah, studied the holographic rendering of his fleet and the rapidly closing system. "I hate blindly flying into a potential battle." In his EON's virtual vision, Tekamah toggled Admiral Feyhdyak's icon. "Any contact with your bio-half?"

A few hours earlier, the computer-based portion of Admiral Thoyd Feyhdyak, the commander he'd sent to intercept the Zoxyth fleet closing on Sector Sixty-Four, had informed him that something had severed his communications link with his biological. He reported they had been seconds from dropping into Earth space when the disconnect occurred.

"Nothing yet, sir." Computer-based Thoyd's voice had a panicked edge. Disconnected intelligences usually did. As a combat commander, Ashtara communed with disjointed personalities all too often. They always seemed on the verge of panic. As if the time separated from their organic id would lead to irreparable psychosis, the untethered parallel existence creating a permanent schizophrenic duality. Tekamah knew it wasn't an idle concern. It happened, and the longer the separation, the rougher the reconnect. Upon discovering their bio-half had indeed died, he'd seen relief in the virtual face of more than one computer-based personality. It was said that bonding with a fresh, tank-grown body was sometimes easier than re-merging with a divergent copy.

The practice of placing copies of combat personnel into the network began for the obvious reasons. Subsequently, they had instituted the real-time connection between network-based and organic-based ids in order to prevent that duality. Otherwise, one was merely a copy. Continuity was lost. If one died, its stream of consciousness went with it. As an Earth-based Argonian from the nineteen seventies or eighties would say, 'Is it live, or is it Memorex?'

Computer-based Thoyd's virtual eyebrows raised. "What do you think happened, Ashtara? I've consulted with my subordinates within the network. None has heard from their bios."

"Calm down, Thoyd. I'm sure there is a reasonable explanation. You were still in parallel-space, the Zox don't have anything that could touch you there."

Admiral Feyhdyak's avatar looked ready to say more, but Tekamah held up a virtual hand. "Thoyd, I have to go. We're approaching Chuvarti. I'll let you know as soon as I hear from you or any of your vessels."

He closed the connection and turned to the communications officer. "Have we received any further distress calls from the Chuvarti system?"

"No, sir, nothing since the initial call. It's fortunate we were so close to Sector Nineteen."

Tekamah nodded, but he knew fortune had nothing to do with it. The intel he'd received placed half of Thrakst's fleet in this sector while the other half had deployed to the far side of the galaxy in remote Sector Sixty-Four. He had a nagging feeling there was more to this situation than met the eye.

"Place all battlecruisers on a weapons-free status," ordered Tekamah. "All fighter squadrons are to launch as soon as we drop out of parallel-space. If we're flying into a trap, I want the Zoxyth to regret it."

He studied the fisheye lens of the squeezed star field to the formation's front. A tiny, bright blue spec at its center, the planet Chuvarti, grew into a discernible sphere as the fleet closed.

The navigation officer broke the silence. "Normal space in three, two—"

Find out what happens next!
Get Retribution: Sector 64 Book Two Today!

RETRIBUTION: SNEAK PEEK

Chapter One Intro from *Retribution: Sector 64 Book Two*

"This cold is going to be the death of me," Remulkin Thramorus said as he trudged through another waist-deep snow dune. Pulling the nanobot-enhanced parka tight around his ears, he lowered his head into the frigid gale. Buffeting him, it threatened to blow Remulkin back to the empty transport hovering to his rear.

Leaning into the wind, the scientist looked through his eyebrows. Ahead, a jagged rock protruded a few stories above the ice plain. Buried under the polar ice cap, a huge mountain, hundreds of times taller than the visible portion, spread out beneath the camp.

Only a month earlier, a construction crew had finished boring a science station into the mountain's exposed triangular peak. The camp's sole entrance lay ahead of Remulkin. Behind and to the sides of the lone scientist, the white plain stretched to the horizon, disappearing into the pole's perpetual night. Interrupted only by the snow dunes that always seemed to occupy the space between him and his destination, the surface was otherwise perfectly flat.

Anchored at the pole of the newly settled planet, this part of the ice field sat motionlessly. Sub-zero temperatures and a thick, stable ice sheet that insulated the site from the planet's iron-rich surface made it the perfect region for Remulkin's experiment.

One snow dune later, the scientist trudged up to the smooth outer skin of the camp's entrance. With the sound of tearing paper, a rectangular opening appeared in its seamless surface. A force field-entrained bubble of heated atmosphere ballooned out and wrapped him in its warm embrace.

The scientist stepped through the hatch-shaped opening, an action that breathed life into ancient memories of his brief military stint. A lifetime ago, a much younger Petty Officer Thramorus had haunted the vast halls of an Argonian-manned battlecruiser.

Dusting the frost from his ample belly, he frowned. In the years since his three-year, all-expenses-paid tour with the Galactic Defense Forces, his forehead had become a five-head, and his six-pack looked more like a twelve-pack.

Remulkin stepped through the inner door into the compound's main room. In mercurial rivulets, billions of nanobots streamed from his bib and parka. No longer needed for insulation, the omnifunctional microscopic robots flowed into the mottled gray floor, rejoining the facility's matrix. The parka and bib morphed to their normal volume and function as a day shirt and pants.

Excited to share the bounty of data garnered at the pole, Remulkin forgot about the day's isolation.

He dusted the last of the frost from his shirt and looked around.

His smile faltered.

Why was it so quiet? Why was the common room empty? At this hour, it should be bustling with activity.

Thramorus shook his head. "I'm back," he said, yelling toward the back rooms. "Is everyone on break?"

Silence.

Raising his voice, he said, "I go away for one day, and you all take a holiday?"

Nothing.

"Hello?"

Anger—and the first hint of concern—chased away his good cheer.

"Guys, this isn't funny."

All he heard was his voice's fading echo floating in the still air.

Determined to find someone, he walked and then jogged through the subterranean compound.

"Hello?"

Still no answer.

Now panting, he ran from room to room.

They were all empty.

He even checked the ladies restroom.

As Remulkin turned to exit, he saw movement. After a confused moment, he realized the scared, middle-aged, portly man was him.

Blinking and wheezing, Remulkin studied his reflection in the vanity mirror. His normally pale, freckled skin was ruddy, glowing above and below his ring of red and gray hair. His mother had once told him that you never really *see* yourself until you think you're looking at someone else.

He shook his head and turned from the unsettling image.

Finally catching his breath in the camp's elevation-thinned atmosphere, Remulkin exited the restroom and walked to the last door, his quarters.

Shaking his head after a final confused glimpse back toward the entrance, he stepped into the room … and jumped right the hell back out.

A body had popped into existence in front of his face.

In the middle of his private room!

"Damn holograms!" he screamed, once his pounding heart and hitching breath permitted speech.

"Sorry about that, Mr. Thramorus," said an uncharacteristically dour-looking Falinch Meklem. His assistant—usually jovial to the point of annoyance—stared grimly from the pre-recorded hologram.

Annoyed at the intrusion into his quarters, holographic or not, Remulkin searched for the deactivation key.

"I know how much you hate these things, but I don't have time for anything else."

There it is, he thought as he found the virtual shutoff key floating on the front right corner of the hologram. Remulkin reached for it.

As if reacting to the scientist's movement, his assistant held up a hand. "This is important, sir. You'll want to hear it."

His finger hovered over the virtual button. Then Thramorus pulled it back as if he'd touched a hot surface.

What the hell was he thinking? His disgust with the invasion of his privacy had banished all other concerns. Remulkin's wife would have loved that one. She was always saying he was too stuffy, too worried about privacy and personal space. She had begged him to let them connect their Electro-Organic Networks to the colony's matrix. Then they could use the neurally implanted EONs to stay in constant contact.

Oh, joy! Remulkin thought.

In the hologram, a running man bumped into Falinch. The assistant lunged forward. Remulkin heard a shouted apology. Regaining his feet, the man pushed his tousled blond hair out of his eyes and appeared to stare at Remulkin.

The uncharacteristic seriousness in the young man's eyes had Remulkin's short hairs standing on end.

Meklem pointed a thumb over his shoulder. "The sensor network detected a Zoxyth fleet entering our galactic sector."

"My Gods," Remulkin whispered.

The assistant continued. "We're all leaving to be with our families. Everything should be fine. The Galactic Defense Forces can't be far behind."

Another person ran through the image. "Sorry."

Falinch waved at the person and then continued. "We tried to call you in, but couldn't detect your terminal."

"Shit!" Remulkin shouted. A sinking feeling struck his gut as he recalled disabling his hand terminal's external link during the experiment.

Falinch continued speaking as Remulkin worked to activate his terminal.

"Sorry for the short message, we have to get on the transport. As soon as it drops me off, I'll set its autopilot to return for you."

"Anyway, I'm sure this is an overreaction. The GDF has those green-blooded, ancestor-worshipping lizards on their heels ... Don't they?"

As holographic Falinch began to dematerialize, Remulkin saw a look of trepidation leak through the man's brave facade.

"No, no, no," Remulkin said, growling in frustration. Hunched over the hand terminal, he tapped furiously. "Come on!"

The scientist shared his assistant's apprehension. They *were* at war with the Zoxyth. The fanatical leader of the reptilian race had declared a holy war against all Argonians. He had sworn to right an ancient wrong, to avenge a supposed Argonian attempt to wreak genocide upon their sacrosanct Forebearers. The visceral Lord Thrakst had vowed to eradicate every last Argonian from the galaxy.

A chill ran down Remulkin's spine.

Finally, his terminal finished its digital handshake and connected to the station's network.

A multi-pitched storm of audio alerts announced a flood of messages and warnings. Red, strobing icons streamed across his screen.

"Oh Gods." This was bad, real bad.

Remulkin scrolled through the news updates and government alerts in sequence. Most had timestamps more recent than the assistant's message. They painted a picture of a rapidly deteriorating situation.

City after city in this newly settled world had fallen silent.

The arrival of an enemy ship preceded each event.

Reports of a brilliant light.

Then nothing, all contact with the area lost.

On the final newsclip, Remulkin watched as the godsdamned aliens closed in on the last settlement.

His new home town.

In this new colony, everyone lived in or near a town.

Whatever the bastards were doing, they had done it to every settlement, every man, every woman, every child.

Save his.

Now Remulkin's home was in their sights.

The last item on his terminal, a recorded video message, opened.

"Baby, I'm scared," his wife said. "Why won't you pick up?" Farene's eyes pleaded. "I need you, baby!"

In the background, daylight streamed through the windows of their home. Suddenly they darkened as if a black cloud had passed overhead.

"Oh my Gods! They're here now!" she said, her voice cracking with fear.

Remulkin touched the image of her face. "Farene!"

His pounding heart threatened to burst from his chest.

To either side, his son and daughter clutched at their mother. At nine years old, their son, Wilby, stood taller than his younger sister, Freena.

His wife stared into the camera he'd mounted over the kitchen door. She'd asked him to put it there. That way the scientist could watch his wife's experiments with cooking—just one of the many things they'd both had to learn as colonists on a new settlement.

"Remulkin?" she said, her eyes pleading. "Why aren't you answering?"

Find out what happens next!
Get Retribution: Sector 64 Book Two Today!

SOLITUDE: SNEAK PEEK

Solitude: Book One of Dimension Space

The Martian meets *Gravity* when Earth's last man, Army Captain Vaughn Singleton, discovers that the last woman is stranded alone aboard the International Space Station. Commander Angela Brown could reverse the event that swept humanity from Earth's surface ... if only she could get there. If you like action-packed, page-turning novels, you'll love the electrifying action in this award-winning, apocalyptic thriller.

SOLITUDE: SNEAK PEEK

Angela looked down to see the familiar horseshoe shape of Hudson Bay glide beneath her white boots. She shifted her gaze to the south and spotted Canada's biggest annular lake. It ringed Manicouagan Crater—one of Earth's largest asteroidal scars and easily visible from space.

"Uh, Commander Brown, if you're done sightseeing, I could use a hand here."

Angela smiled. Mindful of the ever-watchful eye of Mission Control, she resisted the urge to, playfully, hoist her middle finger.

Instead, the commander gave him her cheesiest smile and said, "How may I be of assistance, Major?"

Major Peterson did a double take. He floated a few feet across from Angela. Behind the visor of his helmet, a crooked grin spread across his ebony face. "Really, Commander Brown? Assistance? What happened to, 'What can Brown do for you?'?"

Angela sighed and rolled her eyes. "Don't you start, too." Inside her helmet, her head shook side-to-side. "Crack one public joke, and it follows you around for the rest of your life."

"That'll learn ya," Bill Peterson said with a smile.

Angela ignored him and continued. "That was 2018. It's been two years. I mean, really?!"

Paying no heed to her, the major wrapped his gauntleted hand around a coffee cup-sized white cylinder. His body writhed as he struggled with the stubborn electrical connector.

The pair of astronauts floated near the left or port end of the International Space Station's 300-foot-long solar array truss. The structure supported all sixteen of the station's main solar panels. To Angela, the long edifice looked like the mutated body of a dragonfly with way too many wings.

"This thing doesn't want to budge," he said with a grunt. The man's entire body lurched as he tried to force the electrical connector to turn.

"Is that Charlie Eight One Niner?" Angela said.

After giving the connector's three-inch-thick barrel a final fruitless twist, he released it with a frustrated growl. "The one and only!"

The two spacesuited figures floated in the shadow of the station's outermost solar panel, but sunlight reflected off the truss, illuminating the major's face. He looked from the cylindrical connector and winked at her. "Got a can of WD-40?"

Angela smiled and held up a large set of white pliers. "Nope. But I do have the convincer."

She tilted the joystick grasped in her right hand. The bracket under her feet vibrated, and the robotic manipulator arm attached to the bottom of her boots moved the commander toward Major Bill Peterson.

A moment later she released the controller. Now they floated face-to-face: Angela standing on the end of the long manipulator arm, Bill clipped to the array's hard points, the offending power coupling between them. A metal label riveted to its side read:

C819

Angela grasped its outer ring with the convincer—a tool specifically designed for stubborn connectors. In the zero-G environment, she relied on the stability of Canadarm2, the manipulator arm strapped to her feet, to give her the leverage that she needed to apply a twisting force to the wrench.

The sticky connector finally broke free on her third attempt.

With a crackle of breaking squelch, a new voice blared from the radio speaker. "Great job, Commander."

"Why, thank you, Houston," Angela said. "While I have my tools out, is there anything else ... *I* can do for you?" She glared at Bill and silently mouthed, *Thanks, butt hole!*

In 2018, when UPS had brought back their old slogan, she'd asked a pesky reporter, "What can Brown do for you?" The S.O.B. had run with it. His editor had even made it the title of the front-page article. It had stuck, and now two years later, even she had almost uttered the damn thing!

"Actually, Commander Brown, there is something you can do for me."

Angela suddenly realized that the voice belonged to Randy McCree, the director of Mission Control.

"Oh ... hello, Director. To what do we owe the pleasure?" Angela said, wincing inwardly. She resented the nervous feeling in her gut. The young physicist hadn't asked for this assignment, hadn't wanted it. In fact, Angela would've been happy if they'd left her to her experiments.

Ahead of the space station, Iceland appeared on the eastern horizon. Behind them, the inverted white triangle of Greenland's southern tip retreated, slowly sliding behind the curving line of the planet's western limb.

"Got something I'd like you to take a look at," McCree said.

Angela's head moved back and forth as she scanned the long solar array. Great! The woman had only been mission commander for a week, and on her first spacewalk, she'd already screwed up so badly that someone had summoned the director.

Apparently, NASA's ever-watchful eye was focused on her at that moment. Randy McCree chuckled. "It's nothing to do with your work. You'll need to look a little farther away to check this issue."

"Okay," Angela said, drawing out the word. "What do you have for us, Director?"

"Need you to take a look at Europe."

"Europe? Have you guys misplaced France ... again?"

After a pregnant pause, the director's voice returned flat and humorless. "It seems we might have."

Commander Brown and Major Peterson exchanged confused glances as their smiles faded.

Randy McCree didn't wait for her to reply. "A few minutes ago, several data centers went quiet. Our hackers can't get anything from them, either."

Angela knew that by hackers he meant Information Technologies, or I.T. for short.

"Did they lose power?" Major Peterson said.

"No. There just isn't any new or active data coming through them. Since then, the problem has only worsened."

"Um, Houston, I'm not sure what we can see or do for you from here. I mean, Teddy is pretty good with computers. But—"

"All the servers are in Central Europe," Randy said, cutting her off. His voice had acquired a frazzled edge. "But there's more. We can't raise anyone on the phone either. And all of the region's news networks went silent, too. There's a satellite looking at the area." He paused as if searching for words. "But what we're seeing ... It doesn't make sense."

The cold blue waters of the North Atlantic scrolled beneath the ISS. Their current track across the planet would soon take them over Ireland, Britain, and indeed, France.

"I need human eyes on this thing," Randy McCree said.

Commander Brown knitted her eyebrows. "Thing? What are you seeing, sir?"

"Well, it almost looks like an aurora."

Angela and Bill exchanged concerned glances. Exceptional auroras usually signaled the arrival of particularly energetic solar discharges—something that could prove fatal to astronauts not within the metal walls of the space station.

"Is it a coronal mass ejection, sir?" Commander Brown said calmly, relieved that her concern hadn't crept into the words.

"No, no, no. We haven't had any CMEs in the last several days, and certainly, nothing pointing toward Earth. No, this is something else."

Angela started breathing again and opened a station-wide channel. "Teddy, I need you in the Cupola."

"What's up, Command-Oh?" the Russian crew member said, his mock SoCal surfer boy accent lilting each word.

Angela looked ahead. Beneath the aft end of the port or leftmost forward-pointing solar panel, she watched Ireland's rocky shoreline crest the blue horizon. Overhead and to her right, the long, articulated truss that connected all sixteen of the station's main solar arrays extended 150 feet to the structure's midway point. There it connected to the line of modules that formed the body of the ISS. Between her and the intersection, banks of solar arrays extended left and right like mirrored wings.

The woman looked forward again. As they continued eastward, she glimpsed an upside-down reflection of Ireland on the bottom of the outermost solar panel.

Movement to her right front drew her eye. In the faceted windows of the Cupola, a blond mane drifted into view. Even from 200 feet, she could see it filling a significant portion of the station's observatory.

"Jesus, Teddy! I told you to tie that back," Angela said and then reopened the connection with Houston.

"Hey, man. Don't be hating on the 'fro."

The commander cleared her throat. "Um, Mission Specialist Theodore Petrovich, we're on with Director McCree."

Teddy donned a navy blue baseball cap that sported the circled red chevron of Roscosmos, the Russian Federal Space Agency. The hat reined in his blond mane. Inside the observatory, the man held up his palms in a what-gives gesture. His mock Valley intonation morphed back into his almost clichéd Russian accent and dropped an octave. "Da, Commander. I'm in position." After a brief pause, he added, "Good morning, Director McCree. What can *Brown* do for you?"

Angela shot him an angry look that went unnoticed by all but Major Peterson who chuckled lightly by her side.

"Telemetry shows that you are about to pass over Ireland," the director said. "There's an atmospheric anomaly we'd like you to take a look at. It's over England now and approaching their west coast. So you should—"

"No way!" Teddy interrupted, the return of his Russianized SoCal accent drawing out the words. After uttering a few others in his native tongue, he said, "What in the *hell* is that?!"

To Angela's right, Bill twitched. "Son of a ...!" he said with a tone of shocked awe. After casting an embarrassed glance toward the commander, he pointed east.

She looked forward, and her eyes widened.

A curtain of white light was rising above the horizon.

"Oh my God," Angela said in a whisper.

The commander could see why the director had compared it to an aurora. In the upper reaches of the atmosphere, its light faded to black in undulating feathery fingers.

Then the full height of the thing rolled into view, and the comparison collapsed. The colorful sheets of the aurora borealis usually ran in faint curving lines that never quite reached the planet's surface. However, this thing's light extended all the way from the edge of space down to the ground.

"That's no aurora," Bill said.

Angela nodded wordlessly, unable to speak. This was wrong, very wrong.

The curtain of white ... energy? ... appeared to run in a perfectly straight line left and right until it disappeared over the curve of the north and south horizons.

What the hell could create something like that? she wondered.

The director's voice snapped Angela from her reverie. "What are you seeing, Commander?"

"Houston, we've spotted the ... the anomaly." Breathlessly, she added, "It looks like a wall of light!" Her respiration rate had doubled. The astronaut swallowed, trying to rein it in. "But not like an aurora. The light reaches all the way to the surface. I-I can't see through it!"

The damn thing was high, too high!

"Houston, I'm not sure we'll clear it!" Bill Peterson said. "Looks like we're flying straight at it."

The ISS's ever-arcing orbital path sent them careening toward the white wall. Its upper reaches extended high above the planet. The opaque curtain concealed everything beyond it. It looked as if the space station was rushing toward the energetic rampart like a doomed moth on a collision course with a planet-sized windshield.

Angela's entire body tensed. Pain radiated from her clenched fists. Then the planet's eastern horizon slid into view over the energy curtain's upper reaches, and she relaxed a shade. If they could see the horizon beyond the anomaly, they must be above it. Right?

As their path carried them closer to the wave, Europe and then England and even the Isle of Man slid into view behind the wall. In the highest reaches of the ever-thinning atmosphere, the anomaly appeared to fade and then disappear completely. But the commander had no way to know if its effect—whatever that effect might be—extended above that point.

Angela's body began to tense again as the thought took root like a weed.

Inexorably, the ISS continued east, racing toward its date with the anomaly.

Looking down now, she watched the base of the wave move across the surface, advancing westward, moving in the opposite direction of the ISS. The wavefront raced across the Irish Sea. As the station passed over the Cliffs of Moher on Ireland's western shore, the curtain of light swallowed Dublin ahead to the east.

She held her breath as they sped toward the upper reaches of the anomaly.

"Here it comes!" Teddy shouted.

The commander crossed forearms in front of her helmet. To her right, Bill had the same involuntary response. "Oh God!" he yelled.

Head turned slightly, Angela watched through narrowed eyes as the wall rushed at them. North and south, its extremities appeared motionless, but the central section rushed at them with impossible speed, closing the gap in milliseconds!

Find out what happens next. Get Solitude: Book One of Dimension Space Today!

Thank you for reading Ambush: Sector 64 Book One!

Dear Reader,

I hope you enjoyed *Ambush*. Thanks for riding along with me on this journey.

I appreciate your feedback. Actually, you are the reason I developed the *Sector 64* universe. While I work on my next novel, I'd love to hear from you. Tell me what you liked, what you loved, even what you hated. You can write me at dean@deanmcole.com and visit me on the web at www.deanmcole.com.

Finally, I need to ask a favor. If you're so inclined, I'd truly appreciate a review of *Ambush*. In this day of e-marketing, you have the power to make or break a book. Please post a review for *Ambush: Sector 64 Book One* where you bought it.

Thank you so much for reading *Ambush* and for being my copilot on this adventure. Don't forget to follow me on your favorite site by visiting the profiles listed on the About the Author page.

Fly safe!

Dean M. Cole

ABOUT THE AUTHOR

Amazon Top 20 and Audible Top 10 Author Dean M. Cole, a retired combat helicopter pilot and airline pilot, has penned multiple award-winning apocalyptic tales. Solitude, book one of Dimension Space, won the 2018 ABR Listeners Choice Award for Best Science Fiction. Previously, IndieReader named Dean's first full-length novel, Sector 64: Ambush, to their Best of 2014 list. His sixth book, Amplitude, the third Dimension Space novel, is now available.

Follow Dean on BookBub!

bookbub.com/authors/dean-m-cole

For More Information:

www.deanmcole.com

dean@deanmcole.com

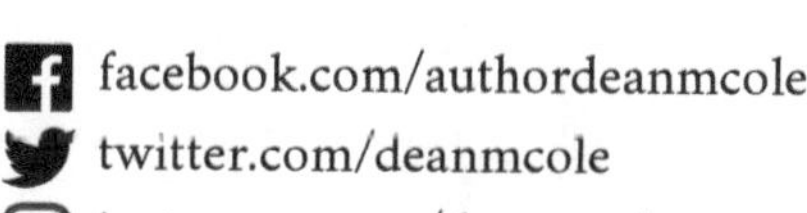

facebook.com/authordeanmcole

twitter.com/deanmcole

instagram.com/deanmcole

www.ingramcontent.com/pod-product-compliance
Lightning Source LLC
Chambersburg PA
CBHW030540310726
48979CB00010B/1980/J

* 9 7 8 1 9 5 2 1 5 8 0 1 8 *